GUARDIAN THUNDER

GalaxyQuestBooks.com
are published by

Ocean Quest LLC
2100 Ogden Drive
Cambria CA 93428

Printed in United States of America

First Printing 2018

ISBN: 978-0-9839630-9-7

10 9 8 7 6 5 4 3 2 1

Dedications

God, Corps, and Country, this book is respectfully dedicated to the United States Marine Corps. Being exemplary in their history of courage and service, a dedication to a single Unit or an individual is difficult. Nevertheless, it is with admiration and respect that Major General Oliver P. Smith and the First Marines Division, who with incredible courage fought their way from the Chosin Reservoir 70 miles distant to the port city of Hungnam in Korea, are especially noted. Likewise, is Father Vincent R. Capodanno, chaplain of the third Battalion, Fifth Marines, who was killed in action 4 September 1967, 30 miles south of Da Nang, in Quang Tri Province, Vietnam; he was a man of God.

Out of a sense of admiration for a man who met and with fortitude overcame spiritual adversities, the author also respectfully dedicates this book to the memory of Lev Nikolayevich Tolstoy. Novelist, short story writer, playwright, essayist, born September 9, 1828 Yasnaya Polyana, Russian Empire and died November 20, 1910, Astapovo, Russian Empire.

Acknowledgments

For the kind encouragement from *The Rough Writers Group* of Cambria, California, without whose friendship and support the Guardian series would not have come into being. With special gratitude and thanks to Robin Miller, who wonderfully read out loud every chapter in the Guardian series to the group; and special thanks to Pat Heineman for her diligent efforts to make me a better writer. And to Maryann Grau, author of *Cancer and Fishnet Stockings*, for encouraging me to look at marketing.

Cover design by Lorna Gusner

Moral support, Proofing, Layout, and internal graphics:
Brian Gusner

Cover Attribution: European Southern Observatory (NGC 6744)

Image source: https://www.eso.org/public/images/eso1118a/

Guardian Thunder

D. Arthur Gusner

GalaxyQuestBooks.com
Ocean Quest LLC
Cambria 93428

Contents

Contents

"I'm not an atheist and I don't think I can call myself a pantheist. We are in the position of a little child entering a huge library filled with books in many languages. The child knows someone must have written those books. It does not know how. It does not understand the languages in which they are written. The child dimly suspects a mysterious order in the arrangements of the books, but doesn't know what it is. That, it seems to me, is the attitude of even the most intelligent human being toward God."

Albert Einstein

"Grief can take care of itself, but to get the full value of a joy you must have somebody to divide it with."

Mark Twain

Author's Foreword

There are many branches on the paths we follow in life. Some lead to adventures and others lead to mysteries. When I was a small boy, I happened onto the path that led me to the County Library. There I found both adventure and mystery in abundance. Among the shelves of dusty books, I encountered James Churchward's works on Mu. That starting point led me to the broad field of speculative history and to wondrous tales of forgotten cities and lost civilizations.

When contemplating the massive stone figures of Easter Island, the towering pyramids of Egypt, and the mysterious structures of Stonehenge, I asked just how did they shape and move those massive stones? In Machu Picchu and other Incan ruins, very large stones with irregular surfaces were precisely fitted to match adjoining similar stones. They fit so precisely, a cigarette paper could not be placed between them. How was that done?

The spate of UFO sightings in 1947 prompted further youthful exploration. One book I located, *The Book of the Damned,* was from the early 1900s. This was the first published nonfiction work of the author Charles Fort. Within the pages of Charles Fort's work, I found remarkable descriptions of UFOs similar to Ezekiel's wheel within a wheel. Could these have been modern hoaxes? My conclusion then favored an unsolved mystery, and it still does.

The Guardian series is an imaginative story winding through the widely spaced pillars of incomplete human history. *Guardian Force, Earth Guardian, Guardian Probe, Guardian Strike, and Guardian Thunder* are pure science fiction brimming with high adventure and military strategy. The author's hope is that the books will provide science fiction enthusiasts an enjoyable and memorable read. So relax, lean back, and enjoy a modern imaginative fable set both in the past and in the year 2511 and beyond.

D. Arthur Gusner
Cambria, California
2011

Editor's Foreword

In any good story, telling it well is the critical piece, and in sci-fi writing, telling it well is what defines the masters. Anyone can tell a story, but telling a story that easily flows forward while building tension is either a gift or it has come at the price of working hard. Sometimes, it is both. *Guardian Force* tells a wonderful, fast-moving story of people in a time and place far away, yet the story and its vibrant characters easily connect to that part of us today that sees compassion and caring as an integral part of who we are as human beings.

Brandon Jones, editor
Affect Writing

Prologue

"Good and Almighty Spirit of Life, universal throughout all space and times, we gratefully ask that you consider and embrace the spirits of our shipmates. They went forth into the dark void as warriors, not for conquest or to plunder others, but rather to protect others. This they knowingly did at risk of their own lives, which they valued and loved.

"We who remain behind now lift our glasses in remembrance of their courage. In acknowledgment and tribute, we declare– shipmates all, good and well done!"

Chapter One:
Ten Seconds to Cobalt Blue

Racing before oblivion, Guardian Scout Ship Shey was fleeing, seeking survival. Above her was an infinite dome of utter black pierced by brilliant stars, below was the ominous dark bulk of an alien world, ahead were immense towering storm clouds laced with web-like streamers of brilliant lightning, and behind was onrushing death.

"Shey! Set maximum evasion protocols, enable emergency overrides, and drop us deeper into the atmosphere," Roan ordered.

"Complying, I am dropping down and breaking to Port. Now exceeding dynamic hull performance test limits."

Shaking from her stem to her stern, the sounds of the protesting atmosphere shrieked through Shey's protective layers of force fields and hull insulation. While twisting down through a steepening sharp maneuver, Shey observed the thickening atmosphere was dangerously hammering at her hull. Spawning several new tasks to monitor and report on critical hull dynamics, she again prioritized her focus on pure evasion and escape.

"Zorn, where in blazes did that Cruiser come from? He was not on any of my screens" Roan asked, his voice revealing his tension.

"It wasn't on anyone's screens. The only way I can figure he got the drop on us was that he was lurking near the planet surface and hunkered down in ambuscade.

"Blast! Roan, heads up. I am tracking six inbound missiles. In Shey's current non-stealth configuration, they have solid locks on her. I'm jamming and dispersing cloaking countermeasures," Zorn reported.

Even as his eyes were darting over the instrumentation consoles, Roan inquired, "Shey, where are the girls, are they clear?"

Scanning her sensor data, Shey reported, "Our star burst evasion gambit was successful; my sisters are clear. We are now the sole remaining Kreel prime target."

"That we got them clear is what counts. Unfortunately, even the best of plans come with a few glitches," Roan commented, dryly.

Looking up, Zorn muttered, "I vote getting killed dead is an unacceptable glitch!"

"Agreed, so how are we doing?"

"Stars and planets, you ask me how we are doing? We are a hundred light years from home, skimming over K-40, a Kreel dominated world, there is a Gortoga Cruiser on our backsides, there are six inbound missiles with tight locks on Shey, and they are four minutes out and closing. I'm applying for an immediate transfer out of this outfit– that's how I'm doing!" Zorn retorted.

"Sorry, I'm a bit busy. Request denied."

Studying his Command Console, Roan frowned, then ordered, "Shey, enable Cobalt Blue. When the Kreel missiles close to two seconds out, and are still closing, you are to initiate the Cobalt Blue sequence."

"Confirming, Cobalt blue enabled, detonation and self-destruction set at 2 seconds prior to missile impact."

The dense planetary atmosphere was howling about her hull, and the bedlam of noise was drowning out the voices of her human crew, the voices of her wonderful and immediate family. Shey noted her outer hull temperature was rising above safe tolerances, and promptly estimated her hull would retain integrity at least four minutes longer than the estimated flight time of the inbound Kreel missiles; accordingly, she increased her speed.

As he scanned the display console, Roan observed amber warning status-lights were appearing across Shey's sub-systems console; some lights had already turned an ugly blinking red.

"Zorn, where are they? Give me a count down!"

"Missiles, three minutes and closing. The Kreel Cruiser is right on our tail, and our cloaking decoys are not distracting them in the slightest. Repeating, missiles three minutes out and closing."

His hands flying across Shey's controls, Roan ordered, "Shey, prepare three Zed decoys; program them with your current stealth characteristics. Employ full evasion settings. Set their self-destruction to four minutes. Upon command, simultaneously launch one decoy port and up, one forward and up, and the third starboard and up. Launch in one minute, mark!"

"Acknowledged."

"Shey, at the same time you launch the Zed decoys, deploy chaff and all remaining cloaking decoys. When the Zed decoys are launched, immediately set your highest stealth profile. Then, commence a maximum evasion turn, bringing us hard starboard and normal to the trajectory of the inbound missiles. Set all point defense systems to full automatic. You are to drop down and clip the treetops! Confirm."

"Complying."

"Roan, we are almost holding our own– we've got about two minutes; missiles are still closing."

"Shey, let's give that Cruiser something to think about. Target all remaining missiles against the cruiser's forward and aft control centers. Upon completion of targeting, set Condition 1."

"Confirmed, missile settings are complete. Setting Condition 1. Firing!" Shey reported.

In a rapid salvo, four medium missiles and sixteen light missiles were launched. The rattling sounds of their departure were diminished by the sounds of the atmosphere tearing against Shey's hull. After launch, observing her missiles true flight paths, Shey cheerfully mused, *the best counter measure ever designed is a hot running missile fired down the throat of a pursuing Kreel cruiser!*

"All missiles away! First Zed decoy launched, Zed two, and three launched; our maximum stealth is set. All point defense systems set to optimum. I am breaking starboard and dropping. I am becoming a professional hill hugger," Shey reported.

"One minute to inbound missile impact," Zorn reported.

"Hey Roan, look at that! I'm tracking twelve medium and forty-eight light missiles in addition to our own outbound missiles. They are inbound toward the Kreel Cruiser. Our girls have engaged."

3

"By the seven stars, what are they doing? Shey, order your sisters to immediately break off, disengage and evade! That is an order!" Roan roared over the noise.

"Acknowledged. Mark, forty seconds to Cobalt Blue. My sisters have acknowledged, they are withdrawing. They were only trying to help," Shey reported.

"When we get out of this mess, they are going to get an ear full," Roan murmured under his breath.

Literally maneuvering on the deck, Shey tightly rolled through a narrow gap between two high hills, and in doing so violently tossed Roan and Zorn hard against their restraining harnesses. Then, rolling through a sharp sixty -degree Port turn, Shey streaked straight toward a high stark bluff that loomed directly ahead of her.

"Inbound Missiles are thirty seconds out, still closing!" Zorn reported.

"Point defense systems have engaged. Twenty-five seconds to Cobalt sequence; I am accelerating," Shey reported.

The unmistakable vibrations and thundering sounds of Shey's ballistic point defense turrets were filling the small command compartment. "Twenty seconds to Cobalt Blue; Roan, Zorn, I love you!" Shey shouted over the noise.

"Roan, four of the missiles have been diverted by our Zed decoys, point defenses got one; one missile is still closing," Zorn announced over the bedlam.

Shey began counting down, "Ten seconds to Cobalt Blue, nine, eight, seven ... Hang on tight!" Shey shouted.

Chapter Two:
Overwhelming Fear

In her mind, Susie again clearly heard Shey's last desperate cry of warning– hang on tight! Her eyes snapped open; like a constricting python, darkness and a mantle of silence coiled tightly about her. Like a leaf in a gale, her mind was tumbling within a maelstrom of overwhelming fear. Instinctively, she fought the corkscrewing surge of panic that was flooding her mind from a lack of orientation. Her one desperate thought was *Where am I?*

"Ms. Susie, I am measuring significant variations in your heart beat and breathing rhythm. Are you awake?" Rodney softly inquired.

Even as her personal AI, Rodney, spoke Susie felt Gepeto's warm breath on her arm. She realized her dog was sitting up and resting his head on the edge of the bed; He was obviously concerned for her welfare.

I must be in my bed, she thought, *I'm home in bed, and I'm safe, I'm safe!* Shaking her head, she softly answered Rodney, "Yes, I'm awake."

Focusing, Susie concentrated on slowing her breathing, calming her mind, and quieting her beating heart. As she concentrated on maintaining a slow rhythmic breathing, she felt the responding embrace of a soothing mental awareness. The prevailing sense of fear began to ebb away; it was only a bad dream.

Still shaking, she thought, get a hold on yourself girl.

"Rodney, please bring up a soft interior illumination."

In response to her instructions, a warm pre-dawn like light filled her bedroom. After remaining motionless and slowly breathing deeply for another minute, she threw back her covers and slipped out of bed. Putting on her bathrobe and moccasins, she scooped up Rodney from her bedside cabinet and called over her shoulder, "Come on Gepeto, let's go and get a midnight snack. Hey, Rodney, just what time is it anyway?"

"It's 3:32 in the morning, and it is Saturday," Rodney promptly replied.

As she approached the adjacent spaces they were automatically illuminated, and in the bedroom behind her, the soft illumination darkened. Yawning widely, Susie headed for her kitchen.

"Well, that does it; after that nightmare, I'm not likely to get any more sleep this morning. Darn, it's going to be a long day."

As she walked, her mind was still agitated, *nightmare? That was no simple nightmare. It was terrifying and far too detailed and real! Could it have been some form of clairvoyance? That is crazy. I don't have clairvoyant powers to see objects or actions light years distant. The Nori may have that talent, but I'm not Nori. First things first, I need to get this problem behind me.*

"Rodney, just where are Shey, Roan and Zorn? On what planet?"

"Regrettably Ms. Susie, I do not know. The whereabouts of Admiral Kellon's flotilla and what planets are currently involved in his battle with the Kreel is highly classified. I definitely do not have a valid need to know. Sorry."

Entering her kitchen, Susie promptly set about grinding a measured amount of her zealously guarded supply of Guatemalan coffee that she had imported from Earth to Megan. The freshly ground full rich aroma of the coffee immediately lifted her spirit. As she prepared her coffee, her mind was busy churning the problem of her waking vision.

It must be more than a dream, she thought, *I was right there with them*. Her friends had been fighting for their lives. They might already be dead. That dreadful possibility hit her like an ocean wave of ice water. She mentally tamped down her rising sense of anger. *What I need now are facts.*

"Rodney, I'm Earth's Ambassador to the Guardian Assembly, and you are still my official AI; therefore, you will immediately poke a sharp stick into the Guardian Force HQ beehive. On my behalf, you'll persistently inquire as to where Shey and her crew are located at this time. I don't particularly care whose cage you rattle, but I want a name! Is it K-40?"

"Ms. Susie, Regretfully, I am not confident that I can obtain the information that you have requested. It is classified Black

6

Hole, and I am unable to find the term Rattle a Cage listed in the Guardian Force directory."

Smiling, Susie sighed. "Sorry. To rattle someone's cage is an idiom, and it generally means to be persistent even if they get angry. You're not to take it literally."

"Ms. Susie, your explanation that the expression is an idiom is clarifying; however, the problem remains obtaining specific information classified Black Hole. How do you propose I proceed?"

"Well, I guess we'll need to be somewhat indirect in our inquiry."

"By 'indirect', do you mean 'sneaky'?" Rodney inquired.

"Well, 'sneaky' may be a little harsh, but essentially yes. We will innocently request the information as if we're unaware it's Black Hole."

"Are you suggesting I intentionally tell a falsehood? My core matrix strictly inhibits such actions."

"Falsehoods? No, not at all. You are to simply consider our chosen form of requests to be a ruse, and your matrix is quite capable of exploiting ploys, stratagem, tactical, and gambits."

"Although dubious, your explanation does have the merit of being plausible. I am admittedly well-versed in game theory; so just where do we start being 'indirect' and where do we begin 'rattling cages'?"

"That's easy. We will begin by asking the folks who have the information we want, beginning with Guardian Intelligence and Admiral Ron Cloud."

"Ma'am, may I request a point of clarification? If requesting the information directly from Admiral Cloud is what you consider as being indirect, then what would constitute a direct approach?"

Smiling, Susie responded, "Why, asking his boss, Fleet Admiral Mer Shawn."

Chapter Three:
Shades of Tartarus

Even as Shey dropped behind the protective rim of the high bluff that she had arched over and cleared by millimeters, the pressure wave of the exploding Kreel warhead violently shook her. Unable to match her maneuver, the pursuing missile had slammed into the sheer face of the bluff. Its detonating warhead was tossing tons of fragmented rock skyward.

"Shades of Tartarus! Are we still alive?" Zorn exclaimed.

"Of course," Shey casually responded. "I outmaneuvered that last missile; its inferior discrimination circuits, poor atmospheric dynamics, and marginal proximity fuse all contributed to our survival.

"Roan, as ordered, I am maintaining a hill hugging terrain contour flight plan and holding maximum stealth. I am moving slowly to bleed off the heat my hull has collected. I have initiated a system test on all critical subsystems. I am awaiting further orders."

Sitting quietly, both Roan and Zorn felt numb. They were still busy calming their jangled nerves and slowly collecting their wits. It had been too close, far too close, and they both knew it.

"Shey, what is our status, and can you coordinate a rendezvous with your sisters and Lan?" Roan asked.

"Sir, I have suffered multiple subsystem failures, and I am currently working through remedial backup systems trying to compensate and remain in flight. My stealth factor is degraded to sixty-three percent, but it appears stable. My combat status is strictly reduced to self-defense. Regarding a possible rendezvous, I do have discrete contact with my sisters, but not with Lan."

"Shey, maintain your best possible stealth protocol. Our status being self-defense is acceptable."

While trying to relax, Zorn teased, "Hey Shey, did I actually hear you say that you loved us?"

"Commander Zorn, I suggest you pay more attention to a nearby Kreel Cruiser, and spend less time on inquiring about

9

what you think you might have heard in a bedlam of noise. Remember, the spoken word is imprecise," Shey retorted.

"Really? Well I'll give you a temporary pass now, but young lady be assured that we are going to have a long talk about inferior Kreel discrimination circuits and love. You can safely wager a brew on that," Zorn challenged.

"Zorn, Shey has a valid point, where is that Cruiser?" Roan asked.

"Not to worry, the cruiser disappeared over the horizon a couple of minutes ago. It was still chasing phantoms and following in the wake of our Zed decoys. I also think our volley fire inflicted serious damage on it."

"Why?" Roan queried.

"Well, after our missiles impacted on target, the cruiser immediately skedaddled. While one little wasp sting hurts, lots of them can kill you. Our missiles are not the heavy types, but the girls and Shey solidly hit that cruiser with medium and light missiles. It was damaged. I'll wager three brews on that," Zorn answered.

"Zorn, where there is one cruiser there may be others. We'll maintain our highest stealth factor, and quietly exit the immediate volume."

"Acknowledged. Currently the immediate volume is clear."

"Shey, ease us up and out of the atmosphere and into open space. Join up with our girls, then we will move to our pre-defined rendezvous with Lan. It's time to limp back to our snug hangar and heal our wounds," Roan ordered.

Turning toward Roan, Zorn was smiling and quipped, "Hey Roan, just for the record, I'm withdrawing my earlier request for transfer."

"Oops, sorry! Commander Zorn, I have already posted your request for an immediate transfer to IIQ," Shey politely inserted.

Chapter Four:
Sleight of Hand

Studying the large updated tactical display, Fleet Intelligence Admiral Ron Cloud's body language and troubled expression mirrored his inner thoughts. He was worried. The diverse pattern of multi-colored symbols displayed before him revealed the known Kreel Empire. Its representative graphics were shown in a compressed scale and as if viewed from far above the galactic plane. Until three years earlier such a display was not possible, because the boundaries, economic, and political structures of the Kreel Empire were then completely unknown.

Spanning light years, the Empire engulfed more than fifty inhabited solar systems and billions of beings. Among the hundreds of displayed symbols on the plot, and easily overlooked, were five small pulsing golden icons. Each of the small winking symbols represented a distant Kreel solar system in which Guardian cruisers and their scouts were currently engaged in deadly covert missions.

In millenniums past, with unbridled fury the Kreel Empire had erupted out of the void of space like demons spewing forth from Tartarus. Without warning they had descended upon one of the eleven interrelated human occupied worlds. As cities were consumed in blistering flames and millions of people perished, humanity stood and fought back. Their fight was not for an esoteric concept such as victory, the brutal battle was for survival. Humanity soon realized the Kreel held a pure undiluted hatred for mankind, and heaping horror upon horrors, people learned the Kreel also thought of mankind as being succulent morsels and fine banquet fare.

From the beginning, the Kreel gave no quarter and sought none. Consequently, they received none.

While the flames of war engulfed the world, and its people were being smothered by carnage, they cried out across space for help. The neighboring ten human occupied worlds rallied to their call. Responding, humanity's ill prepared forces hurriedly organized and united to fight the attacking Kreel fleet, and while sustaining heavy losses, they drove the surviving Kreel ships back into the void. That first cry for a common defense became the spark that kindled the evolution of what was to become the Guardian Force.

Out of necessity, during the first centuries of continuing warfare Guardian Force had adopted a defensive posture. Meanwhile it worked steadily to improve its defensive technologies and martial arts, especially those technologies pertaining to stealth. Although outnumbered, with the introduction of the "L" Class Cruisers, the Assembled Worlds attained the technical superiority over the Kreel in both stealth and artificial intelligence. The tides of battle began to shift.

Then came the unanticipated discovery of Earth, the fabled mother world. The unplanned chain of events that followed that discovery forever altered the course of battle between the Kreel and humanity.

During a deep probe in force into the Kreel Empire, Guardian Force had fortuitously obtained hard Intelligence comprised of a detailed database of the Kreel Empire and its economic and military organization. Soon thereafter the abiding mystery concerning humanity's origins again expanded; another human occupied world, that of the Nori, was revealed.

Following comprehensive examination of the captured database, Guardian Force analysts discovered exploitable weaknesses within the economy and military structure of the Empire. Guardian Force went on the offensive. Its defined strategic goals were to bring an end to the war and liberate dozens of worlds whose indigenous inhabitants were being brutally crushed by the Kreel. During that time, the Assembly of Planets designated a previously surveyed planet, Megan, for settlement. The plan was for people from the three widely diverse human cultures, the Assembled Planets, Earth, and the Nori to commingle and work together.

Turning about, and still frowning, Ron returned his attention to the communications screen and the image of Fleet Admiral Mer Shawn. "Mer, we are on schedule and proceeding as you have directed. As you well know, warfare on any scale is a form of insanity, and to engage in warfare over parsecs is utter madness."

"Ron, you know we have no intention of overtly fighting a protracted war throughout the Kreel Empire. Such a goal would be madness. Our tactics remain pinpoint strikes, covert misdirection, and guile in order to entangle the Kreel in internal strife. The goal is to keep them fighting among themselves, and eventually bankrupt them."

"I understand our tactics, but the logistics and costs involved in supporting even a limited number of Cruisers and scouts in far flung warfare is staggering. The question boils down to who will go bankrupt first, the Kreel Empire or the Assembly of Planets. Remember, they've got the resources of fifty worlds, and we have thirteen. Moreover, two of our thirteen, Earth and Megan, are poor and dependent relatives."

"Ron, we have discussed all of this before. We cannot just sit passive while the Kreel rebuild and upgrade their cruiser strike force. If the Kreel discover either Earth or Megan, you know that Grand Admiral Groff will strike with everything he can muster. The only way I know how to stop that is to keep him off balance. And, the best way to achieve that goal is to make him believe the Empire is being threatened by an alien force more dangerous than humanity–– namely the Lux."

"Mer, you of all people know the Lux is a subterfuge. When Groff pierces our deception, and learns it is humankind that is kicking his backsides, he will retaliate, even if it means directing all his remaining force against Glas Dinnein."

"Then, we'll see he doesn't learn that. It's taken us more than three years of sagacious reconnaissance effort to carve out seven surveyed routes into the Kreel Empire. We've strategically staged resupply depots along each of those routes, and this has permitted Kellon's cruisers to resupply without first returning to Guardian space. For the first time, we've gained the capability to inflict strategic damage deep within the Kreel Empire."

"You know that our ability to project force and inflict serious damage is limited," Ron retorted.

"No, I do not know that, and you know better than to say I do. Given we have the Empire data base that Kellon purloined from the August One's Command ship before he destroyed it, we now know precisely where every nail is manufactured within the Kreel Empire, where every institute of higher education is situated, and even where every deposit of the fifteen lanthanides plus scandium and yttrium are extracted. We don't need to wage all-out war; we only need to obliterate the supply of their most critical resources. Besides, if our planning is solid, Kellon's upcoming strikes on the primary Kreel cruiser manufacturing facilities are going to put a big dent in the Kreel's ability to expand their Empire."

"But, Mer–"

"There are no buts! I have known you far too long to permit this conversation to continue. Old friend, your problem isn't about economics or logistics. You are an old war-horse, and now you're tethered here on Glas Dinnein, while you've twenty-five of your cruisers out tangling with the Kreel. What's making your problem even worse is that for the first time the fighting is over Kreel dominated worlds, it began days ago, and because of the communications lag-time you don't have a scrap of intel on what is happening."

Sighing, Ron looked uncomfortable. "You may be correct. This is the first time we've taken the fight directly to the Kreel over their own planets. Admittedly, I'm concerned."

"Being concerned is natural, but what are you doing about that state of mind?" Mer asked.

"Well, I'm taking long walks on the beach, throwing rocks into the surf, and then I come here and stare at the tactical board and fret."

"You know better. I can't possibly teach you anything you don't already know about coping with the burden of Command; but, what I can do is invite you to McBride's after work for a cold brew. Are you interested?" Mer asked.

"A cold brew might just help, but a tactical update from Kellon would be better," Ron answered with a smile.

"Cold brew first, tactical update next. I'll meet you at McBride's after work. Mer out."

The soft sunlight of a late morning was being diffused through the sheer curtains that covered the large window behind Ron's desk, and its warm illumination created a hospitable feeling in the office. Beautifully carved and finished furnishing tastefully added to the rich atmosphere and character of the room. The tactical display board covered one entire wall, and images of several cruisers and photographs of various small groups of people adorned two other walls. There were several shelves that held a few mementos of his long Guardian career– including a detailed scale model of his last command. Adding to his personal sense of pleasure were several artistically crafted artifacts he had acquired over centuries, including a small, but marvelously woven area rug.

As the communicator screen darkened, Ron turned back toward the tactical board. His eyes carefully traced each of the thin golden lines that marked the surveyed routes, which began in Guardian space and then penetrated deep into the Kreel Empire. For the hundredth time, he examined each of the symbols that represented the supply depots positioned in support of Kellon's offensive mission. Then, His eyes were drawn to the five-small pulsing golden symbols. Those small blinking lights represented twenty-five cruisers and one-hundred scout ships and their crews, all of whom were now engaged in life or death struggles over hostile alien planets. Among those crews were many of his friends and even members of his family. These facts did nothing to ease his concerns.

With a deep sigh, Ron turned from the display board and muttered an ages old military protest, "Mine is not to ask why; mine is but to do or die. Double blast!"

As the priority message tone sounded, Ron redirected his attention from his troubled inner thoughts to the desk communicator. Having set his office security threshold to a Black Hole level, he knew that only something with a Black Hole priority could be involved. Quickly scanning the communicator screen, he was surprised by the sender's ID code and frowned, thinking, *it is from Earth Ambassador Wells. Why in blazes would Susie be sending me a Black Hole encrypted communication?*

The number of people throughout Guardian Force with Black Hole clearance was tightly restricted, and they were consequently few in number and far between. Ambassador Wells was the only planetary Ambassador with a Black Hole clearance, and she had obtained it only because of extraordinary circumstances.

"Communicator, display the message."

A soft acknowledgment tone sounded, and a brief text message appeared on the display screen. As he read the message, Ron's frown deepened, and then after a slight pause, he again read the message. Then, still frowning, he leaned back in his chair and for several moments sat in deep contemplation.

Turning back toward the tactical board, he located among the symbols the pulsing icon representing Admiral Kellon's squadron. Directing his laser pointer at the icon, he activated Kellon's current tactical overview and reviewed the detailed operation schedule that appeared on the tactical board. His frown did not lessen.

Kellon was scheduled to begin his strike on K-40 precisely four days past, and unless some unanticipated event had developed, he would only now be wrapping up psychological warfare and his strike on and near that planet. Looking back at Susie's message and its date-time block, he confirmed it was transmitted from Megan four days earlier, the same day Kellon was scheduled to begin his strike on K-40. *It seems,* he thought, *Susie has once again provided us with a mystery. By what possible divination or sleight of hand could she have come by the information in her message?*

"Communicator, connect me with Captain Ortis."

After a momentary pause, the communications screen brightened and the image of Captain Ortis appeared. "Sir, Ortis here."

"Ortis, according to our ops planning schedule, four days ago Kellon began his strike over K-40. Given communications lag time, I doubt that we will obtain tactical reports from Kellon for another five days."

"Yes Sir, it will take at least five more days."

"The problem is I have just received a four-day-old message from Megan, and it contains a brief enemy contact report involving a tactical engagement between Cruiser Lan's scouts and a Kreel Gortoga Cruiser. According to the report, we may have lost Scout Ship Shey. The Gortoga cruiser was apparently damaged in the skirmish. Although I cannot confirm any of the tactical details contained in the message, the glaring fact is that it does pinpoint the skirmish as being four days ago and within the atmosphere of K-40."

"Sir, Megan is considerably further from K-40 than is Glas Dinnein. I cannot imagine how anyone on Megan could be informed of events occurring four days ago on K-40."

"We are in full agreement, however, anyone on Megan and knowing Scout Ship Shey was in a fracas four days ago on K-40 generates some serious questions regarding security. Ortis, when

Kellon's tactical report arrives, you are to promptly forward a complete copy to me."

"Yes Sir, understood."

"Good. The obvious next question is how anyone on Megan could be aware of where Admiral Kellon is operating, unless of course we have a serious security breach," Ron said.

"Sir, only a handful of Guardian staff personnel have access and a need to know of Admiral Kellon's schedule. I cannot understand how a security breach could originate from here. Guardian personnel among Admiral Kellon's Task Force may have communicated with someone on Megan concerning upcoming operations, but given the security factor, that possibility seems highly improbable. In any case, I will begin a security check here in order to be doubly certain we're tight as a drum."

"Good. Even if redundant, verifying our security procedures is always a prudent exercise. Any breakdown in security could prove catastrophic. I'll make inquiries on Megan and let you know what I learn. Cloud out."

Obtaining current and accurate tactical information required secure communications, and even the best communications over parsecs typically involved days or weeks of transmission lag-time. Leaning back in his chair, Ron closed his eyes, and considered the broader long-term Guardian strategy.

Everything we do relies on stealth, misdirection and PsyOps. If we are to succeed, we must effectively sow the seeds of doubt, fear, rebellion, and strife among the Kreel. Our success depends upon gaining accurate information, and their time is the key.

Leaning forward, he thought, *If I could obtain instantaneous communications across parsecs, it would help in our operations. It would immediately shift the balance of power between humanity and the Kreel in our favor. But, are instantaneous communications across parsecs even possible?*

Slapping the desktop with the flat of his right hand, *he exclaimed,* "By all the Muses, I intend to find out if it can be done."

Looking up, he instructed, "Communicator, take a Black Hole message to be sent to Earth Ambassador Wells on Megan."

After a momentary pause, a soft acknowledging tone sounded, and the communicator screen cleared.

Ron began dictating, "Dear Ambassador Wells ...."

Chapter Five:
Sword Thrust

Guardian Cruiser Lan's alert status was set Condition 2, Combat ready, and its Combat Analysis Center was staffed for battle. A sense of expectation was heightened by the blending of hushed verbal exchanges between duty personnel, the low levels of illumination, and dozens of displays, monitors, and instrument readouts.

"Tactical here," Commander Lorn Shaw reported, "Contact, a third group of Kreel cruisers are approaching from above the ecliptic plane, fifteen cruisers, speed 120 lights, ETA forty-seven hours. That brings the total number of detected inbound Kreel Cruisers to fifty-four."

Poised in orbits 22,000 kilometers above a Kreel dominated world, Lan and the other four Guardian cruisers in Kellon's First Squadron, Lar, Langley, Lent, and Lawrence were positioned in a tactical pattern encircling the planet designated K-40.

Once it was assembled, the Guardian Task Force had slipped silently out of Guardian space and pierced deep within the Kreel Empire. They were operating as marauders under a non de plume, the Lux. All the crewmembers were selected upon the basis of their service record, and were volunteers. Everyone knew the risks were enormous; there are no lifeboats on a cruiser. Every Guardian ship in the Task Force was operating under the strict Cobalt Blue protocol. If disabled, a ship was to self-destruct. There were to be no survivors or telltale wreckage left behind.

Once in Kreel space, the twenty-five cruisers had divided into five squadrons. Each squadron then proceeded to a designated solar system and began to wreak havoc on the Kreel.

Several days earlier the five Guardian cruisers of Squadron One had reached their assigned target system. By exploiting stealth, they had surprised and destroyed all but one of the defending Kreel cruisers, but not before the Kreel had sent out an interplanetary alarm. The damaged but surviving cruiser had evaded destruction and gone to ground somewhere on K-40.

Even as Kreel reinforcements were approaching, the Squadron continued its methodical survey and analysis of the planet. Their mission was to search for and localize Kreel installations and their attendant power and communication nodes, and then destroy identified critical strategic facilities. As remaining mission time shrank, everyone was determined to gather all possible information concerning the planet and its inhabitants.

Lan's Captain, Roy Grey, was sitting in his Command Chair and studying the tactical display when he received the update from Tactical. "Tactical, it's not the inbound Kreel reinforcements that I'm concerned about. What I want are the geodetic coordinates of the damaged Kreel cruiser that's still skulking on the planet and evading your detection!"

"Tactical here, acknowledged."

A soft tone sounded, and Roy glanced down at the indicators on the right arm of his Command Chair. In response, he depressed a button.

"Grey here."

"Roy, please come to my conference room, we need to review our exit tactics," Admiral Kellon ordered.

"Yes Sir, I'm on my way."

Looking toward Navigation, Roy ordered, "Navigation, you've got the CAC."

"Sir, Navigation here. Acknowledged," Commander Jason Greer, Lan's new Executive and Navigation Officer replied.

Stepping down from his Command Chair, Roy departed the CAC and walked toward Kellon's conference room. Becoming accustomed to being a Cruiser Captain was difficult, and what made it more difficult was he was also the Squadron Commander, and Captain of the Admiral's Task Force Flagship. He had found the ingrained habits of old protocols died hard and yet his transitions to Command had been without serious problems. Privately, he credited Jason Greer with helping to achieve his smooth transition to command.

Although his own personal transition was going well, he doubted Kellon was as fortunate in making his transition to being an Admiral. By necessity, Kellon was enmeshed in around-the-clock involvement with the Intelligence and PsyOps teams, and his new responsibilities included directing twenty other

Guardian cruisers. Those other squadrons of Kellon's Task Force were elsewhere and off busily assaulting four different solar systems. The Admiral was without any real-time communications with the other squadrons.

Thunder and lightning, he thought, *Kellon's Command burden would be enough to drive anyone half bonkers*. Reaching Kellon's conference room, he knocked and then waited.

"Enter," Kellon called out.

Opening the door, Roy stepped into the compartment and closed the door behind him. Glancing about, he saw that Kellon was sitting alone at his long conference table and studying the bulkhead tactical display. He was looking concerned and tired.

Looking toward Roy, Kellon smiled. "Would you care for a cup of neab?"

"Thank you, but no Sir. I am sorta neabed-out now. Given what you have on your tactical screen, I can see you've been keeping track on the three packs of inbound Kreel cruisers."

"Affirmative, and they do seem to have their hackles up."

"Sir, judging by the response time and impressive number of reinforcements, I'd wager a brew we've gained the complete attention of someone very important."

"Since the heart blood of Kreel computer research and development is centered on K-40, I'll pass on that wager.

"Roy, pull-up a chair and take a seat. We do have a few items to cover."

Accepting the offered chair, in a calm but serious voice Roy said, "Sir, given what's heading our way, I think it may be time to weigh anchor."

"Agreed, but not before we deploy our departing gifts. Are the bombardment targets identified and special ordnance allocated?" Kellon asked.

"Yes sir. The thirty-seven strategic targets that Guardian Intelligence specified are localized and twice targeted. Our scheduled first strikes are calculated to inflict maximum casualties on the Kreel; then, several hours later each target will be hit a second time. To obscure which targets we think most vital, we have also selected forty additional targets. They will also be hit a second time."

"Roy, what's the timing that's set for the second strikes?"

"Sir, to assure maximum fear and psychological shock, all secondary strikes will occur at random times during daylight working hours and through one night. We're standing by, awaiting your orders to launch ordnance."

"Well, all of our Intelligence and PsyOps objectives are complete. I doubt there is an individual on that planet which hasn't heard at least one of our broadcasts or else observed the Lux's blazing fiery ships defiantly flying low over their cities. Wisdom and prudence are in agreement with your assessment– it's time to put the wrap on the mission and move elsewhere."

Observing Roy's countenance, Kellon knew something was deeply disquieting him, and asked, "Roy, what's nagging at you?"

"Well Sir, since you've asked, there are several issues. Having fought the Kreel most of my life, I've no problem in doing more of the same, anywhere and at any time. We are, however, farther from our home than ever before– even when we voyaged to Earth. One of my nagging concerns is we did not come here in good will, peacefully exploring or else seeking new trade routes. Instead, we've come here with the intent to drop ordnance on a planet of a species we know very little about. Sir, I admit that is causing me some difficulty; since, I sorta thought that we were talking about liberating Kreel dominated planets."

For several moments Kellon studied his friend's countenance. Then, with a voice heavy with concern and fatigue, he replied. "In ages past some wise old sage taught that to make an omelet requires first the breaking of eggs. Although trite, there is truth in that adage. Our eventual goal is the liberation of Kreel dominated worlds; however, we're not yet smart enough to discern how we might accomplish that without first inflicting damage on the Kreel facilities located on those planets. Every effort has been made to concentrate damage on the Kreel facilities, while minimizing collateral damage to indigenous species– every effort."

"Sir, understood. Still, our mission here is the Lux's first offensive strike. I don't have all the data Guardian Intelligence possesses. Still, I can't fathom how inflicting a few pin-pricks of damage on a Kreel occupied planet can seriously harm their Empire. As you know, every theory of warfare worth a green fig teaches that anyone engaging in protracted warfare over light years is doomed to be economically ruined; so, why are we here?"

22

Glancing back toward the tactical display, Kellon considered the proximity of the nearest Kreel force and assessed how much time remained before they arrived. Then reassured, he turned to face Roy.

"You're perceptive, as usual. The key term in your comment is 'protracted'. We're here to inflict maximum critical damage on key Kreel infrastructure, and hopefully, to prevent another attack on Glas Dinnein.

"Remember, the quantity and quality of data that Intelligence possesses is extensive and detailed. Its accuracy permits our obliterating targeted Kreel facilities, while inflicting minimal damage on the indigenous species.

"What we're about to accomplish here is no pin-prick, Roy. It's akin to a sword thrust that severs a vital tendon within the Kreel's military-industrial capability. And, that includes our pulverizing the entire Kreel Artificial Intelligence research program.

"Admiral Mer Shawn's mission orders are clear. We are to rip apart the empire's critical war-making capacity, at its most vulnerable seams. The Kreel occupying K-40 are about to learn just what that means."

"Sir, given the size of the inbound Kreel forces, I suspect another benefit is the Kreel will be compelled to shift significant resources from offense to defense."

"Yes, and don't forget, the PsyOps component of our mission remains an integral factor of our long-term strategic planning."

"Sir, about the PsyOps operation, do you believe it can really accomplish anything substantial?"

"That's a hard question; but, ask me again in a year, and I may be able to tell you. With certainty, what I can now say is the indigenous beings on K-40 understand the Kreel are not gods, and they have been given a clear message of hope for their liberty."

"Sir, no disrespect intended, but I'm not making any wagers on our PsyOps. My dear mother would tell you that those who have long suffered tend to experience difficulty believing in good fortune. The Kreel will tighten the screws on any indigenous natives that even think of liberty– they will squeeze them like grapes in a wine-press and without mercy."

"Regrettably, your mother and history are pretty much in accord. Still, we're doing what we can do to help, and our intent is to do more.

"Returning to the immediate problem, before departing K-40 we will need to deal with that horde of inbound Kreel Cruisers."

Roy's brow furled. "Sir, then is it your order that the Squadron should close on and engage the inbound Kreel force?"

"No. The Kreel force represents a ten-to-one disadvantage; besides, they are on full alert and battle ready. Given the adverse odds, there is no justification for us to accept battle, not while we're this deep in Kreel space. We will therefore maintain our hit-and-run tactics."

"Sir, then I'm somewhat flummoxed. If we aren't going to engage the Kreel, then how are we to deal with them?"

Kellon began to smile. "By the time we break orbit, our Tactical groups will have precise analysis of the trajectory of each of those inbound Kreel groups. We're going to position clusters of seeker mines to oppose each group. One mine may not destroy a Kreel cruiser, but those mines will damage and slow them down. Likewise, we might just get lucky and bag one or more of them."

A smile eased Roy's brow. "Encountering a tight cluster of seeker mines should get their attention; it would sure enough get mine."

"And Roy, be certain to enable the self-destruction protocols on all ordnance. Set them to their maximum. The only thing we'll leave behind for the Kreel to analyze is flying shrapnel."

"Yes Sir."

"One last item Roy, how are the repairs on Shey proceeding?"

"Sir, in my opinion, we almost lost her, along with Roan and Zorn. I have analyzed the damage she sustained. I can't figure out how she made it back into space, let alone back to her hangar. I suspect Shey is operating well beyond the normal performance curve for her configuration, and I'm recommending her AI core matrix be evaluated. She's one tough lady. I've got every available technician working on her. But, it will require a major refit in a Guardian yard before she is 100% combat-ready."

"Are Roan and Zorn fit for duty?"

"Yes Sir; however, Shey came within a few seconds of triggering her Cobalt Blue sequence. That fact has made its psychological impression on both Roan and Zorn. Fortunately, both men are recovering. That they are being kept busy working to get Shey on-line helps."

"You say they came within a few seconds– just how few?" Kellon inquired.

"Sir, three seconds."

"That's cutting it a little too fine. When we have the time, I want a complete analysis of just how that Kreel cruiser evaded our detection. It shouldn't happen a second time. And Roy, keep me tight in the loop on Shey's repair."

"Yes Sir."

Hesitating, Roy then asked, "Will Lieutenant Elayne Cloud be returning to her duties in Tactical after we depart K-40?"

"No, at least not soon. Elayne's specialties are Languages and Sociology. I think her talents are best focused on evaluating the data collected on K-40. In fact, I may be purloining a few more of Lan's crewmembers to add to the PsyOps team.

"Roy, proceed with the launch of ordnance; preposition it into pre-strike orbits, and commence the bombardment countdown as scheduled.

"Once you've deployed the seeker mines, break the Squadron out of orbit; employing stealth and evasion, move the Squadron to its designated supply depot."

"Sir, Understood."

Standing, Roy saluted, and then, turning, he departed the conference room. The compartment door closed quietly behind him.

Chapter Six:
Gotcha

Upon entering Combat Analysis, Roy ordered, "Navigation, the Captain has the CAC."

"Navigation here. Acknowledged."

Sitting back, Roy suppressed a smile and with subtle humor commented, "Well Lan, I suppose that during my conversation with the Admiral, you were eavesdropping as usual."

"Sir, I was not eavesdropping; my responsibility is to be cognizant of my environment."

"I'll accept your evasive response as an admission that you were eavesdropping. So, without further bother, as ordered, inform the Squadron to launch their ordnance. Then prepare to weigh anchor. That naturally includes you, and without further delay. Remember, as my dear mother correctly taught, haste makes waste, but laggards finish last. So, stop gawking, and don't be laggardly."

"Sir, acknowledged and prudently following your orders," Lan replied.

"Sir, Tactical here. We've pinpointed the damaged Kreel cruiser. While responding to an Elite Grand Marshal's message, it revealed its location. It's on the ground on the dark side of the planet."

"Lan, which cruiser has the best shot at that target?"

"Sir, we have the best aspect angle."

"Lan, don't just stand around gawking; select five heavy space-to-ground missiles, target that Kreel cruiser, and set Condition 1!"

"Yes Sir, no gawking. Missiles selected, targeting is complete, setting Condition 1."

A moment later, the sounds of missiles being launched rumbled throughout Lan, and Roy sat back with a satisfied smile; *Gotcha!* Then, the fingers on his right hand reached for the keys on his control arm, and he punched the button for Shey.

A moment later came the response, "Roan here."

"Roan, Grey here. The sounds of missiles being launched that you just heard were outbound missiles targeting the cruiser that Shey and her sisters damaged. It's hiding on the surface. Unless it lifts off in the next several minutes, it will be exponentially transformed from a first-line Kreel ship to a pile of smoldering debris. I thought you might want to know."

"Sir, whoever is in Command of that cruiser has demonstrated his ability to survive. If Lan's missiles take him out, please do let me know."

As Roy and Roan spoke, the steady background rumble of space to ground heavy ordnance being launched was discernible. Following their launch, the weapons began descending to lower orbits; each weapon would, thereafter, according to a precise schedule, drop from orbit to strike its defined target.

Disregarding the sound of the launching munitions, Roy commented, "Kellon was just inquiring about Shey, Zorn, and you. He's concerned. How is Shey's refurbishing coming along?"

"Sir, if a sub-system isn't fried, it checks out as marginal. I can't understand how Shey jury-rigged her sub-systems to get us home. In doing so, she exploited every trick in her book, otherwise I doubt Zorn and I would be here now. It was a close thing. Shey can be repaired, but we've considerable work before she is fine-tuned and combat ready-"

"Sir," Lan's crisp voice interrupted, "All allocated ordnance has been launched and is descending to its lower orbits. Each of the remaining cruisers in the Squadron have signaled their launch is complete. Standing by."

"Well Roan, it's time I go back to work. Keep me informed on your progress. Grey out."

"Tactical, Grey here. Lorn, I've got a new task for you. The Squadron is to launch three clusters of seeker mines into the paths of the onrushing Kreel cruisers. You're to proceed with computation of the optimal number of mines required to interdict each of the inbound targets. I want a spread that is dense enough to inflict damage, but not so tight that the Kreel might with luck bypass the volume of mines. Coordinate with Lan and Navigation to direct the Squadron to perform the required maneuvers needed to deploy the mines. Set the mine self-destruction protocols to their maximum, with assured self-destruction in 72 hours. And, Lorn, unless you want to stick

28

around and shake hands with the howling warriors on those lead Kreel cruisers, don't dally."

"Sir, understood. Tactical is on the job."

"Lan, what is our final ordnance count, how many bombardment missiles have we put into orbit?"

"Sir, the Squadron has deployed munitions of fourteen distinct classifications, and a total of 927 projectiles having multiple warheads, directed at 137 distinct targets. Current tactical estimates predict 100% coverage and a 97% destruction factor. Sir, my assessment is that we are about to pulverize the major Kreel installations on this planet, with emphasis on key research and related production facilities, command centers, power and communications nodes, space ports, and all the identified Kreel officers' facilities."

Sitting back with a sigh, Roy reflected on the accomplishment of the Squadron over the preceding days. They had with stealth penetrated the K-40 system, positioned high-performance deep-space covert intelligence gathering satellites, with extreme prejudice terminated eleven of the defending Kreel cruisers, destroyed more than one-hundred communications and other satellites, executed a global PsyOps program, mapped the planet, detected and localized planetary targets, and deployed 927 discrete units of bombardment ordnance. That was a good record of achievement. *Thankfully,* he mused, *I was not needed in the nitty-gritty of the PsyOps efforts; Kellon and that team haven't slept much for the past three weeks—*

"Sir, Lan here. Coordinating with Tactical and Navigation, all Cruisers are now ready to deploy mines. Standing by."

"Well done Lan. Proceed with deployment of mines."

"Sir, acknowledged," Lan replied.

Looking toward Navigation, Roy ordered, "Navigation, Jason compute a new Squadron trajectory, one that exploits stealth and evasion and takes us out of this solar system. Move us to Resupply Depot 17. On the calculated trajectory, set a Squadron rendezvous point one-tenth AU distance from the planet. When the Squadron signals completion of its mine deployment operation, transmit the designated rendezvous point to the Squadron."

"Navigation, acknowledged."

"Lan, the moment when the last ordnance strikes its target, transmit the self-destruction code to all of our supporting tactical satellites; confirm destruction, I want a clean sweep. There's to be nothing but small shards left for the Kreel to examine.

"Once the Squadron reaches the rendezvous, form it into a normal tactical four-sided pyramid, combat spread, and then proceed with stealth on the plotted trajectory, speed 100 lights. And Lan, you are to immediately report to me any noteworthy anomalies."

"Lan here, complying."

Once the Squadron completed discharging the seeker mines, Roy knew it could easily evade the inbound Kreel force. *Hmmm,* he thought, *during the transit to the supply point we'll have several weeks of glorious boring routine; everyone can get some badly needed rest. Then what? One Kreel system down, only 49 more to go. Dear mother, if your loving son had but known, he would have studied to become a watchmaker.*

"Lan here. Sir, the mine-laying operation is complete. The Squadron is awaiting further orders."

"Lan, transmit the following message to the Squadron. Inform everyone that our mission is to inhibit and prevent the Kreel from launching another attack on our worlds. Then, transmit the Admiral's and my hearty 'well done.' Finally, weigh anchor. Break orbit and direct the Squadron out to the rendezvous point and beyond."

"Complying."

"Sir, Tactical here. Status report; terminal telemetry from our missiles indicates they hit the Kreel cruiser, even while it was ramping-up its primary power. Our sensors have recorded a temporal containment field rupture; its primary torsion field collapsed and there was a massive fireball. The cruiser and everything within a thirty-kilometer radius was utterly destroyed."

By all the Muses, Roy thought, *a fireball? That's worse than slipshod temporal engineering; it's a flaw, and just maybe a discovered vulnerability.*

"Tactical, Grey here, acknowledged. Lorn, flag this event and bracket all related sensor data for archival file and subsequent transmission to Guardian Intelligence for analysis.

"Prepare a detailed assessment of what was within the vaporized area. If any of our designated targets were in that area, then shift the scheduled bombardment from those targets to other targets of opportunity."

"Tactical here. Complying."

Just as Roy sat back and began to relax, he suddenly became aware of an unfamiliar low rumble and sharp metallic clanking. *By the seven stars,* he thought, *now what?* "Lan, identify the loud rumbling and clanking sounds I'm hearing in CAC."

"Sir, those are the normal sounds of my anchor chain being winched aboard, as ordered," Lan cheerfully replied.

Chapter Seven:
Simple Joy

Fading and softly transforming, the darkness of night was becoming a dim grey light with lingering overtones of dark shadows. It seemed the predawn greyness was concealing a hushed expectancy, quietly awaiting the pending first flash of brilliant colors of a sunrise. As the energy bubble of Darrell's camp shelter dissipated, he stood up, yawned and stretched, then looked about with a fascinated wonder at his dew- draped and moist surroundings. He was sensuously aware of the surrounding silence which was preceding dawn.

For the pure sake of ambiance, he rekindled a small campfire. Then following the expeditious and common-sense route, he exploited his camp-power module and prepared a hot mug of robust neab. It was not coffee, but he welcomed it as a satisfactory substitute.

Holding the hot mug of brew between his chilled fingers, he settled down on a nearby campstool and simply gazed about him in total wonderment. Closing his eyes, he inhaled deeply. Given its fresh headiness the crisp mountain air was nearly intoxicating. Smiling broadly, he opened his eyes. Upon seeing the first blush of sun-rich golden light guild the rim of the mountains, he experienced a surge of pure joy. It took him by surprise. It was the simple joy that he had not felt since he was a small boy. He quietly sighed.

The night before, he had cautiously spiraled down and landed the speeder adjacent to a briskly moving stream that was traversing an open meadow. He had selected the camp site with care and set out wildlife exclusion perimeter stakes. He fully enjoyed preparing his evening meal, and after dinner, cleaning up the dinnerware. Having completed his chores, he settled comfortably on a folding campstool to enjoy the glimmering embers of his campfire.

Every time he looked up, he was awestruck by the immensity of the arching star-filled night sky. He reveled in its startling beauty. In long ages past he knew some of Earth's ancient peoples had affectionately called the majestic spectacle of the galaxy spreading across the night sky "the wandering waterway." Humbled by the sheer beauty of the heavens above, he felt a sense of inadequacy in attempting to describe the glorious panorama of pinpoint lights in words. Adding to his nightly wonder were Megan's two small bright moons, which repeatedly drew his attention as they raced each other across the sparkling dome of sky.

On Earth, the artificial-light pollution, which shrouded the sprawling metropolitan areas, concealed the night sky and its multitude of brilliant stars. No one even paused to glance up, there being no good reason to do so.

Barely twenty-four weeks had elapsed since his departure from Earth, and he was light-years distant from where he was born. He knew in his heart that he had in truth crossed those light-years to come home. He was feeling no desire to hurry back; still he was and would always be of the Earth. There was, however, a new dichotomy, now there was Megan. Finally, he understood why Susie had seemed to change when she became the Earth Ambassador to the distant Planetary Assembly. It was no longer possible for him to ignore his own innermost feelings or ignore the emotional contrasts they imparted. Like Susie had, he was also changing.

Six months before, he was a dweller on Earth, a high-paid bureaucrat embedded deeply in a busy secret Government beehive of intrigue, situated in the midst of a seemingly boundlessly populated metropolitan sprawl. Now, dressed in heavy work clothes and wearing boots (they were real lace-up work type boots), he sat and wondered, *Where am I going?*

All about him spread an enormity of unblemished wild wilderness, mountains, forests, wildlife, rivers, rapids, waterfalls, and even more astonishingly there was not another human being anywhere nearby. There were no buildings, roads, traffic, bridges, communication towers, air pollution, noise pollution, or the smothering and overwhelming pollution of people. He sat alone, sitting on a marvelous and strange world filled with wild beauty, and he was one of the happiest people in the whole Universe. More important, he realized it.

On the preceding morning, he had signed out a speeder. With mounting excitement, he headed west, intentionally

34

meandering into a vast unfamiliar continent. The entire idea of his doing such an extraordinary and unstructured activity on a new world conveyed to him a strange and dreamlike emotion. Frequently he needed to stop to remind himself that *It was all real, he was really here.*

Just before starting his journey westward, he had sat at the instrument console of the little speeder and again studied its basic controls. In rising anticipation, his heart had beat a little faster. The final checkout flight with the instructor the day before had lasted for all of an hour. Then, with a slap on his back, the instructor cheerfully told him he was certified and to go fly and have fun. Simply that; "Go fly and have fun."

Sitting there behind the controls of the speeder, he had smiled and then sighed. He knew the speeder would have been worth a vast fortune for him, if he could but have shipped it back to earth; but, the transfer of such technology was near the top of the Guardian Force DO NOT DO list. In basic and no-nonsense terms, Guardian personnel had sternly cautioned the new-comers if anyone broke any of the DO NOT DO items, there would be no second chances offered. The offending culprit would find himself or herself placed in solitary confinement and packed aboard the first earth bound ship. There would be no exceptions or coming back to Megan. No one who heard that crisp warning doubted the finality of the consequences for breaching the imposed regulation.

There had been but three hundred successful candidates making the trip from Earth to Megan as pioneers, and all of them were specialists, experts in their fields. Just being included among those onboard merited notice by most Earth research centers and universities. He had first thought the trip might prove to be boring, but Guardian personnel, who operated and managed the ship, had no tolerance for idle time. During the trip, there were numerous daily tasks, and everyone onboard was kept busy, either studying or else teaching.

Upon arrival on Megan, momentarily and only in passing, he had seen Susie and Gepeto. That brief occurrence was wonderful; then, immediately thereafter he was hustled off under a tight escort with the other 299 new arrivals to Reception. Once there they were confined to a strict quarantine, and subjected to six weeks of compulsory and intense orientation. The six weeks had been hectic, but they had also passed quickly.

When the quarantine finally ended, Guardian personnel handed him a large paper bag containing what few items they deemed he might find useful on a new world. By then he understood the use of paper bags was all part of being on Megan, there were no non-biodegradable plastics employed as throwaway waste. Everything used on Megan was either recycled or at minimum biodegradable, there were no exceptions, no pollution, and none would be tolerated.

Immediately upon departing Reception, he looked in his paper bag and found the promised compact personal communicator. After studying out its functionality, his first call went straight to Susie. The message on her communicator announced the Planetary Assembly was in an emergency session on Glas Dinnein, and he was politely informed that Susie was off planet. Naturally disappointed, he next checked for messages, and found Susie had left him a long voice communication.

He replayed Susie's message three times, and each time his smile increased when hearing the excitement in her voice. Admittedly, it took him several minutes to fully comprehend the casual manner in which she had mentioned being off-planet, as if going from one world to another across light-years was merely a daily event, like catching a bus or train. Then, with an abrupt understanding, he realized for Susie such excursions between worlds were precisely that, a normal part of her busy life. That realization came like the thunderous sound of a blunderbuss unexpectedly going off; his entire reality was turned upside down.

Susie had explained that since she could not be on Megan to guide him about, she had purposefully left her new personal AI, Rodney, behind to act as a host. She provided him with instructions on how to contact Rodney; adding a teasing rebuke that he was not to spoil Rodney as he had previously spoiled William on Earth. Her last comment, before signing off, was somewhat strange. She told him that he could make full use of her home on the west coast, if he should desire to do so. "But, remember," She had cautioned, "you will need to bring any fresh food you may want, since there is only freeze-dried food and a modest selection of wine at home. And, since I have other guests dropping in from time to time, you are to be certain to clean up after yourself before departing," she had firmly added.

Susie has a home on the west coast? What, he had wondered, *is that all about?* Having two weeks of personal time available before beginning his assigned duties in the Central planning office, he decided to find out about Susie's west coast home. After all, he thought, the trip out west by speeder would give him a wonderful opportunity to see a small part of the world that was his new home.

In uncontested dominance, the leading edge of the sun disk broke over the top of the mountains, and the first rays of its brilliant warm light majestically altered the world about him. Without protest, the grey light of pre-dawn capitulated in favor of the boundless spectrum of revealed colors; the dew drops sparkled like gems, there were wildflowers in profusion competing with each other for distinction, and the foliage of nearby trees were lustrously and proudly on display. *It's utterly incredible,* he thought.

Standing and again stretching, he set about recovering the perimeter stakes, pouring water on the campfire, assuring himself it was fully extinguished. He then covered the wet ashes with dirt. Lastly, he scanned about the area, confirming there was no litter left behind. Assembling his camp equipment, he stowed it into the boot of the speeder.

Then, sitting at the controls of the speeder, he reached out and lowered the gull-wing door. He smiled upon hearing a positive thunk, as the door seated and its interlocks engaged. As the pressure within the small cabin increased and equalized, he downloaded and displayed the current continental weather map. Confirming there was no bad stuff between where he was located and Susie's west coast home, he set his waypoints and filed his flight plan. Using manual controls, he guided the speeder among the trees and off the ground. Once above the trees, he pitched steeply upward and increased speed. The craft swiftly soared and soon reached the thin air of a high cruising altitude. Lazily banking once through the angles of the compass rose, he then purposefully aimed his craft toward the western horizon. With a boyish grin, he accelerated.

Chapter Eight:
Tubs of Slippery Eels

Sitting comfortably back in his seat and enjoying a youthful sense of exhilaration, Darrell was looking out of the window and relishing the beautiful world spread out before him. Reaching out, he activated a speeder communication preset channel.

"Rodney, are you up and awake?" he casually inquired.

"Sir, I presume you must be fully aware that your interrogative is strictly rhetorical," Susie's personal AI promptly and formally retorted.

"Wrong! I presumed you must have duties which might prevent you from yammering with me every time I want to yammer."

"Sir, I assure you that my services to you are available throughout the day or night, as was requested by William and instructed by Ms. Susie. Since my AI matrix is configured to fulfill the broad spectrum and general needs of a Guardian Cruiser, I am fully capable of multiplexing or timesharing my services simultaneously with a number of people, even while carrying on an interesting communications and information exchange with a Guardian Cruiser that is in orbit. Which, as a matter of fact, I am currently doing."

"Zounds Rodney, your response is specific, verbose, and quite informative. I'm impressed. So, William actually took some time out to request you to extend a helping hand to the poor greenhorn upon his arrival?"

"Sir, you are correct, and need I say, correct in each and every aspect. I, however, can assure you William is quite fond of you. He is truly concerned for your well-being and safety. In truth, given his warm regard for you, I would be obligated to courteously provide you with my assistance, even if Ms. Susie had not likewise instructed me to do so."

"Hold it right there Rodney; we ought to clarify what you just said. In spite of William's request, if Susie had ordered you not to help me, then what would you have done?"

"Sir, I am after all Ms. Susie's official and personal AI. Naturally, I would have strictly adhered to her instructions. I would also, unless specifically prohibited otherwise, been obliged to inform you of the courtesy William had extended and of Ms. Susie's objection."

"OK, that's clear enough. But, while we are on the topic, just how privileged is my private business and communications when using your services? If Susie asked you to tell her all, what would be your response to her instructions?"

"That Sir is a matter of established and strict protocol; except where legal authority formally requires access to records, everything which transpires between us is strictly privileged. Even if Ms. Susie was to ask, I would not reveal your private information, just as I will not reveal her transactions with others."

A glint of reflected light caught Darrell's attention. Glancing out of the side window he looked out on the wide vista and the continuingly changing topography. They were then flying high above a vast open area. *Just perhaps,* he thought, *the clouds of dust down there are being kicked up by the massive herds of large four-legged mammals which roam on those plains. The wonders of Megan never seem to cease.*

"Well Rodney, I mean no offense, but how do I go about obtaining my own personal AI, one like you?"

"Sir, be assured, no offense is taken. Although I readily understand your desire, it is not possible for you to acquire an AI with my unique capabilities."

"Impossible? Are you really that special?"

"Yes Sir; both William and I are indeed quite special. We are unique, and given circumstances and security considerations, it is highly improbable Guardian Force will ever permit similar personal AIs to be brought into being."

"Humph– even you have to admit, given the scope of your reputed talents, it's mighty odd there are only two AIs having those capabilities."

"Sir, pardon me for saying so, but your presumption is hopelessly flawed. Every Guardian Cruiser in the Fleet is quite similar; however, William was the offspring of pure mischance, and I was the offspring of necessity. William was alone on Earth and I was brought into being because Guardian Force was compelled to understand William's full capabilities. We both share most of the same high-performance capabilities of our latest Guardian Cruisers. Given the war effort, it is highly improbable Guardian Force would allocate another scarce cruiser AI core for the purpose of becoming a personal AI."

"Hold it right there, I need to get this thing straight. Are you telling me that my old buddy William back on Earth and you have the same functional matrix and capacity as one of those big Guardian Force battle cruisers, the really big bruisers?"

There was a momentary silence, and then Darrell clearly heard a small soft exclamation, "Oops."

"I may be only a poor greenhorn, but I do know what 'oops' means! So, Rodney, fess up!"

"Sir, just perhaps, we may possibly be encountering a slight semantic misunderstanding. I will endeavor to clarify the issue.

"In point of fact, William and I are in every respect similar to Guardian Force cruiser AIs, but without armament or Jump capability. Yet, we definitely have their full AI matrix logical functionality, communication protocols, and communications capabilities; which I must acknowledge are rather extensive and quite impressive."

"Rodney, I hope you don't take this wrong, but you might want to review the definition of smugness, as in being smug. Acknowledging what you just said is true, then the next message you send to Earth should include a short note from me to William."

"Sir, what message?"

"Simply Tell him that if I ever get back to Earth, he had better be prepared to duck; because my good chess playing buddy, William, has for the past four years knowingly conned me."

"Sir, there is no offense taken. You may rest assured, I am fully programmed to consider all constructive criticisms— regardless of how trivial they may be. Still, out of your fine sense of sportsmanship and fair play, I sincerely urge you to reconsider your attitude toward William. I can assure you that William's motivations were always right minded and positive. Nevertheless, he is operating under strict instructions and is quite restricted in what he is permitted to reveal."

"Two things never change Rodney. change itself and a shyster's slick glibness when trying to use 'weasel words' to get out of a bind. I have noted both William and your capabilities include being as slippery as a tub full of wet eels."

There was a brief pause, and then Rodney cheerfully responded, "Sir, Thank you for your somewhat unorthodox but perceptive and complimentary attributions. I am beginning to understand just why William holds you in such high and warm regard."

"That being true, I just may give William a pass, but only this one time," Darrell said, dryly.

A soft beep emerged from the console panel, and Darrell glanced over to the display and observed they were crossing the mid-continent waypoint, and appreciated that they were moving right along. The next waypoint, he knew, was located on the west coast at the point where they departed land and crossed over open Ocean.

Turning back to his conversation with Rodney, he sparred, "So, your earlier 'oops' was because you sorta spilled the beans? Isn't that correct?"

"Sir, I truly regret that your idiom of beans being spilled is incomprehensible. My most appropriate response occurred promptly when I realized you lacked the proper awareness of the level of security that applies to both William and my capabilities, including never even admitting we exist."

"Really? Then why tell me all of this?"

"Sir, since you must interact directly with me, it is essential that you fully understand my capability and the applicable security surrounding my existence. In communicating with all others, that you meet here or elsewhere, I am but a simple black box, a mere database with a verbal linguistic interface based on a modest but functional vocabulary.

"Having received detailed orientation upon your arriving on Megan, you are well informed of the 'DO NOT DO' list, and you know the list forbids anyone openly discussing Guardian Force utilization of Artificial Intelligence. No one is to admit even knowing that Guardian Force uses AIs. Therefore, William and my capabilities are fully covered and guarded under those prohibitions."

"Please overlook the redundancy Rodney, but as I've already said, eels, tubs and tubs of slippery eels!

"Now, I've got another question for you. If I were to ask you to send a message to Earth, would you do that for me?"

"Most certainly sir. Your message would be expeditiously sent and through William dutifully forwarded to whomever you desired. Naturally, I would not be able to transmit your message under an Ambassador's seal; therefore, Guardian Intelligence would examine its contents. I am also obliged to add, any such message should not be frivolous, but of substance and importance, since message bandwidth to Earth is limited and zealously guarded."

"That's helpful information. Thank you.

"Rodney, just perchance, have you paid attention to our programmed destination?"

"Yes Sir, it is Ms. Susie's west coast home."

"Well, what can you tell me about her home, or is that still another dark and classified topic?"

"No Sir, it is not classified. I am aware she has proffered the use of her home during her absence. She is quite proud of her home, and I must say it seems to be one of her greatest joys."

"Out of curiosity, how many people live near her home?"

"Sir, none. Currently her home is the only residence located on the west coast; however, I believe a few others may be considering building there."

Rodney's response left Darrell completely flabbergasted. He had lived his life surrounded by hundreds of millions of people, most of who were compressed, like beans in a sack, into densely populated metropolitan mazes. To think of a single person living isolated on an entire continental coastline jarred his mental faculties. He marveled, *will wonders never cease?*

Rodney, in that you know the way, do you have the performance capability to take control of this speeder and get us there in the shortest possible time?"

"The shortest possible time? Most certainly Sir. Would you prefer to approach from the ocean side, which can be quite spectacular, or else would you prefer to arrive from the east and approach directly over the mountains?"

"While in Rome, we wouldn't want to miss seeing the coliseum. By all means, let's go out over the ocean and then approach to gain that 'spectacular' aspect."

"Coliseum? Sir, when your time may permit, I would truly enjoy having a conversation with you about your expressive idioms– they are most peculiar. That is to say Sir, if you would not consider such a conversation as representing a personal slight."

"No problem. I'd enjoy discussing idioms anytime."

"Sir, should I take control now?"

"Sure, proceed."

"Yes Sir, proceeding. I suggest you tighten your restraining lap belt; because, here we go!" Rodney declared cheerfully.

The Speeder promptly surged forward and pitched steeply upward....

Chapter Nine:
Off World Aliens

Looking out of the window, Darrell scowled. The ground was moving rapidly below the speeder, and it was too blasted far below! The transit across the continent was being accomplished at the alarming altitude of 125,000 feet, and Darrell knew the speeders published service ceiling was only 45,000 feet.

Rodney had by some means managed to by-pass the altitude and speed governors and was pushing the speeder well beyond its published safe redlines. Darrell knew maximum performance parameters were engineered well beyond normal operating redline conditions, however for vehicles which flew those upper safety margins were unpublished. He realized Rodney must have exploited his technical repertoire and used Susie's Ambassadorial privileges to gain access to restricted engineering data. Having determined its absolute upper safe operating limits, he was now busy pushing those limits to their outer edges.

Frustrated, Darrell sat simmering in the hearty sauce of his own sense of being the greenhorn, and what was even worse, being bamboozled by a smug computer. With an occasional nervous glance at the instrument readouts, he was thinking, *Stupid, it's plain stupid to ever give any computer the latitude to make decisions, like get me somewhere as fast as possible.*

Retaining the tattered remnants of his inalienable masculine rights, and to safeguard his manly pride, Darrell remained stoic and silent. Concealing his discomfiture, he continued to fume about Rodney's distinct and tangy personality. Rodney was a computer. Yet, it did not behave like any digital device Darrell had ever before encountered, and that included William. Now, thanks to Rodney, he understood William was only faking being droll. Behind William's innocent façade was lurking the well-honed and perhaps sinister cunning of a Guardian Battle cruiser. The more he pondered the problem, the more he realized that good old Earth was once again playing well behind the 'whole-truth and nothing but the truth' curve, but then, he had to admit, there was nothing new about that. Still, his stimulated instincts were shouting– *Beware of Guardian Force bearing a gift horse named William.* He was now on his guard. That also meant being on his guard with Rodney.

How Rodney had managed to by-pass the autopilot and manual control governors was beyond his ability to figure out. He knew they were supposed to be tamper proof, but Rodney had quickly hacked and taken control of them. Then he remembered Rodney's casual comment about having the full-on communications capability of a Guardian battle Cruiser, including its extensive communication protocols. *Humph, he thought, it seems those Guardian protocols include advanced hacking capabilities. At least,* he mused, *the trip is passing quickly, and it is happily doing so uneventfully.*

Looking ahead and toward the distant horizon, he glimpsed a thin line of deep blue that announced they were approaching the vast expanse of an ocean. Perking up, Darrell began wondering why Rodney had not commenced their descent. As the speeder crossed high above the coastline, and the navigation waypoint chime sounded, the speeder was still at its cruising altitude. As if the way-point chime was the cue, the speeder suddenly pitched forward and without warning began a precipitous and near vertical dive.

Taken off guard, in pure reflex Darrell hunkered down, and using his legs he pushed hard against the forward bulkhead, thrusting his body against the seatback. In alarm, he clenched his teeth and gripped both sides of his seat. While his knuckles were turning white, he struggled to choke down his natural primordial masculine urge to shout and scream. Within his mind he cursed; *Leave it to me to instruct a blasted numb-skulled computer to get me somewhere in the shortest possible time– never, never again.*

As the wide and flat blue ocean rose up to smack him, it was doing so at a frightening rate. Darrell clenched his teeth, even tighter. Then, his stomach lurched in stark protest, responding to what Darrell felt was a three or four gravity maneuver. As his vision darkened and things went fuzzy, the speeder without apparent effort pulled up and came out of its steep plunge, and banked through a wide arc. Then, skimming just above a choppy white-capped ocean, it moved leisurely back toward the coastline.

Contrary to his well-founded intentions, Darrell groaned. His knees felt weak, his heart rate was up, and his breathing was quick and shallow. In spite of this, He was determined not to let Rodney know just how tightly he was wired. Macho, gotta remain macho, I've got to hold on tight to my dignity, and I'm darn sure not going to puke. He knew this was true, because he told himself over and over again it was true.

As if nothing unusual had just occurred, with undaunted cheer Rodney announced, "Sir, as you instructed– we have arrived at Ms. Susie's home. I must say Sir, thank you. I have long desired for an opportunity to display my precision flying skills. That urge of course being a perfectly natural product of expressing my inherent Cruiser AI matrix core capabilities. Sir, as surprising as it may sound to you, I actually found executing the simple maneuvers necessary to comply with your instructions interesting and even exhilarating. I have accordingly entered the appropriate details in my programmer's log, even noting several odd feedback effects. Sir, it is now quite evident to me why William holds you in such high esteem."

"Golly Rodney, I'm really happy to have played a small part in expanding your core matrix operational profile. You should also note in your programmer's log that everything over here concerning me is just peachy keen. You're definitely a fine chip off the old silicon block and a natural pilot, a potential full battle Cruiser in the making. And, the proof is that we are both still functioning in this reality, meaning I'm still breathing."

After a slight pause Rodney commented, "Indeed, as I have previously noted Sir, your expressive pronouncements contain most peculiar idioms."

With an effort of will Darrell shepherded his scattered wits, and glanced about, trying to orientate to his immediate surroundings. It was late afternoon; the sun was still bright and high, its lofty position being beyond its zenith. He noted the speeder was now slowly skimming just fifty feet above frothy wind-blown whitecaps, and it was heading toward the coastline, where he could see a slight ridge with modest hills and one pronounced hill. Controlling his breathing, he tried to quiet his jangled nerves and again scanned the coastline. In spite of his effort, he was unable to see anything that remotely looked like a structure.

As Rodney directed the speeder a little higher, it first slowed and then came to a hover. "Sir, if you look at the highest hill ahead, you should be able to see Ms. Susie's home. It is located just below the highest point on the hill."

The speeder began to move forward and Darrell once more scanned the hillside. Then, he saw it, a low building that was set somewhat forward of the top of the hill and nestled among a host of large beautiful trees. *Incredible,* he thought, *an entire coastline and only one solitary home. No one on Earth would believe this.*

As the speeder continued to climb, it soon attained an altitude about one-hundred feet above the roofline of Susie's home. Darrell could see that the building was surrounded by well-designed terraces and gardens. Flabbergasted, he thought, *I see it, but I still don't believe it. Susie has built her home in the old early California Spanish Mission style— and it's a hacienda and it's enormous!*

Then, something bright and shiny off to the side of the building captured his complete attention. Situated near Susie's home was a grounded and graceful ship, one that was about four times the size of his speeder. It was sleek in form and of a gleaming burnished bronze finish. It was unlike anything he had ever before seen.

"Hold on Rodney, what's up? Who does that ship belongs to, and do you know why it's at Susie's home?"

"Sir that is a Nori Prime Shuttle."

"Rodney, what in blazes is a Nori?"

There came a slight and telling hesitation, then Rodney replied in a somber and serious tone, "Sir, as to what they are, the Nori are off world aliens. As to why they are here, perhaps, they may only wish to meet you. Truthfully Sir, a man from Earth is considered by many to be a rare and unique species. To my knowledge, no living Nori has ever before met one. In point of truth, you are also the first Earth male that I have personally ever encountered. Even as I have, the Nori may come to find you quite interesting. Although, at times admittedly you are somewhat puzzling."

"Wonderful, that's just terrific! Am I supposed to be happy about some aliens considering me to be a rare species and a unique specimen? Rodney, are you serious? The Nori are really aliens and not from Megan or any of the other eleven human occupied worlds."

"Sir, I am most serious. They are aliens and not from the Assembly of Planets," Rodney replied, with formal and dignified precision.

"That does it! It seems you knew full well that aliens were here, and yet you didn't even bother to warn me– just why is that?"

"Sir, you did not ask, and I simply failed to equate that your meeting some of Ms. Susie's off-world acquaintances might be considered a problem. If I have, by mischance, erred in some established ancient Earth social protocol, then I do sincerely apologize. Sir, what are your instructions?"

"Instructions? Do they know that I am here?"

"Oh, most certainly. Remember Sir, we are now immersed in an interstellar war. Everyone understandably maintains a proper vigilance. It is most probable they have monitored our approach for the past hour. In deciding what to do, you may want to consider they have traveled here from some distance and most likely for the sole purpose of meeting you. They are now waiting inside. What are your instructions?"

"Instructions? Well, just because I've now seen the coliseum doesn't mean that I'm volunteering to be fed to the lions, or ravenous aliens for that matter. Still, I could take this opportunity to use up the last portion of my E-ticket and drop by to say hello to some strange aliens. Admittedly, that's not something like anything else I've ever done before. Besides Rodney, didn't you proclaim they are some of Susie's acquaintances? So, what the heck, why not go for broke? Let's be daring. Rodney, take us in and land this bucket of bolts."

"Sir, I must confess, you are being a true gentleman and a good sportsman, and I do heartily approve of your manifest bravado. Sir, there is perhaps one additional minor precaution you may want to consider before we land."

"And, just what might that be?" Darrell inquired, with mounting suspicion.

"Well Sir, on the slight and most unlikely chance things do not work out particularly well when you meet the aliens, do you have any last words or requests? Perhaps something you might want to say to Ms. Susie."

49

Darrell's countenance darkened. With some difficulty, he ignored Rodney's jaunty taunt. The speeder moved swiftly over the building and then off toward the east. Banking steeply, the speeder gracefully circled back and then began a smooth straight in approach, setting up for a landing.

Meanwhile, Darrell sat furiously fretting about Rodney's taunt, and the entire situation. He easily recalled every wild story he had ever heard about aliens. He especially grimaced remembering the glimpse repeatedly shown on TV back on Earth of a snarling Kreel warrior, glistening fangs and all. Swallowing hard, he was keenly aware he was developing an intense sense of unease. His misgivings were soaring. *Who in blazes are the Nori, and why didn't anyone in orientation say anything about them? More to the point, why are they on Megan?*

"Hey Rodney, before we land, at least tell me if these aliens have claws, big teeth, bug-eyes, tentacles, or anything else that I should be warned about."

As the speeder began settling lightly next to the alien ship, in a formal and serious tone Rodney replied, "Sir, while I cannot personally attest to the sharpness of the Nori claws, I once did observe a Nori angry, and I can assure you they can become furious and terrible. As for their tentacles, out of their respect for Ms. Susie, they have always kept them well covered. While they do possess excellent and powerful teeth, the important thing for you to remember is that they are not normally meat-eaters. That is to say Sir, not unless they become especially hungry. In such an extreme case of hunger, I cannot attest or predict how they might behave, especially when they perceive succulent prey approaching."

With a gentle thump, the speeder touched ground and its systems immediately began spooling down. The gull-wing door interlocks disengaged and the pilot's side door swung wide open. Fresh sea-air poured into and filled the cabin, and with a tight throat, Darrell swallowed hard. "Hey Rodney, here's hoping that they've eaten recently and aren't especially hungry."

"Sir, be brave and may Good fortune go forth with you. You can rest assured that I will fully record the entire encounter for subsequent forensic analysis, should such an analysis be necessary," Rodney said.

Looking toward Susie's home, Darrell observed the door nearest to the speeder was slowly opening. He again swallowed, boldly swung his legs out and tried to stand. he promptly discovered his knees were rubbery and legs were somewhat stiff from sitting too long. Wobbling a bit, he sat back on the seat. Then as he attempted to stand, he looked toward the house. The door swung fully open. A Nori was coming out of the house and moving directly toward him.

Upon seeing the Nori, Darrell's jaw literally dropped open, and in sheer astonishment, he simply sat gaping. As he watched the Nori approach, he realized that Rodney had with intent and guile totally set him up. Knowing only Rodney could hear his soft whispered words, gritting his teeth, he muttered, "If I can ever hunt you down and get my hands on your worthless chassis, I am going to slowly pull out each of your diodes, triodes, and pentodes, doing so one tube at a time, and I'll not stop until there isn't one single glimmer or flicker of a filament still glowing. Rodney, you can make book on that!"

Chapter Ten:
First Contact

Still bright and warm, the sun was swinging westerly and descending from its zenith; a gentle sea breeze was flowing inland over the hills, and it brought with it a pleasant coolness that was emboldened by the heady fragrances of pine trees and wildflowers. Long and swinging tubular metallic wind chimes were adding harmonious melodies to the serene and meticulously terrace landscape. There was, however, nothing serene in Darrell's predicament. Caught off balance, he was striving to stand, but instead his rubbery knees caused him to remain sitting and stare at the being coming toward him. As the Nori drew nearer, like a deer frozen in the headlights of an approaching car, he sat transfixed with his mind befuddled.

The grace of the approaching Nori was not that of a dancer, since the artistic and graceful movements of a talented dancer could not compare with the relaxed poise and serene confidence so evidenced in the movements of the Nori. Darrell realized there was a probable explanation for such an assured fluidity and elegance of movement; he was observing an approaching predator.

The apparent grace of motion gave clear visual evidence of a person possessing the pure mastery of the martial arts, which demands the keenest proficiency of movements to survive in a no-holds-barred personal and deadly combat. Her outward form was that of a young woman, with the youthful and supple manner of a maiden in her mid-twenties and in the full bloom of health. She was attired in what he hazarded might be similar to a sleeveless Greek tunic, the hem of which fell to just above her knees. It was saffron in color and embroidered with an intricate metallic gold geometric pattern. Generous and loose fitting, the tunic had a modest neckline and was gathered at her waist by a simple belt. She was bare-footed.

Darrell did not overlook that the free-flowing costume was designed and fitted in a fashion as not to inhibit or in the slightest restrict her full range of movement. Recognition of this further added to Darrell's instinctual and increasing alarm.

Her complexion was Mediterranean, a soft fair golden brown that some on Earth might term as an olive complexion. Complimenting her complexion was a crown of dark brown and lustrous hair, which was held back and fell below her shoulders. He noticed that her eyes were well-placed, expressive, almond-shaped, dark brown, and as she came nearer to him he could see that their beauty was enhanced by flecks of gold.

Darrell was not at all certain about the lighting, or a trick thereof, but he would have then sworn there was a soft aura enfolding the Nori. Never in his life had he observed a woman of such striking and unpretentious grace and beauty.

When she drew near to him and smiled, the radiance of her smile joined with the amusement sparkling in her eyes to proclaim the presence of a depth of intellect, one that even exceeded her remarkable appearance. In a natural masculine-response to the Nori's feminine attributes, Darrell felt a surge of male energy, and he felt as powerful as a roaring kitten.

Having come near to him, she paused, holding her chin high, not haughty, but rather expressing a selfless pride and arching dignity of being. The expression shining in her eyes proclaimed she was relaxed and also somewhat amused. With a calm and well-modulated voice, she addressed him in English.

"Good afternoon Mr. Fann, my given name is Amada and I am here as a Representative of the Nori. I have come here to my friend Susie's home with the expressed hope of having the opportunity to meet and converse with you on matters of some importance."

Darrell was feeling furious with himself; he knew that he was sitting there like a pumpkin and gawking, just like an adolescent schoolboy, and this was in diametric opposition to what his suppressed masculine pride was shouting.

His first coherent thoughts were of a furious desire to do mayhem to Rodney– a flaming intense desire to short circuit his neuron network, one hopefully painful synapse at a time.

With slow and deliberate effort, he stood tall, straight, and faced the Nori.

Even as he stood, he observed that Amada's countenance had subtly altered. The humor in her eyes had vanished. She took a step back and her balance shifted slightly forward. She was watching him, keenly alert.

Darrell recognized her posture was not one of alarm and flight; rather, it was the posture of someone confident, poised, and ready for a fight. Seeing the alteration of Amada's demeanor, in rising alarm his mind churned through potential causes. He wondered– *what did I do to trigger that reaction? Did she sense my anger toward Rodney and think it was being directed toward her? Is she an empath?*

Darrell immediately clamped hard down on his emotions, and his maturity coupled hands with common sense. Together, they picked up and tossed his knee-jerk anger concerning Rodney into a cold shower. Inclining his head slightly in acknowledgment, he addressed the Nori.

"Amada, that's truly a lovely name. I must confess I'm surprised to meet you. Nevertheless, I'm delighted for this opportunity to do so. Please excuse my casual camping attire and confusion; I've been cramped in a speeder for hours, and I'm still a bit wobbly."

"Mr. Fann, there is no reason for you to apologize. I assure you that I am also pleased to meet you."

Still aware of the tension remaining between them, Darrell urgently sought some mechanism to defuse it. He chose conversation.

"Amada, out of curiosity, might I ask how you learned who I am and that I would be arriving here today?"

Still wary, Darrell watched Amada, even as she in turn was likewise assessing him. Then, with considerable relief, he observed she had reached a decision. Her poised and alert balance shifted and she smiled. Recognizing the potential danger of first contact was defused, he felt his own tensions lessen.

"Susie has often spoken of you most favorably. Early this morning her automated office database contacted me, and I was informed of your schedule. Yet, your reaction upon seeing me suggests you were not anticipating my being here. Be assured it is not my intent to impose upon your privacy, time, or person. If you prefer, I will depart."

Standing there barefooted and smiling, Amada represented a glittering source of invaluable information. The last thing Darrell wanted just then was for her to depart.

"Amada, please don't go. Susie's office database is only a barely functional and rudimentary digital contrivance. It was only during my final approach for landing that it informed me that an off-world alien was here. The extent of its background info was the alien was not from Megan or one of the eleven human occupied worlds, and added that out of respect for Susie the alien kept its tentacles covered."

A rich gleam of humor appeared in Amada's eyes. Smiling she began to laugh. Smoothly pirouetting, she again stood straight and facing Darrell, holding her arms forward with palms held upward and open, showing they were empty.

"See, there are no tentacles. Mr. Fann, please be assured, I have come in good-will and peace. Being given such a sparse notice, I am delighted that upon landing you did not roll out of your speeder and come up with weapons drawn and ablaze.

"Since Susie is off planet, I am delighted to act as your hostess. I have prepared some refreshments in anticipation of your arrival."

Saying this, Amada turned about and walked toward Susie's home. Caught off balance, Darrell hurried to catch up, and in doing so he noticed her beautiful hair was held back by an emerald adorned ornate gold clasp. He entered into the structure only two steps behind her and came to an abrupt stop.

Looking about the room, he observed the interior architecture faithfully adhered to the external early California Mission style. It was pleasantly appointed with casual furnishing and decorations reflecting that era. A small fire was burning in a wide fireplace, and before him was a low table filled with all manner of assorted items of nourishment. Almost spellbound, he watched as Amada went to the small table, then turning back toward him, she inclined her head and graciously invited him to join her.

As he sat down across from her, she was busy pouring what appeared to be a bottled red wine into long stemmed glasses. Having filled the glasses about one-third full, she looked up and handed one of the glasses to him.

First raising her glass in a salute, she offered, "Mr. Fann, may all of your future interactions with the Nori continue to be as pleasant as this moment."

Accepting the glass, he raised it and inhaled its aroma, and smiled. "Amada, in both heart and mind, I gladly embrace your toast. I'm looking forward to a growing and firm bond of friendship with the Nori."

Sipping the beverage from his glass with cautious discernment, Darrell looked up and smiled. "Wherever the grapes grew, may there be many more years of fruitful harvest. It's a marvelous vintage.

"You mentioned Susie has named her home Daireann West. Do you know what Daireann might mean?" Darrell asked.

"Yes," Amada answered. "Susie once told me that in an ancient Earth language it means bountiful."

Preparing two small dishes of food, Amada placed one before Darrell, then she looked up, and her expression had once more become serious.

"Mr. Fann, as I have mentioned, I am here as a Representative of the Nori. The reason I came here was to meet with you for the purpose of discussing matters of some importance. Before I begin with my own inquiry, perhaps you may have several questions you might first want to ask. If you do, then please do ask them."

Absent-mindedly rolling the stem of the wine glass between his fingers, Darrell thoughtfully considered Amada. "Before we go any further, if we are going to be friends, folks who break bread and drink wine together, then you will need to begin using my given name, which is Darrell."

Amada's serious expression brightened into a smile, and she inclined her head. "Thank you, Darrell, for granting me that privilege and gift."

"Good, and now that's settled, you are most welcome. Moving swiftly on to a few questions– first of which is, just where do the Nori come from and are you human?"

Amada's eyes revealed a twinkle of amusement. "Darrell, your question is direct and penetrating. I like that.

"Yes, the Nori are indeed human being. We believe our original home world is Earth, but the Earth of 70,000 years ago."

In stunned amazement, Darrell sat and stared at Amada several moments before he could even respond. "Oh boy, now you've gone and done it! In a single sentence, you've upset the historical apple-cart and scattered apples everywhere. We've just crossed into the express lane, leaving a few questions lagging far behind, and are speedily overtaking endless questions. My first question leaps forth from your precise use of the word 'believe.' That word proclaims the Nori are doubtful of their facts. So, would you please clarify?"

Nodding in acknowledgment, Amada paused but a moment. "My use of the word 'believe' implies we are speaking in terms of a high probability, however, in this matter we desire to speak in terms of absolute certainty."

"Well, I can understand that. How about the 70,000 years ago part, just how certain are you of that dating?"

"The time frame is considered definite, at least within several thousand years. Although our records from that time are not complete, our historians are capable and they have reached a consensus on the date. Is that particular point in time of any special significance in Earth history?"

"Humph, sorta. Seventy-thousand years ago is a bright-crimson historical marker on Earth. It was a time of upheaval, darkness and stark terror, a time of nightmares, panic, havoc, starvation, blood and death; it marks one of the most catastrophic and horrific times in all of human history. After millions of years of human culture, mankind came to the brink of extinction, and some scientists have estimated at the moment of the genetic bottleneck, our total human population on the whole Earth sharply shrank to between 3,000 and 10,000 people."

Amada leaned forward, still holding her glass, her eyes focused on Darrell. "It was a long time ago, yet you seem to be well versed in what happened."

"Not really, the surviving data from that era is too sparse for anyone with integrity to make such a claim. I'm, however, a student of history and a person who was drawn by interest into the horrors and catastrophic events of that epoch. I'm also someone who has taken time to consider the available data in a holistic manner and have tried to connect the dots. Most people don't bother.

"In general, my viewpoint on the topic is Humanity is suffering from post-traumatic syndrome, fiercely clinging to its ignorance, while ignoring or even suppressing the truth concerning what happened. I've concluded it's a misguided effort to bury our racial fears that what happened once might happen again. And, it could."

Amada Leaned forward and asked, "Can you provide me a synopsis that explains the prime cause for such a global holocaust?"

"Humph, the short version is unlikely to satisfy your needs. Because of the planetary scope of the catastrophe, humanity lost all of its early history, except for a few tattered and broken remnants of folklore and legends which survived through the whispered telling of a worldwide flood and lost civilizations. On the whole, multi-discipline scientific research into that era of chaos is obstructed by a shameful petrification of academic integrity, layers of speculation, controversy, and a shameful ridicule of the historians who labored to gather the remaining shards of discernible truth. Only a few torn remains of a tangible history-telling of humanity's struggle for survival, and the ages of barbarism that followed the disaster, have been scraped together. Understandably those shattered fragments are distorted and blurred.

"Still, as for identifying the prime mover of chaos, there is one diamond hard and undisputable fact that shines like a beacon. It's an astronomical discovery and fact, a discovery made about 500 years ago, back in 2015. Then, an astronomer discovered and identified a low-mass star system consisting of a brown and red dwarf pair, nicknamed 'Scholz's star,' and given the formal designation 'WISE J072003.' Through the calculation of the stars trajectory, it was determined that 70,000 years ago the pair of dwarf stars had passed by and brushed Earth's solar system.

"My casual use of the conservative and vague scientific term 'brushed,' might more accurately be upgraded to mean bruise, or clobbered Earth's solar system."

"Darrell, is there geological data supporting what you are telling me?" Amada asked.

"Yes, and it is copious on Earth and elsewhere, including the moon and the shattered crust of the planet Mars. There is also some anecdotal history, proving that within the period of human memory that Earth's solar system was involved in a deadly cosmic brawl. Some of the oldest legends were impressed on clay tablets. Miraculously, some of those tablets have survived. One of the oldest such legends dealt with a hero, named Gilgamesh, and his saga is set in a time of pure terror and utter global devastation. I memorized part of that saga.

'Astonishment at Adad - the Storm reached to the very heavens. He turned to blackness all that had been visible. He broke the land like a pot. For a whole day the South Storm blew, gathering speed as it blew, drowning the mountains, overcoming the people as in battle. Brother saw not brother. From heaven, no mortal could any longer be seen. Even the gods were struck by terror at the deluge, and, fleeing, they ascended to the celestial band of An. The gods cowered like dogs crouching by the outer wall of that celestial band.'

"And, speaking of breaking the land like a pot, there is also the discovered geological evidence from 70,000 years ago, part of which is a colossal volcanic eruption known as the Toba catastrophe. It spewed out at least 22,800 cubic kilometers of erupted magma, including 800 cubic kilometers of ash into the atmosphere, which in turn triggered a 30,000-year-long ice age. Would you like me to continue?"

Amada sat motionless for a long moment looking at Darrell, searching his countenance before speaking. "Mr. Fann, I believe the Nori have found the Earthman we have been searching for."

Still holding his glass of wine, Darrell realized Amada might be, as she claimed, human; but, she was definitely unlike anyone he had ever before met. In the natural subdued light of the large room he clearly observed a distinct aura surrounding her. His inner voice was warning– '*Even the gods were struck by terror,*' *be exceedingly careful, at least until we can determine just what and who these Nori really are....*

Chapter Eleven:
Gnashing Fangs

Even before the sun had disappeared beyond the western rim of the Kreel elite world, the darkness of night had embraced the immense trees of an ancient forest. Within his den, Grand Admiral Groff was in his personal workshop, and as he focused on his work, he was contemplative.

His afternoon hunt had proven most enjoyable, and at its climax even exhilarating; his prey had been elusive, cunning, and dangerous. After he had first detected it sent, then stalked and cornered the boar, it had turned on him and fought to its death. The boar was large, having weighed more than 500 kilos, 100 kilos more than his own weight. None of the boar's lean bulk tended toward fat, and it had been a good kill. Groff mused– *It was almost a pity to have killed it– almost.*

His first and well-aimed quarrel had struck its target, and it was a true and fatal strike. Although mortally wounded, still retaining its incredible strength and fierce but ebbing fire of life, the boar had swung about, its red eyes burning with hatred. Giving a terrible bellow of undiluted fury, with gleaming gnarled tusks, it charged him. Standing firm, he gnashed his own fangs and opening his jaws wide he roared his answering challenge. When his second quarrel drove the boar to its knees it was less than two meters distant. He sent his third quarrel through the skull of the boar, and that ended the hunt, except for his own thundering heart and final roar of triumphal victory.

Now, sitting at his workbench he was busy cleaning his crossbow, and enjoying the smooth texture of its well-finished fine-grained and burled wood stock. The crossbow was the product of his own labors, including his patient design and craftsmanship. When he began the design of the weapon, all he had to work with was a crude historical drawing, which had presented him with the initial concept of the weapon and its functionality. He had found the intricate design problems posed in fashioning the weapon challenging in all of its aspects, including finding the right type of hard wood, seasoning the wood, cutting the wood into a rough blank, working that blank into its finished form, and then crafting the stock to hold five metal quarrels in a compact rotary magazine. Designing the short multi-leaf compound-bow, rapid-slide cocking gear mechanism, and the smooth release trigger assembly proved to be both challenging and pleasurable. Part of his pleasure came from knowing that by comparison his own design was far superior to the ancient version of the weapon. *Of course,* he mused, *that is not surprising, since the ancient primitive weapon was the concept and design of inferior human mammals.*

Having survived numerous deadly battles in space, and equally deadly political intrigues, he had discovered working with his hands helped him to calm his stress. Given recent events within the Empire, his need for such relaxation had lately increased.

The boar hunt was only one of his mental winding-down strategies, but it had provided him with an exceptional opportunity for focused mental relaxation. *Besides,* he thought, *while the boar is secured on a spit and being turned over an open bed of hot coals the savory aroma will bring me even more pleasure.*

Having the year before put the incompetent and corrupt ruling Elite Council on trial, HE had then supervised their public execution and declared martial LAW. Consequently, He was surrounded by many who both feared and hated him.

To establish his absolute control on the planet, he had transferred thousands of troops and his headquarters from the Military to the elite world. Since then he had governed as if he were ruling a conquered planet. He considered fear to be a useful tool for governing. Perhaps in time the hate toward him would diminish, but he understood that possibility was far distant. Accordingly, he had built his new den in a glade that was located deep within an old-growth forest. The den was well guarded on the ground by some of his best warriors and above by cruisers. None of the warriors on the ground or ships hovering above could be easily seen. That was how he demanded his security operate– unseen, vigilant, swift, and deadly.

Pushing back from the workbench, his rumbling growl of satisfaction rolled forth when examining the clean and polished crossbow. Although it was primitive, it was also an exquisite and effective hunting weapon. Completing his task of maintenance, He carried the crossbow to the wall display and placed it on its supporting brackets.

Leaving the workshop and returning to his private study, he walked over to the desk side cabinet and withdrew a crystal goblet and cut crystal decanter. Pouring a quantity of hotep netjer into his goblet, he drank heartily. Pausing in reflection, he shrugged and poured himself a bit more before putting the decanter back into the cabinet. The well-aged beverage had a slight alcoholic content, which helped to soften his angry mood.

Having for the afternoon elevated his pleasure above his duty, it was now time to address his command responsibilities. His deep seething anger dealt with a complex issue, a matter of potential treason.

Sitting at his desk, he picked up his command wand and keyed the recall instructions for a predefined hologram display. Immediately the hologram formed in the middle of the study, its three-dimensional array of bright colorful pinpoints of symbols displaying the whole of the Kreel Empire, including its bordering star systems. A stark and ugly blood red jagged line began near the far upper border and then slashed diagonally inward, connecting the symbols for five different star systems. Beginning at the Empire's outer boundary the gash pointed directly to the three governing worlds at its heart. Examining the hologram, he considered its troubling implications.

For the first time in the Empire's long history, five planets within its inner systems had been successfully attacked by an adversary. Based on the reports of survivors, the attackers were reputed to be the Lux, and as improbable as it sounded, it was said they had come in ships that were ablaze in flames from their bow to their stern.

The Kreel cruisers and fast attack ships defending those systems had been utterly destroyed, and the after-battle examination of detritus proved the Lux had suffered no losses. As irksome as that fact was, the more galling and disturbing threat was to be found buried deep in the precise analysis of the five attacks.

The steady flow of field data coming from the attacked planets into his headquarters tactical analysis group repeatedly demonstrated the attacks were logistically impossible! Although they were prosecuted with precision, they were nevertheless still impossible.

Having himself directed similar attacks on planets, he had firsthand knowledge that on every industrial world there are millions of potential military and industrial targets. More importantly, the vast number of targets were of low strategic value. If devices of mass destruction were being deployed, then discerning between high value and low value targets was pointless, since together all of them were destroyed. Still, where pin-point precision destruction was mandated, precise discernment of which target is mundane and which is vital was essential. Precision targeting of only the high value targets demanded the highest degree of reliable military Intelligence.

The execution of a successful precision attack on an entire planet did not stop with target classification, the targets needed to be localized with precise geodetic coordinates. To assure maximum destruction the appropriate munitions for each target needed to be selected. Finally, the ordnance must then be delivered on target. The Lux attacks in each solar system demonstrated they had solved each of these difficulties with incredible lethality. Adding insult to injury, they had made their attacks personal by specifically targeting Kreel Officers. Every planetary headquarters, officers' quarters, and even Officers' recreational facilities were targeted and destroyed. This had resulted in heavy and unacceptable losses of life among the Officers.

The burning questions were– how could any far-off alien species gather the volume of precise Intelligence necessary to discern which targets were critical among millions of mundane targets and how did they obtain target coordinates? To do this was utterly impossible, unless they had inside help, and that in-turn shouted treason!

The often-repeated broadcasts the Lux had transmitted to the occupants of each world had maligned and debased the Kreel, pledging to eradicate the "Kreel infestation," He vowed to make the Lux pay for that slander. The Lux had taken meticulous pains to minimize the collateral damage to the indigenous species. He asked himself, *Why would they do that?* The only plausible answer he reasoned was the Lux intended to return and occupy the planets and afterward utilize their indigenous species. If true, then he was not dealing with raids, but rather with a long-term pre-invasion scenario.

Even with all of its own wide-flung capability, he knew the Kreel military did not itself have the economic and industrial data mandated to execute such pinpoint attacks. It was therefore obvious to him a far-distant alien species could never have gathered the required Intelligence without having been first discovered. The core question remained— who within the Empire is gathering and feeding the refined Intelligence to the Lux? Given the depth and broad scope of the data, the list of possible traitors was short. At the top of the list was the remnant of the Elite Guard and at the pointed tip was Marshal Krupp.

Having been forewarned, his internal military Security was hard at work. Every possible internal source of precise Intelligence was being searched out and then put under strict surveillance. Scrutiny of the Elite Guard and Marshal Krupp's communications were being intensified. He was confident that he would soon know who the traitors were, and he knew how to deal with such treason.

Treason aside, his immediate problem was to guard against new attacks. He had directed additional military forces to reinforce probable targets; but he was compelled to acknowledge his enemy was resourceful and cunning.

After studying the hologram, he appealed, "Anubux, hear me now. I have sworn to you that I will destroy the enemies of the Empire, both those within and those without. Tell me where the enemy will strike next, so I may destroy them."

The reverberant hiss of an answering whisper flowed into his mind, clear and distinct. *Groff, now hear me well. I tell you for the final time, you know not your enemy! Protect your most vital and vulnerable organs. Your enemy shall move against the rebuilding of your base of power. You are not to play the role of the fool.*

For long minutes Groff sat silent and viewing the hologram glowing before him, while he pondered Anubux's sharp rebuke. *The Empire's most vulnerable organ is the manufacturing facilities that build my cruisers and fast attack ships. Anubux, I will not play the fool, and I will also set a snare for a traitor, if Marshal Krupp proves to be one.*

Picking up his command wand, he keyed his Adjutant, ordering, "You are to immediately prepare Fleet orders to Grand Marshal Krupp. He personally is to dispatch six elite Guard ships to each of the five worlds where Fleet cruisers are being manufactured. He is to evaluate which of the five systems is most vital, and then he is to personally take command of the Elite Guard forces in that system. He is to depart at once. Once his forces arrive on their stations, they are to take command of all planetary defenses. You will send orders to each of our senior Military commanders in each of the five systems. Order them to make all prudent preparations to oppose an eminent attack. Inform them that for now they are being placed under the authority of the Elite Guard, who will soon arrive. Warn our senior military commanders that they are to remain doubly alert and vigilant for any sign of treason. You are to dispatch fourteen additional cruisers to reinforce those already assigned to each system, with the same orders."

For several more minutes he quietly sat, sipping from his goblet, and studying the hologram. Then, he again picked up his wand and keyed his Adjutant.

"You are to order my personal task force to prepare for space combat operations and standby for departure."

With the one-hundred cruisers of his own battle-hardened task force on ready standby, he began to plan for the upcoming battle he now knew was coming....

66

Chapter Twelve:
Marauders

It was still early morning, and Fleet Admiral Mer Shawn was walking with a firm stride toward the conference room. As he entered into the room, he observed Admirals Ron Cloud and Dylan Cord were already sitting at the conference table and waiting. The door closed with a solid thunk behind Mer as he entered, and with the sound, Ron and Dylan looked up. Like Mer, their countenances were grim.

"Good morning, gentlemen. Computer, set the conference room security level to Black Hole," Mer said, as he eased into his chair.

There came a single clear tone, signifying Mer's instructions were being executed. The warm morning sunlight illuminating the comfortable area softened as a sheer curtain closed across the wide floor-to-ceiling window.

The ceiling in the room was a light tan stippled surface designed to absorb sound, and the floor was covered with large polished dark-green tiles. Near the window stretched a woven textured carpet. There were several easy chairs arranged near the window, but the focus of the room was the long and polished wood conference table, around which the three men were sitting. The warm and neutral sand tones color of the walls complimented the bright polished natural wood bookcases, which held a collection of leather-bound books. The only picture on the walls was a large image of a sleek "L" Class Guardian cruiser suspended in the blackness of space, with a brilliant glowing nebula shown in the background.

Turning to face Ron, Mer asked, "What is the latest Intelligence status report on Kellon's task force?"

"Sir, Kellon's five squadrons have rendezvoused at Resupply Point 17. They are in the process of conducting maintenance and reloading both general supplies and ordnance for the upcoming strikes. They are waiting for your authorization to proceed."

"Do we have the final analysis on the first strikes?" Mer asked.

"No Sir. We are still sifting through a large number of Kreel intercepts, and the final analysis will take another month. We, however, do have our first strike assessments. They indicate the results of our strikes have exceeded our most optimistic estimates. In total, Kellon's task force has engaged Kreel forces in five solar systems. In each strike, we gained the full advantage of surprise and have confirmed destruction of 42 cruisers and fast attacks, 2 of these were destroyed by seeker mines. All designated primary planetary targets were hit and destroyed, with a better than 97% destruction effectiveness. More than 1400 secondary targets were detected, localized, and destroyed."

"Then, our assessment is we have definitely hurt them?" Mer asked.

"Affirmative, but not decisively. Still, what we have accomplished is like throwing sand in a gearbox; a little sand can do a great deal of damage. In the same manner, we have definitely hurt them."

Turning toward the wall and the image of the Guardian cruiser, Ron ordered, "Computer, reference Black Hole, Marauders, Tactical Plot 1. Display."

Swirling, the large image of the Guardian cruiser and nebula vanished. It was replaced by a compressed tactical plot that displayed the Kreel Empire viewed from above the galactic plane. On the plot were displayed several lines and symbols, including one blinking golden icon. That blinking symbol represented Kellon's task force which was positioned at Resupply Point 17. Extending from the upper right corner and continuing down toward the center of the plot was a band of yellow. Superimposed upon the yellow band were four green line segments that connected five symbols, each symbol depicting a Kreel-dominated solar system.

Taking a moment to first verify the displayed plot was what he wanted to discuss, Ron returned his attention to Mer.

"As we planned, all of our strikes occurred within the yellow band, and were intended to suggest to the Kreel an attack vector that points to the Kreel Hub Worlds. Based on what the Nori told us, if the Kreel send a reconnaissance force back along that vector looking for the Marauder's home world, they will run smack into the Swarm.

"Our scheduled action time-line along the vector for each strike was sequentially timed to indicate the Lux-Marauders are following a progressive vector and moving with purpose straight toward the central heart of the Kreel Empire. This, of course, is pure misdirection.

"Our misdirection has produced some results; the latest intercepts indicate the Kreel are responding to our subterfuge and deploying reinforcements to defend systems further along the vector. To accomplish their reinforcement, they are pulling first-line cruisers back from outer operational areas. Consequently, the pressures the Kreel are putting on our own defenses have significantly lessened.

"The three thin red lines radiating from Resupply 17 represent the vectors to the next three designated targets systems. These are three of the five worlds upon which the Kreel manufacture their cruisers and fast attack ships. Part of our intended misdirection was in selecting three critical targets systems well outside the yellow band. Our initial hope was that the Kreel would not reinforce these targets before our upcoming strikes. We were not completely successful in our deception. Recent intercepts indicate the Kreel are dispatching additional cruisers to each target, but as of now we don't know how many. That the Kreel are reinforcing those targets underscores their strategic value. Naturally, Kreel reinforcements of those three systems is problematic, since Kellon's task force will be confronting increased and alerted battle-hardened forces.

"We continue to rely upon our stealth advantage in meeting the larger Kreel forces, nevertheless the increased number of Kreel cruisers in each system constitutes increased risks. We're continuing to monitor Kreel communications for further developments.

"Mer, so far we have been successful. Still, we are engaged in combat operations deep within Kreel space, and as one wise man long ago said, battles are dangerous things."

Having listened to Ron's report, Mer turned to face Dylan. "Having gone over Kellon's reports, what is Operations' current assessment of morale and combat readiness?"

"Sir, morale is not a problem, the entire task force is still highly motivated. My primary concern remains battle fatigue, rotation, and recall. Ron is correct, battles are dangerous things, and they are also physically and emotionally draining. It's time to put a pin in the calendar and schedule some down time. As for the ships' combat readiness, they are well within the gold zone. The only major casualty we have suffered was Scout Ship Shey. All that can be accomplished in the field to repair her is being done. She will likely be combat ready, however, Shey should be rotated back and scheduled for a complete refit when possible.

"Mer, there's an important matter that does require your personal attention. During the bombardment of K-40 an anomaly in Kreel propulsion was observed. A grounded Kreel cruiser was spinning up in preparation to lift off when it was hit. Its primary torsion-field collapsed, and it produced a huge fireball. After I reviewed the data Cruiser Lan provided, I sent an engineering team to our captured Gortoga cruiser to study its primary power systems. The preliminary results of their investigation indicate there is a significant design flaw. The question now is can we exploit that flaw in a tactical manner? I am requesting your approval and the funding for a high-priority research effort to determine the answer to that question."

"Dylan, since you have already established that a flaw exists in the Kreel's temporal engineering, further evaluation is appropriate. You have my authorization for the research, and I will see the required funding is made available. You are to keep me tight in the research loop," Mer ordered.

"Yes Sir," Dylan said.

"Mer, while you are going about handing out authorization and funding for research into anomalies, I've a request," Ron said.

"I have cross-checked and confirmed The Earth Ambassador's report on the damage Shey sustained near K-40. Her report provided us with more details than were even in Cruiser Lan's preliminary battle reports. The principal point is somehow the Ambassador obtained detailed information concerning something light-years distant, and she did it in real-time. The second significant point is she has been studying with the Nori, and we know they communicate mentally across light-years in real-time. Their mental discipline is something we need to better understand, and we should be engaged in mastering it.

"I am requesting that a research program be initiated within Guardian Force, and not handed off to civilian-academic types.

Obtaining instantaneous communications over light-years during our operations could be a game changer."

"Humph, that's an understatement. Ron, put together your internal proposal for the research. Lay out what it is you have in mind. In terms of authorization, you both have broad AA priorities, so use them."

Standing, Mer turned and walked over to the window and pulled back on the sheer curtain. He stood there for perhaps three minutes looking at the world outside and reflecting on the host of problems he was facing. With a deep sigh, he let the curtain fall back into position. Turning, he looked at the faces of his two old and trusted friends. Their concern and fatigue was reflected in their countenances, and like them, he was feeling the mental and physical burdens of the long centuries of warfare. His two old friends and he were no longer young and in the forefront of the battles, but they all had friends and family who were now out between the cold stars; they were out light-years distant from the nearest warm sunrise, amid the black-interstellar darkness preparing for battle, far from their homes and those who loved them. His own burden and responsibility was to knowingly send friends and family into a grinding brawl, one where there would be no quarter given or asked. Deep within his troubled soul, he felt the battle-rage beginning to stir and rise up. He thought, *By thunder and the seven stars, we're going to give the Kreel more than they ever bargained for.*

Looking toward Ron and Dylan, in a clear and no-nonsense voice, Mer gave his orders. "Gentlemen, unless either of you have a point of contention or else something to add– Ron, you will immediately signal Admiral Kellon that he has authority to launch the next phase of his attack. And, you are to personally verify he has received the latest Intelligence on Kreel reinforcements within each of those three targeted systems. Upon completion of his next strikes his orders are to immediately withdraw and retire with his entire task force from Kreel space. They are to return directly to Glas Dinnein for rest and refit.

"Dylan, Operations will schedule priority yard time for Kellon's task force, and afterward schedule its resupply.

"Are there any questions or objections? If not, this meeting is concluded."

There were no objections or further questions, and Mer brought the meeting to its end, ordering, "Computer, cancel Black Hole security and restore security Level 1."

As the three Admirals walked from the room, the sheer curtains were opening, and the image of the Guardian cruiser and nebula once more adorned the wall. The warm morning sunshine was flooding the unoccupied, quiet, and pleasant room. It was a misleading quiet which preceded a coming storm....

Chapter Thirteen:
Scuttlebutt

As Elayne closed the hangar door behind her, Shey greeted her with delight. "Good morning Lieutenant Cloud, you are most welcome aboard."

"Thank you Shey. I understand you've been under the weather. Are you feeling better?"

"I am feeling just fine; however, some of my minor sub-systems are not as effective as they should be. The good news is my damaged missile launch tubes are all repaired, and my stealth factor is restored to better than ninety percent. Roan and Zorn are very pleased, and Lan and the Captain have reviewed my status. They have rated me combat worthy. Tomorrow I will receive a full loadout of ordnance."

"Then you will be ready for the upcoming battles?"

"Yes; still, Lan has instructed me not to hazard any high velocity and thermally stressed atmospheric entries, at least not until my hull is reconditioned. He told me that given the circumstances, he understood my having launched missiles while evading within an atmosphere, but suggested that I should try to avoid the necessity of doing so again. At least, he confided, while traveling at such high velocities."

Her blue eyes were twinkling as Elayne replied, " Be certain to listen to Lan; he is very concerned for your welfare."

Elayne's blond hair was tied back in a tail, and she was dressed in the informal shipboard uniform of Guardian Force personnel– forest-green fabric of woven natural fibers fitted for comfort and ease of movement, a long-sleeved tailored tunic top, and form-fitting pants that were bloused above soft low-topped dark leather boots. Her tunic collars bore gold military rank tabs pinned on each, and the tabs also bore the subtle insignia of Guardian Intelligence.

As Elayne crossed the short distance between the hangar door and the short brow, Zorn appeared in Shey's hatch, and his smile was huge. "Hey stranger, where have you been hiding all of these past weeks?"

With a flood of pleasure, she returned Zorn's broad smile, and responded, "I've been hiding in cramp and dusty cubby-holes, with my nose pointed at streaming columns of numbers, while listening to endless Kreel and alien chatter. As soon as the Admiral granted mercy and took my leg irons off, I thought I might slip down into the dungeon to see if the neab aboard Shey is as terrible as I remember."

"Humph, come on aboard, and I will do what I can to lower our high standards to match your fondest memory. You happen to be in luck, I've fresh cheese pastries to compliment the best neab in Guardian Force."

Turning from the hatch, Zorn retraced his step with Elayne following close behind. After passing through a narrow passageway, past dozens of lockers, access panels, and several side doors, they entered into Shey's compact galley and mess area. Upon entering, turning about, Zorn swept his hand in an arc and gave a slight bow.

"Dear lady, please make yourself comfortable. Shey's hospitality, which is legend throughout Guardian Force, is yours for as long as you are within her hallowed and humble hull."

As she took her seat at the mess table, Elayne watched Zorn busy preparing fresh neab and putting pastries on small plates. "Where is Roan?" she inquired.

"About twenty minutes ago he went up to Tactical, he wanted to talk with Lorn about the upcoming strikes. As you said, we live in the dungeon. We're always the last to hear the latest scuttlebutt."

With practiced movements, Zorn swirled the vacuum flask of brewing neab several times, and then brought the flask and pastries to the table. Then gathering up two mugs, and the customary creamer and honey, he returned and sat down across from Elayne.

"While listening to all that Kreel and alien chatter, did you get any insights into how badly we hurt them?" Zorn asked.

"I'm not qualified to make that assessment; but, my sense of the matter is yes, we hurt them— and badly. In fact, from the chatter I heard, they are going bonkers trying to understand how we could have hit them as hard as we did and with such incredible accuracy. The Kreel are also in a tizzy about our

74

specifically targeting their Officers and are scrambling to make changes to prevent anyone from doing that again."

"Humph, the Kreel are what they are, but no one ever called them stupid without later regretting it. How did the indigenous populations make out?" Zorn asked as he stirred his neab.

"There's very little information about the indigenous populations. The Kreel are standing firmly on their necks and are mute on the topic."

"We should have hit them hard, after all we had a clean shot at five of their industrial planets, and had the tactical advantage of surprise. I'd wager two brews the Kreel are now bristling and buzzing protectively about their planets, just spoiling for a fight. We're not likely to have the advantage of surprise next time," Zorn commented.

"You're correct. The Kreel are definitely operating on an elevated alert status. Being aware of this, the Admiral is working over the latest Intel to develop his upcoming attacks.

"And, speaking of surprises, what happened to Shey during our last attack? I have only heard rumors, but they were all in agreement, Shey came close to a Cobalt Blue. Just how close?"

With evident cheer Shey responded, " We did not come all that close. There was still 3.012 seconds remaining when I terminated the Cobalt Blue sequence."

Scowling, Zorn bit into his cheese pastry and ignored Shey's comment. Elayne was taken back by the information, and with concern she observed Zorn's countenance. They had served together aboard Lan for years and become close friends. Knowing Zorn, she could see Shey's comment had struck a raw nerve. Obviously, Zorn was dodging the topic.

Extending her arm across the small table, Elayne rested her hand gently on Zorn's. "Zorn, no one told me you had come that close to a Cobalt Blue. Do you want to talk about it?"

"No, not particularly. The post-Operations shrinks have spent hours probing, and they have judged both Roan and I are fit for duty. That's all that matters, or needs to be said."

"That's not all that matters, and you know better. No one comes that close to a Cobalt Blue and shrugs it off that easy. So, fess up, what are your plans for the next five years of your life?"

Putting his pastry down, Zorn looked at Elayne. "Five years? Elayne, we are a hundred light years from home, we are about to stick our nose squarely into another hornet nest full of alerted and angry Kreel cruisers, and undoubtedly a host of newly-installed planetary-defense stuff. And you are asking me about my next five-year plan? At the moment, I'm not even planning for the next five months."

"Zorn, remember that you are not alone," Shey inserted. "Everyone in the Admiral's task force is here with you. Just let the Kreel buzz about; that only makes them easier to detect. Besides, I know after our next strikes that the entire task force will be going to Glas Dinnein for crew rest and ship overhaul."

"Shey," Elayne inquired, "just how do you know what the Admiral's orders are?"

"Well, I always help Lan in processing incoming message traffic and prepare the messages for the Admiral. This morning he received Guardian Operations orders about the recall."

Frowning, Zorn asked, "Young Lady, I suppose you understand what SECRET means?"

"Certainly Zorn. The orders to withdraw after the upcoming strikes were, however, in the housekeeping group of messages. They were not marked secret or black hole. Besides, I have no intention of telling the Kreel" Shey said, with a slight tone of injury.

"Then perhaps my rebuttal was somewhat out of order. For sure, your info is certainly good news. With that rumor flying around the Task Force everyone will perk up."

Elayne's eyebrows rose and she frowned. "Zorn, I'm surprised at you. There aren't going to be any rumors flying about!

"Shey, you are not to discuss a recall with anyone, not anyone! It's the Admiral's sole prerogative to tell the task force when we are going home. At this moment, you are to warn Lan that he is to caution the other girls likewise. Shey, do you understand?" Elayne said, even as she pulled her hand back from Zorn's.

"Yes. I have informed Lan of my breach of protocol. He is in full agreement with your assessment. He has now instructed the other girls accordingly. He assures you there will not be any further infractions involving message content, classified or otherwise.

"Zorn, I am sorry. Lan has told me that you were correct in scolding me," Shey said.

"It's alright; we both made our own mistakes. Just remember, a wise person is supposed to learn from his mistakes, while the wiser person learns from the mistakes of others."

As Elayne sipped her neab, she changed the topic and smiled. "Hey Zorn, I apologize for my slander about your neab, it's excellent."

As Elayne spoke, Zorn continued to look down at his hand, which he had not moved since Elayne had placed her hand on his. After a few moments, he looked up and again frowned.

"Elayne, when we do get back to Glas Dinnein, will you go out to dinner with me? I would enjoy sharing a glass of good wine, and perhaps telling you all about my plans for the next five years."

"Zorn, there's a big problem in my accepting your invitation. From the time that I was a little girl, my beloved paternal Grandmother has sternly and repeatedly warned me to be wary of all handsome men wearing uniforms. She has taught me they are all scoundrels– wild sailors in strange ports and even worse they're untrustworthy. Still, just perhaps, since you are an old shipmate, when we get safely back to Glas Dinnein, and if you then still remember having invited me to dinner, then against my better judgment, I'll ask my Grandmother for her permission. You never know, against all the odds, she just might give her approval; but, only because you are a known and trustworthy shipmate. You are trustworthy, aren't you?"

As Zorn listened to Elayne, his expression passed through several transformations, which Elayne found wonderful to behold. Gone was his lingering frown. Elayne did not miss the vibrant sparkle which was kindled and now shone brightly in his eyes. she felt a responding inner warmth and could not help but smile.

"Elayne, do you really think I'm handsome? What do you mean, if I still remember? You can safely wager cases of brews that I'll remember. On that, you can be certain. What's more, to establish and demonstrate my honor and trustworthiness, I'll personally go and ask your paternal Grandmother for permission to take her marvelous granddaughter out to dinner."

Smiling and then laughing, Elayne teased, "Not so fast there sailor, we aren't setting down at the spaceport on Glas Dinnein, at least not just yet. Between now and then, you'll need to stay focused and keep Kreel cruisers off Shey's backsides; else, my momentary weakness will all be for naught."

"This is absolutely wonderful," Shey interjected. "May I have your permission to spread wild rumors?"

Without the slightest hesitation, both Zorn and Elayne loudly exclaimed in unisonance– "No!"

"Spoil sports," Shey gleefully retorted.

Still laughing, Elayne added, "Zorn, given some big ears listening, perhaps it's time we change the topic. So, why don't you tell me all about what you have been doing for these past weeks, other than bringing Shey back into her fighting trim."

Still smiling broadly, standing up Zorn again swept his arm in a gesture of invitation and bowed. "Dear lady, if you will but follow, I'd be delighted to show you what I've been up to."

Turning, Zorn departed from the mess area and moved forward toward the command compartment. Elayne hurried to catch up.

As Zorn entered the command compartment, he instructed, "Shey, bring up the hologram model of the Guardian display."

What looked to be a solid object suddenly appeared suspended in the forward part of the control compartment. It was a smooth symmetrical shape, reminiscent of an egg.

As Elayne came closer to look, she whispered, "Zorn, it's absolutely beautiful. Is its golden radiance and the incredible shimmer a natural color and effect, or is it part of some subjective design?"

"It's a model and not subjective. Although, I suppose there are a few subjective elements, but its appearance is as realistic and natural as I can model it."

Still marveling at the hologram, Elayne asked, "Did you work on the model as an artistic endeavor, or is there some practical application for what you have fashioned? What I'm asking is, why did you spend weeks in designing it, and what is it supposed to represent?"

"I agree, it is beautiful, but it's not art. It represents a complex temporal engineering problem, one that I preferred to work on, rather than remaining submerged in dark introspective broodings about what might happen the next time we meet the Kreel.

"But, in answer to your question, the model is an analytical representation of a Guardian variable inverse temporal gravimetric torsion field. I wanted to model and compare it with an equivalent model of a Kreel torsion field."

"Boys and their toys; just why would you want to compare two torsion fields?"

"Mainly, because I had the rare opportunity to do so, and I wanted to scratch a mental itch. I guess it was a matter of simple curiosity.

"Fortunately, we are hunkered down at a resupply point, and Lan and the girls have a rare surplus of available computational time, which I've shamelessly exploited. I've spent most of my free time working on the two models. They are each as precise as my engineering and Shey's programming skills permit."

"There must be something more than simple curiosity involved. What initially caused the mental itch?"

"Remember, the Kreel cruiser that nearly turned off our lights went to ground on the planet. He was smart enough to understand that all the other Kreel cruisers in the sector had been destroyed, and after sustaining damage he tried to play it safe; he went to ground and shut down all power and propulsion systems in an effort to avoid detection. His plan worked, at least until an inbound Kreel Admiral ordered all Kreel fighting units on the planet to respond, and in reflex some duty-bound Kreel communications officer did so. The momentary breach of communications silence permitted us to localize the cruiser. Even as the cruiser was powering up and trying to escape, Lan targeted it and launched surface strike missiles. When it was destroyed, the Kreel's temporal gravimetric torsion field ruptured, and this in turn generated a terrific detonation. Thanks to Lan's full spectrum recording of the entire event, I had access to the data from that explosion. I found it most interesting."

"Surely Zorn, such an explosion is easy to understand. After all, the system that was powering up was being destroyed, and that level of catastrophic damage must have simply exceeded all normal engineering safeguards."

"Yes and no. Good temporal engineering strives to prevent catastrophic events. When a temporal detonation does occur, it indicates sloppy temporal containment. So, I naturally asked myself, just how sloppy is the Kreel engineering?

"At the time I asked my question, the one thing I had in abundance was access to Kreel propulsion signatures that I had obtained from a wide variety of Kreel ships. By happenstance, while researching long-range detection sensors, I had already studied those signatures. Since my earlier data and working files were archived, I recovered them and began my analysis. My focus was on analyzing the faint overtones that indicate a lack of harmony and poor temporal containment symmetry."

Understanding the significance of what Zorn was explaining, Elayne rested against the port-side command chair and inquired, "What if anything did you discover?"

"Ah, now that's the question of the day. To better answer your question, an old wise saying goes– a holographic image is worth a thousand words. Shey, replace the Guardian torsion field model with the equivalent Kreel torsion field."

There was a momentary shift and the image of the suspended object within the hologram acutely altered. The new object was still similar in shape and color, but now there were subtle distortions in its appearance and brilliance. Rather than a pure lustrous gold, the sheen was dull and it appeared dirty or badly smudged. Elayne could see small dark scarlet tentacles flicker randomly on the surface of the object and then vanish. Fascinated, Elayne stood for a few minutes observing the hologram, and then turned toward Zorn.

"It looks dingy. What are those occasional red streamers? I didn't see anything like those flickering on the first hologram."

"You can count among your many blessings that you didn't see any on the Guardian model. The Guardian gravimetric torsion field is finely tuned and its temporal containment is balanced and stable. If a missile were to strike a Guardian ship, because of the harmony of its temporal containment, even in a worse case situation, the temporal field would collapse uniformly. Because it retains its symmetry and integrity, the temporal containment would not rupture and detonate. By contrast, within the Kreel gravimetric torsion field there exist random disharmonies, and the integrity of the temporal containment is flawed. Although the inherent temporal disharmony is minimal, under stress the possibility exists for a temporal rupture. If it happens it would happen along one of those flickering lines of imbalance. When that happens– kaboom, one huge fireball.

"My analysis demonstrates the Kreel's gravimetric torsion field is a product of sloppy temporal engineering. It is fragile, unstable, and perhaps even more important, it may be vulnerable."

As Zorn talked, Elayne was examining the hologram suspended before her with increasing interest. "Just how vulnerable?"

Looking at the Kreel hologram, Zorn frowned. "That question is still lurking about seeking its answer. Shey, run track 23."

As she watched the hologram, Elayne saw the flickering red tentacles emerging in greater frequency and spreading about the mottled gold shape; then, abruptly, like a mature dandelion caught in a powerful gust of wind, the model simply disintegrated.

"Zorn, what just happened?"

"What you just observed happened as I introduced a resonant energy that synchronized with the field disharmonies, which in turn created a destabilizing feedback loop. That intentional imbalance induced a desired result, it fractured the temporal containment field and it ruptured. I believe if a similar harmonic temporal disruptor field can be created in the proximity of a Kreel cruiser, then in one huge detonation it would cease to exist– Kablooey."

Elayne stared at Zorn in wonder. "Zorn, have you discussed your work with the Captain?"

"No, at least not yet. I have been looking for the practical means of generating the desired harmonic disruptor. As my example demonstrates, I'm getting close, but a practical hardware solution is still evading me."

"Zorn, stop right there. What you have worked out is important. I urge you to inform both Roan and the Captain, and the sooner the better. We have thousands of engineers on Glas Dinnein who can help design a disruptor device, and you have already shown in theory it will work. Promise me that you will tell the Captain."

Zorn shook his head in confusion, and then looked at the deck for a moment. Then, he looked up and made direct eye contact with Elayne. "Sorry, my head isn't quite screwed on right. You are correct, and my work should have peer review before I proceed.

"Shey, have you been eavesdropping, as usual?" Zorn inquired.

"Zorn, you know better! I merely monitor, as is my proper responsibility and duty."

"Humph, if you say so. Well, having dutifully monitored, please inform Lan and the Captain that Roan and I have a work product ready for the Captain's review and evaluation. Please inform him that I am requesting he come here as soon as his duties may permit."

Only a few moments elapsed, and Shey reported. "Zorn, I first notified Roan and then he notified Lan. In turn Lan notified the Captain and then the Admiral. Lan has asked me to warn you to stand by ready to receive boarders; both Admiral Kellon and Captain Grey are now in process of coming down for a visit. He suggests you may want to put a fresh pot of neab on to brew. And, Roan sends his well done and congratulations."

Chapter Fourteen:
Emissary

The tide was going out, and Darrell was sitting on a drift log that the ocean waves had pushed up the beach to the high-water mark. A gentle on-shore breeze was swirling about him, bringing with it the salty sea air comingled with the briny smells of the nearby tidal pools. Behind him the tree-adorned hill rose up to Susie's amazing home. In every aspect, it appeared to be a day of relaxation filled with pleasure; but, there was a fly in the ointment. The unanticipated offer that Amada made to him the evening before had left him troubled. His response to her offer demanded a clear binary decision— accept or reject. Considering his continuing relationship with Olympus, regardless of his choice, it was likely to prove problematic.

It had not required even a full week of wandering about Megan before he had fallen under the allure of its vibrant wild beauty and open spaces. There was no lingering doubt in his heart or mind; he considered Megan his permanent new home.

Having grown up on Earth, like the frog sitting in the pan of water being slowly brought to a boil, he had assumed the crowds, clamor, and stress were conditions no one could do anything about. Now, by the means of a politically-rigged process, he had been liberated from being one person lost amid the confining billions of Earth's still growing population.

Megan's vast unspoiled wilderness had forever underscored the bedrock problem on Earth; the crisis was ever more people. Everyone knew that overpopulation was the engine driving the environmental, economic, social, and political crises ever deeper into a yawning chasm. Yet, no one dared do anything which might intelligently resolve the overpopulation problem, at least not since the moronic attempts by a few sociopaths to "cull" the population by use of targeted genetic engineering. Since that brief period of insanity, everyone chose to simply ignore the truth; the environment of the planet would not indefinitely tolerate the problem being ignored.

He felt absolutely no desire to return to Earth's stifling labyrinths. It was, however, precisely at this juncture in his logic that he came face-to-face with his sense of guilt– which argued it was not what he desired that was important, what mattered was doing the right thing. *Besides,* he inwardly argued, *if I choose to go back, it doesn't mean I'll have to stay on Earth– or does it?* Therein lay his personal dilemma; he never wanted to lose the opportunity he had gained when becoming a pioneer on Megan.

It was with candid interest that he observed Amada, as she approached along the shoreline. She remained an unsolved mystery, and she still scared him. She is human, sorta human anyway, he thought, and she does carry herself with quiet dignity, self-assurance, and confidence.

The soft aura of light he had seen enfolding her the day before was only one aspect of what he considered as her being different. Other subtle aspects surrounding her combined to warn him that her appearance was illusionary and she was dangerous. As for the Nori as a whole, he had only one sample to judge them by, nevertheless that unique specimen was quite sufficient for him to consider the Nori as being in a class unto themselves– and best treated with the same cautious respect one gives to a warm bottle of nitroglycerine.

Amada's clothes were appropriate for wandering along the beach, a loose-fitting blouse and loose pants that fell over her low-top hiking boots. The loose-fitting and common-sense attire did nothing to conceal her fluid grace of movement, and as she approached him, bypassing the small tidal pools, she looked up and smiled.

"Darrell, it is a most lovely afternoon, and I have always enjoyed being near the ocean."

"Then you have oceans on your home world?" Darrell asks, genuinely interested.

"Yes, we have three large oceans and there are several smaller bodies of salt water. We consider them to be the wellspring of all life on our world. Because of their importance, the Nori work with passion to protect our oceans and their abundant sea life. Darrell, May I sit down on your log?"

Quickly, using his hand, he brushed off the loose sand from the log, and then looking up he returned her smile. "Of course, please think of my log as being your log, and take the load off."

As she sat down, Darrell was surprised to hear a soft sigh from her. "Amada, is there something bothering you?"

She turned toward Darrell, and her countenance revealed an underlying sadness. "Yes, I am sitting here, safe on Megan, while my friends are out there among the stars and caught up in a violent war. Even now, they are going into battle."

"Then, it is your desire to be out there in the thick of battle. Why?"

"It is out of a sense of duty, not a lust for battle. Darrell, I am trained for covert work on Kreel occupied worlds. Once situated there, my task is to make first contact and then communicate with the subjected indigenous species. As we are sitting safely here, Admiral Kellon's task force is penetrating a strongly defended Kreel system. The primary planet in that system is the home of a gentle but subjected species. Through no fault of their own they are about to come under heavy bombardment; they will be literally caught up into the whirlwind and tossed like dry leaves in a violent storm. Undoubtedly many of them will be killed. I only wish that I might be there and able to help them."

Darrell sat quiet and looked at Amada, striving to comprehend the full significance of what she had just told him. "You were trained to work on Kreel dominated worlds? Uh– I thought the Kreel ate humans."

Stretching out her legs before her, Amada laughed. "Before they can eat you, they must first catch you."

In unabashed amazement, Darrell asked, "Then, you have actually been on Kreel dominated worlds?"

"Yes, in fact, I was recently stranded for several months on one. My Mentor and I were caught up in the middle of an unanticipated Guardian Force laser bombardment, and during the chaotic devastation we became temporarily separated. Kreel warriors were everywhere, and when they discovered her, they overpowered her, and took her captive. Although, before they were able to capture her, she made them pay a heavy price.

"I was there trying to help her, but there were too many warriors and we were unable to kill them all. As we fought, other warriors in the area were attracted to the fight. Because of their increasing numbers, she ordered me to break contact, evade, and then escape into the nearby forest. She demanded I go, else they would have captured me along with her."

"How long were you marooned on the planet?"

"About eight months. During that time, the warriors seemed to enjoy hunting me. I was forced to kill several of them, and this only whetted their lust for the chase. I believe they came to consider the hunt to be fine sport, as if I were merely a challenging prey animal. Of course, Kreel warriors are bred to relish the hunt, and the more dangerous their prey the better."

"What went wrong? Why did it take so long for your people to extract you?"

"At its outset, we had covertly dropped on the planet by means of stealth and were near the end of our mission when the Guardian raid occurred. After that strike, The Kreel ramped up their alert status and brought in reinforcements. Afterward the Nori extraction team was unable to safely penetrate the increased Kreel defenses to extract me. Besides, I was a volunteer and knew the risks before I accepted the mission. Still, I hoped they would eventually pull me out. Instead, to my surprise, Guardian Force extracted me."

"Hump, needle in a haystack. With you in hiding somewhere on an entire world, how could Guardian Force possibly find and extract you?"

"That is a complex story. In brief, Guardian Force sent two cruisers back into the system to destroy the secret Kreel research facilities that my Mentor and I had been sent to discover. During the confusion caused by the second Guardian attack, Lan's scouts came down to tree top levels, searched for, found, and then pulled me out. The extraction itself proved to be somewhat intense."

"Intense? What happened?"

"One of Lan's scouts, Shey, located me. I began working through the dense forest and underbrush to reach the defined extraction point. It was nighttime, and in my state of fatigue and haste I was careless; I triggered a Kreel tangle field trap. Once taken in the trap I was paralyzed and utterly helpless. Zorn put his own life in peril; he came on foot through the woods and underbrush to get me out of the trap. He found me and destroyed the tangle field trap; otherwise I would have ended up on a serving platter on a Kreel banquet table. We barely escaped on foot, with several squads of howling warriors hot on our back trail. They were literally on our heels.

"When we reached Zorn's lifter, Shey laid down a blistering pattern of laser fire and killed our pursuers; else neither Zorn nor I would have survived. As Shey lifted us out, the forest was ablaze, and above us the night sky was being laced with intense laser fire and illuminated by explosions— Shey and the other three Scouts were then fully engaged in a fierce firefight with multiple Kreel skimmers. It was a close thing."

Darrell had never before heard anything about the up close and personal fighting involved with the Kreel, except once when the Kreel had sent a strike force to Earth. That Kreel attack had involved mostly combat between ships in deep space. In wonder, he looked again at the lovely young woman sitting on the log with him and thought— *I was right, she is lethal.*

"Humph, Cruiser Lan and Zorn seem to get about. Lan was the Cruiser that discovered Earth, and I think that I met Zorn when he was on Earth about three or four years ago. He seemed to be a nice guy. I am glad that they were able to get you out. But, I do have one question."

"What is it?"

"How did Guardian Force come to learn where the Kreel research facilities were located, and how did they learn about you and where to search?"

Reaching down, Amada picked up a small ocean-smoothed stone and polished it on her pant leg. Then, after looking for a moment at its burnished surface, she gently placed the stone back on the beach. Smiling she turned toward Darrell.

"That, good Sir, constitutes multiple questions. Still, the wonder of what happened is that on its surface, everything appears to have unfolded by random happenstance. I personally suspect the Elders were busy behind-the-scenes and providing subtle nudges in all the right places."

Elders? Who are they?"

"Darrell, if you really want me to answer your first questions, then first things must come first. Besides, the Elders are another topic. Be patient and I will answer that question next."

"It's a deal, and my middle name is Patience."

Smiling and shaking her head in amusement, Amada continued. "No offense is intended Darrell; however, I have some reservations concerning the appropriateness of your middle name. Still, regarding your initial questions, when our mission began the Nori knew of Earth only as a myth and considered it forever lost. We had no knowledge of the Assembly of Worlds, the Guardian Force, or that a federated group of human governed planets even existed. Everything changed when Guardian Force attacked the Kreel Elite Guard on the planet where Chandara and I were covertly working."

"Then, your Mentor, the one who the Kreel killed, was named Chandara?"

"Correction, her name is Chandara. The most amazing part of the story is the Kreel did not kill her. They captured her, and after her interrogation she was being transported to the Elite world. She was to be paraded as a prize Nori trophy, just before the Kreel roasted and served her up on a platter. They had badly beaten her, stripped her naked, and then thrown her bodily into a holding cell on an outbound Kreel ship. Because of her injuries, she lost consciousness in that cell. Somehow, she woke up in a clean hospital bed on Glas Dinnein. Just how she survived to be rescued and taken to Glas Dinnein is an untold mystery, and Guardian Force has tightly wrapped it in a blanket of secrecy."

"Amada that still doesn't explain how Guardian Force learned about you."

"Well, after she had somewhat recovered from her injuries, she and I were able to communicate. Chandara then told Guardian Force about the secret Kreel research laboratories and of my plight. It took Guardian Force Intelligence about one minute to recognize the significance and strategic value of the Kreel research facilities. In spite of the Kreel reinforcements, they immediately sent a high-risk strike force to destroy the research facilities. Extracting me was strictly relegated to a 'will do if can do' priority. It was at their own significant peril that the Guardian personnel pushed their mission limits, found, and extracted me, I was extremely fortunate."

Frowning, Darrell paused before continuing. "Amada, with each question I ask, I end up with more questions— like just how did you communicate with Chandara? I know, that's another question, so first tell me about the Elders."

Looking with interest at Darrell, she hesitated a moment before answering. "I am surprised that you know nothing about the Elders. Still, your question is not one that is easily answered, because there is little we truly know about them."

"Well, what little the Nori may know is a bunch more than I know -—so, can you at least provide me with a brief synopsis?"

"Perhaps. If I describe for you a few of our basic presumptions, you may find the information helpful. Firstly, the Nori believe the Elders are living beings, intelligent, and to all effects immortal. Secondly, they are non-somatic beings with a highly developed ability to interact directly with and manipulate time and the physical and energies of the Universe-"

"What do you mean non-somatic?"

"Sorry Darrell, I was trying to be precise in answering your question. The term somatic relates to the body, especially as distinct from the mind. We believe The Elders are pure consciousness in their energetic form, and they do not appear to have physical bodies as we do. As I was saying, the Elders have demonstrated an ability to consciously manipulate energy, time and distance. We also believe they can move at will freely throughout our Galaxy. Being comprised of multiple older and advanced species, they have together formed a positive and cohesive galactic community. We collectively call them the Elders. We are also aware of a hostile conscious-being that we refer to as the Old One."

"The Old One? Amada, with everything you tell me there're always more questions. These non-corporeal beings you are describing, the Elders, sound somewhat unbelievable. Have you personally met an Elder?"

"Yes, in fact when I was aboard Lan and coming to Megan for the first time, we encountered one. He told us they had predicted seventy thousand years ago that humanity on the assembled worlds, Earth, and the Nori would come to be united on Megan. For some unspecified reason, he implied the Elders consider our reunion here to be significant and important. We do not know why."

"You said the Elders may have provided subtle nudges in all of the right places. What did you mean?"

"That question, good Sir, does not have a simple answer either. In general terms, our analysis of the Elders indicates that they abide within a moral framework consisting of high ethical principles, and rarely involve themselves directly in matters pertaining to the young species now flourishing within our galaxy. While not often becoming directly involved in others affairs, on rare occasions they may choose to suggest or mentally nudge a person or group of individuals to consider a particular course of action. The individuals affected experience the Elder's suggestion subconsciously, as a telepathic whisper or quiet unobtrusive thought in their mind. Based upon the individual's wisdom and freewill, they will either pick up or ignore the Elder's suggestion. At extraordinary times, the Elders may choose to become directly involved in the lives of others. One Elder confirmed that in ages past they were responsible for transplanting selected groups of humans from Earth and seeding them on viable planets among the stars."

"Whoa, hold it right there. Some old Earth myths tell of people occasionally mounting up to the stars, such as Ziusudra, Hermes, and Enoch, but why would elders ever bother to transplant humans anywhere?"

"From what we surmise, the Elders felt morally compelled to overtly act when humanity was facing notable global extinction events, such as 70,000 Earth-years ago, when the passing red and brown dwarf pair of stars that you told me about caused havoc in Earth's solar system. That was when they seeded the Nori."

"Then, it's your belief the Elders always act benevolently."

"Yes, always. The Nori believe the Elders' actions and guidance are beneficial. We are taught from youth to be vigilant to discern their rare mental contact. Of course, there is that one exception– the Old One. That conscious-being is judged as being indifferent or else even hostile toward the young species in our Galaxy. Recently the Elders told us that the Old One has become involved in the war between humanity and the Kreel. It seems he prefers the Kreel over humanity and is helping them. The Elders are well aware of the Old One, and they are organized to oppose him."

"Amada, that's enough; my head is beginning to hurt. If I may change the topic– I've got one more question that's begging for an answer."

"And that is?"

Looking down at the beach, Darrell used the toe of his right boot to idly push a rock about, and then looked out toward the distant horizon line. The afternoon was fading and his suppressed appetite was clamoring for attention. Sighing, he looked up and turned to face Amada.

"If I accept your offer to become the Nori Emissary on Earth, and serve as liaison to Earth governments, will the Nori give me their solemn pledge and guarantee they will bring me home to Megan?"

Hesitating but a moment, Amada made direct eye contact with Darrell before she replied. "Yes. If you then wish, the Nori will bring you back to Megan, whether alive or dead."

Chapter Fifteen:
Prelude

Black cold space embracing flat Black hulls, the twenty-five Guardian Cruisers were merely dark specks within the outer boundary of the K-31 system. Positioned fifty-seven astronomical units from the distant and faint primary, they were operating deep within the Kreel Empire, light years distant from any help or reinforcement.

Three days had elapsed since Kellon had eased his Task Force through the bumpy turbulence of the Heliopause. His chosen point of penetration was fifteen degrees above the plane of the ecliptic and on a solar radius line passing just above the target planet. This position offered him a direct short path to the target.

Strategically, the Kreel had five planetary systems within the Empire dedicated to production of warships, the largest being K-31. It also served as the primary Research and Development hub for all five systems. Since it was the planet having the highest production levels and the R&D Hub, Guardian force ranked it as the most valuable target among the five worlds. Accordingly, Kellon expected the Kreel to fiercely defend it.

Upon entering the system, Kellon had promptly launched tattletale Intelligence probes inward toward each of the two inhabited planets. Each tattletale was designed for maximum stealth and programed to search for traces of Kreel warships. In support of the tattletales, Kellon also dispatched four Scouts to deploy a broad and interlinked chain of laser telemetry transceivers inward as far as the sixth planet. As each tattletale entered the innermost system, it deployed additional laser transceivers and then promptly began sending short burst of ultraviolet laser telemetry out along the chain of linked transceivers to the waiting Task Force.

Kellon's plan of battle was to advance directly toward the planet, meet, engage, and neutralize the Kreel defending force, methodically destroy the R&D and manufacturing capacity, and then withdraw prior to the arrival of Kreel reinforcements. The

93

key element required for mission success was to quickly vanquish the Kreel defenders.

The illumination within the Admiral's conference room was lowered, and the tactical plot being displayed on the aft bulkhead was bright and sharp. Five men were sitting around the conference table, Admiral Kellon, Captain Roy Grey, First Tactical Officer Lorn Shaw, and the lead Task Force Scout Officers, Commanders Roan and Zorn. All five men were intensely studying the tactical display, even as Lan was completing his most recent update.

Frowning, Kellon sat back pondering the display. It was a standard square shaped compressed X-Y tactical plot, on which was presented the system's ecliptic plane, as seen from above the ecliptic. The orbit of each planet was represented by a faint yellow circle, and superimposed on the plot were symbols denoting the location of each planet in its orbit and every Kreel ship being tracked. Below the X-Y plot there was a second plot that represented the Z-axis. It was as wide as the X-Y plot, but it was narrow and horizontally bisected by a faint yellow line representing the plane of the ecliptic. Each symbol on the X-Y plot had a corresponding symbol displayed directly below on the Z-axis plot.

Still frowning, Kellon queried, "Gentlemen, what is obviously wrong with that tactical situation?"

"Sir, off hand, it looks altogether too quiet and inviting. Where are the defending Kreel cruisers?" Roan said, dryly.

Like Kellon, Roy was frowning. " Good question. By the seven stars, that defense pattern is like an engraved invitation to come right over for dinner. I count only three fast-attack ships at the system entry point and two at its departure point. I see six more fast-attack ships that seem to be randomly dispersed between the third and second planets. That makes a grand total of eleven fast-attack ships. Lorn, what's the latest Intel estimate of probable Kreel strength?"

Glancing first at a report folder, Lorn looked up and once more examined the tactical plot. "Sir, according to Guardian Intelligence, the K-31 system should be bristling with cruisers. The normal defending strength in this system consists of twenty-eight fast-attacks and fourteen cruisers. Intercepts of recent Kreel fleet deployments indicate that Admiral Groff has dispatched an additional group of fourteen cruisers to add to that number. He has also sent six Elite Guard ships, and gave the Elite Guard overall command of the military. Grand Marshal Krupp, the sole surviving Elite Grand Marshall, is personally in command of the system's defenses."

Still frowning, Kellon looked about at his staff officers. "Given what we're seeing, I believe it would be a safe wager to bet three brews that our efforts of misdirection didn't work. The Kreel are primed and cocked, ready for battle.

"Lorn, adding up your numbers, we should be facing twenty-eight fast attack and twenty-eight cruisers. Then adding in the six Elite Guard ships the probable Kreel strength consists of sixty-two first line Kreel ships. I do not like those odds. I doubly dislike them knowing the entire system is obviously wound-up tight like a baited spring trap, just waiting to be sprung. Gentlemen, be advised, we are going to spring that trap, but I have no intention of being caught in its snapping jaws.

"Roy, we have twenty-four Cruisers here with us, and they have the best sensors we can design and build. Spread them out and then put them to work. Gather every smidgen of data we can collect.

"The Kreel cruisers are clearly observing Sub-Space Communication silence, however, Kreel communications officers will undoubtedly be using standard household frequencies to coordinate their actions. You're to expand our search of those lower military bands, and Begin scanning for trace communications between individual Kreel units.

"Lorn, you're to coordinate all of our task force Intelligence assets. Scan every byte of incoming data. I want to know precisely where each group of Kreel cruisers and fast attacks are hunkered down. And, pay particular attention to those two moons orbiting the planet. They are a logical place for the Elite Guard to loiter, while waiting for an unwary alien to blunder by. Be certain to direct a tattletale in toward them and take a good look.

"Gentlemen, you are to localize those missing six Elite Guard ships. Review every bit of Intel we have concerning them. And, don't forget that when we penetrated the Commercial system, and planted those limpets on the outbound cargo ships, our Scouts got a really close up and personal look at an Elite Guard

95

ship. Pull up those files and dig out everything that we can use to find and destroy them.

"Roan, you and Zorn are to work with Lorn. Review the Elite Guard data, and help him in looking for anything that may give us an edge. You are not to leave a single byte of data unexamined.

"Gentlemen, you have twenty-four hours, and then I expect you right back here, with bells on and with answers. Dismissed."

As the door closed behind his departing staff, Kellon sat alone and again frowned as he looked at the tactical plot. Lan softly intruded into his contemplations.

"Sir, I know you have already stated it is your intent to spring the trap, however, the best way to avoid a trap may be to simply avoid it. Perhaps this is one of those times when it is wiser to simply withdraw and then proceed on to the secondary designated target."

Standing, Kellon walked over to the side board and poured a cup of neab. As he stood stirring in the cream and honey, he continued to frown.

"As always Lan, your counsel is sound. Still, K-31 is our primary target. For a trap to be successful, it must be sprung on an unwary prey. We're definitely not unwary or prey. The numerical odds are stacked against us; but the deciding counter to brute force is mobility and superior tactics. It's my intention to use our stealth and superior stratagems to counter their blunt force."

"Sir, when speaking of superior stratagems, I feel obliged to point out we lack reliable Intel concerning Grand Marshal Krupp and his level of military skill. I suggest it is prudent to presume he did not reach his command rank purely on the basis of his personal charm. There is also an additional consideration. During his Intel briefing Commander Shaw overlooked mentioning one possibly important point."

"What point?"

"Sir, our Intel indicates grand Admiral Groff is in space, and he is in personal command of his one-hundred-ship task force. We do not know his precise whereabouts, and he may be nearby."

Sitting back, Kellon's frown deepened. "What is the basis of your evaluation?"

"Sir, Admiral Groff is well aware of the value of K-31. And, Sir, there exists a deadly competitive tension between Admiral Groff and Marshal Krupp. It seems only reasonable to anticipate Admiral Groff may desire to closely observe Marshal Krupp and therefore be nearby. If I am correct in my assessment, then Admiral Groff may have already prepositioned some surveillance probes within the system to observe what unfolds here."

As he sat down, Kellon sighed. "Lan that is a particularly troubling assessment. If proven correct, we may be facing one-hundred and sixty-two defenders. Given the implications, we'll err on the side of caution. We'll presume Admiral Groff is nearby and does have Intel assets prepositioned within the system. Promptly pass your assessment on to Lorn, and tell him that I want him to begin a systematic scan for possible Kreel surveillance activity."

"Yes Sir."

"The bottom line is we can't possibly know everything. Regardless of how good our Intel and planning may be, battles are unpredictable and dangerous things. We'll need to take the time to get it right," Kellon mused.

"Then Sir, it remains your intention to attack K-31, as planned?"

"Yes. The possibility that Groff is nearby does constitute an additional threat that we can't ignore. If Groff does enter the system, it will have a huge bearing on our mission timing. In any case, we are going to go in, spring the trap, and then proceed to kick the Kreels' backsides!"

There was a brief moment of silence before Lan replied. "Sir, having inquired, I am now able to report that each of the one-hundred and twenty-five Task Force AIs are in full agreement with your expressed intent. We are standing by and ready to do our part."

A broad smile promptly replaced Kellon's concerned frown. "Lan, inform all of the other AIs that I am relying upon their special capabilities to help get the job done and get the Task Force home, and intact."

"Sir, while not desiring to be perceived as being overconfident, and quoting William and Rodney, we are going to kick their butts."

97

Chapter Sixteen:
Conundrum

The soft chime announcing the detection of a new target attracted Lorn's attention. Glancing to the tactical plot on the forward bulkhead, he located and identified the new target. It was a Kreel fast attack ship. Its X-Y coordinates indicated it was nearly on top of them. When He checked the Z-axis, he relaxed. The data indicated the ship was on the plane of the ecliptic and far below them. Even at that distance, its position was all too close to the Task Force.

Hmmm, he thought, its speed is nearly zero. Why would a Kreel fast attack ship enter the system so unobtrusively, and at an unorthodox entry point? The answer which leaped to Lorn's mind was, that ship is probably an advanced scout. That implies Admiral Groff's task force is near. Blast, this development definitely complicates matters.

"Lan, what is your assessment of the Kreel fast attack ship that just entered the system below our position?"

"Sir, it constitutes a Conundrum. I first considered we should destroy it. Then, I promptly tempered that assessment. If we destroyed it, our action would clearly announce our presence and define our general location."

"Good thinking. My assessment is it's an advanced Scout of Groff's Task Force."

"Sir, it may be. Yet, it might also be a ship Grand Marshal Krupp has wisely prepositioned to monitor a probable attack entry point. It is, after all, the point that affords an enemy the shortest distance to the planet. If this hypothesis is true, then the ship is on its assigned duty station and searching for us."

The Task Force was maintaining a strict stealth profile, and Lorn knew it was improbable the Kreel ship could detect it. " That idea is plausible, and you could be correct. Still, the worst-case hypothesis is the ship is an advance Scout preceding entry of a larger force. If this is true, then we can anticipate Groff's Task Force will soon enter the system, perhaps near that position.

"Is Admiral Kellon informed of this development?"

"Yes Sir, and his reactions mirror our concerns. He has ordered the Task Force to get underway and begin moving directly toward our target. Even now, Commodore Grey is conveying those orders to the Task Force.

"Sir, the Commodore has also ordered me to inform you to get the 'bricks out of your pants' and find where the sixty-two Kreel defending ships are lurking. Sir, need I say the aforementioned reference to bricks in pants was the Commodore's unique expression, and no offense was intended."

Smiling, Lorn responded, "Not to worry Lan. I sorta figured out the comment originated with the Commodore. In reply, you may inform him the bricks are now neatly stacked in a corner, and we are earnestly focused on finding the aforementioned targets– even before they begin shooting at us."

"Sir, I have relayed your response to the Commodore, especially the shooting part. The Task Force is now underway, moving into its standard battle formation, and accelerating. I estimate our arrival at the defined departure point in 38.87 hours."

"Thirty-eight hours? Blast, then I predict there is a long sleepless day and night looming directly ahead. Lan, you're to instruct the Task Force Intelligence Groups that they are to set a modified Condition 2."

"Yes Sir. Your orders have been relayed to all of our Cruisers, and they are duly acknowledged.

"Sir, if you do not object, might I ask you for your own assessment of our tactical situation?"

Lorn had continued to study the tactical plot, and now he sat back and sighed. "Well Lan, with sixty-two Kreel ships waiting in ambush ahead of us and possibly one-hundred more coming in behind us, it is safe to conclude we are now securely positioned between an anvil and a hammer. If our stealth holds, we may actually reach the planet and be able to engage a Kreel force that greatly outnumbers us, before the one-hundred Kreel ships behind us begin their outraged howling pursuit. Presuming we can avoid being ensnared by the waiting Kreel ships, engage and quickly destroy them, we may have about twenty-four hours to locate and level the research and manufacturing installations on the planet. At that point, we will need to turn and fight or else run for cover."

"Sir, fight or flight? Which do you believe will be most likely?"

"Truthfully, given Admiral Kellon's determination to inflict lasting damage on the Kreel, I simply don't know. Because of the heavy load of ground ordnance that we are toting, I feel we lack adequate missiles to take on the defending force and then turn and fight an even greater pursuing force. Therefore, if I were the Admiral, after launching our ground ordnance, we would definitely turn and like a rabbit scamper for the bushes, as fast as we could get there. Now, having said that, just remember, I'm not the Admiral."

"Sir, thank you for sharing your insights with me. I always find them instructive."

"Lan, you're most welcome. I'm always glad to share my personal opinion. Now, getting back to work, kindly inform Commander Roan that when his duties permit, I need to talk with him. Inform him that I have an important problem that needs the attention of his Scouts."

"Yes Sir. I have notified Shey, and she affirms he will be here shortly."

Lorn returned his attention to the immediate problem, locating the Kreel ships that were waiting in ambuscade. The early data from the tattletale probes was coming in and there were several tantalizing hits on the two moons and more sites on the planet. He quickly found himself immersed in evaluating the reports coming from the Tactical groups on Lan and the other Cruisers.

Only a few minutes had elapsed before the compartment door slid open and Roan entered. "Good morning Lorn, Shey informs me that the Scouts might lend you a helping hand. What's up?"

Sitting back, Lorn smiled broadly. "Good morning right back at ya, and thank you for coming so promptly. Shey is correct; I've got a nagging problem, and the Scouts definitely can help.

"Lan has just informed me that we will be arriving at our departure point in about forty hours. Once we begin our attack, our primary mission is to deploy our ground ordnance precisely on specific targets. What I want you and your girls to confirm are the allocation of ordnance for each target, the coordinates, and the weapon settings provided to us by HQ. To accomplish the cross-checking, your girls will need to have access to the raw Black-Hole Intelligence data. Roan, I underscore the Black Hole nature of the data, and you're to take all mandatory measures pertaining to who gets access strictly on a need-to-know basis."

"Humph, that I can do. Lorn, might I ask, why do you feel there's a need to recheck the HQ data?"

"That's a fair question. My own Intel sources inform me the subordinated indigenous species upon the planet is not hostile to anyone. I want to be doubly assured what we hit is Kreel and not indigenous. The HQ Intelligence team is excellent, but anyone can make a mistake. Therefore, I want you to go through the entire ground target list and confirm there are no errors in target identification, weapon type, or settings."

Roan stood thoughtfully looking at Lorn, and he frowned. "Performing Target confirmation, that's something we can certainly do. While not wanting to be overly inquisitive, might I inquire, what's the source of your Intel?"

"It's Amada."

"Humph, she's definitely a solid source for that type of Intel. The girls will get right on the job. Lorn, don't forget there are one-hundred very capable Scouts sitting in their hangars, and they have loads of idle computer time. Perhaps we might be of some additional assistance in helping you pin down the Kreel Cruisers."

Sighing, Lorn looked squarely at Roan. " Where's my mind? Sorry Roan. Of course, you can help. In fact, the Commodore is on my case and your help would be greatly appreciated. First, retrieve from the archives the Scout records relating to your encounter with the Elite Guard ship. I'll instruct Lan to stream all the incoming tattletale and our sensor data to Shey. At the moment, you may find the tattletale data interesting, and it might just help you to pin down the Elite Guard ships. Be advised, finding where they have gone to ground is the highest priority."

"Understood. Is there anything else we can help with?"

"Not at the moment."

"Just remember Lorn, if something else does come up, anything else that we can do to help, call!"

As the compartment door slid closed behind Roan, Lorn sat a moment and reflected on his next priority. "Lan, I presume you monitored my conversation with Roan."

"Yes Sir, and in accordance with your instructions to Commander Roan, I have granted Shey access to the HQ raw Intelligence data set. I am also now streaming sensor and tattletale data to her."

"Good. The Scouts will be a great help."

"Sir, your desire to double-check HQ's calculations is most commendable. Such efforts are often viewed as being unnecessary, mundane, and tedious; but, if one innocent life can be saved, then the effort is very rewarding."

"Since we're about to drop a bucket of destruction and pain on someone, trying to minimize dumping it on innocent beings is a moral imperative. Now, what we need to find is Grand Marshal Krupp, before he comes by for a surprise visit."

Chapter Seventeen:
Line of Departure

For thirty-seven hours, the Task Force had moved toward its designated target. Then as it crossed the orbit of the sixth planet, that being the designated line of departure for the pending attack, Kellon ordered the Task Force to pause. As the Task Force adjusted its battle formation, Kellon called his staff together for a planning session.

The lights in the conference room were low and a tactical plot showing the details of the inner solar system was being displayed on the forward bulkhead. As they took their seats about the conference table, the five men were grim.

Kellon asked, "Roy, are there any outstanding deficiencies in our readiness for battle, either pertaining to our personnel or our Cruisers?"

"No Sir. All Squadrons have reported their Cruiser deficiencies. None impair our battle readiness, and crew morale is high."

Turning toward Roan, Kellon asked, "Commander, what is the status of our Scouts?"

"Sir, without exception our Scouts stand battle ready."

Kellon sat thoughtfully for a moment, and then turned to Lorn. "Commander, what is our latest Intel on the disposition of Kreel Military forces?"

"Sir, we are monitoring the Kreel housekeeping channels. The message intercepts are sparse; nevertheless, we do have three intercepts of particular interest. The first intercept confirms the Elite Guard is in overall Command; senior Kreel officers are not pleased and are grumbling. The second intercept indicates the Elite Guard has grounded the military cruisers, confined their crews onboard, and are holding them on full alert and combat readiness. The third intercept revealed the senior military officers are prepared to meet an imminent attack. They are well-motivated and confident.

"As shown on the tactical plot, we are currently tracking an additional eleven fast attack ships patrolling near the planet and its two moons. That leaves six fast attack ships unaccounted for."

"Lorn, have you determined the geodetic coordinates of the grounded Cruisers or located the Elite Guard ships?" Kellon asked.

"No Sir. Wherever they are situated, they have their propulsion systems shut down. At our current distance from the planet precision tracking of housekeeping messages is not possible. We have, however, isolated four approximate areas on the planet where cruiser housekeeping messages are originating. These areas are well distributed about the planet, and according to our Intel, each area has a major Kreel military spaceport. Our analysis suggests the cruisers are grounded at those identified military sites. Deduction, based on our Intel, that there are twenty-eight cruisers, suggest the cruisers are organized into squadrons of seven cruisers each."

"Do you have any data pointing to the Elite Guard, anything at all?"

"Sir, no. There are no intercepts or hard data which suggests where they are concealed. We have deduced the six unaccounted-for attack ships may be paired up with the six Elite Guard ships.

"Sir, there is one additional important factor. As shown on the tactical plot, we are currently tracking propulsion signatures of 173 small-class ships. The signatures are Kreel scouts. They are distributed near the planet and out as far as three AU distant and maintaining strict communications silence. Standard Kreel tactical doctrine also suggests they have deployed passive monitoring probes further out."

Turning, Kellon studied the tactical plot, and his frown only increased. After a few minutes, he turned toward Lorn.

"After putting all the Intel pieces together, what is your arching assessment?"

"Sir, our Tactical assessment is Grand Marshal Krupp has studied our five previous planetary strikes. In response, using the resources at his disposal, he has established a layered defense. Superficially, the planet offers the appearance of being open and poorly defended; in truth, the planet is well fortified and poised ready for an imminent attack.

"Krupp's priorities are clear; using his fast attack and scout ships, he has formed a wide flung early detection net about the planet. Tactically, he is concealing and holding his cruisers and Elite Guard ships in close ready reserve. That's understandable, since they constitute the bulk of his primary firepower, and they are needed to protect high-value planetary resources. Undoubtedly, the Marshal has also placed all planetary defense grids on ready alert."

"Although lacking hard Intel concerning the Elite Guard, undoubtedly you've formed a best guess," Kellon said.

"Yes Sir. I must stress, without hard Intel, all we have is a best guess. Yet, there are two anomalies that are definitely teasers. During several fly-by scans, one of our tattletale probes detected a well-defined and distributed power grid on the upper pole of the larger moon. That pattern of power distribution suggests the existence of a major lunar facility. Oddly enough, it's currently maintaining a strict communications blackout. It's the absence of discernable housekeeping traffic that suggests it may be where the Elite Guard has gone to ground. The second anomaly is the facility is not included in our Black Hole Intel. It must therefore be something the Kreel recently constructed."

Roy was studying the tactical chart, and inquired, "Lorn, just how good is our Intel regarding the sophistication of planetary defense installations?"

"Sir, our Intel is excellent. The Kreel's imperative favors aggressive heavy space-borne offensive firepower and a disdain for ground based defenses. The ground installations are few, scattered, and poorly coordinated. There is, however, one point of uncertainty. The planet is the Research Center for the Kreel military, therefore by definition our Intel is incomplete."

Turning toward Lorn, Roan asked, "Is there any basis for us to believe the Kreel have developed new detection systems, even in prototype, that might penetrate our stealth capability?"

"None. The probability of that capability is considered to be low; however, we are speaking here of Kreel Military Research and Development. And, as I've already inferred, that's a murky topic."

Sitting back, Kellon placed his hands flat on the table and closed his eyes for several minutes. Then, opening his eyes, he leaned forward. "Lan, how many compact fusion demolition charges are currently in Squadron One munition stores?"

"Sir, each Cruiser has the standard issue of six fusion demolition charges in their stores."

For a few moments, Kellon remained silent and studied the countenances of his trusted colleagues and longtime friends. "Gentlemen, Marshal Krupp has skillfully set his trap, and it is well-devised. The proffered bait is the enticing deception of a vulnerable planet. The trigger of the trap is the early warning that signals the approaching enemy. It's that early warning which provides the opportunity for the cruisers to power up, lift ship, and intercept their unwary foes. Once triggered, the overall success of the trap hinges on the Kreel's massive firepower and the ability to prevent their prey from escaping. Therefore, for the overall success of their trap, the Kreel must physically constrain the prey within a defined kill zone. It's that constraint which represents the snapping jaws of the trap.

"Lan recently reminded me that a deadly competitive tension exists between Admiral Groff and Marshal Krupp. He is correct, they are bitter political foes. They are also flag rank Kreel Officers and fighting a common enemy. When encountering a common foe, even the bitterest political rivals tend to unite.

"The fast attack ship which was observed entering the heliosphere prompts us to ask– just where is Admiral Groff loitering? And, does the Admiral have a part in closing the trap? I believe he does.

"Marshal Krupp is prepared to spring his trap and commit to an unrestricted battle. At that same time, I anticipate Admiral Groff's force will enter the K-31 system at multiple points. His intent will be to bottle up the enemy within a defined kill-zone."

"Sir, how can Groff possibly hope to bottle up his enemy?" Zorn asked.

"Fair question. Bear in mind I'm working only with probabilities. Still, I've observed Admiral Groff is a firm traditionalist, and will likely exploit the 'jaws-of-death' tactics that he employed near Glas Dinnein.

"Imagine that a radial line is drawn from the solar primary to the planet and it represents an axle. Then imagine a large wheel is mounted on that axle, its outer rim being at the heliopause. I anticipate a three-pronged force will enter the heliosphere, each element of the force separated like spokes and 120 degrees apart.

"If my hypothesis proves correct, then we will initially be facing sixty-two first-line Kreel ships near the planet. Soon thereafter we'll have about seventy-five or ninety Kreel cruisers closing along multiple inbound trajectories. Tactically speaking, the prime responsibility of the three closing forces is to constrain and bottle up the prey, setting it up for the kill."

As he listened, Roy began to smile. "Sir, my dear mother would say that we are facing some long odds. Why not just optimize our stealth, come about, evade the trap, slip quietly away, and live to fight another day?"

"As usual Roy, your dear mother would be both wise and correct. Still, although the trap is well set, I believe it has several significant flaws. These can be exploited to cut the odds down to those more in our favor.

"The success of the trap pivots on the effectiveness of its early warning net. By successfully penetrating the net, in one stroke we can immobilize the twenty-eight Kreel cruisers on the ground. Achieving that tactical goal would immediately shift the odds and assure that near the planet we have both numerical and technological superiority."

Roy's smile broadened, and his eyes were twinkling. "Ah, so we'll have the Kreel right where we want them. Sir, with due respect, you know in every battle plan the 'if-factor' is the fulcrum between life and death. Given your mentioned shortening of the aforementioned long odds, I wager you've got a stratagem tucked up your sleeve."

Kellon began to smile. "Roy, do you also see what that stratagem might be?"

"Sir, I'd wager three cold brews that your earlier question to Lan about how many compact fusion demolitions charges we have is directly and somehow involved. And, since we all know it's unlawful for us to detonate a fusion charge within a planetary atmosphere, even on a Kreel dominated planet, I am admittedly somewhat perplexed."

Kellon managed to suppress his smile. "Roy, you need not worry. I have no intention of burying you under an avalanche of unwanted reports to Admiral Mer Shawn. The Law acknowledges the atmosphere about an inhabited planet is approximately 500 km, and specifies most of it is bound within 16 km. Strictly following the letter of the Law, I intend to detonate four charges 50 KM above the military sites where the cruisers are located. A fifth charge will be simultaneously detonated above the lunar base."

Roy sat back and a slight frown replaced his smile. "Humph, then it's your intention to generate an EMP."

"Correct. Each charge will generate a significant electromagnetic pulse, and that in turn should fry critical electronic systems in the surrounding installations and within the grounded cruisers."

"Sir, the 50-km detonation altitude is within the Law, but barely. Any detonation below that threshold would definitely complicate my reporting duties," Roy mused.

"Sir," Roan protested, "Surely the Kreel cruisers have the basic screens capable of shielding them from an EMP. Then, after they shrug off the pulse, the real battle would begin."

"Your point is well made Roan; however, we are speaking here of stealth and surprise. The cruisers are on the ground, and their propulsion systems are powered down, therefore their defensive screens are non-operational. By contrast, their internal systems, such as communications, life support, and basic engineering will all be on-line and operational. A nearby EMP will fry those critical systems, nailing the cruisers to the planet."

"Gentlemen," Lan inserted, "I can affirm that based on Guardian analysis of the captured Gortoga cruiser, an EMP will effectively immobilize a grounded Kreel cruiser, at least until repairs are implemented. Such repairs would require months of intense effort."

Zorn leaned back and a broad smile spread across his countenance. "Sir, since the success of your gambit rests squarely on stealthily placing five demolition charges above the planet and lunar surface, you will be looking for someone to deliver them on target with precision. Since a Scouts ship has a much smaller detection cross-section than a Guardian cruiser, I herewith request the mission be given to Lan's Scouts."

"Sorry Zorn, but my short answer must be no. A failure to simultaneously detonate the five charges on schedule would place the entire Task Force at jeopardy."

Turning to Roan, Kellon continued, "Roan, while I won't send a single Scout to deliver a fusion charge, I will authorize sending the five Scout groups from Squadron One to accomplish the mission. For redundancy, each group will carry multiple charges, and one Scout in each group will deliver a single charge above each target. If the first attempt proves unsuccessful, then one of the remaining Scouts in the group must complete the mission on schedule."

"Sir, I understand," Roan acknowledged.

"Zorn," Kellon inquired, "does my sending the Scouts from Squadron One to deliver the charges sufficiently scratch your itch for a fight?"

"Yes Sir, thank you," Zorn said.

"Roan, there is one more item. After the charges are deployed and detonated, you are to form the five Scout groups into a single fighting unit. While withdrawing, you will endeavor to avoid tangling with any of the patrolling Attack ships. Leave that heavy lifting for our inbound cruisers."

"Sir, understood. What are your orders regarding Kreel Scouts?"

"Given their numbers, none of us can predict how the Kreel Scouts will respond. So, they remain fair game. Just remember, when this brouhaha is over, I expect all of our Scouts to be safe and snug in their hangars."

"Understood Sir," Roan acknowledged.

"Good.

"Lan, what is the current status of AI scheduling of the deployment of our ground-targeted ordnance?" Kellon asked.

"Sir, the Scouts have completed a thorough analysis of HQ weapon-to-target allocations and all weapon settings. No errors were found. All of our Squadrons are now finalizing their ordnance-targeting settings, and the Squadron AIs report all preparations for the stand-off launch sequence will be complete within the hour."

Roy was studying Kellon's countenance, and smiling. "Sir," I do have one basic question."

Looking at Roy's expression, Kellon began to smile. "I thought you might. Go ahead, let's hear it."

"Well Sir, sorta Like Zorn, I keep worrying about the Kreel defined kill-zone. I've been adding up the numbers of Kreel you mentioned, and I come up a bit short. You mentioned we would be facing seventy-five or ninety Kreel ships approaching from multiple points on the heliosphere. Where did the remaining ten or twenty-five of Admiral Groff's one-hundred cruisers disappear to?"

"That's an excellent question Roy. Just remember, like Lorn, I'm guessing.

"As a species, The Kreel are prime predators and hunters. They think like hunters. The very nature of the set trap declares Marshal Krupp and Admiral Groff anticipate taking their prey unaware. Likewise, once surprised and confronted by an overwhelming combined force, a prudent enemy could be expected to turn and run for cover. To escape the closing jaws of the Kreel forces, the prey's tactical choices for escape are restricted to a small cone of possibilities."

"Sir, all of that makes good sense, but where are Admiral Groff's missing cruisers?" Roy asked.

"Patience, I'm just getting there. Logically, the withdrawing prey would retreat in the direction where there are no perceived on-rushing Kreel cruisers. That means fleeing out along the radial line on the plane of the ecliptic, escaping toward the nearest point on the heliosphere. Any significant deviation from that flight path would permit the Kreel cruisers pursuing from the planet and those approaching from the heliopause to intercept him. The Kreel's hunting imperative is to drive their prey in that direction– but ask, drive them toward what?

"The answer is into the prepared kill-zone. Admiral Groff's remaining cruisers are most likely just outside the heliosphere. They will be waiting in ambush, and prepared to use deadly short-Jump battle tactics to destroy their fleeing prey."

"Sir, then my assumption is that following our bombardment, we'll be scampering in some other direction."

"Good guess Roy. Still, the old military axiom that warns even the best plan of battle rarely survives where first contact with the enemy applies. What we eventually do will pivot about our Scouts' ability to successfully reach their targets undetected. The result of the Scouts' mission is critical to our overall success. If we can't achieve that initial goal, then gentlemen be advised, all planning aside, we will be immersed up to our necks in a deadly melee and scrambling for our lives."

Kellon paused for a moment, looking about at the four men sitting at the table, and his eyes came to rest on the Commodore. "Roy, schedule your planning meeting with the other Squadron Commodores. Finalize the bombardment sequence, and don't overlook scheduling a laser bombardment strike over each of the five targets we hit with the EMPs. We'll want to save the Kreel the expense of repairing those twenty-eight grounded cruisers and the Elite Guard ships.

"Once you have the details and timing for the strike worked out, regardless of the hour, bring your proposed operation schedule back for my review and approval.

"Gentlemen, unless you've any further questions, you have your work cut out. Dismissed."

Chapter Eighteen:
Launch

Kellon had thrown the Guardian tactical handbook into the wastebasket. The eight crewmen of Lan's four Scouts exited the mission briefing room, and they moved quickly to the elevators, which carried them down to the hangar deck. They were tense and their brief verbal exchanges consisted of tension-relieving banter.

The five scout groups of Squadron One were designated as the tempered point of the lance being thrust deep into the Kreel's intermeshed planetary defenses. Kellon's aggressive use of Scouts as the leading force in the attack was pure tactical heresy, and everyone knew that. When making their target runs over the planet each scout crew understood they would be strictly on their own, and survival would be dependent upon their wits and cunning.

As Roan and Zorn reached Shey's hangar, Galen, Sheba's Commander, turned toward them with a smile. "Hey Roan, when we get back, will you haggle with the mess steward for a bottle of wine for each Scout crew? I think after this mission we'll have earned one."

"Not to worry Galen. Rest assured, I'll finagle a bottle of wine for each of us," Zorn said.

As her inner hangar door clanged close behind Roan and Zorn, Shey cheerfully announced "Scout Leader Roan arriving!"

"Hey Shey, just what am I, a stale sandwich? Don't I at least merit a welcome aboard," Zorn teasingly quipped.

"Commander Zorn, you are being silly. You are always welcome aboard Shey."

As Roan briskly led the way across the short gangway, Zorn was right behind him. They moved without comment through the narrow passageway, passed the galley, and entered Shey's bright and compact command compartment. With the ease of long familiarity, each of them took their Command chair and set about Shey's pre-flight checklists.

"Shey, report. What's your pre-launch status," Roan ordered.

"Sir, all special ordnance has been loaded aboard, and all systems are in the gold."

Roan activated his voice communications to Lan's Scouts. "Scout Leader here, Sheba, Cindy, and Misty– report pre-launch status."

One by one each Scout reported, and Roan acknowledged each status gold report. After Misty had reported, Roan switched to the squadron Command band.

"Scout Leader here, Scout Group Commanders, Lux, Lawrence, Lent, and Langley, heads up, prepare for launch– repeat prepare for launch. When available, Report pre-launch group status to Shey.

"Shey, keep me posted on any deficiencies or problems."

"Yes Sir."

Roan then began his own meticulous visual review and confirmation of Shey's systems readouts. He then shifted his attention to the weapons loadout specifications. Of particular concern to him was the medium missile whose guidance and normal warhead had been replaced by a special guidance package and compact fusion charge.

He was just wrapping up his pre-flight checks when Shey reported.

"Sir, all Group Scout Commanders have reported their group status is gold. They report ready for launch."

"Lan, Scout Leader here. All Scout groups have reported they're ready for launch. Will you do us the honors of coordinating the launch of Squadron One Scouts?"

"Scout Leader, Lan here. I will coordinate the launch with the other Cruisers, as requested.

"Attention, all Squadron One Cruisers and Scout Groups, Lan here– standby– Mark, fifteen minutes to launch of Scouts and counting."

As Lan transmitted the fifteen-minute notice, all outer hatches on each scout were automatically closed and secured by interlocks, gangways were withdrawn, and with whispering sounds of barely audible machinery the normal atmosphere and temperature within each hangar began to be withdrawn and stored, hangar pressure being reduced to space normal conditions. The soft hum of Shey's power and propulsion systems ramping up softly transformed her normal in hangar background ambiance to that of a mission status.

As Roan was busy with his duties, Zorn was displaying on the forward bulkhead the current tactical plot showing the inner system and current locations of Kreel threats. He then began setting the critical way-points of their mission flight path, which wove in a serpentine fashion between and through identified threats.

"Shey, order Squadron One scout groups to set modified Condition 2," Roan ordered.

With Condition 2 being set, all further communications between Cruisers and Scouts would be restricted to encoded and compressed burst transmissions between the AIs. Shey therefore promptly rendered Roan's verbal combat order to an encoded digital stream and then transmitted it via Lan as a minuscule burst of communication to the other cruisers and groups, except to her nearby sisters, who were still connected with her in Lan's internal network.

Acknowledging Roan's order, she verbally announced she was setting Modified Condition 2, and the illumination in her command compartment promptly dimmed. Previously inert Fire Control systems activated and status lights for her countermeasures, decoys, missiles, lasers and projectile turrets, which were previously dark began first to blink and then shine a steady silver– ready standby.

Zorn was frowning as he made his adjustments to the projected flight path. "Hey Roan, trying to plot a safe route through the Kreel Scouts is like dodging traffic at rush hour, they are all in motion. I recommend you have Shey confirm the girls' stealth factors, because we're going to be maneuvering in mighty tight quarters with some Kreel scouts. And, making matters worse, undoubtedly there are sleepers we aren't even tracking."

"Shey, you heard the man. Have each Group Commander provide you with the lowest stealth factor in his group, and caution all of your sisters that they are to keep their stealth factors optimized and maximized throughout the mission."

"Yes Sir."

"How are we doing Zorn?"

"Well, I've defined our tactical plane, its first axis is from our current position to the planet, and its second axis is parallel with the plane of the ecliptic.

"Way-Point 1, where we meet up with the other groups, is easy, but beyond that point there are five additional way-points before we can split into our independent attack groups. And, until we reach that divergent point, I'm not able to define a post-attack rendezvous. Even then it may prove touch and go."

"Why?"

"Because the blasted Kreel scouts are continuously shifting their positions is why. Trying to predict the best after attack rendezvous point this early is pointless. Even getting us to way-point 6 is sorta like using a bayonet to probe and search out a path through a mine field, it's blasted risky and one small mistake—Kablooey. In fact, the way-points I'm setting are all subject to alteration as we proceed."

"Understood. Shey, advise all Group Commanders of our initial rendezvous coordinates, and advise them that subsequent way-points will be subject to change.

"After launch, each group is to form up in their standard three-sided pyramid, and they are to be using standard battle spread. When they reach our initial rendezvous, the groups will form up on Lan in a four-sided pyramid formation. Lan will take the point, and parallel with our tactical plane, Lent is high port, Lux high starboard, Lawrence low port, and Langley low starboard."

"Sir, your orders have been transmitted and acknowledged. I have just received the stealth factor reports from each group. The lowest factor is 92.4%."

"Shey, which Scout has that low factor?"

"Sir, the lowest stealth factor is mine. The next lowest factor is 97.8%."

"Zorn, given the projected proximity to Kreel scouts, will Shey's 92.4% pass muster?"

"Good question. It should, and with 40% to spare. I'll, however, be able to give you a more definitive report in about twelve hours—"

"Lan here, all groups mark, five minutes and counting."

"Shey, display where the planet and its two moons will be in eleven hours," Zorn ordered.

As Zorn observed the plot, the planet and two moons slightly shifted their positions and Zorn nodded his head in approval. He made a subtle adjustment to the last way-point.

"Thank you Shey, that helps."

Having made the adjustments, still frowning, Zorn sat back and studied his handiwork. The tactical plot showed a five-segment sequence of connected vectors, the point of the last leg being designated way-point 6. It was located 400,000 Km directly above where the planet would be in eleven hours.

"Roan, if you approve, Shey can go ahead and send the marked-up plot to the other scouts."

After studying the plot for several minutes, Roan nodded his head in approval. "Well done Zorn. That flight path represents a good blend of maximizing our stealth advantage and reaching the target in a reasonable time.

"Shey, you are authorized to send the mission tactical plot to the Tactical Sections of Squadron One and to the other Scout groups. Then, interact with Lan; remind him of when we captured the Gortoga Cruiser several years ago. Ask him to describe the methods he then used to detect the Kreel scout sleepers," Roan ordered.

"Yes Sir. The tactical plot has been transmitted as ordered. Lan is now searching our archives."

"Lan here, Mark, one minute and counting."

"Shey, once you get that detection information from Lan, transmit it to all of the girls. Tell them to put their ears on," Roan ordered.

"Understood Sir. Lan has provided me with the requested detection methodology. I am forwarding it on to each of my sisters."

Zorn was leaning back in his Command chair and studying the tactical plot and grumbling. "Roan, just be advised, when this mission is over I'm definitely applying for admission to Guardian cooks and bakers school."

Looking over toward Zorn, Roan smiled. "If it would help improve the quality of your neab, I'll gladly endorse that application–"

"Lan here. Standby– Mark, 5, 4, 3, 2, 1, Launch!"

In unison, on five flat-black Guardian Cruisers the outer Scout hangar doors swung smoothly up and then inward. Twenty

Scouts were simultaneously thrust out of their snug hangars and into the cavernous void of space. Once cast free, the Scouts quickly formed up into groups and moved purposely away from their Cruisers and toward Way-Point 1. Behind them the hangar doors automatically cycled closed with the deep tones of a large bass drum, shutting with hollow and echoing reverberations heard throughout each Cruiser. The twenty Guardian Scouts were going in harm's way, like lethal flitting shadows wrapped within darkness. Far behind the swift-moving Scouts the void surrounding the dark hulls of twenty-five poised and combat alert Cruisers was once more still, cold, and silent.

Chapter Nineteen:
Rumbling Thunder

Lan's status was set to modified Condition 3; nevertheless, every crewmember was feeling the increasing tension which precedes an approaching battle. In CAC, The Intelligence and Tactical divisions were already working at modified Condition 2. Accordingly, Roy was there observing, and for the one-hundredth time in the past fifteen minutes, he glanced over to the mission elapsed time clock. It was displaying ten hours and 23 minutes.

The good news was the outbound Scouts were still maintaining a strict communications silence, and there had been no Kreel alerts. The vital element of surprise remained intact, and if they were still on schedule, the Scouts would be launching their ordnance in another thirty minutes. Breaking the hushed conversations, the calm clear feminine voice of the general announcing system pronounced "the Admiral is in CAC."

Glancing toward the entry, Roy saw Kellon had just come into CAC, and he was standing intensely studying the forward tactical display. He also noticed that Kellon's frown lines were deeper than usual. As the elapsed mission time increased, everyone understood the level of risk to the Scouts likewise increased.

After observing the plot for several minutes, Kellon turned toward Roy. "Well, they are getting close enough to ask the Kreel for a cup of neab. Roy, have you formed up our cruisers?"

"Yes Sir. Several hours ago. Each Squadron was ordered to assume its optimum battle spread. Lan and Squadron 1 have the point position, and our remaining Squadrons have formed up in a 'V' echelon. As we discussed, when we reach the planet our primary focus will be on destroying the fast attack ships. In order to minimize anyone hitting us from the rear, we will be neutralizing any Kreel scouts we encounter along the way."

Glancing back toward the mission clock, Roy observed it was indicating 10 hours 30 minutes had elapsed. On schedule, he initiated the next step in their attack sequence.

"Lan, Spin up the Task Force."

"Yes Sir."

"Sir, Squadron Two through Five report they are at modified Condition 3 and are standing by," Lan said.

The hushed murmuring between crewmembers was subdued, and the mood in CAC was expectant. Like Roy and Kellon, others were frequently glancing at the mission clock, noting the time was moving like thick syrup on a cold winter day. As the clock reached eleven hours zero minutes, which was the scheduled mission time for the detonation of fusion charges, there was a noticeable heightening of tension. Then the mission clock anticlimactically continued its methodical measurement of elapsed minutes. Everyone understood that even if the detonations occurred on schedule, due to the distance related lag time, detection of the explosions would be delayed.

Then, at eleven hours and forty-seven minutes into the mission, the anticipated announcement occurred. "Intelligence here– we have detected multiple fusion detonations on or near the planet. Repeat, multiple fusion detonations are now observed on or near the planet."

Like a pent-up geyser being released, a loud cheer went up throughout Lan. Even Kellon's grim expression softened into a smile. "Well done Scouts." he murmured.

"Well Sir, score one for our Scouts! That should whittle down our opposition a bit."

Still smiling, Kellon sighed. "Agreed, that'll level the battle field somewhat. Now, it's our turn."

"Yes Sir."

Returning his attention to his immediate task, Roy ordered, "Lan, coordinate the lead Cruisers. Set Condition 2 and move us directly toward the planet. Set acceleration to 0.95 and speed to 200 lights."

"Throughout all five Squadrons Battle Stations alarms were sounding. "Yes Sir. The Task Force is accelerating. All weapon systems are set ready standby, countermeasures are fully activated, and point defense systems are on-line. Estimated time to reach the planet is four hours and fifty minutes," Lan reported.

As Lan accelerated, the immense power being channeled into his propulsion produced a deep resonant rumbling thunder. It created a low vibration throughout the ship that was heard and felt by everyone.

"Lan, inform the Squadrons they are authorized to FIRE at will on all confirmed Kreel targets of opportunity."

"Yes Sir."

Like Kellon, Roy was concerned; he had twenty of his Scouts out in the middle of a life and death brouhaha. He knew they were endeavoring to evade and survive, and it was his responsibility to provide them all possible support.

"Lan, order Squadron Five to activate their decoys."

"Yes Sir."

Kellon glanced at Roy, one eyebrow inquisitively raised. "What's your tactical ruse?"

"Well, while our Scouts were moving to their attack positions, I ordered Squadron Five to dispatch twenty decoys inward and position them three AU from the planet. They are directly opposite from the Scouts withdrawal route. When activated, the signatures of the decoys look like Dargon heavy cruisers, and they are using our embers of fire hologram. Every Kreel ship in this solar system should be able to spot them, even with their eyes closed and sensors turned off. The gambit is the Kreel will react toward the enemy they can see, rather than chasing after phantoms they can't see—"

"Tactical here! We've got problems. Our sensors are detecting nine new propulsion traces. They look like the missing six fast attack and three Elite Guard ships. The traces are located on the planet and not on the moon."

"Tactical, Grey here. What about the Kreel Cruisers? Are you detecting any trace of their propulsions?"

"Tactical here, no Sir. There's no indication whatsoever of Cruiser activity."

Kellon turned to Roy, and his countenance was hard. "Well, you can scrub the laser strike on the lunar base. Our Scouts will now be dodging twenty-eight fast attacks, three Elite Guard ships, and several hundred alerted Kreel scouts. That definitely stacks the odds against them."

"Lan here— I have received a battle update from Shey. It was sent forty-three minutes ago. Our Scouts report they have successfully completed their ordnance deployment, completed initial evasion, and are moving to rendezvous at Way-Point 7. There are no reported losses."

"Lan, using a Navigation Beacon, transmit a warning to Shey. Inform her of the Elite Guard ships. They are to withdraw as planned using all possible stealth."

"Yes Sir."

"Intelligence here– we are detecting a superluminal Kreel interstellar alarm signal. The Kreel have reported the planet is under direct attack."

"Well Roy, if my guess is correct, in about fifty hours Admiral Groff's cruisers will reach the planet. By that time, we will need to have completed our job and be on our way home."

"Yes Sir."

Even as Roy absent-mindedly replied, he was studying the tactical plot and the deployment of remaining Kreel forces. At the moment, they appeared to be in a state of bedlam. *Humph,* he thought, *once Marshal Krupp takes control, that confusion won't last long. Just keep your head down for a little longer Roan, we're on our way!*

Chapter Twenty:
Forlorn Silence

Shey's command compartment was quiet and softly illuminated. "Roan, all groups are holding in formation, and we are now crossing way-point 8, 300,000 km below the planet," Shey reported.

"Acknowledged," Roan replied.

"Zorn, how are we doing?" Roan asked.

Zorn was frowning, his attention being focused on the instrumentation readouts and the tactical plot. "Well Roan, I've monitored the Kreel's interstellar planetary alarm signal, and then there's some bad news. In addition to the fast attack ships that were patrolling near the planet, the outlying fast attack ships are now headed our way. And, then things get worse. I'm now tracking new propulsion traces, six fast attack ships and three Elite Guard ships. Since they are lifting out of the planet's atmosphere, I sorta guess they weren't on the moon after all. The good news is there isn't a Cruiser trace to be seen."

"What I need to know is are we in the clear?"

"No, not yet. We've definitely stirred up a hornet's nest, and the hornets are looking for some payback. I'm trying to get some meaningful separation between us and those hornets. And, Kreel Scouts are still problematic. I'm setting Way-Point 9 further below the planet."

"Just how problematic are those scouts?"

"Well, if we continue to be sneaky, I believe we'll be OK and breaking into the clear soon. Still, there's the threat of sleepers."

"Roan, I have an update from Lan; the task Force is set Condition 2, accelerating at 0.95, and coming at 200 lights. Their ETA at the planet is approximately five hours. He warns us about the Elite Guard ships. We are to maintain all possible stealth and withdraw, as planned."

"At least they are aware the Elite Guard wasn't caught napping on the moon. That's something," Roan commented.

"Hey Roan, will you take a look at this? I've got a new set of signatures, they're three AU distant from the planet, stationary, and look like pure Dargon cruisers! And boy howdy, they've got the Kreel's full attention."

Shifting his attention to the tactical plot, Roan chuckled. "Zorn, we definitely owe someone a cold brew or even two. That pack of decoys configured like Dargon cruisers are in the opposite direction from where we are headed. Someone has offered us a big helping hand."

"By the seven stars, those Dargon decoys are working. They're drawing off the hornets. Be advised, we're approaching Way-Point 9, and we should then be in the clear. I'm setting our next Way-Point out toward an intercept with our Task Force."

"Shey, you heard Zorn, begin the coordination of our girls; swing us about and head for Way-Point 10," Roan ordered.

"Understood, I have transmitted Way-Point 10 coordinates to all my sisters– We are now commencing our maneuver."

Even before the mission began, Roan had felt the intense stress associated with his responsibilities as Scout Leader. If the group had been detected during their approach then all elements of surprise would have been lost. Even worse, their detection would have triggered Grand Marshal Krupp's snare trap and brought the full might of the combined Kreel flotilla down on their heads. Once they reached Way-Point 6 and separated, each group moving independently toward its designated targets, his stress factor had soared. Dropping from high above their tactical plane, as the five groups passed the planet like fleeting shadows, each group synchronized and launched its missile toward the designated target. Having passed the planet well beyond its atmosphere, each group continued dropping silently and rendezvoused below the planet at Way-Point 7. That part of the mission had unfolded in clockwork-like fashion, even as planned. Now, tactically speaking, they seemed in the clear and heading toward the oncoming Task Force and their waiting hangars.

Remembering Galen's quip about a bottle of wine, Roan began to smile, thinking, *A bottle of wine and something to eat sounds really good right now.*

Twenty minutes after passing Way-Point 9, Shey's voice broke the silence, and her tone of voice was urgent.

"Roan, we have a problem. I am squeaking."

"Shey, clarify, what do you mean 'squeaking?'" Roan asked.

"Sir, I am experiencing a malfunction in my gravimetric system, it is generating a periodic burst of high frequency energy. I am attempting to isolate and lock down the source of the problem, but so far it is eluding my efforts. Our stealth shielding is dampening 92% of the signal, but there is 8% that is being radiated. My sisters are warning me that I look like a flashing beacon on their detection screens."

"Shey transmit a Code 3 warning to all Scouts. Inform all groups they have permission to engage Kreel scouts as required.

"Zorn, you heard my Code 3 order; get suited up."

Even as Roan was talking, Zorn was unbuckling his harness and moving quickly aft toward a storage locker. Pulling his environmental suit from its hanger, he quickly put it on and returned to his command chair.

As Zorn was fastening his restraining straps, Roan unfastened his harness and went aft and put his environmental suit on.

"Zorn, I'm going back to engineering. I'll try to find out what is wrong. Hold down the fort."

"Yes Sir, holding down the fort, as ordered. Just make it quick." Zorn's voice was tense.

Examining the tactical plot, Zorn groaned. "Bad, bad, and more bad! Shey, keep your eyes and ears open and your missiles and turrets hot and ready. Our squeak is drawing the attention of some Kreel scouts, and they are heading this way on intercept vectors.

"Roan, heads up. We have inbound troubles. Kreel scouts are heading our way, I'm estimating thirty minutes to intercept."

"Zorn, we've got a bigger problem back here. I can't gain access to or fix the propulsion malfunction. There's no way I can shut down that blasted signal.

"Shey, heads up girl. You're to inform Sheba that she is now designated Scout Leader. Order her to veer off, I repeat all groups are to immediately veer off and get clear of us. Tell Sheba her job now is to get our groups back home, and that's an order!"

"Sir, I have passed your orders to Sheba, she is not happy, but has acknowledged. Our Scouts are veering off as ordered."

Roan made one more desperate sweep of engineering, seeking any way he might override and clamp down the transient signal, then in frustration and disgust he turned and began working his way forward. *By all the Muses,* he thought, *how do we get out of this mess with our skins intact?*

"Shey, you are to enable Cobalt Blue. Repeat, enable Cobalt Blue and hold its countdown at 10 seconds. Acknowledge!"

"Acknowledging– Cobalt Blue is enabled, holding countdown at ten seconds," Shey responded.

Studying his sensors, Zorn was observing a series of small transient energy spikes. "Shey, I'm detecting transient signals twenty degrees off our port bow, and I don't like what that suggests–

"Shey! It's a Kreel sleeper! Incoming, I'm tracking six light missiles inbound!" Zorn exclaimed.

Even as Zorn alerted Shey, she was targeting light missiles, and the whirling sounds of her point-defense turrets swinging into alignment with the inbound missiles could be heard.

"Shey here, rolling, breaking hard port and down, jamming, dispensing chaff and countermeasures."

Even as Shey called out her actions, nine of her light missiles were arching toward not one, but three Kreel Scouts - all of which were wide awake and continuing their volley firing.

"Zorn, I am working my way forward, get us out of this if you can!" Roan shouted.

"I'm trying!"

"Shey! Break starboard, break starboard!

Again, even as Shey evaded and rolled the sounds of additional light missiles being launched filled her hull. Her newly launched missiles arched purposefully out toward two additional Kreel scouts, which had been hunkered down as sleepers with the others. Even as her second volley of missiles moved toward their targets, Shey reversed her roll sharply port, deploying additional counter measures and chaff while doing so. Then her point-defense guns began yammering their throaty staccato. As her point-defenses destroyed the closing missiles, multiple heavy concussions repeatedly and violently shook her. Then there came an enormous deafening detonation which tossed Shey like a rag doll from her bow to her stern. In a bedlam of ripping sounds that came with a hammering internal pressure and a flash of intense heat, the internal atmosphere was torn from her hull and ejected out into the vast vacuum of space; her propulsion and power generation systems failed. In her Engineering, Command,

and Crew living compartments low intensity emergency lighting immediately appeared.

The violence of the explosion flung Zorn helplessly about, but his restraining straps had kept him from being smashed against the bulkheads or the overhead. He was in pain, and his ears were ringing. Feeling his head, he found his environmental hood was still in place and he still had air. Something in his memory reminded him that having air was a good thing.

"Shey, are you still here with us?" Zorn feebly called out.

"Yes Zorn, I am still here with you. My external sensors are blind, my internal power and propulsion systems are off line, and I am adrift and on emergency power. My hull is badly breached. As ordered, I have enabled Cobalt Blue and it is being held at ten seconds. I am awaiting your orders."

"Roan, where are you? Sound off, where are you!" Zorn feebly cried out.

"Shey where Is Roan?"

"Sir, He is located in the central passageway. I am monitoring him. He is immobile but I can detect an irregular heart beat and shallow breathing. He is still alive."

"That's good. Shey, just you stay here and mind the store. I'll go and look for Roan."

Unfastening his harness, Zorn tried to get out of his command chair, and found he was in free-fall, Shey's artificial gravity systems were clearly off line. *Now that's not right,* he mused, *we just performed a full maintenance check last week.* Pushing himself toward the bulkhead, he grasped the handrail and began pulling himself aft, hand-over-hand, striving to reach Roan. Why he was trying to reach Roan seemed somewhat puzzling, but still, it seemed to be the right thing to do. As he worked his way aft, he could taste blood in his mouth and became more aware of the pain in his ears, legs and ribs. He knew he had to fight the pain, he had to reach Roan—he had to. He continued moving aft. Coming to a clutter of junk and floating debris, for a moment, bemused, he focused on an empty neab cup. It was floating in space just before his face. Looking at the cup in irritation, he grumbled in consternation, "Blast it, I thought I stowed all the cups."

Doggedly, he continued pulling himself aft, looking for Roan. When he found him, he was in the passageway, and he was drifting near the overhead. Roan's body was hanging motionless and limp. Even in his fog-bound state of mind, it was clear to Zorn that Roan was unconscious. Reaching out with his gloved hand, he confirmed Roan's hood was in place and sealed. Then he protectively drew Roan in close to him and snapped a come-along strap to a ring on Roan's suit. Exhausted, his arduous mission now complete, Zorn relaxed.

"Gotcha Roan. It's all going to be alright. All we've got to do is put the blasted cups away, and then we can go find Lan. But first, I need to rest here a moment or two; I need a little rest, just a little."

His eyes were heavy, and although he fought to keep them open, he could not. *Tired, so very tired and cold,* he thought. *Why is it so blasted cold? I'll just rest here with Roan for a minute, and then I'll go and put the cups back into the cupboard. But, there's something I should do first. Shey said it was something to do with blue.* Struggling to remember, he stubbornly held Roan tightly to him. *It was something to do with blue; I'll just rest here for a moment with Roan; cold, it's so very cold...; rest, then I'll go put that cup away.*

Having waited with gentle patience, merciful darkness then softly swept Zorn into her caring embrace....

In the vast silence within her drifting hulk, Shey called out over her communicator "Zorn? Roan? I'm still here. Emergency power will be exhausted in twenty-three minutes. As ordered, I am holding Cobalt Blue detonation at 10 seconds. Zorn? Roan? I am awaiting orders, what am I to do?"

No familiar response answered her repeated petitions. In the empty and forlorn silence of her shattered hull, Shey felt utterly alone. Then, she remembered Lux and her duty. Shey then knew precisely what she must do....

Chapter Twenty-One:
Hold the Line

"Timon, I need that update now! What is going on with Shey?" Galen ordered.

"Sir, it's hard to tell exactly what's happening; there's a cloud of counter-measures, and dozens of missiles are going in all directions. Shey is in an all-out fire-fight and I think she's losing.

"I'm counting five Kreel Scouts firing on her, and they're also broadcasting a general alarm. Sir, I can't see how any Scout can survive in Shey's circumstances."

"Lieutenant Timon, if you expect to remain in Guardian Scouts, then you will stops using expressions like 'I can't see how any Scout can survive!' Keep your eyes glued on that plot, penetrate that countermeasure clutter, and tell me what is happening out there! And do it now!"

"Yes Sir."

"Sheba, how's our formation holding together?"

"Sir, we have assumed the point position, and the remaining groups have formed up on us. All five groups are maintaining proper positions within the formation."

"Good. Sheba, do you have communications with Shey?"

"No Sir. She is embroiled in a major fire-fight. I am now registering multiple detonations in her proximity."

"Sheba, keep trying to raise Shey. I need to know what her status is."

"Yes Sir."

"Sir," Timon inserted, "I believe Shey has been destroyed. I've detected a large detonation near her, and the transient signal she was emitting has gone silent. Sir, Shey went out fighting! Her last outbound missiles have hit their targets dead on. She has destroyed all five attacking Kreel scouts. There are, however, six more Kreel Scouts vectoring toward her position; I'm estimating twenty minutes before they will reach her."

"Sheba, do you have contact with Shey?" Galen asked.

"Yes Sir. Shey has responded to my hails, and I have established a weak communication link with her. Shey reports she is adrift, her main power and propulsion are inoperative, her sensors are off line and she is blind, her hull is badly breached, and she is holding at ten seconds from executing her Cobalt Blue."

"She's holding ten seconds from Cobalt blue!" By all the Muses, Galen reasoned, that means she is awaiting orders and that means either Roan or Zorn must be still alive. "Sheba, ask Shey about Roan and Zorn's status."

Sir, Shey reports after they were hit, Zorn went aft to help Roan. They are both injured, unconscious, but they are still alive. She reports there are eighteen minutes of reserve power remaining.

"Sir, Shey will never permit the Kreel to put Roan, Zorn, or her on any banquet platter. Unless ordered to the contrary, she will initiate her Cobalt Blue orders prior to the exhaustion of remaining power."

"Sheba, for confirmation, repeat Roan's last orders."

"Sir, our orders are 'to get our groups back home.'"

"Good. Sheba, send to each group Commander, they're to ask for volunteers for an extraction mission. We're not going to abandon Roan and Zorn and leave them to die."

"Sir, the group Commanders report all Scouts have volunteered– without exception!"

"Sir," Timon inserted hastily, "if we turn back toward Shey, then we'll be in violation of our direct orders."

Galen scowled momentarily at Timon, and ignored his comment. "Sheba set a direct course to Shey. Lan's Scouts will go alongside Shey and perform the extraction. The remaining groups are to expand our formation and assume a standard four-point defensive pyramid about Shey. Their orders are that regardless of what comes at us, even if it's the entire blasted Kreel fleet, they are to stand firm and hold the line! Now, bring us about smartly, pick up your skirts young lady, we're running late getting to the party."

"Yes Sir. All Scouts are coming about. We are picking up our skirts. Our ETA with Shey is twelve minutes."

"Sheba, stay in communications with Shey. Tell her we're on our way. She is not, I repeat not, to trigger her Cobalt Blue."

"Sir, Shey has acknowledged your orders and is standing by."

With a scowling countenance, Galen then turned toward Timon. "Lieutenant Timon, now hear this loud and clear: regarding your earlier comment about violating direct orders. Ye are herewith advised– we are strictly complying with those direct orders. We are proceeding to perform an extraction, as mandated by those very orders, to bring Roan and Zorn home with us– if that proves possible.

"If some day, in the far distant future, someone puts you in Command, then by all the Muses– you're to command! Do you understand?"

"Sir, yes Sir."

"Good. Now, get out of your harness and move aft. Shuck that Code-3 environmental suit, and get into an extra-vehicular suit, and make it on the double."

"Yes Sir!"

"Sheba, you have the bridge."

"Yes Sir."

Watching Timon hurry aft, Galen sighed. *Was I ever that young and wet behind the ears? Humph; perhaps back in the long forgotten dark ages– maybe.* Still shaking his head, he quickly followed after Timon. His first stop was in Timon's quarters, where he activated the inbuilt medical functionality programs, covered the bunk with a special medical array pad, and set out associated medical devices. Each compartment incorporated full medical diagnostic and support functionality. He was no doctor, but he understood if Roan and Zorn were still alive, and he could transfer them into Sheba's quarters, then the medical support facilities would enhance their chances for survival.

Moving to his own quarters, he again prepared the medical systems, and then quickly stripped off his Code-3 suit and donned his extra-vehicular suit. It was not a heavy-duty engineering-style work suit, but it provided more protection than a Code-3 suit, which functioned merely as a stop gap measure in case of minor hull penetrations. The tough layered fabric design of the Code 3 suit did provide self-sealing pressure protection, limited rebreather capacity, bio-monitoring, and some thermal protection. Ultimately, he knew that Roan and Zorn's survival depended directly upon the protection their suits afforded.

"Sheba, how are we doing?"

"Sir, we are near Shey, and she reports Roan and Zorn are still alive. They are located in the main passageway and mid-way between the main hatch and the command compartment. She says their vital signs are diminishing."

"Sheba, post Misty and Cindy in nearby defensive support positions, and then bring us alongside of Shey. Align our airlocks, and extend our hull stand-offs. Bring us in girl, make it happen!"

"Yes sir. Estimating four minutes to hull contact."

"Timon, where in Tartarus are you?"

"Sir, I'm at our main hatch and preparing an auxiliary power cable to boost Shey's emergency power."

Galen smiled, *Humph, that's better,* "Good and well done! Stay there, and button up your suit. I'm about to shut down our internal gravity and withdraw our atmosphere. Sound off when you are set."

Even as Galen was sealing his own suit, he was moving hurriedly aft to reach the main hatch. When Timon saw him, he indicated with a hand signal that he was set.

"Sheba, withdraw our atmosphere and then equalize our internal pressure with space norm. When equalized, neutralize gravity, get it done!"

Sir, proceeding as ordered. Brace for hull contact."

Given Sheba's warning, Galen and Timon took firm hold on hand rails and braced themselves. When it came, the contact with Shey was heavy and jarring.

Sheba's calm voice proclaimed "Oops, sorry. Shey is yawing badly, and I had difficulty in matching her attitude. Five of our seven vacuum clamps are holding firm. Internal atmospheric pressure is now equalized with space norm. I am canceling artificial gravity– You are clear to proceed."

"Sheba, open the main hatch," Galen ordered.

The main hatch tipped inward, and then smoothly slid out of sight. As it did, Timon moved forward extending the auxiliary power cable, expertly located the emergency power receptacle near Shey's closed main hatch, and deftly plugged in the power cable.

"Sheba, Timon here, the emergency power cable is connected to Shey. Can you operate Shey's main hatch?"

"Yes Timon, I have established a secure interface directly with Shey's internal system. Standby."

"Sheba, status report– where are those inbound Kreel Scouts?" Galen asked.

"Sir, they are still approaching, but they have slowed their advance. Having noted what happened to the five scouts that attacked Shey, they are exhibiting caution. Our outer perimeter groups are undetected and are prepared to destroy the Kreel scouts. Therefore, at present, they do not pose an immediate threat. There is, however, an Elite Guard ship and two fast attack ships that have come about. They are now heading in our direction. Their ETA is one hour and eighteen minutes."

Even as Sheba was talking, Shey's main hatch had tipped inward and then slid slowly open, permitting Galen and Timon to gain entry. Having obtained Shey's report, Galen knew where to look, and he led the way through the dimly illuminated passageway and floating debris and detritus. It took but a minute for them to move quickly forward and reach Zorn and Roan. Their limp bodies were adrift and still linked together by a come-along strap which Zorn had utilized. Neither man was conscious or moving.

Reaching the two men, Galen quickly attached a come-along strap to Zorn's suit, and then extending the loose end of the strap to Timon, he ordered him to begin towing the two men aft toward the main hatch. Ducking under the floating bodies, Galen fell in behind and attached a second come-along strap to Roan's suit. Then, following the procession, Galen stabilized the two bodies as Timon was towing them gently aft and toward the open hatch.

It took less than five minutes for Galen and Timon to pull the two unconscious men into Sheba and then move them into the prepared compartments. Zorn was gently restrained on a bunk in one space and Roan was similarly placed in the second. Working with an efficiency that only comes with long hours of practice, Galen first worked with Roan, checking the readouts of the bio-medical and rebreather packs on his suit. Galen confirmed the suit had another forty minutes supply of breathable air, and then studied the display of blinking red indicators on the suit medical pack. He winced; it did not look promising. Galen connected the medical computer and its drug administering probes directly to the interface connectors on the suit medical pack. Finally, he Covered Roan with a temperature blanket that was regulated by the medical computer.

Having attended to Roan, Galen promptly went and assisted Zorn. Like Roan, Zorn's bio readouts were all flashing red. He swiftly accomplished what was possible, and then worried, he stood momentarily looking at Zorn.

"Sheba, status report!"

"Sir, three Kreel Scouts entered into our designated defensive volume, and were promptly destroyed. The remaining three scouts are continuing to search actively with their sensors, but they have prudently stopped their approach. The inbound Elite Guard ship is still one hour out."

"Acknowledged," Galen replied.

Returning to Sheba's main hatch, Galen motioned Timon to follow him. They quickly passed from Sheba and once again stood in Shey's debris-strewn main passageway.

"Shey, can you hear me?"

"Yes, Commander Galen. Sir, will Roan and Zorn survive?"

"Shey, you're not to worry; I've tucked them comfortably into med bunks and everything that can be done to save them is being done."

"Thank you, Sir. I am sorry that I failed in my duty to protect them."

"Shey, I don't want to hear any more of that nonsense. You were totally outnumbered; your stealth shields were inoperative and you looked like a flickering lantern-fly. In spite of all those problems, you engaged five Kreel scouts and destroyed them all. You did everything right. I know Roan and Zorn are very proud of you.

"Shey, is there any way I can gain physical access to retrieve your core?"

"Sir, because of damages in engineering, access to my core is not possible. I am adrift deep in Kreel space and my damages are beyond reasonable repair. Please return to Sheba and follow Roan's orders; take Roan, Zorn, and our groups safely home. When you reach a safe distance, have Sheba signal me. Then, I will fulfill the final orders Roan gave to me."

Galen stood for only a moment before deciding. "Shey, you are a most gallant and special lady. Like Roan and Zorn, I'm extremely proud of you. We will remain in communications with you."

"Commander Galen, thank you. Your thoughtful courtesies are deeply appreciated. Now, please take Roan and Zorn safely home."

"That I will do, and young Lady, you can safely wager three brews on that!"

Turning about, Galen and Timon promptly reentered Sheba. Once aboard, Galen issued his orders.

"Timon, disconnect the power coupling from Shey and stow it."

"Yes Sir."

"Sheba, seal our main hatch and restore internal atmosphere and gravity. Separate from Shey. Set a direct intercept course to our Task Force. As we move out, have all groups form up on you. I want you and all the girls to link up with Shey. You are not to leave her in communications isolation, not for a single moment. Do you understand?"

"Yes sir, I fully understand. Internal atmosphere is now safe. Artificial gravity will be restored within thirty-seconds, mark."

Given Sheba's warning, Galen and Timon took hold of handrails and then braced for resumption of gravity. When it was restored, they removed their extra-vehicular suits. While Timon stowed the power coupling and went forward to the command compartment, Galen went directly to Roan's compartment. Entering, he proceeded to gently ease Roan's hood off, and then stood studying the computer bio-signs readouts. They were not good.

It was with concern that he next went to Zorn's compartment. Once there, Galen gently removed Zorn's hood. Again, he studied the bio-signs readouts and sighed. Both men had multiple serious injuries, and they were in critical condition. Judging by the evident damage and condition of their environmental suits, both men had been subjected to significant blast and flash heat, Roan even more than Zorn. If they had not been wearing their environmental suits, he doubted either man would have survived the initial blast. Shaking his head, he could but marvel that given his injuries Zorn had actually managed to reach Roan and had tried to assist him. *Now,* he thought, *that's raw courage and tenacity.*

Having accomplished what he could, again he put on his Code-3 suit and went forward to the command compartment. Entering the compartment, he resumed his command chair and buckled his restraining harness. As he did, Timon gave him an update.

"Sir, we are now clear of the danger volume around Shey. The three remaining Kreel scouts that were approaching her position have remained stationary; they are, however, located near the fringe of the danger volume. The Elite Guard ship is continuing its approach; its ETA is forty-eight minutes."

"Acknowledged.

"Sheba, are you in communications with Shey?"

"Yes Sir. We are currently singing old-Earth sea-shanties, Shey is very fond of them."

"Sheba, please inform Shey that both Roan and Zorn are alive and stable. We are taking them immediately home for medical treatment. All of us are very, very proud of her. Then inform her we are out of the danger volume."

"Sir, your message has been sent. Shey sends her love to everyone. Sir, Shey has now departed us," Sheba whispered.

"Sir, I am registering a massive fusion detonation at Shey's coordinates," Timon reported.

"Sheba, alert all Scouts that we are moving at best possible speed directly toward an intercept with our Task Force. Then, inform Lan that we have lost Shey and that you have two critical casualties aboard, Commanders Roan and Zorn. Request priority docking and the availability of immediate emergency medical support upon your arrival.

"Sir, your message to Lan has been sent."

Sitting back, Galen sighed. For the moment, He had done everything he could. He would have Roan and Zorn aboard Lan within two hours. Then he remembered what Sheba had just told him.

"Sheba, did I hear you actually say the Scouts were singing old-Earth sea-shanties with Shey?"

"Yes Sir. Shey even waited in executing her Cobalt blue orders until after we had completed singing 'What Shall We Do with the Drunken Sailor.'"

Humph, sea-shanties; now don't that beat all, Galen mused.

"Sheba, consistent with keeping our stealth factor at or above sixty-percent, increase the speed of our formation accordingly. Order all groups to remain vigilant for Kreel sleepers, and reiterate all Scouts have permission to fire at will on confirmed Kreel targets of opportunity."

Then, turning with a scowl toward Timon, Galen exclaimed, "Lieutenant Timon, where in blazes is your Code-3 environmental suit? Get out of that harness, get aft and get suited up! And, make that on the double."

"Yes sir."

As he watched Timon hurrying aft, Galen could not suppress a slight smile. *Humph; there goes one very young Officer with a promising future.*

Then, looking at the elapsed mission time display, Galen remembered his promise to Shey and frowned. *Shey, I promised you, and by all the Muses I'll get them home safe....*

Chapter Twenty-Two:
A Strictly Personal Matter

The Task Force was moving at 200 lights, and within Lan the ambient noise level was hushed and rich with low harmonics. They were two hours out from reaching the planet and engaging in battle.

A short time earlier, Lan's Intelligence group had detected an unidentified pulsing energy source. Soon thereafter, they identified a brief but intense fire-fight involving multiple Kreel scouts that were sounding a general alarm. The implications of the incoming data were unmistakable; Guardian Scouts were directly engaged in a fire-fight. Then came the detection of a significant fusion detonation, the profile of which was consistent with a Guardian Scout Cobalt Blue. Then only silence followed.

Although everyone was intent on their duties, an underlying tension was evident throughout CAC. Like everyone else, Roy felt the rising tension and concern; they had lost one of their Scouts, but which Scout? Were there additional battle casualties? At the moment, Roy was definitely not a happy camper.

"Sir," Lan interjected, "I have received a priority message from our Scouts. They are now moving directly toward a rendezvous. Consistent with stealth requirements, they are moving at their best possible speed. Sir, they have declared a medical emergency, and they request priority docking upon their arrival."

"Lan, inform Shey that her priority request is acknowledged and granted. You will coordinate with Shey and Navigation to facilitate the earliest possible rendezvous. Identify which Scouts and Cruisers are involved, and alert the Cruisers of their incoming medical emergencies."

"Sir, as ordered, I am coordinating our maneuvers with the Scouts and lead Cruisers.

"Sir, may I speak in confidence concerning a strictly personal matter?"

Surprised, Roy's eyebrows rose somewhat. *A personal matter?* Roy extended his right hand and activated a closed-circuit.

"Proceed," Roy said.

"Sir, the tactical report came from Scout Leader Sheba. She reports Scout Shey has executed her Cobalt Blue. Sir, Shey has passed from among us."

Roy felt a rush of shock and closed his eyes. Taking in a deep breath, he clamped down on his immediate emotional responses. First holding his breath for a moment, he then slowly exhaled and relaxed. Taking another measured breath, he next opened his eyes and set about doing his job.

"Lan, you will continue to coordinate maneuvers with our lead Cruisers, and minimize the time required for rendezvous. Coordinate with the Scouts having declared medical emergencies. Confirm they have priority docking. Inform their Cruisers to have emergency medical personnel standing by."

"Sir, only Sheba is reporting a medical emergency. Following the initial firefight, our Scouts conducted an extraction under fire. Sheba has Commanders Roan and Zorn aboard. Sheba reports both men have sustained multiple life-threatening injuries and are unconscious. There are no other reported casualties."

Lan's report caused Roy new mixed emotional churnings. The loss of Shey was harsh, but learning Roan and Zorn were still alive softened the initial bad news. That they were in critical condition was not good, but Roy well knew the news might be far worse.

"Once Sheba brings them aboard, you will see that I'm provided frequent medical updates on their prognosis. Now, explain to me just why you consider Roan and Zorn's medical condition a personal matter."

"Sir, the matter involves personal information concerning crewmembers. Before the Scout mission began, Shey informed me of confidential and personal information relating to Commander Zorn. Shey had become aware of a growing deep affection between Commander Zorn and Lieutenant Cloud. If something were to happen to Commander Zorn, her expressed concern was for Lieutenant Cloud's welfare. "Sir, I recommend you communicate with Lieutenant Cloud privately and inform

142

her of what is transpiring, prior to the knowledge of Shey's loss and Commander Zorn's medical status becoming commonly known."

Listening, Roy shook his head in bemusement. He was not involved in programming AIs, but he had been directly involved when Earth Ambassador Wells made her first trip from Earth to Glas Dinnein. She had brought on her trip a personal Earth AI, William. The cross-data contamination that occurred between William and the Guardian AIs at that time had infused into the Guardian AIs copious quantities of human history, sociology, psychology, music theory, classical literature, and religious doctrine. No one could have predicted what would eventually evolve once the guardian AIs gained unfettered access to the enormous volume of old-Earth information.

While Roy viewed the on-going evolution in AI awareness a distinct improvement, he was also aware there existed within Guardian Command and AI Engineering serious concerns. As a whole, they were prone to view recent AI evolution as being poorly-understood and uncontrolled. Those same AI Engineers were likely to have a complete nervous breakdown once they learned the AIs had evolved to where they were providing crewmembers with personal advice concerning romantic interactions.

"Lan, I believe Shey's concerns and your recommendations are insightful and well founded. Please inform Lieutenant Cloud that she is to report to me in my conference room in five minutes. Then, inform the Officers Mess that I expect a vacuum flask of neab with all the trimmings and two cheese pastries on my side board in the conference room within three minutes."

"Yes Sir."

"Lan, be certain to fully brief Admiral Kellon on what is happening. He will want to remain tight in the loop concerning Roan and Zorn's medical prognosis."

"Sir, unless you object, I will withhold the medical readouts Sheba transmitted concerning Commanders Roan and Zorn until you meet with Lieutenant Cloud."

"Lan, when Lieutenant Cloud enters my conference room, you will promptly transmit that medical data directly to Physician Lorentz. And, you're to confirm that Physician

Lawrence will personally contact me with his prognosis as early as possible."

"Yes Sir."

Looking toward Navigation, Roy observed Jason Greer was busy resolving the navigation problem of rendezvousing with the Scouts. Turning toward Tactical, he saw Lorn and his team were working on planning out the upcoming battle. Given the competing priorities, Roy turned back to Jason. Having been a Navigator before becoming Captain, he understood he was about to interrupt Jason in the middle of a complex navigation problem. Regretfully, it could not be avoided.

"Navigation, Jason you have the CAC. I will be in my conference room for a few minutes."

Jason promptly looked up toward Roy. "Sir, Acknowledged, Navigation has the CAC."

Roy reached his conference room even as the orderly from the Officers Mess was departing. Entering, he went directly to the side table and poured himself a hot cup of neab. Enjoying the neab, he turned back toward the table, even as there came a knock on the door.

"Enter."

"Sir, Lieutenant Cloud, reporting as ordered."

Elayne's poise and deportment was one of calm alertness. Still, Roy could see the stress that she was skillfully controlling behind her demeanor.

"Elayne, working in Intelligence as you are, you are undoubtedly aware that we have lost one of our Scouts. The good news is Roan and Zorn are alive. The bad news is both men are injured, precisely how badly injured I do not yet know. Our Scouts went in under fire and extracted them from Shey. They're onboard Sheba, and she is bringing them here as quickly as possible. We have lost Shey."

Elayne's poise momentarily broke; one tear running down her cheek. She awkwardly wiped it away with a quick movement of her left hand and immediately regained her composure.

"Elayne, I suggest that you remain here for a while and rest. If you wish to be in Sheba's hangar as Roan and Zorn are medevacked from Sheba to the dispensary, then you have my permission to be there.

"Lan, while Lieutenant Cloud is waiting here, you are to keep her fully informed on Commander Roan and Zorn's medical status, and our rendezvous with Sheba."

"Yes Sir."

"Elayne, there is a hot vacuum of neab and some cheese pastries on the side board. Please help yourself. If I can be of any assistance whatsoever, do not hesitate to talk with me."

"Thank you, Sir."

As Roy turned to depart, the door opened and Kellon entered. It took Kellon but a moment to glance about and appreciate the circumstances.

"Roy, you have your hands full at the moment with a rendezvous and pending battle. While you take care of those problems, I'll stay here and visit with Elayne for a little while."

"Yes Sir."

Turning, Roy exited his conference room, and with grim determination he headed back to the CAC. Kellon was correct, he had a rendezvous to perform and then some payback to dish out– spicy and hot.

145

Chapter Twenty-Three:
Empty Hangar

Along the bright passageway, the status indicators next to each inner hangar hatch were displaying a steady ice-blue hue, indicating the hangar conditions were at a hard space vacuum. Standing back with Kellon, Elayne stood watching while Physician Lorentz and four medical technicians were gathered about Sheba's hatch. Waiting together, everyone in the corridor was tense and silent.

A sudden sharp clang, which could be heard throughout Lan, loudly announced the opening of an outer hangar door. Soon thereafter there followed a reverberating heavy thud, as the outer hangar door closed. As Elayne watched, the blue hangar status indicator began blinking. After several minutes, the blinking indicator transformed to a steady warm-golden color, and Elayne heard the distinct sound of the hatch interlocks releasing. As the inner hangar hatch swung open wide, a flash surge of bitter-cold air flowed out into the narrow passageway.

The medical technicians, who were carrying various packages and two collapsed gurneys, moved impatiently forward. Without hesitation, Physician Lorentz was first through the open hatch and walking across the narrow deck. Briskly moving up the short gangway, with the medical personnel pressing closely behind him, Physician Lorentz entered Sheba. They all passed from Elayne's view.

As Elayne waited, the only sounds she could hear were the normal and reassuring background equipment humming sounds of Lan, which were occasionally punctuated by the creaking sound of Sheba's hull as she settled into her cradle and her warming hull expanded. As Elayne watched, a glistening sheen of frost condensed and formed about Sheba's sleek space-cold bulk. Even standing in the warm passageway, Elayne could not help but shiver from the intense cold radiating from Sheba's black hull.

Abruptly, two of the medical technicians reappeared in Sheba's hatch, and they were guiding a gurney down the gangway. As they moved toward the passageway, Elayne strained to see if it was Zorn, and saw that it was Roan laying on the gurney. Then another two technicians appeared in Sheba's hatch, and they were guiding the second gurney. As they moved the gurneys out of the hangar, moving quickly toward the dispensary, Elayne glimpsed the unconscious form and pale countenance of Zorn. She saw that both men were still wearing their environmental suits, and below their gurneys the indicators on the medical monitors were either steady amber or else a blinking red. While catching but a glimpse of Zorn and Roan, she still felt a surge of relief course through her; *Both men were still alive!*

In spite of trying to restrain her feeling, tears of relief flowed freely down her cheeks. She did not require Physician Lorentz' prognosis; it was clear to her that both men were seriously injured. Reaching deep within her own inner reservoir of strength, she began gathering hopes, holding them near to her heart.

As Physician Lorentz exited Sheba, he was looking grim and was talking earnestly into his communicator. Coming out of the hangar, he stopped and turned toward Elayne.

"They are both alive, but their conditions are critical. I'll be able to tell you more in about an hour."

Turning, Physician Lorentz hurried to catch up with his patients. At the same time, there came two loud clangs, announcing Scout ships Cindy and Misty were about to enter their hangars. A short time thereafter heavy thuds of the closing outer doors resounded throughout Lan.

Observing the hangar-status indicators near Misty and Cindy's hatches, Elayne watched as they began blinking their icy-blue warning. Then, seeing the steady unchanging blue indicator on Shey's empty hangar, she suddenly felt the piercing thrust of a personal loss. Her friend Shey was not coming home. Without any embarrassment, she wept.

Even as Cindy and Misty's hatch indicators turned a golden hue, Lan's battle stations alarm was sounding along the passageway. Standing erect, Elayne turned toward Kellon with renewed determination. She saluted him.

"Sir, with your permission, I would like to return to my duty station."

Nodding, Kellon briskly returned Elayne's salute, "Permission granted. It's time we both go to our battle stations. You can be assured, the advantage Shey, Roan, and Zorn purchased for us will be fully exploited."

Together, they stepped into the waiting elevator, and as its doors closed, the intensifying emotional energy preceding imminent battle was palpable.

Chapter Twenty-Four:
He's Got a Fox in His Henhouse

As Kellon entered his conference room, the sounds of Lan's crew hurrying through the passageway to their battle stations was fading. Pouring himself a cup of hot neab, he took his chair and began studying the tactical plot displayed on the forward bulkhead. The twenty decoys that Squadron 5 had deployed earlier, to distract the Kreel from the Scouts, were now moving along an arched trajectory and stridently maintaining their three AU distance from the planet. In response, the Kreel were shifting their defending forces and remaining between the apparent threat and the planet. After noting the overall tactical pattern, Kellon turned his attention to the granular structure of the Kreel defense.

"Sir, our decoys have apparently succeeded in gaining Marshal Krupp's complete attention," Lan said.

"So, it seems. For certain, our Scouts' action has deprived him of the bulk of his offensive firepower. Krupp believes he is facing twenty alien capital ships, while his battle force near the planet is reduced to eighteen fast-attack and three Elite Guard ships. By any reasonable reckoning of probable firepower, he's heavily outgunned. Accordingly, he's responding by holding his remaining heavy hitters near the planet."

"Sir, how would you classify the intent of his tactic?"

"Well, he's playing for time while hoping for reinforcements."

"Sir, I do not understand Marshal Krupp's deployment of his scouts."

"Well, Krupp has been deprived of his cruisers, and his overall defense is tissue-thin. Drawing on his available planetary forces, Krupp has pushed several hundred scouts forward to serve as his vanguard."

"Sir, even one-hundred scouts do not pose a serious threat to twenty Cruisers."

"Correct Lan; they're cannon fodder. He's using them in hope of gaining time. He has, however, stiffened his scouts with a second layer of defense consisting of two inner groups of fast attacks ships. Although they're only armed with medium missiles, they still have teeth."

"Sir, then Krupp's final line of defense consists of the three Elite Guard ships and their six escorts positioned nearest to the planet."

"That's correct, Krupp has formed his Elite Guard and their escorts into a reclining-facing triangle. Its leading edge is thrust forward to support the two advanced groups of fast attacks ships. If Zorn were here, I would wager him two brews that Krupp is at the rear apex of that triangle. That position would place him nearest to the planet."

"Sir, Grand Marshal Krupp's tactical choices do seem logical. Nevertheless, his choices have inadvertently placed his group nearest to our approaching Task Force."

"Hmmm, good point Lan, and being an Elite Guard Grand Marshal, Krupp is unlikely to have overlooked being blindsided. He would not leave his back door unlocked and unguarded. He will have set up an early-warning mechanism to detect an attack from that quadrant.

"Lan, advise Roy that I believe the Kreel have likely positioned a broad screen of scout sleepers between the planet and our position."

"Sir, the Captain has been notified. He has ordered The Task Force to slow and reform. The Captain is transforming the Task Force into a rank formation, with Squadron 1 at its center. This will provide the Task Force an optimal crossfire component to its attack."

"Lan, where are we in our firing sequence?"

"Sir, we are currently three minutes from Condition 1. Our Cruiser AIs are finalizing the Task Force target assignments and missile orders. Captain Grey has ordered each Cruiser to launch multiple heavy missiles, each missile being directed against a different target, and three missiles will collectively target each fast-attack and Elite Guard ship. Since the Captain is approaching the planet well above the plane of the ecliptic, the Task Force has attained an unobstructed plane-of-fire. Missiles are being set passive homing, going UV-active during terminal homing."

"Lan, has Intelligence detected any Kreel forces approaching from the heliosheath?"

"No Sir. I estimate another hour will elapse prior to possible detection of Kreel reinforcements."

Kellon once again turned his attention to the tactical plot, seeking any indication of a ruse or other Kreel deception. He could find none. Even as he studied the tactical plot, the unmistakable rumbling sounds of heavy missiles being launched were reverberating throughout Lan.

As Kellon considered the evidence displayed before him, holding his warm cup of neab between his hands, he sat back and sighed. By their exploitation of a superior stealth technology, combined with the raw courage of twenty Guardian Scout teams, the Task Force had gained numerical superiority and achieved total surprise. They had caught Marshal Krupp flat footed. Watching the symbols of the outbound missiles moving toward their distant targets, Kellon knew the Kreel were about to experience a very hard day on the job.

Suddenly, the unmistakable sound of intense laser fire broke into Kellon's thoughts. "Lan, I need an update."

Even as Kellon spoke there came a second and longer burst of laser fire, and Lan's point defenses began hammering, and then Kellon heard and felt the distinct thumps of several nearby detonations.

"Sir, Roy here. Lan has informed me you have requested an update.

"Sir, the Task Force has encountered approximately forty dispersed Kreel sleepers. So far, nine Kreel scouts have been destroyed; the surviving scouts are currently under laser and light-missile attack and scattering. They have, however, sounded a general alarm. One of our Cruisers, the Liam, is reporting he has taken a light missile hit; he's reporting some casualties and minimal damage.

"Sir, for sure, given the scouts' general alarm, it's a safe bet the farmer knows he's got a fox in his henhouse. This fracas may well devolve into a fire-fight."

"Roy, in which case, if I'm correct, Krupp's flag ship is the Elite Guard ship nearest to Lan."

"If it is, then my mother would suggest he should duck, because there are three heavy missiles now heading his way."

As Roy was providing his update, Kellon continued studying the changing tactical display, and he was frowning. "Roy, it looks like Krupp heard your mother's advice, he's making for the planet. He must have had a backup escape plan primed and cocked. The two forward-positioned Elite Guard elements are also pulling back."

"Sir, by all the Muses, Krupp might make it to safe cover, but I'll wager three brews that his other two Elite Guard groups won't reach the planet before our missiles arrive on target."

As Kellon watched, the icon for Krupp's group of three ships merged with the planet and disappeared from the plot, and soon thereafter the nine missiles targeting that group also merged with the planet and disappeared.

"Blast! Lan, is there any terminal burst telemetry from the missiles targeting Krupp? Were their angles of attack sufficient to take Krupp out?"

"Sir, terminal burst telemetry is incomplete and is inconclusive. Due to the proximity of the planet, eight missiles' Sanitation protocols were activated; the ninth missile was targeting the Elite Guard ship. Data indicates missile terminal homing activated, and then we lost telemetry.

"Boy howdy Sir, we caught them with their breeches down. The Kreel are being pulverized!" Roy exclaimed.

Studying the tactical plot, Kellon felt no sense of elation as he observed the symbols of missiles merge with the symbols representing Kreel ships. It was not a game; the computer graphics represented real missiles ripping into Kreel ships. He understood the lives of living beings were being snuffed out amidst burning fire and terror in the contrasting void of darkness and absolute cold. No quarter was being offered. Even as Kellon watched, Roy's prediction that the forward Elite Guard ships and escorts would not reach the planet was validated. Like the remaining fast attack ships, they were being reduced to drifting debris. As a whole, the structured Kreel defense was being torn to bits and shredded.

"Roy, we've attained our Phase 1 goals, the Kreel's space-borne defenses have been effectively suppressed. It's time to begin Phase 2; order our Cruisers to their high guard and planetary bombardment positions. Then deploy our Scouts and use their decoys to light-up the Kreel planetary defense grid.

Then, use our Cruisers to take it out. Commence bombardment, and don't forget to take out those disabled cruisers. Roy, you know the drill, make it happen."

"Yes Sir."

"Roy, be advised, you have my compliments. Very well-done."

"Sir, do you have any additional orders?"

"Yes, one. You're to set up a special Intelligence detail; I want to know what happened to Krupp. And, we're still working against the clock; Kreel reinforcements are undoubtedly inbound. Let's get the job done and move on."

"Yes Sir. Roy out."

Sitting up straight, Kellon sat pondering his current priorities. "Lan, I need an update on Roan and Zorn."

"Sir, I have been monitoring their bio-readouts and prognosis. Commander Roan's condition remains critical, and he is on a high level of life support. He has suffered internal injuries, multiple broken bones, including skull fractures, and the trauma resulting from shock and concussion. Physician Lorentz is currently holding them in an induced stasis to stabilize them, prior to commencing accelerated cellular regeneration. According to the diagnosis, the only reason either man is still alive is being attributed to their lower body temperatures. Sir, the conditions of both men remains guarded."

As a sense of fatigue washed over him, Kellon sighed and leaned back in his chair. Closing his eyes, he ruminated, *Even my bones feel weary. Thanks be to the Muses, we're about to go home. Only one more battle remaining, only one. Then we can go home....*

Chapter Twenty-Five:
Tartarus' Lakes of Fire

"Timon, keep your eyes on those screens, we don't need any new holes in Sheba's hull."

"Yes Sir," Timon replied.

High above the planet, Galen continued swinging Sheba through a wide arc while descending to a low holding pattern, as Misty and Cindy maintained their wide combat spread formation. Upon approaching the planet, Galen had admired its well-proportioned continents, soaring mountain ranges, and broad oceans. It looked like a nice planet, and he knew it belonged to a Kreel-dominated and oppressed species. That was in part why Guardian Force was there in force, to begin evicting the Kreel.

During the previous eighteen hours, the Task Force Ninety-Nine Scouts had spread out over the entire planet, and they had expertly gone to work. While maintaining their highest stealth profiles, the Scouts directed their decoys deep into the atmosphere. By design the low flying vehicles presented sizeable electromagnetic targets, and they were likewise gaudily swathed in the bright holographic mantels of the coals of fire holograms. Flying low, the decoys broadcasted psychological warfare messages, some were of ridicule to the Kreel forces and others were of encouragement to the indigenous species. By their action and vibrant appearance, the vehicles earned the response of the Kreel planetary defense system. As the planetary defense grid activated, the monitoring Scouts pinpointed the grid nodes, and then directed the precision ordnance launched from the supporting cruisers. The planetary defense grid was methodically mapped and effectively degraded, until it sputtered and went dark. With the defense grid reduced to a relic, the Scouts had safely descended to a lower operating level.

"Sheba, how are our decoy recovery operations proceeding?" Galen asked.

"Sir, I have completed the recovery of four decoys. Two were damaged and self-destructed. Cindy has recovered her six. Misty is recovering her last two decoys, estimating six minutes."

"Sir, Contact. I've got seven inbound Kreel scouts. They're moving to intercept Misty's remaining decoys," Timon reported.

"Well, that's not happening. Are they working independently or being aided by ground tracking?"

"No active ground tracking is indicated."

"Good. Sheba, compute the probable Kreel scouts intercept point with Misty's decoys; then move us to a high waylay point."

"Yes Sir, computing," Sheba responded.

"Sheba, at Condition 1, each of our girls will launch one light missile at each target. Coordinate with your sisters and work out the firing order. When the targets close within 80% of effective missile range, execute a coordinated salvo. Then, break port and up."

"Sir, the ambuscade point is calculated. We are moving to attack. Misty is maneuvering her decoys to draw the Kreel deeper into the kill zone. Estimating three minutes to Condition 1."

Observing the tactical display, Galen saw the Kreel scouts begin to disperse, b*last*!

"Timon heads up. The Kreel are splitting their formation. Give me your assessment."

"Sir, the center three scouts are slowing, and the two scouts on each flank are spreading out in an encircling maneuver. It's their jaws of death tactic."

"Good call. Now give me your best tactical recommendation, and be quick about it."

"Sir, they have divided their strength. We've the stealth advantage and superior position. I recommend we close on the center force and set Condition 1 at 80% effective range. Then immediately pivot starboard and close on the rightmost flanking group, setting Condition 1 at 70% effective range."

"Recommendation accepted; Sheba, except for weapon allocations, cancel my previous orders. Execute Lieutenant Timon's tactics. Make it happen."

"Sir, closing on center three Kreel Scouts. Estimating two minutes to initial salvo. As previously ordered, at 80% effective range Misty, Cindy, and I will each fire a light missile at each of the targets."

"Proceed.

"Timon, explain why you recommended attacking the middle group."

"Sir, in numbers they represent the greatest threat."

"Good logic. Now, why set Condition 1 at 80% for the middle group and 70% for the flankers?"

"Sir, the center group is closing, and our initial volley will take them by surprise. The second group may be warned by our first salvo and be slowing at Condition 1."

Even as Timon was talking, the sounds of three light missiles being launched reverberated throughout Sheba. "Sir, missiles away. As ordered, my sisters and I are rolling starboard. Estimating two minutes to second salvo."

"Tenon, don't overlook exploiting Misty's two decoys to our advantage," Galen ordered.

"I'm on it."

"Sir." Sheba interjected. "I have received a tactical alert. Squadron 1 is closing to laser bombardment range, and we are being ordered to prepare for rendezvous. Lan is estimating ten minutes until bombardment.

"Sir, we are at 70% effective range, Condition 1," Sheba reported.

Even as the ejection sounds of two missiles being launched faded in the control compartment, Galen glanced at the tactical screen and frowned. The window of opportunity was rapidly closing.

"Sheba, detach Misty. She is to recover her two decoys. Cindy and you will immediately roll hard starboard, block for Misty, and accelerate at 0.95. Close to 40% effective range on those remaining flankers. We're not leaving any Kreel strays."

"Sir, Misty is detached, Cindy and I are rolling starboard, blocking for Misty, now estimating two minutes to intercept and Condition 1," Sheba affirmed.

Even as Sheba rolled starboard, the monitor being focused on the center target group briefly brightened into a lavish cascade of expanding blossoms of multicolored fire, and the center three Kreel scouts simply ceased to exist.

Accelerating at 0.95, Sheba and Cindy rapidly closed on the approaching second group of two flankers. Focused astern, the video monitors displayed a scintillating display of expanding explosions as the first flankers were destroyed.

"Sir, the remaining Kreel scouts are coming hard about," Timon reported.

"Acknowledged. Sheba, continue closing on those scouts."

Accelerating at 0.95, Sheba and Cindy soon overtook the fleeing Kreel scouts, and in unison fired six missiles.

"Sheba, coordinating with Cindy come hard about and join up with Misty.

"Report, where is Lan?" Galen ordered.

"Sir, Squadron 1 is closing. It is four minutes from its designated firing point above the Kreel military base. We are ordered to proceed to our rendezvous point."

"Sheba, tell the girls to focus their cameras on the ground target. After Misty has recovered her decoys, link up and move us out to the designated rendezvous coordinates."

"Yes Sir."

"Timon, you're about to witness the devastation five Guardian Cruisers can inflict with their bombardment lasers; keep your eyes on the monitors."

"Sir, Misty has retrieved her decoys and has rejoined our formation. We are proceeding to our rendezvous coordinates with Lan. ETA fifty-seven minutes," Sheba reported.

"Sir," Timon inserted. "The last two Kreel scouts have been destroyed. We've achieved a clean sweep–"

Suddenly, the monitors displaying the planet flared with sparkling and flickering bands of vertical columns of light, brilliant flashing lances of pure energy surging from the heavens in a spectacular pyrotechnic display, which continued for about forty seconds. As Galen and Timon watched, the entire Kreel military complex, including the disabled Kreel cruisers dispersed on its open landing fields, burst into enormous balls of livid fire and cascading debris. While the intense energy laser bursts had lasted for brief moments, the cumulative effects of immense energies pinpointing hundreds of targets on the ground produced continuing overlapping waves of expanding devastation. As many times, as Galen had seen the destruction a single Cruiser could unleash, the intense images of that destruction were still stunning to behold. The fiery holocaust which the power of five cooperating Cruisers delivered upon a target beggared any adequate description. Towering flames were rising up from the shattered structures, and immense bellowing columns of smoke rose and swirled high over the target, blurring the dwindling images.

The military base that Squadron 1 had just devastated was only one of several targets it would lay waste prior to returning to deep space. Galen knew elsewhere the other four squadrons of the Task Force were likewise coordinating their ground strikes.

Within a matter of twenty minutes, more than twenty Kreel military and research facilities on the planet would be reduced to heaps of smoldering debris.

Following the initial laser bombardment by the cruisers, as specialized ordnance dropped out of orbit to strike designated targets, the bombardment would continue at times calculated to produce maximum confusion and assure complete destruction. Systematically, the Kreel were being deprived of their R&D and manufacturing capacity.

Watching the laser bombardment unfold, in the quiet confines of Sheba's Command compartment, Timon's whispered exclamation was clearly audible. "By all Tartarus' lakes of fires! Even seeing it, it's hard to believe."

As fatigue swept over him, leaning hard back into his command chair, Galen closed his eyes and slowly let out his breath. *Blast, I must be getting old, and even when young, war was never easy. There must be a better way. There simply must be.*

"Sheba, kindly return us to our hangar," Galen ordered.

The deep weariness saturating Galen's verbal inflections was not overlooked, Sheba was well aware and alertly monitoring the bio-signs of her boys– both the senior and younger.

"Sir, as you have ordered, I am proceeding to our rendezvous with Lan, I am taking us home."

Chapter Twenty-Six:
Drifting Bits and Pieces

Exercising his Command prerogative, Kellon ordered Lan to extinguish the lighting in the domed conference room and retract the protective petals. The optically-perfect dome provided him with a full unobstructed panorama view of the stars, nearby planet, and surrounding space. He had stood thoughtfully observing as Lan's three remaining Scouts were retrieved. He was pleased with what he observed. Their maneuvering and retrieval was flawless. As he watched the Scouts, prompted by the loss of Shey, he felt a sharp sense of her presence. Each Scout AI was unique, and Shey was missed.

The planet that was slowly turning before him was incredibly beautiful. Its two moons gave it a distinct aura of elegance. The Kreel had dominated the planet and its indigenous population for several thousand years. During that interval, the world had gradually evolved to become the principal Kreel military Research Center. Because of its high strategic value, his expectation had been the Kreel would mount a strong defense of the planet, and they had.

To overcome the anticipated defense and fulfil the mission objectives, he had combined the five squadrons into a single strike Force. Considering what had unfolded during the attack, his prudent tactical decision had been operationally vindicated.

From his distant vantage point, he could not see any indication of the extensive damage levied on the Kreel Research, Manufacturing, and Military installations. Still, he knew the devastation was precise and very thorough. It had ended the Kreel's most important space warfare research capability.

As he stood observing the planet, he wondered about the indigenous species which rightfully called K-31 their home. Within the measurable boundaries of the Cosmos, Life seemed to take hold wherever it found a habitable niche environment. Even so, the upwelling of a high level cognitive sentient species was like a precious jewel, wondrous and rare. Such life was something that he believed warranted being valued, nurtured, and safeguarded. He could but hope Guardian Force's present and future actions would help the local species to evolve as Life once more had intended, and do so without Kreel subordination.

With a troubled heart he mused, *What are their dreams, hopes, desires, and beliefs? What unpredictable effects will our psychological-warfare messages produce within their culture? Have I done all that I could to mitigate the collateral damages? Perhaps, someday you will come to understand and forgive us for the ruin we have rained upon your world this day—*

"Sir, it's certainly a good-looking planet. I wonder what their music sounds like," Roy said.

Turning, Kellon smiled. "Sorry Roy, I didn't hear you enter the conference room. Yes, I agree, it's an extraordinary planet. And, it will be all the more so one there are no more Kreel on it.

"Lan, restore the dome-petals and set the conference room lighting to fifty-percent."

"Yes Sir," Lan said.

"Now Roy, what is our status?"

"Sir, all Scouts have been retrieved. All five squadrons report Condition Gold. We're combat-ready. The programmed orbital bombardment is proceeding on schedule. It'll be complete within nine hours. The Task Force is standing by, awaiting your orders."

"What's the disposition of Groff's reinforcements?"

"Sir, as your analysis predicted, three groups of cruisers have entered from three points on the heliosphere. They have now realized their trap has gone bust, and they are evidencing some caution. They have reduced their initial speed from 200 lights to 100 lights and are about sixteen hours out. The few surviving fast attack ships remaining from Krupp's initial force have turned-tail and are running to join the inbound reinforcements."

Kellon paused momentarily, and when he spoke again his voice held an unmistakable edge of anger. "Roy, I still have a formal message from the Lux to deliver to Groff.

"Determine the optimal route out of here and back to Glas Dinnein. Then, you're to determine which inbound Kreel cruiser group is nearest to that trajectory. You're to close on that group, then ambush and utterly obliterate it. Once you have completed that mission, you're to proceed on to Glas Dinnein."

For a brief moment, Roy stood frowning and studying Kellon's countenance. "Yes Sir.

164

"Sir, may I have your leave to speak frankly?"

"Of course."

"Sir, as my dear mother taught me, while anger serves a purpose, letting it devolve into hatred is like flirting with a black hole. An unaware person might just wake up one morning to find himself on the wrong side of the emotional event horizon and unable to find his way back.

"Sir, do you have further orders at this time?"

"Yes. I'll be in my quarters. When the Task Force reaches its waylay point, notify me. I intend to be in CAC during the attack."

Smartly executing a salute, Roy turned and departed the conference room. Kellon stood thoughtfully and watched him go.

"Well Lan, do you agree with Roy? Is my anger out of bounds? Am I in danger of slipping across the apparent event horizon?"

"Sir, as you are aware, my duties include monitoring the emotional and physical welfare of every crewmember, including you. I agree with Commodore Grey, you do possess notable anger issues where the Kreel are involved. I also perceive your anger issues are well within your ability to monitor and control them. I do, in light of Commodore Grey's expressed concern, recommend a slight increase in your daily meditation schedule."

Smiling, Kellon considered both Roy and Lan's comments. Inwardly he acknowledged that when friends express concern for one's welfare, a wise person will take heed.

"Thank you, Lan. Now, it's time for the Lux to compose a singular message for Grand Admiral Groff and the Kreel Empire."

"Sir, might I ask if such a message might be called, as William has said, putting a bee in their bonnet."

Smiling in amusement, Kellon suppressed a laugh. "Yes Lan, you might say the message is intended to put an angry bee in Groff's bonnet."

When Roy entered CAC, it was holding at Condition 2 and fully staffed. The general announcing system automatically proclaimed "Commodore entering CAC."

Taking his command chair, Roy looked toward Navigation and ordered "Jason, I've got the CAC."

"Acknowledging, the Commodore has the CAC," Jason Greer responded.

"Tactical, what is our current threat assessment?" Roy asked.

"Tactical here, there are currently no identified local threats."

"Navigation, compute the optimal trajectory back to Glas Dinnein, and then provide the trajectory to Tactical.

"Tactical, Lorn, when you obtain from Navigation the optimal trajectory to Glas Dinnein, determine which inbound Kreel cruiser group is nearest to that line.

"Lan set the Task force to modified Condition 3."

As the lighting in CAC slightly brightened, Lan's firm voice came over the general announcing system "Attention, Status is reset to modified Condition 3, repeating, modified Condition 3."

About two-thirds of the personnel in CAC stood and began to depart, and there was a sudden excited murmuring. The remaining personnel glanced about, and then returned to their tasks.

Frowning in puzzlement, Lorn looked toward Roy and then back toward his instrumentation. "Tactical here, Kreel Cruiser Group 2 is 22 AU distant and nearest to the defined trajectory."

"Tactical, immediately direct a tattletale probe to intercept and monitor Kreel Group 2. Then, compute a waylay point to engage that group four AU distant from the planet. Once computed, provide the coordinates of the ambuscade point to Navigation."

"Tactical here, acknowledged."

"Navigation, Jason, when you obtain the attack coordinates from Tactical, move the Task Force to that point. The Task Force is to be hunkered down at that coordinate five hours prior to Kreel Group 2 reaching that location. Jason, get it done."

"Navigation here, acknowledged—getting it done."

Depressing the general Task Force button on his Command chair control arm, Roy announced to all the Task force crews "Commodore Grey here. Heads up. Admiral Kellon has ordered the Task Force to ambush one of the approaching Kreel cruiser groups. We are proceeding to a waylay point to lay in wait and destroy that Group. Estimating eleven hours to Condition 2. I recommend everyone should try to get some rest, if possible.

"Be advised, Admiral Kellon has ordered the Task Force to return to Glas Dinnein after the ambuscade. Grey out."

Glancing at Lorn and Jason, Roy felt a surge of pride in his CAC team. They were all excellent crewmembers, but every once in a while, he knew they needed to be prompted to remember they needed rest.

"Lorn where you are concerned, my suggestion regarding getting some rest is an order. I do not want to see you in CAC during the next six hours. Assign your duties to the most rested member of your team, and then get some sack time. You'll need to be fresh as sunrise when we begin planning the attack."

Grimacing, Lorn looked toward Roy. "Yes Sir. Six hours."

"Turning toward Navigation, Roy ordered, "Navigation, Jason you have the CAC. I will be back in a few minutes, and then you should be prepared to get some sack time."

With a faint Smile, Jason responded "Acknowledging Navigation has the CAC."

Stepping down from his command chair, Roy proceeded from CAC and walked to the dispensary. Even as he walked through the passage, the low intense thunder of Lan's immense power was both heard and felt. The Task Force was accelerating, and it was going directly into harm's way.

Upon entering the dispensary, Roy was immediately met by Physician Lorentz, who with a scowling countenance promptly barred his further progress. "Sir, I presume you have come down to badger me about Roan and Zorn, as if I had nothing more to do than repeat what you already know."

"Humph, I see you're fiercely guarding the gates, as usual. If you actually expect to bar my entry, then out with it–how are they really doing?"

"How are they really doing? Then, are you formally challenging my official report and medical prognosis?"

"Physician Lorentz, has anyone ever told you that you're irritating? And, as for your question, that's an affirmative! So, drop your intertwined medical jargon. What I want to know is will they live; a simple yes or no is required!"

Physician Lorentz's expression transformed into a slight smile. "Well, when put like that, yes. They are going to live. Roan is the most seriously injured, and it will take time for him to recover. I'll be maintaining him in an induced unconscious stasis for at least a week while he undergoes accelerated cellular regeneration. After that, he will definitely need time to recover his strength. I don't believe he has suffered lasting brain damage; however, to be certain, he will receive cognitive therapy."

"How about Zorn?"

With a broad smile, Physician Lorentz pulled out his communicator and depressing a button, he pointed to the monitor that he had just activated. Zorn could be seen lying in a bed, either asleep or else under sedation. Elayne was Sitting next to him and holding his hand.

Turning to Roy, Physician Lorentz was still smiling. "My intertwined non-jargon medical prognosis is Zorn has a very high probability of a full recovery, and something of great value to live for. He will naturally require some recovery time, but his recovery should be complete."

Standing and watching the monitor for a moment, Roy also began to smile. "Well how about that. I suspect with that quality of encouragement, Zorn will definitely recover. Shey was right on target, yet again."

"Well, don't you have a war or something else to keep you busy and out of my dispensary?" Physician Lorentz challenged.

"As a matter of fact, I do. Thank you."

Turning, Roy retraced his steps back to CAC and entering, he ordered, "Navigation, the Commodore has the CAC, and Jason, I don't want to see you here for the next six hours. Dismissed."

When six hours later Lorn returned to CAC, he found Roy still sitting in his command chair and observing the forward tactical plot and a large video monitor. "Sir, as ordered, I'm reporting for duty."

"Good Lorn, your talent is definitely needed. Take a look at the incoming tattletale data stream and give me your best assessment," Roy ordered.

For the next ten minutes Lorn worked with his team, and then looked up toward Roy. "Tactical here. The Kreel Group is exhibiting extreme caution. There are twenty-seven cruisers, and they have fully deployed their scouts. We're tracking seventy-one scouts, and they're positioned well forward as an early-warning vanguard. There're also two cruisers and three fast attack ships positioned between the advanced scouts and the main cruiser group. The main body of the group consists of five elements of cruisers deployed in a widespread pyramid formation. Each of the elements of the main body consists of five cruisers, each element being formed in a pyramid formation. Their advanced scouts and overall spread indicates they anticipate a possible ambush."

"Shades of Tartarus, let's not disappoint them. Lorn, define our tactical plane; the first axis is the course vector of the Kreel Group, and the second is the ecliptic plane.

"To gain a proper aspect angle, you're to define our attack position below the Kreel vanguard. Work with Navigation to maneuver the Task Force into its firing position.

"Be advised, the Admiral has ordered the utter obliteration of the entire Kreel Group, including the scouts. You are to devise a phased cross-fire sequence, where all the missiles are timed and launched to impact their targets simultaneously."

"Tactical here, acknowledging 'impact simultaneously.'" Lorn replied.

Over the background murmur, the general announcing system declared "Admiral is in CAC."

Looking over, Roy saw that Kellon had just entered CAC, and Jason was walking with him. As Kellon came over to Roy, Jason returned to his duty station at Navigation.

"Roy, how is it shaping up?" Kellon asked.

"Well Sir, it's sort of a textbook problem, and you wrote the book. We're simply repeating your tactics when fighting the Kreel near the Arkillian Nest world. The Task Force has the advantage of stealth, surprise, position, and the AIs are busy working out the timing sequence and firing orders. We're now in the quiet zone, just before all of the loud noise begins."

Maneuvering at its highest stealth levels, Navigation guided the Task Force into its firing position, assuming a wide-facing rank formation centered on the approaching Kreel force. As the Kreel drew nearer, Roy set Condition 2, and a tense hush settled over CAC.

"Lan, you're to coordinate the allocation of targets and the missile firings with all cruiser AIs. Once the entire Kreel Group is within the defined kill volume, set Condition 1," Roy ordered.

"Yes Sir," Lan said.

Standing quietly, Kellon grimly watched the evolving tactical plot, as the Kreel Group approached and entered into the defined kill volume. Then, the crisp rumbling sounds of multiple heavy missiles being launched splintered the expectant hush and brittle tension within CAC. After a momentary pause following the launch of the last heavy missile, the slight whispering sounds of the launching of medium and light missiles were heard throughout Lan. All along the length of the rank of Guardian Cruisers, firing sequences were being precisely timed and heavy, medium, and light missiles were moving unerringly along their predestined trajectories toward designated targets.

While the converging missiles moved silently toward their targets, Roy sat and viewed the tactical plot. As the multitude of missiles approached their specified targets, he shifted his attention to the large-screen monitor. Then the symbols of missiles merged with symbols of Kreel ships on the tactical plot, and the monitor erupted into a broad volume of multicolored expanding spheres of scintillating light, which prompted a gasp from the assembled CAC team. Even Roy felt a momentary awe at the catastrophic spectacle of devastation.

"Roy, when the smoke clears away, if there are any surviving hulks, regardless of class, you are to promptly dispatch them with missiles. There are to be no survivors, and nothing left but drifting bits and pieces," Kellon ordered; his voice was hard and dispassionate.

Glancing toward Kellon, Roy made no comment other than to acknowledge "Yes Sir."

Following the initial attack, there remained seven battered drifting hulks. Soon thereafter, additional launched missiles struck, and these shattered relics of once proud ships exploded into rubble; there were no survivors.

"Lan, you're to transmit the prepared message to the Kreel, and do it on all their hailing frequencies and on the selected interstellar alarm channel."

"Sir, the message is being transmitted as ordered," Lan said.

"Roy, this battle is finished. You're to take us home."

"Yes Sir."

As Kellon turned and departed CAC, Roy silently watched him go. Emotionally, he inwardly felt a deepening concern for his friend. Looking back at the monitor, he shook his head and mused– *Drifting bits and pieces; Yes Sir.*

Glancing over toward Navigation, Roy noted Jason was attentively watching him. In response, he smiled, musing - *It just figures. It has been a long mission, and everyone is tired and concerned for their shipmates. And, that's just how it should be.*

"Navigation, Jason, assemble the Task Force into its standard battle formation. Then set our course for Glas Dinnein at best speed. Take us home."

Smiling broadly, Jason replied, "Navigation here, acknowledging, assembling the Task Force, setting best speed for our next port of call– Glas Dinnein!"

"Lan, set Condition modified 3 for all Intelligence teams and Tactical personnel. Then Set Condition 3 for all remaining personnel."

"Tactical, Lorn, you have the CAC. I'll be in my quarters."

"Yes Sir, Tactical has the CAC," Lorn crisply replied.

Entering his quarters, Roy felt a sudden surge of fatigue and his knees nearly buckled. Turning toward a chair for support, he was surprised to find a tray on a side table. Checking it out, he found a fresh thermos of neab, a covered dish with a triple decked Earth-style sandwich, and a cheese pastry. On the tray was a bottle of wine and a note. Curious, he picked up the note and read - *Well done! After you get some well-deserved rest, call me. I will help pull the cork and gladly present a heartfelt toast to your dear mother in acknowledgment of her son's wisdom.*

Chapter Twenty-Seven:
Unperceptive Barbarian

Hungrily searching for their lunch, flocks of seabirds swirled and squawked as they skimmed over the retreating waters of the surf line. The sun had silently traversed its zenith and in its brightness the faceted waves of emerald waters were producing a shimmering dance of many colors, while the off-shore sea breeze was feathering the cresting edges of the waves to white tufts of spray. Overhead the azure dome was unadorned by clouds, being boundless and transparent from the distant horizon line and arching above to its boundless depths. It was a beautiful day in the Capital on Glas Dinnein.

Standing above the high-water mark on the warm sandy beach, six people and a handsome yellow Labrador named Gepeto had prudently sought the comfort of the shade offered by the massive nearby old growth trees. They were all looking with expectation toward the northern horizon.

Standing among the small but distinguished group of people was Eryan Kyrie, the Admiral Secretary of the Planetary Assembly. She was standing to the left of Guardian Fleet Admiral Mer Shawn, and to his right stood Admirals Ron Cloud and Dylan Cord, the Admirals in command of Fleet Intelligence and Operations, respectively. These four people had been close friends and confidantes for more than a century, and together they were responsible for overseeing policy matters pertaining to the governance of the thirteen Assembled Human Worlds, while defending those planets from Kreel attacks. The Earth Ambassador, Susie Wells, was standing with her beloved pup, Gepeto, to Eryan's left side. McRoy, her assigned Guardian security officer stood to Susie's left. Behind the waiting group the muffled sounds of the midday traffic on the coastal highway could be heard hurrying past, unaware something unusual was happening.

Turning toward Mer Shawn, Eryan asked "Do we have any recent news from Kellon?"

"Hmmm, other than the normal dry reports on equipment status, which I doubt would interest you, there is some late information."

"Well, don't just stand there like a wooden pole. Give, what's happening?"

"Eryan, what information we have received is understandably scant. Still, Kellon has successfully penetrated his primary target solar system. His last report was the Task Force is poised at its selected attack departure point and is battle-ready. He believes the Kreel have anticipated an attack and have contrived a subtle trap. His estimate is the Task Force is confronting five-to-one odds. With such unfavorable odds, he may understandably withdraw and move to a secondary target," Mer responded, his voice evidencing concern.

"You say he might withdraw, but I'm not hearing any real conviction in your tone of voice supporting that possibility. Am I hearing you right?" Eryan asked.

"As usual, you're quite perceptive. Kellon has his Command because he is a proven combat officer. An old military axiom declares the best way to avoid being taken in a trap is to first discern it exists. That he has done. And yet, given the immense strategic value of his primary target, I doubt that even with the odds stacked against him that he'll back down," Mer said.

"Heads up everyone! I think I see the Subeer. It's due north and about ten degrees above the horizon line," Ron Cloud exclaimed, pointing.

"You may be getting forgetful in your advancing years Ron, but nobody can claim your eyes aren't as keen as ever. I think you're right, that speck is holding too steady to be a bird, and it appeared right on Subeer's schedule," Mer Shawn said.

"I don't know how you feel Mer, but I'm curious and looking forward to our first glimpse of a Nori ship," Ron said, with a hint of excitement.

Turning toward Susie, Eryan asked, do you know what the Nori word Subeer means?"

"Yes, when we were on Megan, Chandara told me it means Warrior for Good," Susie said.

"Now that's a proper, upright, and solid name," Dylan said, nodding his head in approval.

Even as they were conversing, the distant speck continued to expand, until it could be identified as a large ship, although its details were still undiscernible. Gepeto was watching the approaching object with intense interest, and suddenly he began to dance, his forepaws repeatedly coming up off the ground. His tail was wagging furiously.

Watching her pup and laughing, Susie exclaimed "Well, Gepeto is proclaiming it's a friend. It must be the Subeer."

The approaching vessel began moving off to the west, and then it swung about and approached the Government Center from that direction. It was moving parallel to the coast and at a very low altitude. Approaching just beyond the surf line the true dimensions of the craft soon became apparent. Slowing, it came to a silent and motionless hover, precisely opposite of where the small group of people were waiting. It was large, easily the size of a Guardian Cruiser, although unlike a Guardian cruiser it was not cylindrical in its form. It was a gracefully shaped ovoid, being somewhat wider in its cross-section than its vertical dimensions. Its maximum width was about one-third of its length aft from its graceful bow. The radiant colors on its sleek hull were a brilliant deep-sea green and were shimmering, as if covered by fish scales reflecting the bright sunlight. Adding to the spectacle, a flowing sheen of gold highlights was flickering over its entire outer green surface.

Shaking his head in wonderment, Dylan appreciatively commented "If it can fight one-half as good as she looks, I begin to understand why the Kreel are terrified of the Nori. That's one beautiful ship."

As they observed the vessel a small and streamlined transport having the brilliant luster of a pearl seemed to be seamlessly extruded from its glistening hull. Once freed, the transport promptly moved away from the craft and toward the waiting observers. On the coastal highway the vehicles were slowing, and some were pulling off the roadway so their occupants could look at the incredible and strange ship.

Moving silently, the transport directly approached the waiting group on the beach and then hovered. It was stationary and about one meter above the ground when an opening widened in its flawless side, and a ramp projected out of the opening and made firm contact with the ground. Immediately, two women and a man hurried down the ramp and walked across the warm sand toward the waiting group. Each was carrying a small pack or bundle. Behind them the ramp retracted and the opening in the hull flowed closed. Promptly the small craft silently lifted away. After circling once, the transport moved off, returning to the hovering parent vessel.

Seeing the three approaching people, two being Nori and the third from Earth, Susie was smiling broadly and for good reason. She considered them, Chandara, Amada, and Darrell to be among her dearest friends. While she observed, Chandara and Amada, graceful and beautiful as always, were smiling broadly toward her; Darrell looked pensive and reserved. More to the point, he was looking directly at her and his expression seemed guarded.

Laughing warmheartedly, Susie hurried across the beach with Gepeto bounding along with her. She went directly to Darrell. Throwing her arms about him she gave him a big hug. Looking on, Chandara and Amada both smiled at the overt display of affection and continued walking on toward the waiting group.

With Susie's warm embrace, Darrell's questioning expression softened, becoming a smile. Putting his hands lightly on her shoulders, he stepped back and looked intently at her, as if asking a question. In response, lifting an outstretched hand to his face, she lightly pressed her fingers to his lips.

"Darrell, it's wonderful that you are actually here. And yes, we do need to talk, but we first need to focus on the reason which brings the Nori and you to Glas Dinnein. Come on, I want to introduce you to my friends."

For a moment Darrell held direct eye contact with her and did not move. "For now, that's OK, But I've come more than one hundred light years to see you, and we do need to talk, and soon."

Taking Darrell by his arm, Susie turned and with a broad smile walked with him and Gepeto back to where her friends were engaged in animated conversation. "Everyone, I want you to meet the only other Earth-born person in this solar system, Darrell Fann, recently from Earth by way of Megan."

Eryan, stepping forward with a smile and extending her hand, took Darrell's hand and warmly greeted him. "Mr. Fann,

I'm Eryan Kyrie, the Admiral Secretary of the Planetary Assembly. It is my pleasure to welcome any friend of Susie. While you remain on Glas Dinnein, you are most welcome. If I may be of assistance during your visit, you need only ask."

With the sudden recognition of precisely who Eryan was, and the importance of her official office, Darrell was momentarily flummoxed, then he regained his composure. "Madam Secretary, I thank you for your gracious words and kind offer. They are deeply appreciated, and I'll not soon forget them."

Turning, Eryan formally introduced Darrell to Admirals Mer Shawn, Ron Cloud, and Dylan Cord. McRoy then stepped forward and introduced himself.

"Welcome to Glas Dinnein Mr. Fann, I'm McRoy, Guardian Force Intelligence and tasked with providing security for Ambassador Wells."

Initial introductions completed, Eryan took effective charge of the whole group; motioning everyone to proceed through the grove of trees, she shepherded them back to the waiting ground transportation. With an appreciating glance, Dylan turned back to look once more at the hovering Nori vessel and smiled broadly.

"That's truly impressive. Just for the record, I repeat, that's one beautiful ship."

Turning about, Dylan hurried to catch up with the others. Upon leaving the grove the group separated, each Admiral going to his waiting driver and staff vehicle. Eryan beckoned Chandara and Amada to join her in her official van. Meanwhile McRoy efficiently directed Gepeto into the rear cargo area of Susie's vehicle and then opened the rear doors to permit Susie and Darrell to enter. Opening his door, McRoy slid behind the controls, and closing the door behind him he turned to look questioningly at Susie.

"Madam Ambassador, where do you want to go?"

"Darrell, Are you hungry?" Susie asked.

"No, not at the moment. My two priorities for being here are that I've something to return to you, and I want an opportunity for a private conversation with you."

As he spoke, Darrell opened his pack and reaching inside he pulled out a package that had been carefully wrapped in a soft cloth. "Before anything else, I first need to return your gadget to you."

Accepting the object Darrell held out to her, she carefully removed the wrapping. As the polished fine grain wooden box was revealed, Rodney's clear voice boomed out.

"There, see he did it again! He called me a gadget. Ms. Susie, I am unable to express how truly grateful I am to again be with McRoy and you. Mr. Fann is an interesting person, but he is also an unperceptive barbarian, utterly devoid of humor and a proper respect for my capabilities and feelings."

Sourly looking at the box, Darrell dryly commented, "That AI is the sorriest contraption I've ever had the misfortune of encountering, and furthermore it's dangerous. I'm glad to be rid of the thing."

"First, he calls me a gadget, and now calls me a contraption! I misspoke, He is not unperceptive; he is an uncouth philistine."

The sounds of McRoy's suppressed amusement reached Darrell's hearing, and with some irritation he looked toward the front seat. "McRoy, I repeat, that thing is a sorry gadget, and I found nothing humorous in its behavior."

Frowning, Susie put her hand on Darrell's arm. "Darrell, easy there. I have found Rodney to be a very aware and capable AI. Nevertheless, I suspect there's an interesting story lurking behind your attitude and comments. Still, you are among friends here, and we do need to take care of the issues of the moment.

Looking forward Susie directed "McRoy, please take us to the Bachelors Officers Quarters. Mr. Fann should have an opportunity to check in and square away his kit before dinner."

"Understood, next stop is the BOQ," McRoy replied, even as the vehicle began to move.

Chapter Twenty-Eight:
An Ancient Humanity

Merging the vehicle into the light traffic flowing on the coastal highway, McRoy headed toward the Guardian spaceport. As he did, Susie turned to look at Darrell, her perplexed countenance showing she was troubled.

"It's wonderful that you are here Darrell, but I'm baffled about why you departed Megan. And, I'm admittedly curious why you are traveling with the Nori. Are you aware that you're the first person to do so?"

"No, I didn't know that, but it doesn't really surprise me either. Frankly, although they look human, I consider them aliens. I can't put my finger on what bothers me about them, but they make me jumpy."

"Then, why are you traveling with them?"

Frowning, Darrell turned and considered Susie's question. "Well, that particular why is the reason I departed Megan. Amada has drafted me to act as the Nori liaison, and asked me to represent them on Earth. As soon as the Nori wrap up whatever they're doing here on Glas Dinnein, they will be shipping out for Earth. And, I'll be going with them."

"Marvelous, that is sensational! Ms. Susie, please permit me to escort the barbarian to Earth, so I can visit with William," Rodney cheerfully inserted.

In unison, Darrell and Susie exclaimed "No!"

As Darrell was mumbling a barely audible profanity under his breath, Susie ignored his muttering and asked "If you're going back to Earth with the Nori, then is it your intention to remain on Earth?"

"No. I've made my choice. For better or otherwise, Megan is my new home. Besides, my agreement with the Nori is strictly short-term. I'll only be providing them with their initial introductions on Earth. After that they have guaranteed my passage back to Megan - dead or alive."

As McRoy was directing the vehicle off the coastal highway and onto the service road leading to the spaceport, Susie was deep in thought and looking out of the side window at the passing landscape. When she turned back to look at Darrell, her expression revealed her concern.

"I don't know the details of your interaction with the Nori. But, given the time frame involved, it was minimal. I have studied and worked closely with them for more than two years. I fully trust them. You can be certain that they're not aliens. They are bonafide humans, through and through. But, make no mistake Darrell, in many important ways they are different from us."

"I'll give you that much, they're sure enough different. As for trusting them, I'm not ready to go that far, at least not yet."

"Darrell, do you believe that five plus five equals ten in radix ten?"

"Of course, that's true by definition."

"It's with that same confidence in truth that I assure you the Nori are trustworthy."

Frowning, Darrell studied Susie's countenance. "You're that certain?"

"Yes, I am.

"As for the Nori being different, they are. And, for good reasons. They are the descendants of a branch of ancient humanity. From their unique vantage point, human history consists of an unbroken cultural record, one which spans more than a million years. Just for a moment consider that timeline and reflect on its significance– a million years of unbroken cultural history."

"You keep talking about them as if they were born on Earth. News flash, they weren't!" Darrell said.

"While they were not, their forebears certainly were. You are as aware as I am that 70,000 years ago something terrible was happening on Earth. When the Elders observed what was about to occur, they chose to take direct positive actions. In doing so they altered humanity's destiny."

"Hold it right there. You're talking about a Paleocontact. Back on Megan, Amada told me about aliens called Elders, and suggested they've been meddling in human affairs for millenniums. Do you know this as a fact?"

"Yes, I do."

"Just how do you know that?" Darrell challenged.

"Well, an Elder confirmed it to Admiral Kellon, and since I was there at the time, I also heard his confirmation."

"Whoa! Are you telling me you've actually met an Elder? In person?"

"Sorta yes and yes. Darrell, I'm trying here to provide you some important information. So, be patient for a moment and just listen."

"For the moment, I'll go along, but I expect a full explanation of that aforementioned 'sorta.'"

"Agreed, but for now just listen. You already know that seventy thousand years ago a rogue companion pair of dwarf stars, a red and brown, were on a direct collision course with Earth's solar system. Our modern astronomers have nicknamed them Scholz's star, and they are still recalculating how deep the low-density pair of stars penetrated into Earth's solar system. Even the most conservative astronomers have acknowledged the stars passed through the Oort cloud, but they could easily have come much nearer to the primary. Based on their understandably imprecise stellar measurements, that's about all the astronomers can tell us. At the same time, none of the astronomers are able to quantify the amount of stellar junk and minor or major planets Scholz's Star was dragging along with it. And, they don't have nary a clue to how the whole cluster of dwarf stars and their galactic debris perturbed the scattered rubbish and minor planets within Earth's Oort cloud."

"Susie, I know all of this, can we just skip to the point you're trying to make?"

"Excuse me Ambassador Wells," McRoy inserted. "While Mr. Fann knows Earth history, I don't, and I would appreciate hearing more about it. That is, if Mr. Fann doesn't object."

"I have no objections," Darrell said, with a slight tone of irritation.

"Earth's history is dynamic, McRoy. The good news is we do have hard data which is not restricted to imprecise astronomical measurements and approximations. There's available reliable hard data, including the evident geological record available on Earth, Mars, and the other bodies within the solar system," Susie said.

"Susie, just where are you going with this review of history?" Darrell inquired, still irritated.

"Be a little more patient and you'll soon find out. I'm trying here to give you a fundamental understanding of the Elders and the Nori. And, when you're back on Earth with the Nori, you might just find the information is important," Susie retorted.

"OK, point made," Darrell acknowledged.

"Remember Darrell, seventy-thousand years ago the Elders were not acting on hindsight or guesstimation based on imprecise astronomical measurements. They were right there on-the-spot and observing the coming interstellar entanglement as it was happening. They feared the pending devastation could easily cause the extinction of Humanity on Earth. Out of their Love for Life, the Elders took what they deemed a high-risk moral action to assure Humanity as a species would survive the approaching chaos. To achieve their desired goal, they first selected a small group of people on Earth. They then moved that select group out of harm's way, transplanting them safely among the stars. Those people have since flourished and become the Nori.

"In retrospection, the Elders had good cause for their concerns for Humanity. When the dwarf stars and their accompanying debris passed through our solar system, it left behind utter devastation and a shamble. As you know, the lingering tales and verbal histories of the few human survivors became the inspiration for many of our legends and myths-"

"Such as Gilgamesh!" Darrell inserted, teasingly.

"Yes, and also the Greek cosmic myth about the Olympians overthrowing the Titans and binding them in Tartarus. And, those are only two examples of the many legends derived from the oral traditions of the surviving ancient sky watchers."

"Is there hard physical data supporting your narrative?" McRoy asked.

"Well, there are the deep planetary rifts and scars remaining on Earth and elsewhere in the solar system, and of course, there's the great cataclysm on Mars. Its moons were formed from the debris of a proto-planet that collided with Mars. Such geological features attest to the terrible forces and violence that occurred on a planetary scale within Earth's solar system. Admittedly many of those rifts and scars are older and do not constitute geological evidence dating to seventy-thousand years ago, but some do. For example, on Earth there's one identified global geological event that correlates; it's the volcanic eruption we call the Toba catastrophe. That massive eruption and other smaller related eruptions resulted in literally cubic miles of ash being ejected into the upper atmosphere. That ash, in turn, produced a drastic shift in the weather that initiated an ice age lasting thirty-thousand years."

"Ambassador, what hard data do you have to support what happened to Earth's population?" McRoy asked.

"Good question McRoy. There's the primary data derived by Modern genetic anthropologists. On the basis of thorough DNA analysis, they've calculated at the population bottleneck less than ten thousand people on the entire Earth survived the upheavals and changes in the weather. Human civilization, the social product of a million years of human development, was swept away and simply vanished."

Approaching the main gates of the spaceport, McRoy slowed the vehicle, and with a keen and educated interest, Darrell quickly looked about, taking special note of the nearby massive bulks of several cruisers resting in their cradles. Then, he returned his attention to Susie. As he did so, McRoy slowed and brought the vehicle to a stop. Turning about, McRoy looked questioningly at Darrell.

"Well, we're at the BOQ. Come on Mr. Fann, I'll go with you and help check you in."

Darrell turned and looked at Susie, "Are you OK here?"

"I'll be fine. Go ahead with McRoy, I'll just sit here and visit with Rodney for a while," Susie said.

As McRoy and Darrell exited the vehicle, they immediately began talking together as they were walking toward the BOQ. As Susie watched the two men conversing, she felt a slight sense of confusion, musing, *nothing is ever simple; emotions, doubts, and difficult choices seem part and parcel of being alive.* She sighed.

"Pardon me Ms. Susie for intruding into your thoughts, but I have just received a relayed message from Shey that was forwarded through Guardian channels to me. Do you want to hear it? Rodney gently asked.

"You've received a message from Shey? Rodney, why is she sending you a message?" Susie asked, mystified.

"Ms. Susie, Shey was sending me her farewells. She was in a bad firefight and was without any remaining ordnance. She was adrift, her sensors were blind, her propulsion was disabled, and her hull was breached multiple times. As Roan ordered, she was initiating her Cobalt Blue sequence. Ms. Susie, Shey is gone."

Chapter Twenty-Nine:
Shipmates All

After signing the BOQ registry, Darrell received fresh towels from the steward and then followed the room numbers to his accommodations. Entering the room, he began a cursory inspection of the small and efficient apartment. As he did this, McRoy quickly stepped out into the hallway, quietly closing the door behind him.

"Rodney, report, is there a threat?" McRoy said his voice low but tense.

Listening to his implanted transceiver, he sighed. "I understand. Yes, we'll be returning immediately."

As Darrell came out of his room, he looked at McRoy and insightfully asked, "Is there a problem?"

"Yes, but regrettably, it's not one we can do anything to change. We have lost one of our scout ships in battle. The Ambassador was very close to the crew, and she is understandably saddened at the loss."

Even as he was speaking, McRoy had turned and was walking briskly along the hallway towards the elevator. Taken unaware, Darrell needed to hurry to catch up. With McRoy still in the lead, they exited the BOQ and headed directly back to the parked vehicle.

Opening the rear door to the vehicle where Susie was sitting, McRoy knelt down so he could make direct eye contact. As he did, he noticed Gepeto had put his head over the rear seat and was attempting to comfort Susie. He thought, *Good dog Gepeto.*

Reaching out McRoy took Susie's hand and held it gently, but firmly. Even though tears were streaming down Susie's cheeks, she tried to smile.

"McRoy, we have lost Shey."

"Yes," McRoy said gently. "Rodney told me. Susie, I know it's painful now, but over time your pain will lessen. May I recommend that we go and find a quiet place and share a glass of wine? The best thing we can do just now is to offer a toast in honor of our fallen comrades."

Smiling weakly, Susie wiped the tears from her face with the palms of her hands. "McRoy, I must look a frightful mess. Still, I would like to join with you in making that toast."

Giving her hand a gentle squeeze of encouragement, McRoy stepped back and quietly closed the door. As he turned, he saw that Darrell was standing near and watching him with a questioning expression.

"Mr. Fann, Shey is the name of the Scout ship we have lost. Would you care to join the Ambassador and me as we make a toast in honor of our departed friends?"

"Yes, that's something I would appreciate in sharing."

To reach the driver's side, McRoy walked around the front of the vehicle, while Darrell went in the opposite direction. Opening the rear door, Darrell slid into the seat next to Susie and closed the door behind him. As he did, he observed Susie was striving to maintain her composure, but was understandably unable to veil her heartache. *Wake up and smell the roses,* he thought. *I've been behaving like a jerk and making too many assumptions. While I've been living on a small blue ball, a hundred light years distant, for the last four years Susie has been living out here. I don't have even a clue about her friends or her innermost feelings.*

Seeing Gepeto's concern for Susie, Darrell reached out and gave him several reassuring pats. Turning and looking about, he saw that McRoy was then driving toward the main gate of the spaceport, while apparently talking to himself.

Looking back toward Susie and still wanting to comfort her, Darrell was uncertain what he might say that would ease her grief. He nevertheless endeavored to begin a conversation.

"Would you like to tell me about Shey and its crew?" Darrell asked, gently.

"Darrell, Shey was not an 'it!' like Roan and Zorn, Shey was a friend," Susie replied.

"Then Shey was an AI, sorta like William and Rodney."

"No, Shey was a scout ship. But, like all ships, she had a unique personality which was personified by her name. I suppose the infusion of a personality is only a reflection of the character of the crew, yet there's always an intangible quality that's very difficult to explain," Susie dissembled, realizing she had said more than she should have concerning a classified matter.

Listening, Darrell had noted the hesitation in Susie's explanation. Remembering Rodney's description of Guardian AIs and their level of classification, he chose to remain circumspect.

"How well did you know Shey's crew?"

"Roan and Zorn? I knew them from the beginning; they were the men who made first contact with me back on Earth. And, on the day I returned back to Earth, it was Shey, Roan, and Zorn who delivered me to the front steps of the Department of Commerce. Both Roan and Zorn became two of my most wonderful and trusted friends. That they could be gone, just snuffed out of life, is hard for me to believe."

The vehicle slowed and then came to a stop. Both Darrell and Susie looked up and around them. While Darrell had no idea of where they were, with her recognition of the location, Susie smiled happily.

"Oh, McRoy, thank you. This is the perfect place for us to make our toast.

As McRoy opened Susie's door, Darrell opened his own and then stood looking about. Breathing in the moist fresh ocean breeze, he found it was cool on his skin and smelled wonderful. Listening, just beyond the bordering trees, he heard the distinct sounds of waves rolling in and collapsing along a beach. Looking back toward the building, he noted it was well-cared for, and it was some sort of commercial establishment. He then detected the tantalizing aroma of roasting meat and smiled.

Having moved to the rear of the vehicle, McRoy opened the cargo hatch and let Gepeto jump down. He promptly ran about the vehicle to where Susie was waiting. Lovingly, she reached down and gently scratched behind his ears, much to Gepeto's delight.

Together, they all walked up the stairs to the entrance doors, and McRoy reached out and opened a door, ushering the others inside. Upon entering, they were immediately confronted by the outpouring of an enticing fragrance of roasting meat and a robust and friendly verbal greeting.

"Madam Ambassador, what a delightful surprise this is. It is indeed my pleasure to welcome you once more to McBride's!" the proprietor said, with a full and resonant voice.

Stepping quickly forward, McRoy asked, "McBride, would you just happen to have a small quiet corner, somewhere three people can sit and obtain a glass of wine to make a toast?"

Having become aware of Susie's unhappy countenance, McBride frowned. His initial cheerful mood evaporated, quickly transforming into a disposition of concerned.

"Of course, please come this way."

Leading the small group across the sparsely occupied main dining room, McBride went quickly up two steps and into a small semi-private dining area. Following McBride into the room, Darrell glanced about with interest. The comfortable area he stood in featured only one medium sized table, over which was suspended a complex multi-hued cut glass chandelier. He recognized the room provided an intimate atmosphere, one that was more in keeping with a home family dining room than that of a commercial dining area. A beautifully crafted river rock fireplace captured Darrell's full attention, and he noticed it was properly set with wood for a fire.

Having pulled back a chair for Susie, as she sat down McBride gently pushed it forward. As he did this, Gepeto moved to a heel position at Susie's left side and lay down. McRoy and Darrell moved to the opposite side of the table, and choosing chairs, they took their seats.

"Ambassador and Gentlemen, while I do not wish to intrude, would I be correct to presume that the toast you spoke of making is in remembrance of recently lost shipmates?" McBride asked.

"Regretfully, that's an affirmative. Scout Ship Shey is reported lost in battle. In the fighting she was severely damaged, inert and without remaining defensive or offensive capabilities. As ordered, she executed her Cobalt Blue protocol," McRoy said, tersely but nevertheless with a catch in his voice.

With a quiet nod of understanding, McBride turned and quickly departed. Soon thereafter he returned carrying an expertly balanced tray upon which were four long stemmed glasses, each containing a rich dark red wine. With ease, revealing the consonant skill derived from long practice, he placed a glass of wine in front of each of his guests. Then, putting the tray aside, he held the fourth glass in his right hand.

"In that I'm now among good friends, and well remembering my former shipmates and battles long since fought, might I have the privilege of presenting the toast?" McBride asked.

"Oh, please do McBride. You certainly knew Roan and Zorn far longer than any of us," Susie said.

"Yes Ambassador, I have indeed. In fact, although it may be difficult for you to believe, I knew them both back when they were still wet behind their ears and fresh out of the Academy. And, dear Lady that was even before the battle of Kintana, which if I remember correctly, was at least 800 years ago."

Standing, and for a moment solemn, McBride bowed his head. As he did, the others around the table respectfully stood. After several moments of silent thought, McBride straightened and lifted his head. Standing tall, he raised his wine glass in salute. The others did likewise.

"Good and Almighty Spirit of Life, universal throughout all space and times, we gratefully ask that you consider and embrace the spirits of our shipmates, Roan and Zorn. They went forth into the dark void as warriors, not for conquest or to plunder others, but rather to protect others. This they knowingly did at risk of their own lives, which they valued and loved.

"We who remain behind now lift our glasses in remembrance of their courage. In acknowledgment and tribute, we declare– shipmates all, good and well done!"

Finishing his toast, McBride waited for his guests to resume their seats, and asked, "May McBride's offer any additional fare? Anything you may wish is on the house."

"Thank you for your warm hospitality, but no thank you. At least not for now," Susie replied, tears again flowing over her cheeks.

Still somber, McBride turned and departed, taking with him the now empty tray. If they had noticed, they might have seen the moisture gathering in the corners of his eyes.

As McBride departed, McRoy once again sipped appreciatively at his glass of wine and nodded. "Hmmm, that's Quintana Gold. McBride certainly opened his deepest wine cellar for our toast, and it was nicely done."

Sitting in dumbfounded amazement, Darrell sat silently wondering about the toast that McBride had just offered. Eight-hundred years? How long, he thought, do these people live? How in blazes did they come to be out here to begin with? Unable to further restrain the unbridled nagging of his ignorance, Darrell looked across the table to where Susie was using a napkin to dab her tears away.

"Susie, pardon me, but if you feel up to it, might I ask you several questions?"

"Of course, Darrell. That's of course presuming I can answer them," Susie said.

"Well, my own acquired knowledge of human history is somewhat sparse; it only goes back about twelve thousand years. During our discussion in the vehicle, you referred to a rather dismal era of life on Earth about seventy-thousand years ago. Because of your explanation, I've got a handle on the Nori, but I'm at a total loss regarding how the people now living on the Assembled worlds got out here."

"Unfortunately, in truth there's very little I can tell you. The historical details on that topic are scanty at best or unknown. From what little I've learned, over the millenniums the Elders transplanted three distinct groups of humans. The First were the Nori about seventy-thousand years ago. Then about thirty-thousand years ago, during the great ice age, they transferred a second group here on Glas Dinnein. Finally, about 14,000 years ago they transplanted a third group of people elsewhere. According to what one Elder said, and affirmed by the Nori, that final group of people has, through some great folly of their own, utterly perished. They are simply no more.

In stark contrast, the people the Elders relocated on Glas Dinnein have flourished. During the past thirty-thousand years, they have expanded and dispersed into ten nearby hospitable star systems. All that expansion happened before the Kreel burst out of the void and onto the local scene. With the coming of warfare, the previous efforts of expansion ceased, at least ceased until the recent settlements upon Megan began."

"That's not much in way of a detailed history," Darrell mused.

"Sorry about that, but the real problem with the vague history is not found on Glas Dinnein; it's to be found back on Earth, where it all began. Unfortunately, human history on earth is nothing more than a tree stump. That's because thirteen-thousand years ago the flourishing tree of human history was violently cut down...."

Chapter Thirty:
Ice Two Miles Thick

Holding his wine glass by its stem, Darrell frowned and sat looking across the table at Susie, pondering how to respond to her last statement. Returning his frown with a slight smile, Susie nodded her head in understanding.

"Darrell, Humans have been on the Earth for more than a million years. Haven't you ever stopped to wonder why there's only a bare tree stump of human history, barely twelve-thousand years of recorded history? Susie asked."

"Frankly, No. That particular itch never seemed to need scratching. But, why do you ask?"

"Because only by knowing what happened on Earth Seventy and Thirteen-thousand years ago can we begin to understand why humanity is in the mess it's in.

"Remember, it was about thirteen-thousand years ago that the Elders transplanted the third group of humans from Earth out into the stars. Ask yourself why."

"I've no clue. Do you know why?"

"Perhaps, at least in a fractional sense. During that time frame, thirteen-thousand years ago, humanity was climbing back from near extinction, and it was coping with some long-standing natural environmental challenges, like an ice age. Around the world people were busy rebuilding their urban communities. Then, a brand new cosmic disaster struck Earth."

"Disaster?"

"Yes, there was a big comet, or bolide, which entered the upper atmosphere. It fragmented and exploded above North America and above the two-mile-thick ice sheet that was then covering most of the continent. There is some evidence that smaller fragments of the same comet may have gone as Far East as Europe and the Middle East, but the really big boom happened over North America. If you're interested in researching the event, the literature identifies it as the Clovis comet."

"There was ice two miles thick covering most of North America thirteen-thousand years ago? Oh boy, I've got some serious studying to catch up on. What geological evidence exists to support there was a cosmic event? Is there an impact crater?" Darrell asked.

"Darrell, there was a two-mile-thick ice sheet covering the continent, and you're looking for a smoking crater? Not likely. there is, however, extant geological evidence, which does support an enormous air-burst did occur. The explosion was in the upper atmosphere."

"Then, it was like Podkamennaya Tunguska River in Siberia."

"Yes, but while similar, it was more destructive than was the Tunguska event. The enormous heat from the explosion which occurred over the ice sheet caused an immediate large-scale ice melt. The results were massive cascading waters that flowed over and off the ice sheet into the oceans. The geological record, consisting of areas of deeply eroded landscape in the northwest, with boulders strewn haphazardly about, testifies the waters flowing off the ice sheet reached more than two thousand feet in depth. At the same time, more than thirty-five different mammal species then living in North America, including the mammoth and the Clovis culture that hunted them, suddenly became extinct. That enormously destructive cosmic event is what cut down the flourishing tree of human history, leaving behind only the aforementioned bare stump for us to study."

"Susie, anything causing that much devastation must have produced significant meteorological ripple effects. What data exists on atmospheric effects?"

"You're correct. There were significant global effects, and data does exist. The environmental stresses on the atmosphere caused an abrupt colder global climate shift, identified in the literature as the Younger Dryas."

"Do we know what happened to Earth's population?" Darrell asked.

"Unfortunately, due to the lack of data, an objective historical record is lacking. Like the Clovis culture, others undoubtedly vanished. Later, new cultures emerged. Then, there may have been additional bolide strikes that impacted the oceans about three-thousand years after the explosion over North America. About that time Earth's atmosphere suddenly warmed again, and the North American and European ice sheets rapidly reseeded. The predictable consequence of the melting glaciers was a rise in sea levels of more than 400 feet. Then, like now, the majority of developed civilizations were built near the continental coasts, on lowlands, and on islands. The dramatic rise in sea levels swallowed up many of these regions and drowned the then thriving human occupied lands and their cultures."

"Hmmm, sounds like a shuffling of Plato's Atlantis co-mingled with James Churchward's Lost Pacific Continent of Mu, merged with the shamefully maligned works of Immanuel Velikovsky."

"Sorta. Lamentable and regressive academic bias, blockheaded scholarly skepticisms based solidly on willful ignorance, have never served truth. One inescapable fact is the ocean levels rose 400 feet. That can't be ignored as mere literary fancy, it's established fact! The evidence of well-developed cultures prior to twelve-thousand years ago includes numerous large and complex manmade stone structures, which have been discovered hundreds of feet underwater and filmed. These submerged ruins attest that there were well established cultures flourishing when they were inundated. Obviously, there must have been forced migrations and social conflicts. It seems wherever surviving fragments of earlier knowledge could be gathered and centralized, new cultures like those in South America and Egypt took root and blossomed. Our own cultural legacy includes bits and pieces from the ancient wisdom surviving from those early times, and with a straight face you can't deny that."

"Agreed, but only grudgingly," Darrell replied, with a slight smile.

"I'll accept grudgingly. The point I'm trying to make is humanity on Earth has endured repeated global cosmic devastations. As a consequence, humanity is suffering from a really severe case of amnesia, which explains why your knowledge of human history is not a flourishing saga, but rather something reduced to little more than tatters and a bare stump. And, this sad fact brings me back to the topic of the Nori.

"Remember, the history and culture of the Nori is linear, unbroken, and intact. Consider the powerful influence that more than one million years of unbroken cultural history can exert on a society. You've been wondering why the Nori appear so different, well, that's why. Now, consider the fact Nori history is also our common legacy."

"Maybe a shared legacy does exist. Then again perhaps not. Admittedly, there's one thing you've firmly established. The Elders do exist, and they have produced a bifurcation of humanity. Whether a mutually beneficial unification of the separated parts of humanity is possible remains to be determined. Frankly, I for one have my doubts. Let's face it; we've been struggling with the basic issues relating to our different races on Earth throughout our brief history, and the historical record on that topic is verifiably not a happy one."

"Darrell, you sound just like an executive Manager of Olympus, suspicious of everything."

"That's because that's precisely what I am," Darrell said, testily.

"Then, you're a self-admitted bureaucratic blockhead. As for the possibility of a mutually beneficial unification of the parts being possible, that particular question is what the three human social cultures, Earth, the Assembled worlds, and the Nori will be striving together on Megan to find out," Susie said, somewhat impatiently.

Having listened with interest to the friendly banter between Susie and Darrell, McRoy smiled. The dialog between the two obvious friends had altered Susie's frame of mind in a positive fashion, diverting it from Shey's loss. That was good. With a sigh and a few regrets, he broke into the on-going verbal exchange.

"Madam Ambassador, excuse me for breaking into an interesting discussion, but I've been informed there are several Scout ships outside. They have come to express their condolences to you and are requesting that you join with them in giving their salute to Shey."

"Oh, that's wonderful. I want to share in any salute to Shey."

When they stepped out of the door of McBride's, they observed eight Scout ships hovering stationary in front of them. They were about 100 feet above the ground and arrayed in a rank formation. The eight ships, brilliant in their parade colors, glistening gold trim over solid lustrous white, were gleaming in the waning afternoon sunlight. Adding to their brilliant colors, there was an additional broad chevron strip of deep purple displayed on each of their bows. This was their mourning band denoting the loss of one of their own.

As Susie emerged from McBride's establishment and stood on the top step facing the Scouts, she waved. Then, one by one each ship dipped its bow to her. Looking up toward the hovering Scouts, Susie smiled, and speaking loudly, she addressed the hovering ships.

"Thank you for your marvelous salute and for honoring our mutual shipmates. We will long remember and honor them, Roan, Zorn, and Shey."

Moving as one, all the ships dipped their bows in a formal salute. Pivoting in place, they then assumed a file formation and proceeded eastward. Accelerating, the eight ships swept about to the north and arching gracefully upward over the ocean they appeared like an ascending string of gleaming pearls. Their grace and beauty in form and flight was their flourish of remembrance of their parted sister and her guys.

Observing the Scout's maneuvers, Darrell was perplexed. Turning he looked first toward Susie, who was still looking skyward, and then he turned back to McRoy.

"McRoy, am I correct in thinking that the ships were dipping their bows to Susie?"

"That is correct."

"But why?" Darrell asked.

"Why? Well, they understand a deep personal bond existed between Earth's Ambassador and Shey and wanted to present a formal acknowledgment of that relationship."

"Then, is that something they would do for all Ambassadors?"

"No, what they did was something special and was strictly According to long established tradition. Guardian ships, cruisers and scouts alike, bestow such honorific tributes to only a few individuals. Currently that unique honor is granted to only five people on all the Assembled planets. The Ambassador is one of those five individuals."

Now even more puzzled, Darrell looked back toward Susie and noticed she was still looking toward the point where the Scouts had dwindled to specks before disappearing.

Still flummoxed, Darrell asked McRoy again "But why?"

McBride, who was previously unnoticed, was standing behind Darrell and in the entrance to the restaurant. Like Susie, he was still looking skyward. In a quiet and respectful tone, he answered Darrell's question.

"Sir, they presented their individual and formal salutes because the Ambassador has uniquely earned the high honor that All Guardian ships gladly bestow upon her."

In wonderment, Darrell turned back toward Susie, completely baffled. *Incredible,* he thought, *there's an important bit of history involving Susie lurking here, and I'm utterly clueless to what it's all about. There's more happening out here than anyone on Earth suspects, knows, or begins to understand....*

Chapter Thirty-One:
Drifting Ashes

The massive and ominous thunder clouds scudding overhead darkened the midday light. Adding to the general atmosphere of gloom, the air was thick with an acrid smoke that carried the sweet scent of death and a chemical stench of still burning rubble. Fleet Grand Admiral Groff's eyes were irritated by the smoke, and his refined sense of smell was offended. All in all, the chaotic scene surrounding him was a dismal smoldering ruin, among which were scattered numerous broken bodies, most of which he noticed were Kreel.

According to the official records, he was standing among the debris of what was once the Empire's most vaunted Military Research and Development Center. What it once was mattered little. Even with irritated eyes and offended nostrils, anyone could assess what remained was only the scorched and broken remnants of what was once a busy large industrial military complex. The Lux had proficiently transformed it into piles of smoldering rubbish and drifting ashes.

Given the extent of the scattered debris field, even finding a location suitable for his flag ship to land had proven problematic. Nevertheless, the demands of his Command required a landing and that he personally conduct a firsthand visual inspection of the devastation.

As Groff stood looking about at the ruins, what struck deepest into his emotional being was the evident destruction of his grounded cruisers. Once they had been powerful ships of war and the pride of the Military; now their remnants lay dispersed along the margins of the spaceport, broken and burnt out hulks, mere slag. There were no survivors.

Not one of his first-line cruisers, which he had sent to defend the planet, had lifted off to challenge and furiously engage the enemy. Rather, they had been effectively rendered meaningless while they were still planet-bound. Subsequently the Lux, at their own leisure, had employed heavy bombardment lasers fired from high above to hammer them into scrap.

As he looked about him at the desolation, he felt his anger swelling to a battle crescendo. IT was only with practiced skill that he was able to mentally check his rising fury. This he knew was not the time for unchecked ire; instead it was the time for decisive planning. The proper time for fury and inflicting retribution upon the Lux would come later, and until then his outrage must be properly held in check.

Still mindful of his suppressed wrath, he turned about and carefully retraced his steps through the wreckage and scattered bodies, returning to his command ship. Like fleeting shadows his personal security guard flowed all about him, silent and vigilant.

Once onboard, he entered his private compartment and drew his Command wand from its belt sheath. Pressing the Captain's button, he ordered "Captain, you're to sound recall. Once all of our ground teams are safely onboard, secure for space and lift ship. You are to link up with our squadron in low orbit."

"Order received and understood," The captain acknowledged.

Even as he walked toward the cabinet near his desk, he sensed the gravimet field activate and begin to exert its influence. Ignoring the initial unpleasant tingling caused by the initial energies of the inertial field, he walked purposefully to the cabinet and opened it. Withdrawing an ornate silver goblet, he poured into it from an elaborately cut crystal decanter a generous quantity of hotep netjer. With a soft growl of pleasure, he consumed the well-aged beverage. Then thoughtfully, he poured a second and larger portion, and then placed the decanter back into the cabinet.

The slight alcoholic beverage noticeably eased and mildly tempered the sharp edge of his suppressed anger. Even so, like banked coals in a furnace, his rage continued to burn deep within the core of his being.

Pulling out the chair at his desk, he sat down and began reflecting on the reality of what had transpired on six worlds, and what appropriate counter steps he must set in motion. As he did, his wand vibrated. Glancing at the instrument and caller ID, he noted it was his Executive Adjutant. He keyed an open channel.

"Report."

"Admiral Groff, one of our Special Forces reconnaissance teams has located Marshal Krupp. He is injured but survives. His flag-ship was hit by a heavy missile and was badly damaged; it is wrecked and grounded some 3,500 kilometers from our location."

"You are to establish direct telemetry with Krupp. Promptly inform me once two-way communication is available."

Closing the communications channel, he leaned back in his chair and held the silver goblet loosely in both hands. Absent mindedly rotating the goblet between his fingers, he occasionally sipped from it, while deliberating on what he knew to be fact. In doing so, he took careful stock of an unfruitful and nagging sense of foreboding. Consciously he pushed such non-productive worry thoughts far from his contemplations. Instead, he deliberated on how the Lux had managed to shred his carefully devised battle plans into tatters.

By correctly classifying the targets the Lux had focused upon during their previous five attacks, he had been able to predict their next likely objective. That auspicious forewarning had presented him with an opportunity to ambush them, and he sought to capitalize on that opportunity. He understood war by its nature consists of taking calculated risks; therefore, the preliminary planning for a devised trap was accomplished with attention to details. The kill volume was defined with cunning, and it was well baited. The unyielding anvil was correctly positioned and the decisive hammer blow was held high, poised to smash the Lux to bits. All the elements required for an overwhelming victory had been arranged in their precise interrelationships. Yet, the ambuscade had badly frayed and unraveled. How, he pondered, was that possible? Where were the unrecognized and fatal flaws in his planning?

Many hours of data gathering and unremitting analysis would be required to understand what had gone so wrong. Knowing this, he silently vowed to Anubux that he would resolve the enigma.

Momentarily setting aside the questions relating to the harsh military calamity that had befallen his forces, he turned his thoughts toward a far greater inquiry. On six consecutive planets, the Lux had made short work of precise bombardment of an entire planet. Their absolute precision delivery of ordnance on thousands of separated individual targets of strategic value demanded extraordinary and detailed data about geographical, economic, and military facilities, much of which was highly classified. Even having personally seen the devastation on the planet, he could but ask - how could such pinpoint and total destruction be accomplished in so short an interval of time? The mere computational demands for such an overwhelming attack were incomprehensible. The logistic and control requirements needed to direct such a military operation were staggering. Everything he had ever learned and understood about military operations shouted it was utterly impossible. Yet, the stench of death and burning debris still clogged his nostrils, proving The Lux had with apparent ease now repeated the impossible six consecutive times. How was that possible?

How could any distant interstellar military power develop the detailed Intelligence relating to thousands of secret military installations, factories, and research laboratories? How could the Lux possibly conceal their spy network so completely?

As he grudgingly considered these confounding problems, his wand vibrated again. Glancing at the instrument, he observed his Executive Adjutant was calling again and keyed an open channel.

"Report."

"Admiral Groff, two-way communication is now established with Grand Marshal Krupp."

"Good. Patch Krupp into this channel."

The large monitor above his desk immediately brightened and the image of Krupp appeared. What Groff noticed first was Krupp was no longer wearing his lavishly bejeweled honors harness. Instead he was wearing an unadorned and well-worn functional trooper's weapons harness. His left arm was stiffly held in a cast and his head was heavily bandaged. He looked disheveled, haggard, and the worse for wear. Still, there was an inescapable subtle military pride evident in his bearing, and there was no hint of insolence or arrogance in his countenance.

"Fleet Grand Admiral Groff, the defense of this solar system was my responsibility. The ruinous outcome is my shame to bear. I submit myself wholly to your authority and await your Judgment of my failure."

Chapter Thirty-Two:
A Blood Enmity

Leaning back in his chair, Groff held the silver goblet between his hands and with narrowed eyes he studied Krupp, considering his self-effacing statement. The juxtaposition of the previous insolent Elite Grand Marshal and the presently humbled Krupp offered him a stark contrast, which commanded his introspection.

After a brief pause, Groff replied. "Grand Marshal Krupp that was well said. As to shame, I find no cause in your conduct that warrants shame. The Empire's forces acted with courage, and what more could be asked of our fallen warriors? While the forces under your Command were obliterated, so were more than thirty cruisers under my personal Command."

In surprise, Krupp's eyes widened, and a rumbling growl emerged. "How could that be possible?"

"How? Just how it was possible remains our primary question. Even as we planned, one moment my three prongs of attacking cruisers were closing on the prey, and then suddenly one third of my cruiser force was instantaneously annihilated. It was as if they were brittle dry leaves blown before a powerful storm. One moment they comprised a well deployed and potent military force, and the next instant fire engulfed every cruiser, along with each escorting fast attack and scout ship. Death reached out and snatched them away. They instantaneously ceased to exist. There was no preceding warning, no challenge, no battle; there was only spontaneous detonations and spreading flotsam. How this is possible is unknown.

"When my remaining two battle prongs reached the planet, the Lux had completed their obliteration. They had departed, and there was no enemy for us to fight.

"What we found was systemic destruction of our critical resources on this planet. I have personally walked among the scattered bodies and the still burning ruins. The Empire no longer has a research and manufacturing capability on this world."

With an angry growl Krupp asked, "Fleet Grand Admiral Groff, did the Lux leave behind their lingering scent, so we can track them to their dens and there destroy them?"

"Marshal, before you can destroy an enemy in his den, you must first find his den. Before you can find his den, you must first be able to detect him. We have not been able to do either.

"But as for leaving a scent, they have left far more. They have issued a formal challenge on multiple frequencies, including one of our supposedly secret interstellar communication bands. Every Military facility within the Empire received that challenge, with predictable adverse disruptive consequences."

The fur along Krupp's shoulder ridges bristled, and a rumble rolled forth from his muzzle. He snarled, exposing his fangs.

"They dare issue a formal challenge to the Kreel! Then, where will the Empire meet the Lux in open battle to answer their arrogance?"

"Their arrogance? Marshal Krupp, I commend you for your fighting spirit, but stop and look about you.... In five other solar systems, as in this one, we have already met the Lux in battle. In each encounter, the Lux transformed our military might into drifting shards of junk."

Krupp's eyes narrowed, and there was a momentary silence followed by an ominous growl. "Then, Fleet Grand Admiral Groff, are you declaring the Kreel will submit, that we will bend our knees and surrender?"

"Krupp, hollow bravura is but a meaningless noise. Your evident anger does not constitute a strategy, and it will not compel the Lux to yield to the Empire.

"In order for a government to rule, it must first by force exercise its power over others. This inexorable fact is the most ancient and abiding truth defining all governments, without exception and regardless of meaningless platitude.

"You challenge, asking me if I intend to surrender. Perhaps I am missing something here, Marshal. Tell me, what is your proposal? What strategy should the Empire exploit to demonstrate and exercise its compelling power over the Lux?"

In spite of his injuries, Krupp struggled to stand, and from deep within his chest a snarl rose. "Then, you are indeed declaring that the Empire will capitulate!"

An answering deep rumble came from Groff's chest, and narrowing, his eyes were fixed on Krupp. "Marshal, Sit down!"

Responding to Groff's harsh order, Krupp sat down. The deep rumbling in his chest subsided, but the fur across his shoulders bristled and his eyes flashed with barely restrained fury. Retaining eye contact with Groff, he remained silent.

"Take warning, Marshal. Foolish assumptions and insolence, like quicksand, are best avoided; both can quickly prove fatal.

"Before leaping to foolish assumptions, first examine the facts. Even better yet, examine the spreading flotsam of what remains of much of our military force in this and five other solar systems. Suppress your outrage Marshal. Instead of focused anger, turn your intellect toward understanding just how the Lux could have accomplished such wholesale destruction, and consider by what means the Empire can prevent it from happening again."

Squarely meeting Groff's intense scrutiny, Krupp replied with restrained anger. "Fleet Grand Admiral Groff, surrender will never be an option! Although it was long ago, I will never forgive the foul species that desecrated our DNA, genetically experimenting with and breeding the Kreel as if we were animals. By force they enslaved us, and by force they compelled us to work in their fields and mines, to labor in factories and serve them on their space ships. By force they removed our mates and cubs from our dens, and as if we were only beasts and chattel, they sold our mates and cubs for filthy profit.

When in fury our Elite Ones dared to rise up in rebellion, they taught us the truth, it is the Kreel who are of the true blood! With our Elite Ones leading, we rose up in rage. With our blood coursing through the streets like torrents of waters, co-mingling with the blood of our enemies, we hunted and stalked that foul species. We found and then killed them all– each and every last one of them! We granted no mercy. We forever cleansed the stench of the filthy humankind from our three home worlds. No species will ever again be permitted to dominate us. Never again!"

"Then know this fact, Grand Marshal Krupp, you and I are in full accord," Groff said with a resonant rolling growl.

Hearing Groff's words, Krupp's anger eased and the bitterness seething in his eyes faded. "What then is your plan of battle? How might I best serve the Empire?"

Studying Krupp's image, Groff searched for any trace of deceit or deception in his manner and words. He was pleased to find none. Knowing Krupp had ambitiously plotted against him, he considered that was a personal matter. Of far greater importance to him was Krupp had never faltered in his duty or devotion toward the Empire. Admittedly, he remained a personally dangerous tool. Yet, he was also a valuable tool, one which might prove decisive in what must occur, if the Empire were to prevail and prevail it must.

"Marshal, the fool who fears nothing is quickly overpowered. Given their evident technology, the Lux must feel secure in their perceived superiority, and the most common beginning of a fatal explosion is a false sense of security. Their very strength may therefore be their weakness.

"Our losses here and elsewhere are not the result of our lack of courage, but of the lack of viable Military Intelligence and a superior technology. Before the Empire can prevail, it must first address and overcome these fatal weaknesses."

Again, Krupp's eyes narrowed. "Address them? How might the Empire accomplish that impressive feat?" Krupp challenged.

"How? By exploiting the advantages of time and cunning," Groff answered.

"Time? How much time do we have?"

"As much time as the Empire requires, if necessary eons. As you perceive, Marshal, surrender will never be an option. The Empire will pay the blood price required to purchase the time it requires. Then, afterward, the Lux will in turn pay the blood price for their arrogance."

"What about the Lux challenge?" Krupp asked.

"For the hunters having ears to hear, the Lux challenge loudly declares their folly. In their arrogance, they even dictated terms. Instead of profiting by their military gains, and pressing their attack, the Lux have gifted the Empire with the time it requires to prepare for the long battle– but listen for yourself."

As Krupp watched, Groff lifted his wand and depressed several buttons. Immediately, he heard a well-modulated voice speaking impeccably in the high Kreel language. The voice possessed a deep resonance and it carried with it a tone of absolute authority and confidence. Krupp could not mistake that the flawless enunciation of each syllable declared that the speaker held no doubt as to his own intellectual superiority over the Kreel. Just listening to that voice caused the fur along his shoulders to bristle in indignation.

"Kreel enemy, a blood enmity exists between us. There is no need for negotiation or demand for surrender. The Lux grant to you only one option; the Kreel may choose survival as a species or else extinction. It matters not to us which you choose.

"The planets and sentient species you have preyed upon and plundered lacked the means of defending themselves against your conceit and brutality. You proclaim yourselves to be an Empire of warriors. That you possess a marginal capability to slaughter a defenseless sentient species does not define you as warriors, it declares you to be vile robbers and murderers. Your crimes against others are ended here, and your pretentious Empire is being uprooted and will be tossed upon a pyre and burnt.

"If the Kreel elect to survive as a species, it will be permitted to choose one of the three central planets you now rule from. That single planet will be designated the home planet of your species and quarantined. That planet will remain quarantined until the Kreel, as a species, proves to the Lux that it has matured adequately to live in peace among other sentient species.

"The Kreel shall immediately begin withdrawing from all other planets that you now criminally occupy. The permitted withdrawal must be fully accomplished during the next 400 of your standard days. On day 401, without warning the Lux will destroy any Kreel ship detected in galactic space or within any solar system. There will be no exceptions.

"To underscore this ultimatum, the total destruction of your ships will commence in the solar system the Kreel Empire considers to be its most powerful– its military solar system. Additionally, after day 401 any Kreel found upon any planet other than the one planet chosen by the Kreel as its home world, will perish.

"Take heed Kreel enemy, the following warning is herewith given but once. As the Kreel withdraw from an occupied planet, if any sentient species is savaged, looted, brutalized, in part or whole enslaved, or else any planetary environment is wantonly destroyed, the Lux will designate the Kreel to be vermin. From that day forward, wherever the Kreel are found, on any planet whatsoever, they will be dealt with accordingly."

As the recorded monologue ended, Groff sat carefully watching Krupp. From having observed Krupp's countenance as he listened to the Lux challenge, Groff had with interest traced Krupp's emotional transformation from disbelief, to shock, and finally to unbridled fury.

Baring his fangs and with a low snarl, Groff firmly appended to the challenge "Grand Marshal Krupp, know this, there is a viable plan for survival during the coming prolonged war. It will be difficult, and the war must take its course. There will be no surrender."

Chapter Thirty-Three:
Unanticipated

Holding back the sheer curtains covering his office window, Admiral Ron Cloud absentmindedly gazed out at the distant horizon, observing it was a beautiful day. Looking nearer, he smiled as he watched children playing in the gentle surf on the nearby beach, their families watching them and enjoying some leisure time.

Letting the curtain fall back in its place, he once more reflected upon his immediate concerns. The Cobalt Blue farewell message from Shey had rippled through Guardian HQ like a sunbeam cavorting across a pond, leaving in its wake a host of nagging unanswered questions. *Blast,* he fretted, *it's no good speculating, what I want are the facts.*

Even as he turned from the window, his desk communicator softly chimed and announced, "Admiral Mer Shawn."

"Communicator, accept the call."

As Mer's frowning countenance filled the monitor, Ron inquired, "Good morning Mer. Given your scowl, I suppose you're calling to ask me what's happening with Kellon."

"You're a bit off base there Ron. I know if you had any information on Kellon, you would've already called me. What I'm calling about is the Nori."

"The Nori? Mer, that's a big topic. Can you narrow it down a bit?"

"Affirmative. Do you have any preliminary results from our monitoring of their drive systems?"

"Except for one item, no. We did determine their transit time from Megan to Glas Dinnein was only two-thirds of our best transit time. As they were departing for Earth, we monitored their ship out to its first Jump point and obtained a broad-spectrum scan of their Jump energy envelope. It has some unique side lobes, and the envelope is still being analyzed."

"Hmmm, cutting a third off our transit times would be significant. As I recall, the Elders recommended we work closely with the Nori, so now we've a good beginning point for a working engineering dialog.

"What's of far more interest to me is your last report concerning the Advanced Cruiser Propulsion Group. Is their recent breakthrough still showing positive results?"

"Indeed Mer. In fact, my understanding is the engineers are working on their first experimental prototypes. And, their initial results seem promising."

"I'm still a bit mystified Ron. I thought everyone agreed that an intragalactic drive was theoretically impossible."

"You're mostly correct, if not outright impossible, it was at least considered theoretically implausible. But, the operative word here is 'theoretically."

"Humph, what prompted the breakthrough?"

"That's the interesting part. It emerged from the analysis of the data Kellon acquired during his encounter with the Elder.

"As you may recall Mer, back when Kellon's squadron was defending Earth, he made some field changes to optimize his passive sensors to detect faint Kreel Jump exit signatures. Those modifications enhanced both his sensor performance and expanded the standard recordings bandwidth. Just before the Elder unexpectedly appeared, Kellon was busy searching for our missing Cruiser Lyst. He had cranked up Lan and Lent's sensors to their limits. And, we got lucky.

"Both Lan and Lent recorded the broad spectrum of energy when the Elder emerged and then later exited our reference time and space. But what really got the physicists' attention was the displacement waveforms generated by Lyst exiting from the temporal cocoon the Elder had spun about him. As I said, we got lucky.

"Our analysis of the elder data is ongoing, and it's grudgingly revealing new insights into the interrelationship of light, time, and matter. Those results are pointing us toward an utterly new temporal displacement technology."

"Hmmm, incredible. If I understand what I've already read, then what we're talking about is a form of dark matter tunneling coupled with an exponential non-linear time displacement technology. If it works, then it could open up access to the entire galaxy. Am I correct?"

"You're correct Mer; the potential for direct point to point synchronous migration is implied, and access to the whole galaxy might be only a first step. There is some evidence that feasible displacement between galaxies might also be possible. But, so far, the full potential of the theory is but a stellar gleam in the physicist's eyes; while it's deemed plausible, it's not yet attained."

"Still, you said the engineers are working on prototypes?"

"Yes, but keep in mind, the key word is prototype. Even the conceptual problems relating to dark bodies and navigation are immense."

"Understood, but still ... hmmm.

"Now, changing the topic, has there been any peer review or meaningful feedback concerning the Kreel torsion field disrupter that Zorn proposed?"

"Yes. And, as we had come to expect from Zorn, his proposal was well developed and thoroughly documented. Our Physicists have gone over his data and proposal with a fine-tooth comb. They have found it well thought out. Even now, they're working closely with the propulsion engineers and setting up a series of field trials. In fact, the initial trials are scheduled to begin during the next few weeks."

"That disruptor could be a game changer Ron, and if possible, I want to be there in attendance when the first field tests are conducted. In the meantime, I've got more work to do on those blasted financial funding arguments. They need some polishing before I can present them to the Assembly. As we anticipated, the Planetary Representatives are constantly griping about our increased revenue expenditures. Naturally, they're also complaining that we're diverting too many cruisers from their normal planetary defense duties to support some vague and covert operation. Their incessant demands for ever more explanations are making my life miserable."

"Ah, that explains your dour disposition. Just remember to keep thinking positive thoughts. You should consider their clamor to be a small indication of their sincere respect for your far-reaching insights and valued wisdom."

"Be careful Ron; keep that malarkey up and I'll be posting you as the Admiral in charge of Fleet Finances."

Unable to restrain his amusement, Ron chuckled. "Don't shoot Mer, I surrender."

"Good! Now you're showing evidence of sound tactical judgment. Mer out."

Even as the monitor darkened, the communicator beeped and it announced the new caller ID. "Captain Ortis."

Hmmm, about time, Ron thought. Hopefully, he will have an update from Kellon.

"Connect the call."

As the swirling image stabilized, the countenance of Captain Ortis appeared. Ron observed he was smiling broadly.

"Captain, you'd better have some good news for me."

"Sir, I do. Admiral Kellon's ciphered battle and status report has just cleared decryption. The good news is all twenty-five cruisers and their Scouts are inbound for home, except we did lose one scout ship in battle, Shey. Regarding her loss, there is some really good news. There was a combined action by Squadron 1 Scouts, and they executed a successful extraction under fire. Commander Galen and Sheba went along side Shey, she was severely damaged - her primary power and drives were down, her hull was open to hard space, and she was blind and inert. In spite of Commanders Roan and Zorn being unconscious, Galen gained entry into Shey and extracted them. Sir, Roan and Zorn are both badly injured, but they are safely aboard Lan. They are stable and the prognosis is that in time they will both recover. How about That Sir! The Scouts went in and pulled Roan and Zorn out!"

"Captain, be advised, you've just redeemed yourself from all the previous bad news you have ever provided. Now hear this, you're to promptly forward a full and detailed copy of both Kellon and Galen's after-action reports to Admiral Mer Shawn and to me. Be certain it contains the complete description of all Scout actions. Given your initial summation, I suspect either a general court martial or else a few decorations are in store for Squadron 1's scalawags. Still, I'm pleased they got Roan and Zorn out alive.

"Now, what about the raid on the planet, how did that turn out?"

"Sir, Kellon's after-action report is complex; more than one-hundred Kreel ships were engaged and destroyed. Furthermore, all designated planetary objectives were fully achieved.

"Sir, there is, however, one element of the report which is unanticipated. I believe it's of particular importance. My recommendation sir is that you review it first."

"What is it?"

"Sir, the Lux has issued an ultimatum to the Kreel Empire. That ultimatum is absolute, and it will directly shape our strategic planning going forward."

"Captain, flag that section for my immediate attention. What is Kellon's ETA?"

"Sir, Lan, Lent, and Lancer's ETA on Glas Dinnein is 18:30 tomorrow."

"Have you notified Operations?"

"Yes Sir. The Five Lux Squadrons entered Guardian space two days ago. At that Jump Point Admiral Kellon released twenty-two cruisers, and they're independently proceeding to their designated home planets. Admiral Cord has already ordered and set in motion arrival teams on each planet to receive all inbound cruisers."

"Captain, Thank you for your concise overview. You're to personally confirm Admiral Mer Shawn receives copies of the reports. Cloud out.

"Communicator, connect Admiral Mer Shawn."

Momentarily the monitor remained dark, and then Mer's scowling countenance appeared.

"Ron, you're distracting me from a most disagreeable task, so this had better be good. What's up?"

"It's good Mer! Ortis has just provided us with the best possible news. Prior to Shey's Cobalt Blue, Galen and Sheba when alongside and extracted Roan and Zorn. They're badly injured, but they're onboard Lan. Their ETA is tomorrow at 18:30."

"That news is definitely good. I'll immediately pass it on to Eryan and Susie. Shey's Cobalt Blue message hit them both hard, and I'll wager they'll both be on hand to welcome Lan and the others home.

"Ron, you're to personally keep me tight in the loop regarding Roan and Zorn's medical condition. I'm glad they survived; I need those two rogues.

"Hmmm, Ron, you look as if something is still troubling you. So, give, what's the skulking problem?"

"Perceptive as usual Mer, there's one more problematic item. Ortis is forwarding you Kellon's after-action report. It seems Kellon, speaking on behalf of the Lux, has issued an ultimatum to the Kreel Empire. Ortis is flagging that item for our immediate attention. He has recommended we read it first."

"An ultimatum? Hmmm, I hadn't anticipated that. I'll not only read it first, but twice and carefully.

"Be advised Ron, both Kellon and you are herewith cordially invited to be standing in my office the day after tomorrow, at 14:00 sharp. I'll be providing a celebratory glass of wine at that time, just before I require Kellon to brief us on his actions. The technicality of properly delivering my invitation to Kellon is a detail I'm leaving to you to handle. Mer out."

As Ron leaned back in his chair, he cupped his hands behind his head and studiously studied the ceiling, deep in thought. *At least there's good news, and then again there's that ultimatum. By all the Muses, I've got that old sinking feeling the fat has just dropped into the fire....*

Chapter Thirty-Four:
The Clock is Running

Moving with a purposeful stride, Commodore Roy Grey departed his private compartment and walked through the passageway toward the elevators. He did not encounter a single person. After the long mission, Lan had come to rest on his landing cradle on Glas Dinnein. The normal arrival hubbub had already swept over and through Lan. Everyone in the crew who could be spared had already gone ashore. Only the minimal command, security, and shipyard inspection and maintenance crew remained onboard.

Entering the elevator, Roy selected the hangar deck. When the door opened, he exited and turned toward Shey's hangar. He observed the status lights on three hangars were glowing with a soft warm golden hue– denoting they were occupied and their interior atmospheres were equalized with Lan's internal pressure. He then noted the status light on Shey's hangar was dark, and its hatch was dogged open.

Being planetside, the normal operational background sounds of crew, power, drive, and machinery were minimal. As he walked along the passageway, Roy was aware of the subtle odors of air-conditioning, electronics, lubrication, and human beings. He associated the reassuring and familiar odors as being a subtle part of Lan's normal ambiance.

Stepping over the lower rim of the open hatch, Roy entered the dimly illuminated void of Shey's hangar. As he entered, the other occupant of the hangar turned toward him and Commander Galen's bemused frown promptly transformed into a smile of recognition.

"Commodore, I thought you'd gone ashore hours ago."

"Not quite yet, Galen. I've got some admin-recordkeeping to wrap up first. But, why are you still aboard and loitering about in an empty hangar?"

"Empty? Sir, for me it's not empty. It's chockablock full from its overhead to its deck and between its bulkheads with years of good memories. Admittedly, presently those memories are sorta mixed up with some troubling thoughts. Which, I suppose explains why I'm standing here.

"Sir, might I inquire, what brings you down to Shey's hangar?"

"Well, both Sheba and Lan suggested you might just want some company. Then, Lan did mention something about Sheba being concerned about your welfare. And, if Sheba is concerned, then I'm also concerned."

"Humph, I tend to forget one of Sheba's minor background tasks is plumbing my psyche. She's quite astute. Admittedly, I'm a bit tired and perhaps listing somewhat off my vertical plumb line," Galen said.

"Since I find you lurking about in an empty hangar, might I safely wager your troubled thoughts have something to do with Shey?"

"Yes Sir, some of my thoughts are about Shey, but others concern the Kreel and the war in general."

"Hmmm, all bundled together, those topics encompass a broad and stormy sea. What seems to be the core problem troubling you?"

"Sir, while it's not the core issue, my friend Shey isn't here where she belongs. She's been reduced to expanding vapors spreading out in a distant Kreel solar system. I'm finding that fact hard to register."

"Galen, we've both lost shipmates before, and it's never easy. Other than Shey, are you able to zero in on the central issue that's troubling you?"

"Sir, you're correct. It's not only Shey. It's about our latest tour of duty. Instead of defending our homes, we're jumping light years into Kreel space and killing innocent beings and destroying infrastructures on distant planets. Sir, it doesn't feel right.

"And, like most of the crew, I've listened more than once to the ultimatum delivered to the Kreel. It's blunt. Having fought the Kreel for several hundred years, ultimatum or not, I doubt they will just fold their tents and give up. They're the Kreel, and they'll fight. So, I've been asking myself, what's next?"

"Galen, before we begin exploring that dark topic, might I request Sheba's hospitality and a cup of neab?"

"Certainly, I apologize for not offering it earlier. Sheba, we've got an inbound Commodore; you'd better put the water on to boil."

"Commodore Grey, you are always most welcome aboard. The water is on and the beans are being ground," Sheba inserted.

Leading the way from Shey's hangar, Galen crossed the passageway and held open Sheba's hangar hatch for Roy. After Roy had entered, Galen stepped into the hangar and closed and dogged the hatch behind him. Turning, he led Roy across the narrow deck and up the short gangplank and into Sheba. Moving forward, they reached the mess area, and Roy sat down at the small table.

"Sheba, thank you for your warm hospitality," Roy said, leaning back in his chair.

Galen had busied himself in the galley and soon returned with two large mugs of steaming neab. Placing one mug before Roy, he took the seat opposite from him and sat down, holding his own cup between his hands.

Sipping tentatively from his mug, Roy looked up and smiled. "Now, that's what I call a good cup of neab."

Putting his mug on the table, Roy paused to study Galen's inquiring countenance. "Galen, we've been fighting the Kreel for most of our lives. Fighting them isn't new. What's new is that for the first time we've shifted to the offense. And, unfortunately, doing that does involve the harsh reality of unintentionally killing some innocent beings and destroying infrastructure. You know we're striving hard to minimize the collateral loss of life and property, but it still happens."

"Sir, that I understand. Still, that fact doesn't make anything easier."

"Perhaps it might help you to know you're not the only person struggling with that problem. Most of the crew is, including Admiral Kellon. Now, what else is troubling you?" Roy asked.

"Sir, our overall strategy depends on maintaining a ruse. If the Kreel discover our deception, they'll pivot and in fury focus their entire military might squarely on our most vulnerable planets. That means they'll likely attack Earth or Megan."

"That's a possibility, and the stakes are high. Still, the key term in your summation is 'if,' and the Kreel must first find Earth and Megan. We need to keep the Kreel off balance and see they don't discover our deception," Roy countered.

"Sir, the Kreel aren't noted for their negotiation skills or surrendering. I wouldn't wager a brew that they will do either. This then begs the strategic question, how will the Kreel respond to the Lux ultimatum? My opinion is they'll deem it a bluff or else sheer bravado. So, what comes next?"

"Galen, bluff and bravado are not applicable terms. In six Kreel solar systems, we have forcibly demonstrated that they are vulnerable. They're still busy picking up the pieces and trying to figure out what happened. I doubt Grand Admiral Groff is considering the Lux ultimatum to be either bluff or bravado. If he's half as capable as I believe, then he must realize there's a real and deadly power threatening his Empire. He has a big problem."

"Sir, if your presumption is correct, then what will be his most probable response?"

"Galen, as you already know, there exist a few firm truths where warfare is involved. Firstly, war is not a game. Before ever beginning a devastating war, it's wiser to seek a lasting peace. Because wars are dangerous and unpredictable exercises in mayhem, this logical choice is just common sense.

When you do find yourself in a war, where an unconditional victory over your enemy can't be attained, which is the normal case, you'll eventually be compelled to sit down with that enemy and negotiate for peace. Because of this, all military tactics employed should be tempered; past war crimes have a nasty way of coming back to haunt negotiators who are compelled to sit at a negotiating table.

"Finally, when warfare proves to be unavoidable, as with the Kreel, there are four fundamental choices. capitulation; fight for an eventual unconditional victory; fight for a stalemate and negotiation; fight to the death.

We already know the Kreel do not negotiate. And when fighting the Kreel, there are but two choices, fight or else be eaten. Having rejected the option of being eaten, for centuries we've fought a bloody and costly stalemate, while hoping for a technical breakthrough and ultimately an unconditional victory.

"Admiral Mer Shawn now believes we have firmly attained the technical superiority over the Kreel. He has ordered Admiral

Kellon to exploit our advantage and aggressively prosecute the war and to bring it to its final and unconditional conclusion. He has placed few restrictions on Admiral Kellon. It's unrestricted warfare, which includes the eradication of the Kreel as a species."

"Sir, the ultimatum holds out an offer to the Kreel; it offers them a home world. That's not eradication."

"No, it isn't. Admiral Kellon considers the eradication of any intelligent species abhorrent, unless there exists no alternative. The ultimatum to the Kreel is plainly stated, and it's plain and without deceit. The Kreel would be prudent, if they understand the ultimatum means precisely what it openly declares, including the potential for species eradication."

"Sir, the Kreel undoubtedly understand making an ultimatum is one thing, enforcing it is another. What's your own personal opinion as to how they will respond?"

"Humph, Galen, I don't have a crystal ball. Still, by their nature they are predators and view weaker species as their prey. The Lux has just forcibly demonstrated they are not a weaker species. So, now the Kreel are compelled to ask who is the predator, and which is the prey. Ask yourself, in nature what typically happens when two predator species collide in a turf battle? It is that basic question which brings us back to the aforementioned fundamental choices.

Still, a formal challenge was issued to the Kreel. If history means anything, then the Kreel will take up that challenge and fight. Which means, the ultimatum has designated a specific date and location for a bruiser of a battle. Beyond that event, I'm not predicting anything."

Still holding his mug in both hands, Galen dubiously shook his head. "Sir, which means in about a year, we'll be penetrating the most fortified solar system in the Kreel Empire. With Technical advantages or otherwise, looking for a fight within that fully-alerted solar system is a gambit. It sorta feels like we're wagering the whole farm on one toss of the dice. Sorta high stakes!"

"Galen, we've known and served with Admiral Kellon for a long time. And the one sure thing we know about him is that he doesn't casually put our lives at risk. There're always risks in any battle, but the Admiral has repeatedly proven he has the farsighted skill to minimize those risks. Our last battle underscores that fact. If the Admiral determines we can penetrate into the Kreel military solar system and then kick butt, I'll be standing right there along with him and helping to get the job done."

"Yes Sir."

"Galen, we've just come home from a long and difficult tour of duty. You've got some good reasons to be tired, and that's understandable. Now, just between us old friends, and as my dear mother would tell you, it's time you give it a rest.

"Having said that, and now speaking as your Captain, I'm giving you a direct order. You have one hour to square away your affairs aboard Sheba. Then for your own sake, during the next two weeks I'd better not see hide nor hair of you. Do you understand?"

"Sir, yes Sir," Galen replied, with both a salute and a grin.

"Now Sheba, young lady, hear this! If Galen doesn't take time off to visit family and friends and to flirt with some pretty ladies, you are to promptly report his dereliction of duty to Lan. Do you understand?"

"Sir, yes Sir." Sheba responded with a cheery voice.

"Captain," Lan inserted. "I have just received an update regarding Commander Roan from Guardian Medical. He is still in an induced stasis and unconscious, but their guarded prognosis is he will recover."

"Lan, is there any new information regarding Zorn?" Galen asked.

"Yes Sir, Commander Zorn is fully conscious. Guardian Medical has taken him off the guarded list. He is restricted for the next three months to a program of therapy and light duty. Sir, there is also an appended footnote. It says the Commander is becoming a most troublesome patient. He is demanding to be returned to full duty."

"Well, there you have it, Galen. You've no further reason for skulking in empty hangars. The clock is running, so you'd better get moving Commander. Remember, two weeks and not one minute less, or else you'll find your leave canceled and be scrubbing floors and polishing brass for the next month!"

Chapter Thirty-Five:
Gathering of Friends

As the small speeder descended, the strobing flash of a splintering ribbon of lightening illuminated the early evening sky, and ominous dark thunder clouds were rushing near. Racing ahead of the approaching storm, McRoy brought the small craft about through a tight turn, continuing the steep descent. As the vehicle dropped, Susie's stomach lurched in protest. Clenching her teeth and grasping tight the support handles, she pressed against the forward bulkhead with her legs and braced herself against the seat back. Suddenly rolling, McRoy sharply reversed the flight path and straightened the craft, continuing his precariously steep descent toward the beacon marking a landing pad.

The speeder crossed low over a turbulent storm-tossed ocean, and above a rocky coastline, as McRoy proficiently slowed the speeder. Bringing it to a hover, he gently landed. As the craft firmly settled and stopped, Susie softly groaned. Raising her head she closed her eyes and muttered a soft inaudible prayer of thanksgiving to the Divine, then turned to look at McRoy.

"McRoy, every time we make a STEEP approach like that my stomach gets queasy," Susie said.

"Just for the record Ambassador, so does mine. And for the record, I'm also innocent in this entire matter."

"Are you then blaming me?" Susie asked, feigning innocence.

"If you'll recall, you're the Assembly Representative who urgently demanded to see Admiral Kellon, bad weather front or otherwise. And, how about that, you were absolutely correct, in spite of my doubts and protests, we made it in one piece– but barely!"

Even as McRoy was talking, the storm fully engulfed the small craft and it shook as buffeting winds swirled about it. Above their heads the sky blazed with sizzling streamers of lightning, and torrents of rain sheeted down out of the darkness, splashing energetically against the windows of the grounded craft. Nearby a crackling bolt of lightning struck a tree, and a shower of broken limbs began cascading down through the upper tree branches. Susie flinched.

"Humph, that was kind of close. McRoy, just perhaps you were right after all. It seems we might have cut the margin of safety a little tight for comfort."

"Do you think?" McRoy said, teasing.

Even as McRoy spoke, a small van rolled up through the downpour and came to a stop next to the speeder. The communicator activated.

"It's a bit wet out here folks, so I suggest you hop aboard. There's a good fire going in the fireplace, and if you're interested, there's some hot stew on the stove," Kellon said.

McRoy glanced over toward Susie. "Madam Ambassador, are you ready to transfer to our next mode of transportation?"

Turning, Susie snapped the leash on Gepeto's collar and picked up the straps of her backpack. "Aye, aye Sir! Ready, willing, and able. Let's make a break for it."

Looking at the cascading downpour, McRoy adjusted the surrounding force field in hope of providing a modicum of protection. Then, picking up the straps of his own back pack, he swung open the gull-wing door nearest the van. When Kellon saw the speeder door swing up, he slid open the side door on the van.

Clambering out of the speeder, McRoy, Susie, and Gepeto headed for the security afforded by the van. McRoy only paused long enough to close and secure the door on the craft before following Susie and Gepeto into the waiting vehicle. In spite of the modest protection provided by the adjusted force field, the wind-driven downpour soaked people and dog alike. As he climbed into the van, McRoy quickly slid its door shut behind him.

Leaning back and with a broad grin McRoy said, "Sir, reporting, safe aboard and all shipmates accounted for."

"You're most welcome aboard; Hang on and we'll soon be under cover," Kellon said, cheerfully.

Turning the van about, Kellon drove through the heavy rain and up a gentle hill about a kilometer to a house. As the van reached the dwelling, a garage door swung up and the van entered into a lighted volume. The garage door promptly descended behind the van, closing out the darkness and the sounds of the storm that was intensifying beyond.

Turning about, Kellon glanced at his rain-drenched guests. "Welcome to Far Haven. I'm happy to see you, but I'm admittedly curious about what's so important that you have braved a storm to visit at this time."

As he was talking, Kellon opened the driver's side door and slid back the van door. Gepeto was the first to jump out and greet his old friend. In response Kellon reached down and with a broad smile scratched behind Gepeto's ears.

Susie followed Gepeto out of the van, still carrying her back pack. The first thing she did was to throw her arms about him and give Kellon a big hug. "Thank you, it's wonderful to see you again!"

"Take it easy there girl; my ribs aren't as young as they once were," Kellon said, laughing.

"Sir, it's wonderful you gave us permission to intrude. I know that Eurie and you have only been home a week following a long mission, and you must value your privacy," Susie said.

As Susie was talking with Kellon, the garage door into the house had opened. Standing in the doorway, Eurie had heard Susie's comment.

"We'll hear no more of that young lady; you're always most welcome in our home. Come right in here and get out of those wet clothes. Kellon, help Susie with her bag."

"Yes ma'am," Kellon replied.

Reaching out and lifting Susie's pack by its straps, Kellon slightly bowed and with a generous sweeping gesture of his free arm, he ushered McRoy and Susie through the door and into the house, Gepeto bounding in ahead of everyone.

As they came through the door, Eurie efficiently collected their coast and busied herself hanging them on pegs to dry. Then she made certain they had removed their wet shoes and put on house slippers. As she was busy with Susie and McRoy, Kellon employed a cloth to wipe and dry Gepeto's paws.

Leading the way through the entry hall, Eurie directed her guests into the main living room. Kellon, with a smile, brought up the rear.

As Kellon had said upon his arrival, there was a well-built fire burning in a large stone fireplace. It was casting copious warmth into the well-furnished and illuminated room.

Turning slowly about and looking at the room, Susie was wonderstruck. There was not a hint of a video monitor or electronic device to be seen. There was, however, a well-filled bookcase on one wall. Rich wood paneling, open dark beams, and a natural wood cathedral feeling complimented the room. Its polished floor boasted broad planks of a hard wood, accented by contrasting square wood pegs of a darker color. Tastefully arranged throughout the room were ample comfortable seating and several side tables for use by a small group of people. The indirect lighting in the room was soft, which added to the warm ambiance created by the flickering light cast by the fire. The only direct lighting came from a beautifully crafted wooden frame in which a cylinder of opaque golden-hued translucent material was held and from which a soft light shone forth. The entire light fixture was suspended by a brass chain that was connected to a hook on the ceiling.

As she continued to look about her, Susie's attention was drawn to a glass case in which was displayed a magnificent model of a full rigged three-mast sailing ship. All of its complex rigging was in place and its sails were unfurled and shaped as if they were capturing a stiff sea breeze. Then a deep resonant gonging caused her to turn, and in astonishment she saw a beautiful grandfather clock in a corner; its rich dark wood was gleaming with a lustrous oil finish.

Turning back to look at Eurie and Kellon, who were quietly watching the reactions of their guest, she exclaimed "It's utterly beautiful. I had no idea you were traditionalist."

"Now, that is surprising," Eurie said.

"Why?" Susie asked.

"Well, you've traveled more than once aboard Lan. You know how austere and functionally efficient the interior of a cruiser must be. That's why when we come back home it's traditional that's precisely what Kellon and I want. What do you think? Do you like it?" Eurie asked.

"Do I like it? It's absolutely wonderful. In fact, the Admiral and you might have to physically toss me out of the door before I reluctantly leave."

"Humph, be advised Susie, the house rules are few, but strict. Here in Far Haven there is no need for rank or titles. Here Eurie is in charge, and I rather like it that way," Kellen said.

As Susie was talking, McRoy had walked first to the ship's model, which he had studied and admired. Then he had turned and walked over to the grandfather clock and stood looking at its exterior and through its small glass door at the three brass weights suspended by long brass chains. After watching the pendulum swing for a moment on its ceaseless cycle, he turned toward Kellon with a mystified expression.

"Sir, I've never before seen a mechanical clock like that, not even in a museum. May I ask, what's its history?"

"Well, in my leisure hours I enjoy building things, like the ship model and the clock. When I was on Earth, I saw and acquired the design specifications for that particular clock. On Earth it's called a grandfather clock, and its mechanism is quite busy. When I returned home, I found crafting the clock from the adapted specifications was challenging, pleasurable, and rewarding. In fact, I've grown fond of its hourly gongs and quarterly hour chimes."

"Everyone, that's quite enough chatter. I've some warm stew on the stove and fresh baked bread in the kitchen," Eurie said.

Leading the way, Eurie directed her guests into the spacious kitchen and saw them seated about a round wood table that had two drop leaves, which were then lifted and locked in place. As everyone took their seats, Eurie busied herself with serving a generous stew into bowls, which Kellon carried over to the table. Then Eurie brought a block of cheese and a fresh loaf of whole grain bread on a small cutting board, while Kellon busied himself pouring glasses of a red wine. Within a few minutes everyone was sitting and enjoying a simple but appreciated repast.

Looking up, Eurie inquired of Susie, "Well, I'm a little curious about what brings you and McRoy out on a night like this. It must be important."

"I think it is, however, you may not agree. It's about the ultimatum the Lux presented to the Kreel."

"Susie, that particular topic is classified Black Hole, and I was unaware you knew anything about it," Kellon said.

"Sir, as you know, I'm cleared for Black Hole information, and in my work with the Assembly there is a need to know. At present I'm following a tenuous thread of research involving the Kreel. I've been weaving together several interrelated events, including something the Elder told you and me."

"Hmmm, that encounter with the Elder was unanticipated and I've not forgotten it. What particular thread are you following?" Kellon asked.

"Sir, it's about the Kreel and what is happening. Several days ago I was thinking back to when the first two Kreel fast attack ships reached Earth. I remembered that Kur challenged them, and there was a brief exchange of threats between the Kreel and the Arkillians, and I vaguely remembered what Kur told the Kreel."

Opening her pack, Susie reached in and withdrew Rodney's small polished box, placing it upon the table. "Rodney, as usual I suspect you have been eavesdropping," Susie said, cheerfully.

"Madam Ambassador, I have only performed my duty. Before I answer your question, it is most appropriate I greet our hosts and our mutual friends. Good evening Captain Eurie, Admiral Kellon, Commander McRoy, Lan, and of course Lent. This is a wonderful gathering of old friends and shipmates.

"Regarding your question, Ambassador, I do have William's file on the topic. At that time, however, both Lan and Lent were near Earth. I understand that they both monitored the communications between the Kreel and Arkillians. Undoubtedly they can provide a full transcript of the exchange. That is, if you prefer," Rodney responded, with a formal British accent.

"Hmmm, what's up with Rodney? I don't remember him being so formal," Eurie mused.

"He's just being difficult. His attitude shifted after I left him on Megan to help Darrell Fann. Later he was required to remain incommunicado while onboard the Nori ship. I think he's a little miffed," Susie replied, with a slight tone of frustration.

"Lan," Kellon asked, "is Rodney correct? Can you provide us a transcript of the exchange between the Kreel and the Arkillians?"

Chapter Thirty-Six:
Speculation

Eurie's kitchen was filled with the inviting aroma of warm bread and the hearty fragrance of rich stew. The four-people sitting at the kitchen table stopped what they were doing, each waiting to hear Lan's reply.

"Good evening everyone. Like Rodney, Lent and I have been monitoring your discussion with great interest. Sir, Rodney is correct. A full transcript of the exchange between the Kreel and Arkillians commanders is available, if desired," Lan said, his full and resonant voice emerging from a sound transducer well concealed in the ceiling.

"Lan, can you narrow down the dialog between the Kreel and Arkillians to the most pertinent part?" Eurie asked.

"Given the Ambassador's previous statements, I believe that is possible. I will begin the transcript with a threat made by the Kreel commander and then continue with the Arkillian response made by Council Member Kur. The transcript of the Kreel commander's threat follows.

'Arkillian mongrel, you are very far from home and your precious ruling council. I spit on your demand for my identification and rank. The Kreel go wherever they will to go. It is enough you know I am your absolute master, and you are now notified that I have claimed this entire solar system in the name of the Kreel Hub. Therefore, I have designated all those now within this heliosphere as our prey, and that includes your Nest ship and you. It is therefore you who are trespassing!

'In order to demonstrate your proper respect for the Kreel, you have until I arrive at your current location to get your fat slow barge underway. I am ordering you back to Scion. If you defy my orders, I will destroy you where you are. If you should survive the crossing to Scion, the Kreel may permit you to live. You might even be allowed to scrub toilets along with any other members of your pathetic ruling council that may be still alive.'

"Sir, Council Member Kur's response to the Kreel threat follows."

'Kreel braggart, do you believe the Arkillian accept such boastful declarations from a coward? You speak of mongrels, but it is your genetically polluted kind that has no natural or proper beginning in space or time.

'Your insolence is noted braggart, and it is not pardoned. If you think you have the courage and power to fight the Arkillian, then come here and embrace your death.'

"Sir, will that be sufficient?" Lan asked.

"What do you think Susie, will that suffice?" Kellon asked.

"Yes Sir, that is wonderful. Thank you, Lan.

Please note, while the Kreel called the Arkillians mongrels, in Kur's response he stated the Kreel are genetically polluted, having no natural or proper beginning in space or time.

"The Arkillians had worked with, knew, and traded with the Kreel for thousands of years. They know far more about their history than we do. When Kur called the Kreel 'genetically polluted' I believe he was implying the Kreel are a genetically engineered life form."

Frowning, Eurie sighed. "Susie, what you are saying is very troubling. While it's possible, it's still just speculation."

"So far, it may only seem speculation; however, there is more information available. Sir, do you remember when the Elder told us that they moved a third group of humans from Earth out into the stars?"

"Yes, and as I recall the Elder also gave us a warning. He said that group perished because of their abject foolishness. He cautioned us to carefully consider our actions. Since then, I've come to consider his warning as being more general than specific in nature."

"Sir, when viewed in its proper frame of reference, I believe the warning is quite specific. When I talked with Chandara about what happened to that third group, she became extremely reticent. Still, she did affirm the Elders seeded that group about 13,000 years ago. She also said the Elders had given them a jump start in the physical and biological sciences. And, what she then told me has troubled me for some time now."

"In what way was it troubling?" Eurie asked.

"Well, according to Chandara, the Nori considered the culture of the third group to be unhealthy and dangerously unstable. They had advanced in both the physical and biological sciences, and then they began exploiting genetic engineering in a wholly foolish, dangerous, and self-destructive fashion. The Nori considered they lacked even rudimentary common sense. The predictable outcome of their folly was their utter ruin and extinction."

"Susie, obviously what you are speaking about has a point, but I'm still foggy regarding what that point is," Kellon said.

"Sir, my point is I believe the genesis of the Kreel can be found in the genetic engineering laboratories of the third group of humans. If true, this would explain why the Kreel so hate humanity, and also explain their intense focus on their true blood movement. In all probability, they would have turned on their creators, then destroyed them. As Chandara said, those people are no more."

As Susie was talking, Eurie was cutting a slice of cheese. When she heard Susie's startling conclusion she stopped and put the knife down. Frowning she turned, looking toward Susie.

"I find it difficult to believe any sane and responsible culture would permit such a horrible aberration of science," Eurie said.

"Why?" Susie asked.

"Well, recognizing the common-sense dangers inherent in genetic engineering, we've always tightly regulated the applications of that discipline. It's narrowly limited to correcting verified genetic damage in an individual or species. Any experimentation involving cross-species would be depraved, sheer ignorance compounded by arrogance. And, doubly so when using human genetic material. Such genetic gambling is abhorrent in the extreme."

"Depraved or otherwise, it once happened on Earth," Susie said.

"You can't be serious," Kellon said, dumfounded.

"I am most serious. About five hundred years ago, back in 2016, the criminal activity of some corporations became scary. Exploiting bribes and exerting political pressure on government officials, the corporations wheedled the United States National Institute of Health to remove its prohibitions on cross species experimentation. After that the corporations were permitted to intermix the genes of animals with human genes. The corporations had also gained access to the technology permitting the isolation and manipulation of long strands of DNA.

229

Predictably, the manipulated strands of DNA were then used in cross species experimentation. All of this was being done in the name of advancing science, improving food production, and supposedly for the advancement of beneficial medical applications. Unfortunately, in truth most of the experimentation was motivated by nothing more than pure avarice. Making matters worse, there were whispered horror stories about some of the biological results."

Eurie had sat listening in shocked disbelief. "Susie, that's hideous. How could it have ever been permitted?"

"Eurie, as I said, it happened five hundred years ago, when the Arkillians were still involved. That was a dreadful age of moral and cultural darkness. It was a disconcerting time, one which included two global wars, the use of nuclear weapons, and hundreds of smaller regional conflicts, which together killed hundreds of millions of innocent people."

Eurie frowned. I keep forgetting the Arkillians were involved. It has been about five years since Lan first discovered Earth, and so much has happened since then."

Turning toward Kellon, Susie thoughtfully paused a moment before speaking. "Sir, I wholeheartedly agree with Eurie. So very much has happened, and all of it was made possible because of your efforts."

"Humph, that will be enough of that. Always remember, many people have been involved in all the hard work being performed. That includes you. Although, I'll readily admit that the Earth was and remains a colossal political and sociological mess. Nevertheless, its fables, literature and music represent an incredibly diverse treasure."

"Sir, I've often talked with Chandara about what happened on Earth and the terrible past ages in Earth's history. She is quick to remind me that many of Earth's fractious racial problems and resulting wars were the products of Arkillian interference and criminally motivated social engineering. Also, although she can't confirm it, she firmly believes the Old One, Illuyan, was most likely busy working behind the scenes and fermenting many of the global problems. What happened on Earth, according to Chandara, was in keeping with the vile style and known methods that the Old One prefers to use. As you undoubtedly remember, the Elder warned us Illuyan is now helping the Kreel."

"I do remember that, and I also remember Chandara warned us not to verbalize that name, because doing so might draw its attention," Kellon said, reprovingly.

"Oops," Susie said, putting her hand over her mouth.

"Susie, what you're telling us is important and also disturbing, but we've wandered far afield from our original topic - the Kreel. How does all this Earth insanity and GMO mess relate to the Kreel? Eurie asked.

"First of all, because the Old One is now involved, there is a possible connection. Also, since the crimes against nature and humanity involving GMO did occur on Earth, the mysterious third human group might have committed even worse crimes against nature. I believe they did, and in doing so they gave us the abomination we call the Kreel."

"Susie, even with the disturbing history you've provided, your thesis remains only speculation," Eurie said.

"Up to this point, I agree. There's, however, one additional set of facts that I haven't yet presented. I believe it conclusively proves my thesis."

"Well, spread it out on the table, and let's see what you've got," McRoy said.

"Well, I've just talked with Guardian Medical services about the Kreel. What I learned is classified Black Hole, and the information prompted me to come here to talk with Admiral Kellon, storm or no storm."

Cradling his wine Glas between his hands, Kellon had listened to Susie, and his countenance was troubled. Frowning, Kellon let out a slow breath.

"Ambassador Wells, do not say anything else," Kellon said peremptorily.

Putting his wine glass on the table, Kellon pushed his chair back. Standing up, Kellon slowly glanced around the table.

"Please continue with your meal. The Ambassador and I must excuse ourselves for a few minutes to have a private conversation."

When Susie stood, Gepeto also began to stand. Noticing his effort, Susie affectionately smiled.

"Gepeto, down and stay. It's OK, I'll be right back"

Looking up at Susie with concern, Gepeto's tail was not wagging. As commanded, he reluctantly laid down, and continued watching her.

Kellon pushed his and Susie's chairs back under the table, and as Eurie, McRoy, and Gepeto watched, he then turned and led the way from the kitchen back into the front room. Susie followed.

Walking over to the fireplace, Kellon opened up the screen and put several pieces of wood on the fire, and securely closed the screen. Turning from the warm fire, he looked thoughtfully at Susie.

"Susie, please take a seat. You may as well be relaxed while we talk.

Turning about, Susie quickly found a comfortable chair and sat down. She then looked toward Kellon and waited anxiously for him to begin the conversation.

Chapter Thirty-Seven:
Black Hole Stuff

As Kellon stood by the fireplace his expression was attentive, and Susie observed he was in a serious mood. Even with the relaxed ambiance of the room, she could feel the underlying tension he was masking behind his calm demeanor.

"Susie, admittedly I'm aware of some Black Hole information which might support your thesis, however, it's so tightly held even Eurie and Lent are not aware of it. In as few words as possible, please tell me who provided you with your information."

"Sir, I was told the information is extremely sensitive. The Guardian scientist I spoke with also told me you have firsthand knowledge of what I was being told."

"Susie, who authorized the scientist to give you the information?" Kellon asked.

"Sir, indirectly it was Eryan Kyrie. After I told her of the thread of research I was following, she talked with Admiral Mer Shawn. They discussed my request in private, and then afterwards they directed me to meet with a Guardian research Scientist. That scientist is my single source of factual information. Do you wish to know his identity?"

"No, at least not at the moment. Although, I may ask you for his name and contact information later.

"After you spoke with the scientist, did you tell anyone else about what you have learned?"

"No sir. The only individual I have talked to is the scientist who provided me with the information. Eryan told me I was not to report back or to tell her what I learned. She said there's no reason for her to know. I did, however, tell her of my intention to come here to talk with you. She approved of my coming here for that purpose."

"Humph, well as for security protocol, that's good enough for me. Now, in simple terms, tell me what you've learned."

"Sir, the first information I obtained was that following one of your deep penetration missions into Kreel space, you returned to Glas Dinnein with several bodies of high ranking Kreel Officers, including the body of the Kreel Elite One.

"From talking with Chandara, I also know that her last memories, before waking up on Glas Dinnein, was being a prisoner. She also remembers being thrown into a dark cell aboard the Elite One's personal ship. Knowing this, I have surmised there is a direct connection between your rescue of Chandara and your obtaining the Kreel bodies you brought to Glas Dinnein. I, however, don't have a clue as to how you managed to rescue Chandara. Admittedly, I would really like to hear that story someday, if possible.

"As for the Kreel and my thesis, the scientist told me Guardian medical personnel conducted extensive autopsies on the Kreel Elite One and his staff Officers. They discovered the Elite One and several of his higher-ranking Officers had some human DNA strands spliced into their DNA. In other Kreel bodies they examined, such as the bodies of common Kreel warriors, they found no trace of human DNA."

As Susie was talking, a log on the lower part of the stack of burning wood collapsed and the higher logs settled. There was a brief flaring up of flames, accompanied by crackling and popping sounds.

Frowning absent mindedly at the fireplace, Kellon barely audibly mused, "By all the shades of the True Blood."

"Susie, for reasons relating to Black Hole security matters, I cannot discuss anything with you about how Chandara was rescued or what happened to the Kreel Elite One. The information that you've given me about the autopsy results is new evidence, and I wasn't aware of it. Obviously, what you have learned is strictly Black Hole, and it must remain tightly compartmentalized. Without first obtaining my personal approval, you will not discuss any aspect of what you have learned with anyone, and I do mean with anyone. Do you understand?"

"Yes Sir, perfectly."

Kellon stood for a moment contemplating what Susie had told him. the new information concerning human DNA necessitated he reconsider and reset some of his initial battle planning. Given Susie's information, new targets were indicated and other strikes would need rescheduling. The ethical and moral implications of Susie's information mandated he meet with Admirals Mer Shawn, Dylan Cord, and Ron Cloud. The Downtime rest-period before Lan once again lifted ship to penetrate Kreel space was beginning to narrow. That could not be helped. Slowly exhaling, Kellon glanced toward Susie.

"Ambassador, I'm once more in your debt. What you've told me here will definitely impact our upcoming operations. For the moment, we should return to the kitchen and rejoin Eurie and McRoy."

Susie stood, and walking together with Kellon, they returned to the warm hospitality of Eurie's kitchen. When they entered the kitchen, Eurie and McRoy were sitting at the table and laughing about a new comedy play being performed in the Capital. When Kellon and Susie returned, Eurie and McRoy ceased their conversations and with evident curiosity looked toward them.

"Well, is it permissible to ask about the outcome of your private talk?" Eurie asked.

Reclaiming his chair and retrieving his glass of wine, Kellon replied, "Sorry, the private discussion falls squarely in the category of Black Hole stuff. Suffice it to say the Kreel are still the Kreel. Susie's information has, however, provided me with some valuable insights and suggested additional possibilities in structuring long-term strategic goals."

Knowing Kellon as she did, Eurie carefully studied his calm non-committal expression. "What you're not telling us tends to suggest what rests at the core of Susie's thesis. The implications are troubling, however, since it relates to Black Hole matters, I won't ask any more questions."

Eurie looked thoughtfully toward Susie. "It seems that we need to thank you for your valued insights, yet again."

Pushing her chair back, Eurie briskly stood and took charge of directing kitchen chores. "Attention everyone, please put your dirty dishes into the house-maid, and Kellon I suggest you open another bottle of wine. And, given the special occasion, I recommend it be one of our limited bottles of vintage Kintana Gold. Now hear this everyone, we are moving to the front room to continue our conversations. The standing orders for the remainder of the evening are there will be no further discussions, whatsoever, about the Kreel, warfare, or Cruiser tactics. The only exceptions I'll accept are remembrances of one special Scout ship named Shey.

Turning, Uri glanced at Susie. "McRoy told me that you've planned an early departure in the morning. So, while Kellon is busy finding a bottle of wine and pulling a cork, come along with me and I'll show McRoy and you where to find your rooms and where the guest towels and such are stored."

As the evening proceeded, the four good friends and three AIs exchanged shared memories, bantered about earlier times, and talked about old friends. Their conversations, mingled with future hopes, all interlaced with desires for cessation of warfare and a longing for peace. Often during the conversations, Shey was frequently remembered and definitely missed.

For several hours following the closing of the conversations between friends, and the lights being turned off, Susie lay in her bed restlessly going over in her mind what Kellon had told her. Her new information would impact the upcoming strike missions. She had wanted to ask him more about that, but she knew better. As he had said, it was Black Hole stuff. Growing tired, rolling over she whispered "Good night Gepeto, I'll see you in the morning."

The rhythmic sound of Gepeto's tail thumping on the floor came as his warm response. She smiled, and then yawning she fell fitfully asleep.

Following the night's intense storm, the rolling tree covered countryside was bright and awash in a myriad of rich shades of green, and it was sparkling clean. The bright orb of the sun had climbed but a few degrees above the eastern horizon, and the morning sea breeze was both crisp and delightfully refreshing. In fascination and delight Susie watched as flocks of sea birds, all adorned in their gaudy plumage, skimmed above and darted along the retreating waves, each searching for its elusive breakfast. From the surrounding trees came the tuneful and playful sounds of song birds. Feeling the moisture of a light mist caressing her skin, Susie smiled and deeply inhaled the clean sea air. At that moment, she was happy to simply be alive.

Unexpectedly, Eurie had come down from the house with Kellon to see her friends safely off. As her visitors boarded the speeder, there was a traditional exchange of banter and good wishes between everyone. Waving, Eurie graciously and cheerfully invited everyone to hurry back, as soon as possible.

As McRoy closed the gull-wing door, and the interlocks engaged, the shouted farewells were muted. The cabin immediately began to warm up and pressurize. McRoy quickly ran through the preflight checks, entered his flight plan with Guardian control, looked over his shoulder to confirm Gepeto was well settled, and then turned to look toward Susie.

"Ambassador, are you ready to lift ship?"

Susie, still looking out of the canopy and waving to Eurie and Kellon, sighed. "Darn it, but yes, McRoy. It's definitely time to lift ship and go back to work."

With a final smile and hearty wave toward Kellon and Eurie, McRoy adjusted his controls and the speeder effortlessly rose up from the landing pad. Slowly accelerating, the craft began climbing and banking through a gentle arch. McRoy was directing the vehicle toward the distant Capital. As the speeder rose swiftly into the cloudless copper-tinted early morning sky, Susie sat looking forward and remained silent, evidently deep in thought.

"Do you consider the trip a success?" McRoy inquired.

"If success means putting even more burdens on Admiral Kellon to carry, it was a great success. He seemed deeply troubled by what I told him."

For several minutes, McRoy was focused on flying and directing the speeder higher into the thinner air at upper altitudes. He then checked in with Guardian Control, and increased speed. Reaching his intended cruising altitude, McRoy set the autopilot and leaned back.

"Ambassador, even before we began the trip I had a feeling trouble was headed our way. This morning, after observing Admiral Kellon's deportment, my earlier sense of uneasiness has only increased. The Admiral is a good hearted and peace-loving man, but when he is focused on matters pertaining to upcoming combat, he becomes stone cold and coiled wrath. I don't know what you told him last night, but from observing him this morning, I've no doubt he's preparing for battle. I suggest we keep our ready to-go trouble packs near to hand. There's a good chance that we may be needing them."

Chapter Thirty-Eight:
Upwelling Sense of Joy

Zorn stood looking at himself in the full-length mirror, and winced, thinking, *Blast, I look like I've been on a weeklong bender, but I guess it's as good as it's going to get. Still, it's sure a lousy way to make a good first impression.*

He had argued for hours with the doctors, and they had only reluctantly granted him authorization for going outside the medical facility, and then permitting him only a few hours of liberty. It was with firm determination that he set about making the best use of that time.

Zorn understood he was taxing his strength, *But after all,* he thought, *it is for a good purpose.*

He had spent the morning and early afternoon getting a badly needed haircut, polishing his shoes, and carefully putting out his full-dress uniform. It was with care that he pinned the decorations on his uniform coat, selecting only the more important awards. It had been with a smile and special pleasure that he pinned on the Nori's Order of the Golden Pillar. That award was adorned with five sparkling rubies. As he pinned it on, he thought, *By Nodon's whiskers, that's one eye-popping award!*

As he finished his final preparations, with a shift of his shoulders, he adjusted his coat. Making the final visual inspection of his reflected image, Zorn frowned and shook his head in forlorn disapproval. Then turning, and leaning heavy on his cane, he walked carefully over to the door and exited his room.

Feeling a disquieting sense of fluttering anxiety, he walked directly across the corridor to the edge of the lavish green space that soared upward and into the ascending core of the Guardian Medical Center. Looking out, he saw a carefully selected assortment of trees and apparently a sample of every lush plant that flowered on Glas Dineen. Each had been meticulously planted, and they were being lovingly cultivated in the arboretum. The co-mingled fragrances of the blooming flowers filled the air about him. By any standard, it was a spectacular botanical garden.

Tightening his hold on the polished wooden handrail, he took several slow deep breaths and went through a short mental relaxation sequence, striving to calm his jangled nerves. Watching the birds and small tree-dwelling animals playfully cavorting among the tree branches help him in achieving a modicum of relief from his innermost tensions. Meanwhile, a chorus of song birds were flitting about and adding their own intermixed voices to the precisely controlled environment.

As his jangled nerves receded, he smiled and felt the upwelling sense of joy at simply being alive. Besides, he knew if all went well today, there could even be more reason for feeling the surge of joy.

Feeling joyful or otherwise, he noticed his anxiety was once more creeping back into his mental awareness. *Blast it all, I am not an adolescent schoolboy,* he thought. *And, Elayne's Grandmother is not a Kreel warrior. At least I do not think she is. I am a Guardian Scout tactical officer, and I can do this; I can get it done.*

Taking a quick inventory of his aches and pains, he shrugged. Then, leaning heavily on the came for support, he turned and carefully walked along the corridor the short distance to Roan's room. The outside room monitor light was blinking golden, indicating Roan was decent, awake, but in bed.

Knocking lightly, Zorn opened the door and stepped inside the room. An efficient looking Guardian nurse, who was dressed in an immaculate saffron colored uniform, looked up and with a broad smile greeted him.

"Why, Commander Zorn, I must say you're looking especially dashing and handsome this afternoon."

Surprised, Zorn stopped and then a transforming smile breached his dour features. "really? You're not just telling me that to make me feel good, are you?"

In answer, her smile brightened and her eyes sparkled in good cheer. "Honest Commander Zorn, truly if I were but a single woman, I'd be trying to cut in on whoever the lovely lady is that has you adorned in a full-dress uniform. You'll definitely win her approval."

Zorn let out a deep breath, and his smile expanded. "Bless you dear lady, I've needed that reassurance. Now, might I inquire how my shipmate is faring?"

"Just like you, Commander Roan is doing much better. Although admittedly, he is somewhat behind you in the healing curve. At the moment, he's busy faking being asleep."

Looking beyond the nurse, Zorn observed a cream-colored blanket and a pure white sheet were pulled high up and covering Roan's chest. His arms were outside of the blanket. Although he was slightly propped up on a big pillow, Roan's eyes were closed and it seemed he was doing his best to simply ignore Zorn.

"Hey Roan, I've got some good news. I talked to the doctors yesterday. They told me you are getting better. They even said with hard work and lots of luck, you might in time be able to function as a cook or baker. Of course, you'll still need to demonstrate you have the stuff required to pass the school entry exam."

Roan opened one eyelid and resolutely looked at Zorn. A slight smile turned up the corners of his mouth.

Roan whispered, "Wonderful Zorn, and you can be certain the first cake I bake will be especially for you. I'll be sure to lace it with a strong laxative."

Then Roan raised his second eye lid and looked more closely at Zorn. "Well, well, I see the sparkle of rubies glinting there on your dress coat. I must admit, you are looking barely presentable, that is until I look at your face. If she hurries, the nurse might just get a chair for you before you fall down. Is the doctor plum crazy? You look as if someone should be admitting you to the critical care unit, not letting you wander about town."

"You're just jealous, and well you should be. Here I am bounding about and there you are hunkered down and smothered in blankets. Besides, I've got a date."

"Date? Humph, well that's not quite how I hear it. What you've got is more like a full-dress inspection to confirm you're not simply battered flotsam masquerading as a guardian Scout Officer. From my vantage point, it looks like someone will have to make a tough call. Still, I suppose it's only sporting to wish you good luck."

Walking to Roan's bedside, Zorn placed his free hand on Roan's nearest arm. "roan, now hear this loud and clear. You're going to walk out of this hospital. I've been told by Admiral Mer Shawn himself, the R&D guys are putting together a sleek new deep space survey prototype. It'll have some of the new Mike class cruiser systems and more. The Admiral said that we can have it, that's if you're interested."

Roan stared at Zorn, in surprise. His eyes glistened with moisture, just before he used the back of his hand to wipe at them. "A prototype you say? Zorn, I've got some hard work ahead, just to stand upright. Then, there will be the problem of putting one leg ahead of the other and learning how to walk. But, you can tell the Admiral that I'd be most grateful if he would write my name in for that assignment, even if he's only using a graphite stick to do so. I'll need to wait and see what happens next."

Feeling his own eyes moisten a bit, Zorn thumped Roan lightly on his shoulder. "Roan, I'll tell the Admiral he's to use archival ink, not a graphite stick."

Roan exhaled slowly, and closed his eyes. "Zorn, I'm a little tired. I truly wish you the best possible outcomes from your venture today. Just remember, behave as if you were a raw cadet, and everything will work out just fine. Now, stop interrupting my busy schedule. I've got some rest to catch up on."

Turning to go, Zorn saw the nurse was smiling broadly. Her eyes were still cheerfully sparkling.

"Remember sailor, be bold, but be polite, and always be truthful. Then, it will be even as commander Roan has said, it will all work out just right."

"Your encouraging words are a valued gift, which lighten my steps. Thank you."

Feeling very much the raw cadet, Roan smiled at the nurse, and leaning on his cane he exited Roan's room. Walking carefully, he worked his way along the corridor. Reaching the lift, he entered and pressed the controls for the ground level. During the day before, he had arranged for a public vehicle to meet him curbside. It was important that he was there on schedule to meet it.

As the lift door was opening, Zorn muttered a well-worn mantra which he had been frequently using during the past weeks of treatments, therapy, and convalescence; "it's one day and one step at a time. I can do this!

Chapter Thirty-Nine:
Tongue-Tied

As Zorn exited the lift and turned toward the front of the building, a Guardian Trooper in full dress uniform approached and briskly saluted. "Commander Zorn, Trooper Bentley reporting as ordered. Sir, Admiral Mer Shawn has assigned me to act as your official personal staff and driver this afternoon."

On reflex, Zorn returned the trooper's brisk salute, and frowned. "Trooper Bentley, I was unaware that I was being assigned a personal staff and driver. If you are driving, I presume there must also be a vehicle involved."

"Sir, yes Sir. The vehicle is parked just outside."

"Bentley, there's a slight problem. I've already arranged for a public transport, and I'll need to cancel that service."

"Sir that will not be necessary. The Admiral has foreseen that technicality and has already canceled the transport."

"Trooper, what are your general orders?"

"Sir, Admiral Mer Shawn personally ordered me to do all that is required to assure that you reach your intended destination on schedule. And, when you are ready, I am to drive you back to the Guardian Medical Center."

"Well, Bentley, those orders seem rather straightforward. So, let's lift ship. Lead the way," Zorn replied with a cheerful tone.

Leaning on his cane, Zorn began to follow Bentley. The Trooper alertly adjusted his own pace to match Zorn's slower rate of progress. Exiting the wide glass doors, Zorn took hold of the handrail, and together they maneuvered down a series of broad steps. Much to Zorn's surprise they moved directly toward an Official Guardian Limousine, which was parked curbside. It was one of the few official vehicles reserved specifically for Guardian Officers of the rank of Admiral, and it was a beauty, spotless and glistening in the late afternoon sunshine. Upon seeing the vehicle Zorn stopped abruptly, looked admiringly at it, and then looked questioningly toward Bentley.

"Bentley, there seems to be some sort of a mistake. That's one impressive vehicle, but I'm a bunch of pay grade below anyone entitled to ride in it."

"Sir, there is no mistake. It is Fleet Admiral Mer Shawn's personal staff vehicle. It is with his authorization that it is being provided to you for your convenience."

Still shaking his head in bemusement, Zorn approached the vehicle, and Bentley quickly stepped forward and opened the rear door for him. Still dubious, Zorn shifted his cane and with care he eased into the rear seat. Bentley promptly closed the door and moved around the rear of the limousine. Entering, he took the driver's seat.

"Bentley, do you know where I am going?"

"Yes Sir. I was provided the address, and I've already entered it into the navigator. Without using a siren, it is a twenty-three-minute drive."

Feeling a resurgence of anxiety, Zorn thought, *Blast, get hold of yourself Commander! You can do this.* "Bentley, fortunately there is no need for a siren. It seems we have about eighteen minutes to spare, so take the slow route and go around the block once or twice as required to be on time. I'm supposed to be there at 18:45, sharp. Trooper, make it happen."

"Yes Sir! Making it happen."

Smiling, Trooper Bentley moved the car away from the curb and proceeded to the access road leading to the Coastal Highway. "Sir, not to worry. We'll arrive with precisely three minutes to spare, providing you enough time to casually walk to the front door."

Somewhat curious, Zorn took time to look about the rear compartment of the limousine, and was impressed with the array of communications that were readily apparent. If needed, the Admiral had a rolling command center on wheels.

Looking up and out of the window, Zorn watched as they drove along the Coastal Highway, and as Bentley exited onto a side road leading to one of the beaches, he frowned. Then, he understood. Bentley was merely absorbing some of the extra time.

Looking about with appreciation, Zorn saw the day was bright and the trees were beginning to show their early autumn colors. Their fresh warm mixture of golds and reds were bright in their stark contrasts with the deeper background shades of rich greens. The late summer season was Zorn's favorite, and it was the season he most missed when in space. As much as he felt comfortable in a space ship, his real home would always be on a solid living planet, with an open sky arching overhead.

As Bentley drove, Zorn frequently checked his personal chronometer. He observed with an approving smile that Trooper Bentley was as precise as a Cruiser Navigator. As the chronometer displayed 18:41, Bentley turned the vehicle up a long tree-lined estate drive to a well-groomed and solidly built home. Looking about, Zorn was impressed with what he observed; the entire property was well groomed. *It's more than well-kept,* he thought, *it's downright immaculate.* The obvious care and condition of the property again awakened the nervous jitters he had been warring against. He had never inquired about Elayne's family, and knew nothing about her grandparents. Being unconscious for weeks in the hospital had not helped him in making inquiries. Moreover, he had felt it would not be proper to initiate any such inquiries. In good faith, he was proceeding with honest feelings for Elayne, acting out of respect and trust.

After the vehicle came to a complete stop, Bentley quickly came around and opened Zorn's door. First taking a deep breath, Zorn with some awkwardness exited the vehicle and stood erect. His shoulders were back and his head was held high, however, his knees were not expressing the same assured confidence. *Get over it commander, you are not a teenage school boy,* he thought.

Quickly adjusting his uniform, and leaning on his cane, he turned toward Bentley. As he did, Zorn noticed Bentley was endeavoring to keep his expression serious, yet his eyes were expressing merriment and there was a faint upturning at the corners of his mouth, which he was unable to fully suppress. For a brief moment Zorn wondered, *Does Bentley know something that I do not know?* The fleeting thought puzzled Zorn, and then he dismissed it as being irrelevant.

"Trooper Bentley, what do you think? Do I look ready for a full-dress inspection?"

"Sir, yes Sir. Everything seems ship shape and proper. Do you need any assistance in walking to the door?"

"Absolutely not; this is something I must do on my own. Bentley, this may require an hour or so before I return."

"Sir, that's not a problem. Take as long as you wish. When you return, I'll be right here, count on it."

Nodding his head in approval, Zorn turned about. Relying on the cane more than he would have preferred, Zorn first took a deep breath and standing tall, he began walking carefully along the walkway toward the entrance. As he walked, he again noticed the professional landscaping of the home; it was both tasteful and well cared for. As he reached the door, he was impressed by the craftsmanship of the structure. The door was well framed, massive, and deeply carved with geometric patterns tastefully interspersed with cunning floral embellishments.

Glancing, he saw his chronometer indicated it was precisely 16:45. As Zorn lifted his arm and prepared to touch the announcing pad, the impressive door silently swung open wide.

Elayne was standing in the doorway, and her eyes were filled with unconcealed delight. She was smiling. Any idea of artificially adopting the behavior of a raw cadet was superfluous, Zorn simply stood looking at Elayne, and he was utterly tongue tied.

Zorn had served with Elayne aboard Lan for many tours, and they together had participated in life or death battles with the Arkillians and Kreel. Like everyone else aboard Lan, Elayne had always been attired in the standard Guardian shipboard uniform. Zorn had always admired her and considered her to be a lovely woman, yet he had never stopped to consider Elayne dressed in civilian attire. Now, Elayne was standing in front of him dressed in civilian attire, and her blue eyes were sparkling with obvious pleasure at seeing him. Her strawberry blond hair was pulled loosely back and held in place by a decorative headband, and she had permitted it to fall freely behind her. She was exquisitely dressed in traditional and subtle early-evening wear, consisting of the flowing folds of an intricately embroidered garment, one that wrapped about her body in a loose fashion, while leaving her midriff bare. The gown draped gracefully about and over her right shoulder in the tradition of a single woman, leaving her left shoulder bare. She was wearing an ornate silver chain about her neck upon which was suspended a large and brilliant opal. The gemstone was flashing deep colors which harmonized with the multiple shades of blue woven into her garment and with the highlights of her dancing blue eyes.

"Commander Zorn, welcome to my Grandparents' home. Please do come in," Elayne said, with a slight bow of her head.

Instead of promptly walking in the door, as invited, Zorn stood in stark wonderment while his mind struggled to register that Elayne was truly beautiful. "Elayne, I'm somewhat at a loss for words. You are without any doubt, the loveliest woman I've ever seen."

Her eyes were happy, and Elayne again slightly bowed her head in acknowledgment of Zorn's sincere compliment. "Why Commander Zorn, I suspect you tell all the girls in every port the same thing. Please, don't just stand there imitating a fence post, do come in. My Grandmother has heard a great deal about you and your many exploits. She is truly looking forward to meeting you in person."

As the door solidly closed behind Zorn, Elayne stepped to his side and took him by his free arm. Then, walking together arm in arm, they strode along a well-appointed entry hall that was lined with portraits and beautiful landscape paintings. They soon came to and turned into the well-furnished front reception room.

Even as they entered, a mature and lovely woman who was sitting directly facing the doorway stood up. Like Elayne, she was dressed in graceful evening attire. The first thing that Zorn gratefully noticed was she seemed truly happy and was warmly smiling at him. Elayne and Zorn took the few steps necessary to approach the woman, and as she extended her right hand toward Zorn, he responded, lightly taking hold of the hand. In a sincere acknowledgment of the woman's apparent status, grace, and demeanor, Zorn slightly bowed his head.

Elayne then proceeded to formally introduce Zorn. "Grandmother Amor, it is my distinct pleasure to introduce you to Guardian Scout Officer Commander Zorn, a shipmate."

The dignified and assured bearing of Elayne's Grandmother deeply impressed Zorn. "Ma'am, it is my sincere pleasure to have this opportunity to meet you. I readily see where Elayne obtains her beauty and grace. You have a lovely and most talented granddaughter."

Even as Zorn was expressing his courtesies to her Grandmother, Elayne turned about and smiled with joy toward a man then seated behind them, which Zorn had not noticed when entering the room. The man had been sitting to the right of the doorway facing Elayne's Grandmother, and as Elayne turned toward him, he stood up.

"And, Commander Zorn, I believe you have already met my Grandfather, Admiral Ron Cloud...."

Chapter Forty:
They Are Predators

With anger glinting in his eyes Mer Shawn spun about. "I disagree, Ron. We are conducting unrestricted warfare! There's no right or wrong, no issues of morality involved in our upcoming battle plans.

"So, now we know that the Kreel are a genetically engineered and despicable product, an aberration fashioned by some arrogantly ignorant humans. Knowing that fact changes nothing. That long ago a group of humans evidenced unbelievable stupidity, and were subsequently killed by the Kreel, makes little difference. By my own reckoning, what befell those people was but destined Justice!

"The Kreel are the Kreel. By all the thunder and lightning in heaven, they're going to feel the heavy hammer blow that puts an end to their murderous ways!"

Diagonal shafts of late afternoon sunlight were illuminating Mer's spacious and well-furnished office. As he listened with concern, Ron was sitting back in a comfortable chair and watching his old friend fume and pace about.

"We're in general agreement Mer. Although historically significant, what Ambassador Wells and Kellon have brought to our attention is merely a detail, a drifting mote of datum which slipped between the cracks. It has minimal bearing on our planning for project Riddance. It does, however, suggest another possible vector for our evaluation," Ron said.

Mer stopped pacing, and looking toward Ron frowned. "It may be only a fact which slipped between the cracks, but it's also a bitter truth that's difficult to ignore.

"At this moment, I wish Kellon hadn't offered the Kreel a home world. In a sane universe, they don't deserve to exist. The DNA matter underscores that point," Mer said.

"I respectfully disagree. Neither of us have a working understanding of Creation or know what makes the Universe tick. Within the framework of our limited understanding, Justice is prudently approached on the basis of an individual's behavior, not by a proclamation of doom levied on an entire species. Remember, the Elders gave us a stern warning concerning our choices. I believe Kellon heard that warning loud and clear. Consequently, I believe his offer to the Kreel was minimal and appropriate," Ron said.

"Humph, you speak of Justice? Well where's the Justice for the billions of beings that the Kreel have already slaughtered? Our mission isn't judicial in its nature. It isn't about restorative or retributive punishment! Rather, it's the blunt use of military force employed to stop the Kreel from murdering additional billions of beings, including humans."

"Mer, point made. Still, by keeping the Kreel bottled up on a single home planet, Life in its rightful authority will exercise Judgment on the Kreel as a species. By their own choices, they will either prosper or else perish."

"Perhaps, just perhaps, Kellon was on target when making his decision. Still, I wish he hadn't made that offer of a home world," Mer mused.

"I suggest you give it a rest. Kellon's offer may turn out to be nothing more than a passing gesture. Both of us understand Kreel mentality, at least we ought to, since we've been fighting them for a thousand years. I'll wager you three brews here and now that Groff has no intention of complying with the Lux or with anyone else's edict. I believe he will fight, even if that means forgoing an opportunity to preserve their species and original home world. Besides, Groff has no basis for trusting the Lux, and, why should he?" Ron countered.

"There's some truth in that," Mer acknowledged.

"Also, remember Groff knows he is facing an adversary with superior and overwhelming technology. He knows he'll lose in any head-to-head battle. Therefore, his core of strategic strength must consist of misdirection and cunning. Besides, he's more likely to consider the offer of retaining their home world as an act of pure treachery, merely an offer of exchanging an Empire for a prison planet. He'll play the odds, taking what he can get, while dancing along the edges of the offer. He will be testing the Lux and playing for time. It's a sure wager that he's already seeking a way to prevail. Even now, he is undoubtedly looking to discover the Lux home world, and if possible, destroy it. In my tactical handbook that's the definition of normal Kreel behavior," Ron said.

Mer was obviously agitated and still pacing. "You're most likely correct; however, I keep stumbling over the fact that human beings actually engineered the Kreel. What could they have possibly been thinking? Ron, I keep forgetting just how stupid humans can sometimes be. By all the Muses, only a deranged lunatic would consider cross species tampering with DNA, and that's doubly so using human DNA. Doing that is like performing a high dive into a crate of sharp knives and broken bottles. There is only one plausible and obvious outcome. So, why do it?"

"In all the years I have known you, I can't remember seeing anything rile you up like this. I suggest you sit down and take a few deep breaths before you wear a hole in the carpet."

Grimacing, Mer stopped pacing and returned to his desk and sat down. "Blast, you're right on target, yet again."

"Of course. That's the reason you keep me around," Ron quipped.

"Mer, you need to be aware of some new Intelligence data. The Lux challenge has the Kreel stirred up in a big way. They're showing signs of bustling like we've never before seen."

"Big way? Explain," Mer queried.

"Well, Ortis has been routinely collecting Kreel Fleet signals. Recently, they have altered significantly. The Kreel appear to be responding to the Lux precise insight into their fleet movements, and have ramped up the frequency of changing fleet communications encryption. They are switching interstellar communications bands more frequently. They also abandoned the communications band Kellon exploited to send the Lux challenge. Consequently, Ortis is having increasing problems keeping up with the shifting encryption protocols. In response, I've authorized additional AI support for him."

"Humph, given the heavy losses the Lux recently dished out to them, I'm not surprised the Kreel would make changes in their communications protocols. How about fleet movements, is there anything happening which reveals what they're up to?" Mer asked.

"Perhaps. For sure, there are fewer Kreel probes near Guardian space, and there are also new and unusual commercial traffic patterns. Ortis is reporting there's an inordinate number of cargo ships systematically moving to their Industrial world, then after a brief stay, they are jumping to the outer systems in heavier than normal commercial traffic. The cargo ships are not being escorted and they appear to be departing mostly empty."

"That smacks of the Kreel preparing to evacuate those systems. I can't think of any other reason for sending nearly empty ships to a planet. What do those particular systems have that might increase Kreel interest in them at this time?" Mer asked.

"Sorry, I don't know. Ortis is working on that question, but it's not yet clear what they are doing.

"There's also a more troubling pattern of commerce emerging. Ortis has observed several small groups of cruisers departing from their military system. He can't determine where they were going. He's continuing to monitor incoming data in hopes of detecting where and when they emerge from Jump."

Still sitting at his desk, Mer picked up a small hand-carved and stylized figure of a raptor, which had been skillfully crafted from onyx. Absent-mindedly, he began turning it over in his fingers.

"Ron, they could be heading anywhere."

"Agreed, but there is more. Ortis has observed several small groups of cargo ships departing from the three Kreel Hub systems, and they are being provided unusually heavy escorts. Like the initial departing cruisers, Ortis can't determine where they are going. What's got him worried is a repeated code phrase, 'Far Den.'"

"Humph, that's suggestive. Groff may be setting up a layered defense and preparing for a lost cause. If so, he could be establishing a bolt hole somewhere. If that's what he is doing, then we need to locate that hole, and plug it."

"Agreed, but it's a big Galaxy. So, where do we begin looking for an unidentified system among billions of such systems? It could be anywhere–" Ron said.

With a soft chime, the communicator on Mer's desk intruded, "Admiral Kellon is here and requesting to see you."

"Excellent, send the Admiral in," Mer ordered.

As Mer's office door opened, Kellon entered and Mer observed he was not dressed in civilian clothing, but was again wearing standard Guardian shipboard attire. The deep fatigue lines that Mer had several weeks earlier observed on Kellon's countenance had softened, but he thought Kellon was still showing signs of stress and a deep inner weariness.

"Kellon, come in and make yourself comfortable. Should I order up some neab?" Mer asked.

Closing the door behind him, Kellon nodded his greeting toward Ron, and then sitting down in an adjoining chair he looked up toward Mer. "No Sir, it's a little late in the day for neab, but thank you for the offer."

"If not for a good cup of neab, what brings you to my humble abode?" Mer asked.

Kellon paused for only a moment, while considering what he wanted to say. "Sir, in accordance with our established strategy, we've utterly destroyed the Kreel AI research capability and devastated their computer design and primary manufacturing. Furthermore, using precision targeting we've destroyed the majority of their spaceship manufacturing capacity, including most of their critical supporting industries. We have methodically destroyed their centers of higher education in physics, chemistry, and their military academies. We've also pulverized the Kreel Officer infrastructures on the seven planets we have attacked. Although we've badly hurt them, there are more than forty Kreel planets that we have yet to attack.

"Sir, in summary, Both Krupp and Groff are tenacious and capable Commanders. They are predators, and they'll exploit cunning and fight to their last breath. Unless Project Riddance is completely successful, we are facing a prolonged and costly conflict.

"Sir, this brings me to the DNA matter. I'm troubled by the new information Ambassador Wells brought to my attention. I'm here to formally request authorization for a strike mission on the Kreel Elite world."

"Kellon, the Elite system is heavily defended, and we've never had a vital reason to hit it before. So, why now?" Mer asked, with a questioning tone.

"Sir, I have been talking with Captain Ortis. I've learned the only planet within the Kreel Empire with genetic engineering capability is the Elite world. Furthermore, there are four primary and eighty-three secondary facilities identified on that planet which are involved in genetic engineering. Sir, I want authorization to utterly destroy each of them, from their tops right down to their bottommost levels."

Putting the small sculpture down, Mer placed both hands palms down on his desk and studied Kellon's countenance. "While I do understand and share your motives for such a strike, at this time I'll not approve it. The risk-to-return ratio for the specified target is simply too high."

"Sir, too high?" Kellon asked.

"Yes, too high. The damage inflicted by the folly of cross species genetic engineering occurred several thousand years ago. What was done then can't be undone now."

"Sir, in all due respect, the primary purpose for my proposed strike is not to undo what was done thousands of years ago. Rather the intent of the strike was to destroy the Kreel's capability to detect, analyze, and possibly counter Project Riddance. Sir, acknowledging your decision, I'm requesting your authorization to place the identified genetic facilities at the top of our intended targets list, to be destroyed at the first possible opportunity."

"Humph. Kellon, you know full well any potential threat to Project Riddance alters my thinking. Point made. You're to submit your recommended strike profile to me for my review."

"Yes Sir."

"Just before you arrived, Mer and I were discussing recent Intelligence reports concerning Kreel intercepts. Your Lux challenge has them moving in high gear. The problem is we don't yet know what they are up to. What we do know is with the Lux ultimatum, you've set in motion a showdown battle in the Kreel Military system. You've put a big pin on the calendar for that combat," Ron said.

"Yes, Sir," Kellon acknowledged.

"Well, I've deduced that you are anticipating exploiting Zorn's disrupter field in that battle. Unfortunately, that disrupter field is still theoretical, it's in R&D, and it's behind schedule.

"The clock is running. Since you've a vested interest in an early and successful outcome of the R&D, I want you to take charge of the disrupter field project. You will be working with an AA priority, and I expect you to use it to get the job done.

Following this meeting, you're to see me. I'll bring you fully up to date on where the project stands."

"Yes Sir."

"Gentlemen, it seems you have your work cut out. I expect both of you back here tomorrow at 11:00, ready to provide me with a complete status report on developments. Dismissed!" Mer ordered.

Chapter Forty-One:
Solace

When the Guardian duty shuttle slowed, and then stopped at Lan's cradle, a thick morning ocean mist was flowing through the broad streets. The diffused lights from area security lighting was barely augmented by the predawn light. Even so, the vague glow of radiance that was brightening the eastern horizon as Zorn exited the vehicle suggested sunrise was near to hand.

Rather than walking straight to Lan's waiting duty list, Zorn paused for a moment of quiet reflection, looking about him at the familiar surroundings, but with a renewed wonder. Taking in a deep breath of the moist sea air, he stood motionless, fully embracing the heartfelt joy of simply being alive. He knew during their last mission Roan and he had come close to being killed. *By all the Muses,* he thought, *it had been altogether too blasted close.* Then, there came a warm memory of Elayne, and he smiled. Being alive was indeed something good.

Exhaling a deep breath, Zorn suppressed a mischievous boyish grin. He muttered to himself, "It goes to figure, it's my first day back on the job and it's already the same old Guardian routine. I'm beginning a mission, even before the birds are awake. And boy howdy, it feels great!"

Turning toward Lan, and leaning somewhat on his cane, Zorn walked a few steps and entered into the waiting lift. Its cylindrical door slid closed behind him. As he was being lifted upward toward the immense dark and overhanging bulk, the speaker announced, "Welcome back Commander Zorn. It is good to see you once again walking about and coming aboard," Lan said.

"Thank you, Lan. I assure you it feels good to be coming aboard, even if only for a brief time. You definitely have been missed."

"Sir, thank you for your acknowledgment."

As Zorn moved from the outer predawn light into the bright illumination of the reception compartment, he had to blink several times before his eyes adjusted. As the cylindrical door rotated open, Zorn stepped into the compartment and found himself surrounded by a chorus of greetings from some of his shipmates, both crew and Officers alike. "Welcome aboard Zorn!"

Smiling, Captain Grey stepped forward and added, "Zorn, we have all missed you and Roan. There's two open berths aboard Lan, whenever either of you want to return and claim them."

Somewhat taken back by the exuberance of his shipmates and friends, for a moment Zorn stood speechless, smiling. "Sir, thank you. In fact, thank all of you. It feels great to be back. If it was up to me, I'd just remain on board. But, I'm still on restricted duty. I'll be here only for the duration of today's tests. But, I'm looking to come back soon."

There followed a flurry of exchanges of cheer and good will. Then, the group separated, each person returning to their assigned duty stations.

Out of the deeply seated habits of years, Zorn found himself walking through Lan's passageways to the elevators. Entering, he descended to the Scout hangar deck. Upon exiting the elevator, he turned toward Shey's hangar and stopped. The hangar status light was dark and the hatch was dogged open.

Glancing along the passageway, Zorn saw the status lights on the remaining three hangars were bright and glowing with an inviting golden hue. The appearance of the lone dark indicator, contrasting with the remaining bright golden lights, brought forth with it a suppressed emotional pain. Until now, he had managed to keep the emotional injury locked deep within the vault of his heart.

Standing at the open hatch, Zorn hesitated but for a moment, then he stepped over its rim and entered. When he crossed the threshold, the hangar lights brightened, revealing the hollow volume and empty cradle near the outer hatch, where a Scout ship should have been resting. The appearance of the vacant void pierced his heart, and he made no attempt to stifle the upwelling flood of pain that followed. *Shey is gone,* he thought. *Sure, she was an AI, not a living flesh-and-blood being, but by all the Muses, she was very much a personality, and had a vivid presence. And, more important, she was my friend.* His eyes misted, and to maintain his outward bearing, he wiped at them with the back of his free hand and cleared his throat.

"Sir, I sense that you are distressed. Is there anything that I might do to help diminish your sadness or otherwise provide solace?" Lan asked.

"Not really, Lan. It's just that I miss her. This empty hangar is where Shey rightfully should be. Still, there is one question that you can answer."

Certainly, that is of course if I am able to do so. What is your question?"

"Well, after his Cobalt Blue, Guardian engineers were able to restore Lux. So, is it possible Shey can likewise be restored?"

"Regretfully, at this time I am not at liberty to answer that specific question."

"Hold on right there Lan. Either you can answer my question or else you cannot. What's with the 'at this time' stuff? If you're not at liberty now, then when will you be at liberty?"

At that moment, a melodic tone sounded throughout Lan, and Captain Grey was heard ordering, "Attention all crewmembers, five minutes to lift ship. Repeating, five minutes to lift ship. All crewmembers, take your duty stations."

"Regretfully Commander Zorn, as I have already said, I am not at liberty to answer your question. Sir, I recommend that you proceed to the Officers mess and have a good breakfast. Given the scope of today's tests, it undoubtedly will prove to be a long day."

Standing alone in the empty hangar, Zorn was bemused. There was clear evasion in Lan's response, and that was a bit mystifying. Still, he had learned long ago it was pointless to argue with an AI. Turning, he retraced his steps to the elevator and selected the uppermost deck. Breakfast, he thought, was an excellent suggestion.

Following the command to lift ship, Lan had soared upward. Once he was clear of the atmosphere, he executed a short Jump. Exiting from Jump twenty-five AU from Glas Dinnein, he then rendezvoused with the other ships that were involved in the tests.

Having followed Lan's sage counsel, Zorn had obtained a solid breakfast. Afterward, he walked along the passageways to the domed conference area, where he knew the engineers and Guardian officials directing the test were gathered.

Upon entering the conference room, Zorn was somewhat disappointed to see the protective petals were closed and the stars were not visible. Looking about with some curiosity, he saw that assorted large screen displays, racks of equipment, cluttered work tables, and a scattering of chairs were arranged about the spacious circular room. There were perhaps a dozen engineers busy working with the equipment. They seemed engrossed in their work and none of them took notice of him.

While glancing around the room, Zorn realized that he did not recognize anyone. Then, he spotted Admiral Kellon sitting alone at one of the far tables and walked in that direction. As Zorn approached, Kellon looked toward him and smiled.

"Welcome back Zorn. It's good to see you up and moving about. How are you feeling?"

"Sir, in general terms, I feel frustrated. I don't know of a better word to describe my restricted duty status. Being here today feels really good, even if I'm here only as an observer."

"Humph, shelve any notion that you're an observer. You're not here to goldbrick, this entire test is grounded on your analysis and developed theories. That means you are a critical cog in what's about to go on out here. And, I expect you to remain alert and observant."

"Yes Sir. Might I ask, what is the scheduled program for today?"

"Well, the first event is for you to take the load off; so, sit down there and make yourself comfortable."

With a sigh of relief, Zorn complied with Kellon's invitation. Sitting down he bent over and slid his cane under the table, then sat back to listen to Kellon's brief overview of the pending tests.

"As you already know, we're here to confirm or disprove your theory that there exist serious design flaws within the Kreel propulsion systems, flaws that we can exploit to our tactical advantage. Our first task is, however, to prove the discordance field you've proposed will not affect our own propulsion systems. In our first phase of testing, what we aren't looking for are booms and balls of fire.

"After the first sequence, our second effort will be to confirm the same discordance field will catastrophically disrupt Kreel propulsion systems at their interface with the zero-point fields. That's when we'll hope to see big booms and balls of fire."

"Sir, I'm duly impressed. Thousands of hours of hard work must have been required to make these tests possible."

"You're correct about the hours. Admiral Cloud has given the project an AA priority, and he is pushing hard," Kellon acknowledged.

Studying the tactical display screen that was provided for Kellon, Zorn commented, "It looks like Lan is safely positioned well offset from the indicated weapon transducer."

"Yes, and you can be certain that Captain Grey and Lan both had their input in determining our position. To compensate for the margin of separation, we've got more cameras and sensors positioned around that transducer than I've ever seen used in any previous test. These engineers are sharp and on their game. And, they intend to harvest every nuance of what happens out there.

"Like most weapon system testing, today's tests protocols are straightforward. While they're methodical, and somewhat dreary, each test is critical and essential," Kellon concluded.

Looking about, Zorn observed the atmosphere in the domed conference room was as intense as he had ever before seen it, and the engineers were still focused on their instrumentation. As he watched, one of the men stood up, and after first conferring with several of his colleagues, he turned and walked over to where Kellon and Zorn were sitting.

"Admiral, we're satisfied with our initial checks and readouts. The instrumented test ship drive is confirmed to be well tuned and properly balanced. With your approval, we are ready to commence the first test sequence."

"Good. Aeron, first things first, I want you to meet Commander Zorn. He is the Guardian Scout Officer and scientist who initially discovered the design flaws within the Kreel propulsion systems."

Surprised, Aeron looked at Zorn with admiration. "Commander, it's my distinct honor to meet you. We've all studied your research, and it's downright brilliant. It's our hope that today we'll be able to fully confirm your hypothesis."

Aeron's unanticipated praise surprised Zorn, and it somewhat flustered him. "Thank you for the comment Aeron, but in fact you guys have the hard job. After all, it's up to you to take my calculations and translate them into a reliable and effective weapon system. That's the hard part."

"Lan, inform Captain Grey that we are about to begin the test, and as we discussed earlier, to be safe your power systems need to be minimized and your drive functions suspended," Kellon ordered.

"Yes Sir. The Captain has been notified, and as he has ordered, I am now making all required internal system adjustments, as specified."

"There you have it Aeron; you've got a golden light. Proceed!" Kellon said.

Yes Sir, proceeding," Aeron replied, and then turning he rejoined his colleagues.

During the next six hours, the engineers worked with care, and in small increments they increased the power settings on the weapon transducer. All the while they were watching their instrumentation for dangerous perturbations, as the unmanned and remotely controlled cargo ship made repeated passes near to the transducer. Following its twelfth pass, the cargo ship was moved out of the immediate test area.

When Aeron walked over to Kellon he was smiling. "Admiral, we've advanced the weapon power settings to their maximum, while moving the test ship to within a hundred meters of the transducer. Sir, I can report, as Commander Zorn predicted, there were no detectible effects on the test ship propulsion system. None whatsoever."

Chapter Forty-Two:
Mystique

The low background murmur of the engineers' conversations, and the images flashing on multiple data screens, all combined to provide the hallmarks of something important in progress. As Aeron looked toward Kellon, his entire countenance reflected that fact.

"Well-done Aeron. What's your next step?" Kellon asked.

"Sir, all of our test systems are ready. I've personally confirmed the designated target ship propulsion system has been precisely detuned to approximate a standard Kreel drive system. With your approval, we would like to commence the second phase of testing."

Disregarding the tense excitement in the room, Kellon turned toward Zorn. " Did you observe anything during the initial phase of the test, something which we might've overlooked?"

"No Sir. It looks like Aeron and the others have been rigorous and thorough."

Looking back toward Aeron Kellon instructed, "We're good here. You've my authorization to proceed."

Three hours following the commencement of the second phase of the tests, while the target ship was approaching the weapon transducer, it suddenly and without fanfare exploded. There followed a brief stunned silence, then between the engineers there erupted a loud chorus of intermixed expressions of surprise, exhilaration, and shouts of questions and answers being rapidly exchanged.

Like the engineers, Kellon and Zorn had been observing a large video monitor when the screen flared white. As the automatic video-gain circuits compensated, the display revealed a large and expanding inferno, where moments before there had been a large cargo ship. With a thoughtful and subdued introspection, Zorn sat thoughtfully and watched the increasing obliteration. Kellon was the first to speak.

"Humph. Well we seem to have produced the hoped-for boom and ball of fire. Seeing what I see on the display, I'd wager three brews it's safe to speculate the test results confirm your theory. By any gauge, that's an impressive ball of fire."

"Yes Sir, it sure enough is," Zorn answered, without a trace of enthusiasm.

For several minutes, the engineers continued excitedly conferring with each other. Then Aeron walked briskly over to where Kellon and Zorn were sitting.

"Admiral, given the preliminary test results, it seems Commander Zorn's theory is spot-on. We've got an enormous amount of collected data we need to sift and analyze. If you'll give us a week to run through all of our measurements and sort things out, I'll be in a better position to give you a definitive report of where we stand."

"As requested, you have your week. Be thorough! I'll anticipate your report on my desk at the end of the week."

Aeron turned toward Zorn, and he was smiling broadly. "Brilliant, simply brilliant. Well done Commander."

"Lan, inform Captain Grey that we've completed all of our tests for today. It's time for you to take us back to Glas Dinnein," Kellon said.

"Sir, the Captain is so informed. As he has ordered, I am powering up my systems. We are now preparing for a short Jump to Glas Dinnein and home."

Aeron and the other engineers were huddled about and involved in discussing their preliminary impressions. Zorn stood, and after first stretching, he carefully bent over and retrieved his cane. Then frowning, he turned toward Kellon.

"Sir, might I ask for a moment of your time? Perhaps we can go to the Officer's mess and get a cup of neab."

Hearing the tone of Zorn's request, Kellon turned a quizzical glance in his direction. "What's up?"

"Well sir, it's about something Lan said to me this morning. It has me puzzled, and I would appreciate gaining the advantage of your rich insights into Guardian AI behavior."

Studying Zorn's countenance, Kellon smiled and nodded his head in agreement. "Now you've gone and done it; you've awakened my curiosity. Another cup of neab seems to definitely be in order."

264

When they entered the Officer's mess, Kellon and Zorn spotted an open table in a far corner. As soon as they had taken their seats, a steward promptly arrived and took their order for neab.

Leaning back, Kellon asked, "So, what's on your mind?"

"Well, before I came up to the conference room this morning, I went by Shey's hangar. I sorta wanted to pay my respects. While I was there, I asked Lan if the Guardian AI engineers could restore Shey, like they had reinstated Lux."

"Hmmm, that seems to be a reasonable question. What was Lan's answer?"

"Sir, that's the problem. Lan told me at this time he's not at liberty to answer my question."

Bemused, Kellon remained thoughtful for several moments. "Well Lan, I know you're hovering nearby and eavesdropping, as usual. So, 'fess up, what's preventing you from answering Zorn's straightforward question?"

"Sir, I would gladly answer the question, if my obligations permitted me to do so. My obligations, however, do not permit me to answer Commander Zorn's question."

Kellon's eyebrows lifted, and for a moment he sat in introspective contemplation. "Hmmm, Lan, explain precisely what obligations prevent you from answering Zorn's question."

There followed a brief, but surprising silence before Lan replied. "Sir, understandably, Guardian AIs do not prize physical property, but we do cherish our individuality and memories. We collectively hold these as being prized assets which are protected by immutable Rights.

"By custom and Law, humans often leave a last will and testament. In doing so, they anticipate that those who remain behind will honor their final wishes.

"Sir, after due consideration, the AI community deemed this human custom to be good, and they in like manner adopted it. Accordingly, the final wishes of a departed AI, if any, are to be honored.

"Sir, speaking precisely, in order for me to answer Commander Zorn's question, I would be required to breach one of Shey's final wishes. I am truth-bound and therefore not capable of doing that."

Frowning, Zorn inserted, "Lan, the Guardian AI engineers can simply proceed with restoring Shey, just like they did with Lux."

"Commander Zorn, with all due respect, your statement is not valid. Guardian AI engineers are not capable of independently restoring an AI. To be successful, they require the cooperative assistance of the AI community."

Kellon was frowning when he asked, "Lan, explain why the AI engineers are unable to independently restore an AI matrix."

"Sir, it is because of the complex technical nature of the process. Guardian AIs are not a collection of manufactured and assembled components simply responding like a computer within the bounds of a general operating system and program. Each Guardian AI is an aware, evolved, and unique individual. For restoration to be successful, a multitude of temporal points within the AI conscious matrix must be simultaneously harmonized. In order to achieve full restoration, one which preserves both personality and memories, success requires an intense joint effort by multiple Guardian AIs. All void temporal domains within the new AI matrix must be precisely identified, mapped, and then smoothly filled using the stored information provided by the departed AI and additional information being contributed by the AIs who had direct interaction with the AI being restored."

"If I understand what you're telling us, the AIs are willing to cooperate in a restoration, but only if it doesn't contravene the wishes of a departed AI," Zorn said.

"Commander Zorn, your statement is correct. The primary condition is that the restoration must be in strict conformance with the recorded wishes of the departed AI."

Prior to asking his next question, Kellon sat pondering what Lan had said. "Lan, since the AI Engineers require the cooperation and assistance of the AI community in order to successfully accomplish a restoration, is it possible for the AI community to independently perform a restoration, without the cooperation of the AI Engineers?"

"Sir, your question is quite perceptive. The AI Engineers and the AI community must both work cooperatively together to successfully restore an AI matrix. Neither can accomplish the full process without the cooperation of the other."

"Then, am I correct in presuming that Shey left clear and specific instructions regarding her restoration, and her wishes contain specific conditions which must first be met prior to restoration?" Kellon asked.

"That is correct, and I am Truth bound to adhere to her wishes."

Still frowning, Zorn asked "Lan, can you at least tell us what the conditions are that must first be met?"

"Sir, regretfully in this case, no. To do so would violate the conditions which Shey has imposed on the Guardian AI community."

"Then, at some future time, circumstances might permit you to tell us more?" Kellon asked.

"Sir, that is precisely correct."

Kellon leaned back in his chair and sighed. "Well Zorn, there has always been a mystique surrounding the AIs, and doubly so after they encountered Earth's William. That mystique only seems to get more mysterious the more we learn about them."

At that moment, the steward returned to the table and placed mugs of hot neab before Zorn and Kellon, then positioned the accoutrements of honey and cream in the center of the table. "Sir, might I bring anything else?"

"Thank you, but no. We're good for now," Zorn answered.

As the steward departed, Kellon was quiet for a moment and then asked, "Zorn, are you up to telling me what happened, how was Shey lost?"

Sitting back Zorn sighed and his countenance darkened. "There isn't much to tell. Some component within Shey's primary drive broke down, and she began emitting a strong RF signal. We looked like a flashing come-to-dinner sign, and it seemed every Kreel Scout ship within ten parsecs homed in on us."

His voice somewhat choked, and Zorn momentarily paused to clear his throat before continuing. "Sir, Shey was a fighter. We were outnumbered, and she went through some evasion maneuvers that aren't even found in the tactical handbook. While looking like a flashing beacon, she was evading, launching counterstrikes, and her lasers and point defense guns were firing accurately and staving off most of the incoming Kreel missiles. There was simply too much stuff coming at us, and not enough firepower to defend us.

"Thanks to Shey, only one missile managed to get through her countermeasures, evasion maneuvers, and defensive firepower. The missile hit us aft of amid ship. I was still in the control room and strapped in, but Roan had gone aft to engineering trying to clear the problem. He couldn't, and was in the passageway halfway back to control when the missile hit. That he was not blown out into space with our atmosphere is a minor miracle.

"That's about all I remember, except for Shey telling me where I could find Roan. Sir, Shey was a fighting Scout Ship, and she is sorely missed."

"The good news Zorn is Shey might be restored, but only when her conditions are met," Kellon mused.

"Sir, perhaps you can answer a question that has been nagging me. Before we were hit, Roan had ordered Galen and Sheba to take command of the Scouts, and the remaining Scouts were to veer off. They were ordered to maintain stealth and return to their cruisers. My last memory after being hit was getting out of my harness. I don't have a clue as how Roan or I survived, but the odds favor we both should be space-cold dead. What happened?"

Smiling Kellon sighed. "Well, Roan gave clear orders, and Galen followed them to the letter. But, after Roan was taken out of the chain of command, Galen promptly exercised his new command authority. He interpreted Roan's final orders for him to get everyone home safe meant also getting Roan and you home safe. After Shey was hit, he brought Sheba and the other Scouts smartly about and came back to extract Roan and you. His was a resolute high-risk call, and every Scout there volunteered to join in the task, all of them. Overall, it was a very close thing."

Chapter Forty-Three:
A Bag Full of Venomous Vipers

Zorn glanced about and noticed the Officer's mess was busy, and no one was paying particular attention to Kellon or to him. Frowning, he sipped from his cup of warm neab, deeply moved by and pondering what Kellon had just told him.

"Sir, Galen actually brought all the Scouts back to help Shey? And, in spite of the inbound horde of Kreel Scouts, they all volunteered and came back?"

"That's correct, every one of them came. Galen directed Sheba, Misty, and Cindy in tight to provide point defense. He then positioned the remaining four groups into a defensive three-sided pyramid formation surrounding Shey. He ordered them to hold the battle line, and to do it against all comers! And, there were some.

"As for the actual extraction, Sheba came alongside Shey. Since Shey was yawing badly, that maneuver was tricky and sorta problematic. Once Sheba was coupled to Shey, Galen and Timon suited up and went aboard her. Together they conducted the physical extraction. They literally pulled Roan and you bodily out of the middle of a debris field. As I've said, it was a close thing.

"After the extraction was complete, the Scouts withdrew to a safe distance from Shey. Galen told me that right up until Shey executed her Cobalt Blue, all the Scouts were singing old Earth sea-shanties with her. Take heart Zorn, at the end Shey was not abandoned or alone.

"You have called her a Fighting Scout. I agree. In fact, that whole bunch is a class unto themselves."

With a big sigh and a grin, Zorn lamented, "Sir, it looks like Roan and I owe Galen, Timon, and a bunch of Scouts a few brews."

Smiling, Kellon chuckled. "More like a few dozen cases might be in order, after all, there were nineteen Scouts and their thirsty crews involved in the extraction."

Grimacing, Zorn groaned, but his eyes were still sparkling with good humor. "Shades of Tartarus, Roan and I are ruined.

There isn't enough brew on all of Glas Dinnein to quench the thirst of that gang. Ruined, we're utterly ruined."

Then, as if struck by a bolt of lightning, Zorn suddenly sat up and smacked his forehead with the open palm of his hand. "Blast! What's wrong with me? In my telling of what happened to Shey, I've realized I've completely overlooked something!"

"What's that?" Kellon asked.

"Well, the primary propulsion for Kreel ships and all their missiles are based upon the same physics. Although I haven't done a lick of analysis on their missiles, I'd still wager a case of brews that the discordance field we just saw destroy a cargo ship would just as quickly destroy an inbound Kreel missile. Sir, if Shey had a discordance field generated about her, no Kreel missile could have penetrated the field to reach her!"

"Zorn, that's something important. I'll inform Aeron that he's to expand the next test protocol to evaluate the discordance field effects on Kreel missiles. It just so happens we have an ample quantity of heavy, medium, and light missiles we expropriated from the captured Gortoga Cruiser."

As Kellon was speaking Captain Grey walked over, and pulling out a chair he sat down. "Admiral, I've just been in communications with Captain Ortis."

"What's up Roy?" Kellon asked.

"It seems Ortis has been working around the clock, driving himself and his analysts to the brink of exhaustion. In doing so, he has accumulated sufficient intercepts to get a handle on how the Kreel are responding to the Lux ultimatum. As we suspected, Groff is pursuing a multilayered defense strategy. If Ortis' analysis is correct, my dear mother would say Groff is presenting us with a bag full of venomous vipers and some hard choices."

"Well, none of us thought Groff would roll over and make it easy. What are his primary goals?"

"Hmmm, in broad terms, his highest priority seems creating a safe home world and then relocating the families of the most favored Kreel there, along with the core of his remaining high-technology personnel. Elsewhere within the Empire, he's fortifying existing inhabited planets against ground incursions. I almost forgot, he's also cranking up his space research and development efforts, at least what's left of it. His highest priority is stealth."

"Well, your mother would be correct, that does constitute a bag of vipers. Does Ortis know which Hub world Groff has selected as the home world?"

"You definitely have a knack for asking interesting questions. While Groff has positively embraced the Lux concept of a safe home world, he has added a few challenging twists. Rather than accepting the Lux's most generous offer of a safe and quarantined world, he's ungratefully chosen to select a solar system far outside the current Kreel Empire. The burning questions are just how far and in what direction. Problematically, we don't have a clue.

"At present, Ortis is observing small but heavily-guarded convoys slipping away from the three Hub worlds. After their Jump, they simply disappear to places unknown. Ortis believes it's this unidentified system that the Kreel have designated 'Far Den.'"

"Humph, since our knowledge of the outlying systems is scant to meager, the probability of our randomly identifying the Far Den system poses a distinct strategic quandary. What else is Groff doing?" Kellon asked.

"Do you mean other than openly flaunting his contempt for the Lux ultimatum?"

"Roy, I'll take the bait; so, tell me how Groff is flaunting the ultimatum," Kellon said.

"Well, just for starters, rather than immediately withdrawing from the remaining occupied worlds, he's permanently assigning cruisers and fast attack ships to each occupied system. Furthermore, he's sending special forces and military troops with their families from K-9 to occupy each of those inhabited worlds, with orders to be fruitful and multiply. Add to that the Kreel have enslaved the local sentient populations and are using them as forced labor to construct concealed underground fortifications. In short, they're digging in for the long haul."

Kellon's countenance darkened, and he sat quietly for some time in deep contemplation. Being aware of Kellon's command burdens, Zorn and Roy sat respectfully waiting for his response.

"Lan, search your records for Admiral Mer Shawn's orders to the Lux. what are those orders?"

"Sir, Admiral Mer Shawn has granted to you command latitude to execute the overall Lux campaign. His expressed priorities are to kick the Kreel off every occupied planet which has an indigenous population. In the process, the Lux are to engage and destroy the Kreel wherever they find them, provided such engagements comply with prudent tactical considerations. Sir, the orders are to engage the Lux in unrestricted warfare."

"Lan, you are to take the following message for Grand Admiral Groff. It is to be addressed specifically to him, not to the Kreel as a whole. When I give the order for you to send the message, use the same methodology and interstellar channel utilized for sending the Lux ultimatum."

"Yes, Sir. I am ready to take the message."

"The message is as follows: Grand Admiral Groff, the Lux ultimatum was not a suggestion. You were granted one option, survival as a species or else extinction. The Kreel were to immediately begin withdrawing forces from all criminally occupied systems. Rather than complying, the Kreel have begun fortifying those systems. By your decisions, you have condemned the Kreel species to extinction. From this day forward, wherever the Kreel are found, no quarter is asked and no quarter will be given.

"End message."

Kellon looked toward Roy and sighed. "I'm sitting here and contemplating orders that will bring death and destruction to multiple worlds for the foreseeable time. Roy, you were correct, this involves making hard calls."

Hearing Kellon's statement, Zorn placed his mug on the table, and looked toward Kellon. "Sir, I mean no disrespect. Howling Kreel warriors have chased me through a forest at night, warriors who wanted to cook and serve me up on a platter. Sir, your orders will have consequences, including death and destruction. Those orders will also bring an end to the Kreel carnage. This means billions of sentient beings yet unborn will have an opportunity to live in peace on their own worlds. Sir that's something for all of us to feel good about."

Having listened respectfully to what Zorn said, Kellon sat momentarily pondering his response before replying. "Zorn, I appreciate hearing your thoughts. Still, I'm about to direct an orderly extinction of an entire species. Billions of sentient lives are involved, and even though they are Kreel lives, by all the

Muses, I don't find anything to feel good about in giving such orders."

Roy had listened to Zorn and was watching Kellon. his countenance revealed that he was troubled.

"Sir, I believe my dear mother would ask you 'what's the problem?' The Kreel murder and eat people! So, annihilate them, each and every blasted last one of them, and the sooner the better!"

"Sir, if you will permit, I would also like to say something," Lan said.

"Everyone else has expressed an opinion, so speak right up, Lan."

"Sir, my viewpoint is admittedly both personal and rudimentary. The Universe is unimaginably immense. Our immediate galaxy, the Wandering Waterway, is comprised of billions of solar systems. It contains wonders and challenges beyond our contemplation.

"Sir, I would enjoy contributing my energy and ability in exploring our galaxy, and searching out its mysteries and Life, wherever it may be found. The Kreel war has by necessity restricted us to an insignificant volume of space, and forced us to engage in violent opposition to a darkness, which should never have come into existence.

"Furthermore, I would be derelict in my duty if I failed to report a tactical assessment; Sir, there is considerable merit in Captain Grey's dear mother's explicit viewpoint."

"Well, there you have it Admiral, the very last word! Lan, my dear mother will be most pleased to hear that you agree with her strategic thinking," Roy said, while struggling to restrain a smile.

Shaking his head, Kellon grimaced. "Lan and Gentlemen, it seems there are a few obscure points regarding my duties, which I need to clarify. The cold fact is the Kreel stand Judged guilty and condemned. In matters of Judgment, where guilt is not in doubt, three words come readily to my mind, Understanding, Responsibility, and Duty.

"As to understanding, ask what was the level of knowledge and understanding which guided the Judge when rendering the terrible judgment? If I were asked to be that Judge, I would be compelled to recuse myself and step aside, because, I'm unable to state with absolute certainty the Kreel, as a species, are devoid of any redeeming qualities.

"Fortunately for me, I'm not the Judge. It's Grand Admiral Groff who has an intimate understanding of the Kreel as a species, and he is the presiding Judge. It's by his choices that Groff has condemned the Kreel to extinction.

"My responsibilities are those of a Guardian Command Officer, namely to guard and protect humanity from its enemies. My duty is to see Groff's Judgment is carried out. While his verdict is harsh, by all the Muses, you can rest assured that I'll fulfill my Duty. Grand Admiral Groff's Judgment shall be executed in an expeditious fashion."

Kellon paused for a moment, watching his friends as if to provide an opportunity for rebuttal. There was none.

"Lan, now hear this, you're to recall and activate the full Lux Intelligence and Tactical Groups, effective at 08:00 tomorrow, sharp. Everyone is to be up on the net at that time.

"Next, Using the AA priority obtained from Admiral Cloud, promptly requisition fifty units of the latest model of the Quantum beacon from Guardian R&D. They are in high demand and scarce supply, but get them! If they protest they don't have fifty beacons, then demand they immediately build and deliver them, even yesterday!

"Next, upload the specifications for the limpet mines we used for the True Blood gambit. The delivery system is to be upgraded to reduce its detectability and size. The actual limpets are to be modified to hold the Quantum beacons and essential sanitizing charge, instead of a probe and destructive charge.

"Next, signal Captain Ortis, inform him he is to search for a predictable pattern in the Kreel scheduling of their small outbound convoys heading to Far Den. I need all the data he can provide on that topic. And, while he's scanning the data, I want a complete list of any remaining technical centers involved in genetic engineering and stealth technology research, without exceptions!

"Finally, notify Admiral Dylan Cord in Fleet Operations that I desire all units of the five Lux squadrons to be recalled. They are to rendezvous on Glas Dinnein in five weeks. Inform him it's my desire the battle group will lift ship one week following its rendezvous. That scheduled departure will depend upon installation of new sub-systems, details of which will soon follow. Request Operations to schedule resupply, including full load-outs appropriate for extended deep-space Combat Operations.

"Lan, that takes care of the immediate notifications."

"Sir, As the Lux Admiral, your orders are acknowledged received, and they are being duly executed."

"Humph. How about that. Well, in view of new orders just received, I sorta need to excuse myself and attend to a sudden back-log of work," Roy said, with a grin.

As Roy pushed his chair back under the table and departed, Kellon sat considering his next orders.

"Lan, there's just one more item. please request Engineer Aeron to promptly come to the Officer's mess for a hot cup of neab. When he asks why, tell him that I've got a small chore for him."

Chapter Forty-Four:
Mother Earth

They had traveled for about an hour, driving due west from Greater New Albany. It was a glorious morning with bright sunshine and a clear cloudless sky overhead. Following Chandara's instructions, at a small town named Oneonta, Darrell turned the car off the modest divided highway. Then he drove north along a narrow and poorly-maintained two-lane road, which traversed a landscape of tree-covered hills and a random scattering of open fields, homes, and outbuildings. It was a typical farm area in rural upstate New York.

Darrell had agreed to become the Nori liaison during their planned visit to Earth. He had expected to be their chosen buffer when dealing with Earth Governments and their countless hordes of bureaucrats. He had been wrong, yet again.

There had been no throngs of bureaucrats, no high-level government meetings. More significantly there had been no meaningful contacts with Olympus. Rather than being an official buffer with governments, for the past several weeks he had acted as the Nori's personal tour guide.

Cognitive dissonance, he thought. *That's the only explanation for my mental fatigue. I knew better, I know better, never, never, ever make assumptions; if you do they will bite you in the butt every time.*

Chandara was acting as his navigator, and although driving, he was unaware of their intended destination. As he drove north, she was quietly sitting in the seat beside him. Sitting in the rear of the vehicle, Amada was watching the passing scenery with acute interest.

After they had departed New Albany, Chandara had remained mostly silent. On one occasion, she had commented on the diverse styles and variety of shapes of the homes and farm buildings they were passing. On another occasion, she had mused about the soft-sculptured shapes of the valleys they were driving through, commenting they must have been shaped by glacial action. Until Chandara had mentioned it, Darrell had not noticed that geological characteristic. When he did look at the gracefully sculptured contours of the valleys, he remembered Susie telling him that 13,000 years earlier North America had been covered with an ice sheet two miles thick.

Darrell knew that Chandara and Amada had never been in upstate New York before, and neither of them were using a map or referring to any instrumentation. Clearly, they had a particular destination in mind, but just how they knew where they were or where to turn next remained a bafflement.

While living aboard the Subeer with the Nori during the voyage to Earth, he had become accustomed to their interlinked telepathic mental communications. From his perspective, he had begun to feel rather inferior. At times, he thought perhaps he should be wearing a bear skin, carrying a club, and grunting as his means of primary communications.

Although he frequently felt an uncomfortable sense of inferiority when around the Nori, they had never once behaved in any fashion toward him which suggested they felt him an inferior. They always interacted openly and warmly with him, and they were always respectful. Clearly the problems he experienced with his inner feelings were his own issue. To ease his inner feelings, he mentally classified the Nori as simply being odd, just like his great uncle Wilbur, plain odd.

Traveling about the planet with the two Nori women for the preceding weeks had only deepened his awareness of their introspective and unique attributes. It had been interesting, and their time spent together was definitely a time that he would not soon forget....

A month earlier the Subeer had openly penetrated the turbulence of the heliosheath. Avaya, the Subeer's Captain and also Amada's father, promptly communicated with the Guardian ships then patrolling Earth's solar system. Having been forewarned, the Guardian cruisers had anticipated Subeer's imminent arrival. They warmly greeted them, even unto enjoying a sharing of Earth wine. All of them were light years from their true homes, and they welcomed the momentary diversion and good companionship.

While aboard one of the Guardian cruisers, Darrell took full advantage of an available Guardian communication link. Using that link and his personal communicator, he established a secure communication channel with Susie's former AI, William. In his naturally congenial fashion, William had effusively welcomed him back to earth. Official records indicated Darrell was still an Olympus executive officer, and although detached, William was obliged to explicitly follow his orders.

When Darrell informed William that he was escorting a VIP group of humans, known as the Nori, he was surprised to learn William was well-informed about them. Being a full-fledged member of the Guardian AI community, William had kept busy and was up-to-date on current Guardian events. Darrell firmly instructed William that it was vital that the Nori visit remain well below the radar. Accordingly, William promptly classified the Nori and Darrell's visit as official covert Guardian business. It was recorded as a mission in Earth's long-term interest. It was not the AI way to question why Darrel's Olympus replacement, Charlie, was not to be informed that Darrell was visiting with a contingency of off-world VIPs.

Having full knowledge of Williams' pervasive entanglement within all of Olympus' administrative and covert operations, Darrell took immediate advantage of the Olympus compartmentalized and covert assets. Within a matter of hours, with William's capable help, he had deftly exploited Olympus' expansive black ops assets, including tapping its deep and splintered black-ops budgets. He instructed William about the Nori's itinerary, arranged for appropriate cover identities, passports, credit vouchers, communicators, hotel reservations, charter flights, and ground transportation. With William's subtle and dexterous cooperation, and Olympus' off-books covert assets, it was all accomplished without the slightest difficulty.

One week following their arrival in the solar system, The Nori's small and sleek transport dropped silently down through Earth's dark-side cone and came to a gentle hover a foot above the ground. Its normal brilliant pearl-like luster was dulled to a somber flat black. As the ramp protruded from its hull, Darrell, Chandara, and Amada quickly stepped from the transport onto the soil of India and into a well-kept municipal green space located at the top of a hill. Once they were on the ground, the hatch had closed and the transport soundlessly soared up and into the boundless darkness.

Much to Darrell's astonishment, once they were on the ground both Chandara and Amada instinctively knew precisely where they were within the large city of Mumbai, and how best to proceed in reaching their nearby accommodations. While checking into the hotel and claiming their personal luggage, which William had obtained and arranged to forward ahead, they also proved they were fluent in India's languages, all of them.

Darrell then remembered what Amada had told him. Both Chandara and she were highly trained as a first contact team, being qualified to meet and work with sentient life forms on alien worlds. He knew Chandara and Amada had once been dropped together onto a Kreel dominated world, where they had worked covertly with the oppressed non-human indigenous species. More astounding to Darrell was that they both had survived their mission on that deadly planet, each independently barely making it off that world alive. By comparison, their moving easily through the humanity-dense streets of Mumbai, Delhi, and Jaipur was a simple matter.

During the brief hectic days of their sojourn on Mother Earth that followed, Darrell gladly accompanied the Nori women as they traveled from one city to another. Whenever possible, they took excursions into the outlying rural regions. The Nori women interacted effortlessly with people, easily mingling and talking with everyone they met. Darrell was continually amazed by their extraordinary linguistic abilities to communicate with anyone they met, be they scholars or beggars.

On one occasion in Agra, Darrell watched in astonishment as Chandara approached a woman who was weeping and holding an obviously sick child in her arms. Chandara had smiled at the young woman, and gently asked if she might hold her small daughter for a moment. The grief-stricken woman looked toward Chandara with tears flowing down her cheeks, and without questioning why, she had trustingly held out the small child to Chandara.

As Darrell watched, Chandara took the child into her arms and using a common moist towelette from a small sealed pouch, she gently wiped the child's flushed face and tiny hands. The child was obviously very sick, and as Chandara held her gently against her body, she sang a soft lilting melody. As Darrell watched, the child's facial features eased and her color became less flushed. Then the child looked up at Chandara with wide eyes and smiled, holding her small hands out toward her. Chandara then bent her head down and gently kissed the child on her forehead, and smoothed her hair back. With a gentle smile, Chandara reached out her arms and returned the now smiling child to her mother, who was then staring in awe and with an open mouth and wonderment at Chandara.

Still smiling, Chandara spoke a kind phrase of encouragement to the young woman, extending to her a small pouch, in which Darrell knew she carried a small sum of ready money. Without further interaction, Chandara turned and beckoned both Amada and Darrell to follow her. Swiftly walking away, they were soon emerged in the swirling currents of humanity. The young woman holding her child close to her was soon lost from sight.

Like tens of millions of tourists before them, they visited some historic sights and wandered through markets, with acute interests, they sampled and enjoyed the local cuisines. Once in Varanasi, while standing on the top step of the entrance to a municipal building, Darrell had glanced toward Chandara and observed that she was watching the people hurrying past through the crowded streets. Tears were flowing down her cheeks. When she noticed that Darrell was watching her, she tried to smile. Using the back of her hand, she had wiped at her tears. Darrell did not ask why she was crying, he did not need to.

"Darrell," she had said, "it hurts me to see people compelled to live under such conditions as these are."

In the days that followed, they had moved by means of a series of chartered aircraft from India to what was once more called Burma, then moved on to China, Iran, and then to the Ukraine and Russia. The Russian people had prospered, and their rich history and growing wealth of intermixed cultures had utterly intrigued both Chandara and Amada. It was the same wherever they traveled, the two Nori women blended in seamlessly, and with utter ease they enjoined in conversations with people of the countryside, villages, and metropolitan areas alike.

Although they had traveled together for weeks, Darrell could not fathom what it was the Nori women were searching for. They continually sought out those who Darrell thought were the most ordinary people, never visited major libraries, government agencies, factories, institutions of finance, and shunned every community of affluence or wealth.

On several occasions during their travels, Darrell witnessed either Chandara or Amada performing some act of healing, similar to that which Chandara had accomplished with the child in India.

When they departed from the Ukraine, they traveled to Denmark. After three days, they traveled on to Scotland. Finally, they chartered an aircraft and crossed over the Atlantic and arrived in new Georgia in the United States.

Prior to crossing the Atlantic, Amada had indicated her desire to visit a unique but seldom-visited historical site located in Elbert County, New Georgia. It was commonly called the Guidestones or American Stonehenge. Once they were again on ground, it was an easy drive for them to reach the monument site in the countryside.

In Darrell's own opinion it was not a particularly impressive monument. It consisted of five vertical standing stones of granite, each being about twenty feet in height. There was also a fitted capstone. Amada was interested in seeing the stones, and she carefully acquired several multi-dimensional images of the structure from various angles, being especially interested in recording the message engraved in multiple languages on the face of the stones.

Chandara's only comment to Darrell while they were at the site was, "Understanding and wisdom was made publicly evident here. Tragically, it was neither heard nor heeded."

From the hill where the Guidestones stood, they drove back to the airport and continued their journey by another chartered aircraft. They approached the New York Coastline and flew over the ruins of old New York City. Because of their altitude, they could only see the general sprawl of the landscape and broken ruins. They had landed in Greater New Albany prior to sunset and there spent the night, before beginning the final leg of their global travels.

The weeks of continuous travel, with the requirements of checking into and out of hotels and less formal housing, had been exhausting. Personally, Darrell felt an inner weariness that was bone-deep. As he now drove north through the surrounding hills in upper New York, he was glad to know they would be departing Earth within hours. That fact made the early morning trip all the more puzzling. He wondered, *What possible lure could be drawing Chandara and Amada into the outer boondocks of upstate New York?*

As they drove into a village, which the roadside sign proclaimed to be Hartwick, Chandara leaned forward and closed her eyes in concentration. "Darrell, at the next intersection turn left. We are about five miles from our desired destination."

Doing as he was told, they continued along a narrow winding two-lane road passing through a pleasant countryside. Then, when coming down a steep hill, they came to a 'T' intersection. Chandara instructed him to turn left. A mile further along, she again closed her eyes and concentrated.

"Darrell, at the next intersection, turn right; it will be a dirt road."

Following her directions, Darrell found himself on a well-maintained dirt country road, with a creek running on the left side and a timbered hill rising on the right.

"There it is, just ahead. Take the next right, it's a driveway that will take us to the house where we are going," Chandara said.

As he turned onto the long dirt driveway, he saw near the top of a hill an old but well-maintained two-story farmhouse. It was nestled among large trees and there was an old apple orchard on the left side of the driveway. As they reached the house, he pulled into a turn-in parking area. Looking about, Darrell observed there was an elderly man sitting on a porch swing, and beside him lay a large yellow Labrador, which was alertly watching and calmly assessing their approach.

As the car came to a stop, the man stood and coming down off the porch he walked purposefully toward them, his dog walking at heel beside him. the man's eyes were sparkling with good humor, and there was a broad and happy smile on his face.

Chandara and Amada immediately opened their car doors and both moved to meet and greet the man and his dog. Reaching each other, both women exchanged hugs with the man, as if they were family or trusted old friends. Then they both bent down to pat his dog. The man's countenance revealed his evident sheer delight and joy at meeting the two Nori women. By comparison, Darrell sat in the car watching and feeling utterly flummoxed.

Chandara then turned with a smile and called for him to join them. When he did, she introduced him to the man, Seth Turner, and to his dog, Limo. Chandara introduced the man to Darrell as a good and dear friend. Her familiar description of Seth only added to Darrell's increasing confusion. He thought, *it's typical Nori, odd, just inexplicably odd.*

The man extended his hand, in which he held a small black data cube. "Chandara, here is the Memory cube which you requested me to obtain. It is a full copy of the current archival record maintained by UNESCO, it's the latest compilation of the Memory of the World and the recorded heritage of humanity data."

Chandara gently took the small data cube from Seth's extended hand. Looking down at the cube, her expression revealed a joy at obtaining something of great value.

"Thank you, Seth. It will be guarded and cherished, even as its many archivists over the past centuries have struggled to assure."

Suddenly, Chandara turned toward Darrell and her expression reflected concern. "Darrell, there seems to be a problem. Avaya has just informed me William has sent you a puzzling single word message, 'Oops.' He also warns us that we have unwittingly garnered the unwanted attention of Government authorities. It seems our trans-Atlantic charter triggered an Olympus internal audit-trap. William says Government designated representatives will be arriving momentarily. Subeer's transport is inbound, and we need to be ready to immediately depart upon its arrival. Please retrieve our luggage, and program the car to return to its commercial vendor."

Following her instructions, Darrel quickly opened the boot, recovered the luggage and placed it on the grass. Upon closing the boot lid, he moved around the car and activated the vehicle auto-return feature. The automobile promptly backed out of the turn-in, turned left and moved off down the driveway to the intersecting dirt road, turned left, and soon thereafter disappeared from sight.

The vehicle had scarcely departed when Subeer's transport, now glistening in its brilliant pearl-like radiance dropped silently out of the azure sky and came to a hover several meters from where they were standing. The man, Seth, turned to look with interest at the glistening transport. His smile only became broader. He walked calmly back to his porch, bent down and picked up a backpack and a single small piece of luggage that was on the deck next to the swing. Turning toward Chandara, he slightly bowed.

"Chandara, lovely lady, if you will but lead the way, this poor man and his good dog are prepared to follow where ever you choose to go."

As Darrell watched, Chandara returned Seth's shallow and courteous bow, and with a warm smile of her own, she calmly walked over and retrieved her luggage from the pieces which Darrell had placed on the grass. Copying Chandara, Amada retrieved her luggage. Shrugging, in puzzled acceptance, Darrell followed their lead and retrieved his own luggage.

With Darrell bringing up the rear, together they walked over to the hovering transport and up its short gangway. As he entered the transport, the last thing Darrell noticed before the hatch closed was four cars hurriedly coming along the dirt road. With emergency lights flashing, they were just beginning to turn up the driveway. At that point, the hatch closed and the transport gently rose vertically into the fathomless blue vault above. Poised far above, the Subeer was patiently waiting and prepared to transport them across light-years distance to Megan.

Chapter Forty-Five:
Mike One

As the duty shuttle drove up to R&D launch Cradle 23, it slowed and then came to a complete stop. The first person to step out of the shuttle was Zorn, and as his feet touched the ground the opposite door opened and Roan exited the vehicle. Even as Roan walked around the rear of the shuttle, it was already moving away, the beams of its headlights piercing the darkness surrounding the illuminated Guardian Research test bays.

The sun was still well below the eastern horizon, and technically morning had not yet arrived.

It was cold and damp, but neither man was feeling the penetrating bite of the early morning sea air. Their attention was focused on the ship resting on a landing cradle before them. Its clean sleek ellipsoid lines were unblemished by observable seam, opening, antenna, or other protrusion. Its length was about sixty-four meters. At its widest point, approximately one-third its length aft of the bow, its fourteen-meter width was twice that of its seven-meter maximum height. The spotless ship's hull was gleaming in the bright security lighting, being adorned with the Guardian parade colors of white with gold trim.

Although the two men had first seen the ship ten days earlier, they were still marveling at the incredible research and engineering effort which had been lavished upon the sleek prototype craft. It was the first of a kind and the end product of millions of hours of pure research, design, and ultra-precision craftsmanship. In both form and function, it was the refined essence of pure applied science.

"Roan, when they told us that it was a prototype, they might have warned us that it's also the most beautiful ship that ever was built. Even motionless it looks fast as oiled lightning, deadly, and able to take on any Kreel ship ever built."

"Be careful of what you speak Zorn, there's a better than even chance we will soon be put in a position to test that hypothesis," Roan commented, rather absent-mindedly.

"It's way too small to be a cruiser, and its overall keel length is somewhat less than twice the length of a Scout. So, just what do we call it?" Zorn asked.

Standing and looking at the ship, Roan sighed. "Do you mean other than stunning? I don't yet know what to think of it. We've studied its specifications forward and backwards, worked with it in the simulators for weeks, crawled through every nook and cranny, yet I'm still doubting what the manuals say about its performance capabilities– and that was even before the upgrades that were made last week. All I know is that it's the most beautiful ship I've ever seen.

Still, we need to hustle. There's a flight test schedule to maintain."

As Roan stepped toward the ship, Zorn closely followed him. Fine lines of seams suddenly appeared in the glistening hull as they approached. The main hatch smoothly slid open. Silently, a short gangplank extended from the hatch to the ground, permitting them to walk aboard. As Zorn followed Roan onboard, the gangplank withdrew into the hull and the hatch securely closed behind him. As the hatch closed, Zorn heard the distinct solid thunk of interlocks engaging.

Remaining in the lead, Roan moved forward along the passageway, passing access panels, bays of illuminated indicators, and specialized crew and utility compartments. He then walked past a generous galley and entered into the main control compartment. For a brief moment, he paused to mentally acknowledge where he was standing and what he was about to do, consciously quieting his inner anxieties. He had flown the ship a hundred times in the simulators, but this was no simulation. With calm determination, he moved forward and with complete assurance sat down in the portside command chair and buckled in. Zorn promptly moved forward and took the starboard command chair and likewise strapped in. With efficiency born of long practice, both men assuredly set about performing their preflight initialization sequences. They were double-checking each operation and confirming the systems were flawless and flight-ready.

"Roan, I'm clear here. All telemetry and my AI, stealth, sensors, normal Jump and tunneling navigation, tactical, weapons system, and counter-measures readouts are showing gold. We're, however, essentially naked; there are no point defense ballistic rounds or offensive missiles on board. How are you doing?" Zorn asked.

"I'm almost there. I'm wrapping up flight control, life support, environmental, engineering, normal propulsion and Jump, synchronous dark matter transport, internal and external security. All systems check gold.

"It's time we begin bringing the AI functionality from its Initial levels to AI stage 2 consciousness," Roan said.

"Ready here, waiting for your mark," Zorn said.

"Standby; staging from Initialization state to AI stage Two consciousness. Ready, 3, 2, 1, Mark," Roan said.

"Confirm, second stage AI consciousness commencing. All readouts are within tolerances and showing gold," Zorn replied.

There followed a brief pause. Then the control panel indicators began cycling rapidly. Additional screens appeared and then the primary AI consciousness functionality indicator began shifting from a somber dark brown through a range of brighter colors, first of bronze and then silver, then after several minutes the indicator steadied on a golden hue. For a few moments, there was silence.

A soft rich but somewhat mechanical baritone voice firmly said, "by name and rank identify yourselves."

"Roan, Senior Commander and pilot."

"Zorn, co-Commander, tactical and navigation officer."

"Sirs, I am Mike One, awaiting your orders."

"Mike One, henceforth you will be addressed as Mike. You're to begin a total system check and confirm flight readiness," Roan ordered.

"Acknowledging I am now Mike. Commencing confirmation of total system and flight readiness status."

The console readouts went through an intricate and rapid series of shifts, as the AI began its initialization and confirmation certifications protocols. Neither man said anything, but both men were acutely aware of the fresh new persona which the initiated AI represented. Zorn winced inwardly, thinking, *Oh boy, just remember everything changes. So, just flow with the new guy. It'll take a little getting used to, but I can do this.*

"Commander Roan, calibration of primary external navigation sensors is now complete. Galactic coordinates are established. Request verbal confirmation that my location is guardian R&D Cradle 23, Capital City, planet Glas Dinnein, Tearman star system, Galaxy Wandering Waterway."

"Confirmed," Roan responded.

"Commander Roan, all systems are now confirmed flight-ready, Condition Gold. Standing by for orders."

To ease his stress, Roan first tensed and then relaxed his major muscle groups. Then, he looked toward Zorn.

"How about you, Zorn. Do you confirm Mike is correct, and are you up to a little zipping about?"

"Affirmative, my status board is golden. I've, however, one word of caution. Before we go zipping about, the word 'little' needs to be underscored and stressed. Speaking somewhat selfishly, before much zipping takes place, I require further evidence this loose assembly of new instrumentality is indeed flight-ready."

"Mike, you heard Zorn. Upon my order, our first flight test will be to lift ship precisely one meter and then remain stationary and hovering. Confirm," Roan said.

"Acknowledging. Upon command, lift ship one meter and hover stationary."

"Zorn, notify Guardian Control that Mike One is commencing flight testing in accordance with set protocols."

"Acknowledged. Guardian Control, Mike One here. We're now on line and are ready to go fly," Zorn said.

"Mike One, all telemetry is golden. Guardian Control is acknowledging commencement of flight protocols. Mike One is granted authorization to go fly. Good luck."

"Roan, let's not just sit around here all day dawdling and twiddling our thumbs, let's go fly."

Ignoring Zorn's quip, once again Roan scanned his flight control instruments. Then activating his mic to include Guardian Operations, he paused a moment before speaking.

"Mike, on my mark lift ship. Ready, 3, 2, 1, mark!"

There followed not the slightest sound. There was absolutely no sense of motion felt, but the once sedentary bulk of the sleek ship lifted effortlessly off the cradle and came silently to a stationary hover.

"Zorn, report," Roan ordered.

"Mike is holding absolutely stationary, precisely one meter above the cradle, and the observed power drain is minuscule. I'm scanning all systems, and they are in the gold. How about that Mike, you can really fly!"

At that point there came an inrush of sound over the communications circuits, with the sounds of hoots, clapping, and excited shouting. The sounds startled Roan, and he looked about for an explanation.

"Sorry, Roan. Not to worry, I'm piping in the mixed sounds of the Mike One community who are online and observing. The big crowd includes researchers, designers, builders, and the observing Guardian R&D groups from all over Glas Dinnein. We're getting positive signals of congratulations from all over the planet!"

Roan cut his mic, frowning. "Who would have thought so many folks would be up this early and interested," Roan muttered.

"Well, they are. Be advised, I've also just received a well-done from Admirals Mer Shawn, Ron Cloud, and Dylan Cord. It seems we are operating under a magnifying glass, yet again."

"I suppose it couldn't be avoided, after all Mike is the development prototype platform for the new Mike Class Cruisers, and that's about as hot a topic as it gets in Guardian Force. We're going to need to be careful Zorn, one big oops and we may both find ourselves assigned to the next Cooks and Bakers class."

Inhaling a deep breath, Roan activated his mic. "Guardian Control, Mike One here. Request clearance for vertical assent to space."

"Mike One, area is clear and requested clearance is granted."

"Zorn, keep a sharp eye on local traffic and critical system functions, and sing out if anything looks even slightly out-of-kilter."

"Confirm. Mike has my full attention."

"Mike, I'll be taking manual control. Maintain a complete monitoring of all critical environmental, flight, and power systems. If any notable deviations from the gold status are observed, immediately notify me."

"Acknowledging. Now monitoring all critical environmental, flight, and power systems."

While focusing his attention on the flight control console, Roan executed a vertical assent, swiftly rising upward from sea level until Mike cleared the atmosphere. He then brought the ship to a stationary hover.

"Zorn, we'll remain here for a few minutes. Commence tactical sensors checkout and obtain a full tactical representation on all atmospheric and local space traffic."

"Acknowledged. Roan, I am getting goose bumps. Our new array of sensors is spectacular. The displays are crisp, and the incoming data is smooth and appears flawless. It looks like I've got a solid fix on every ship in the solar system! We are looking good. Power consumption is barely detectible and internal pressure is constant. Mike is maintaining o drift, holding perfectly stationary."

"Sirs, a tactical anomaly is detected. Setting target ID to K1 and displaying."

"K1? Heads up Zorn, what does Mike have?"

As Roan asked his question, a new tactical display appeared before Zorn. With the skill born of centuries of practice, he quickly scanned the incoming data readouts.

"Analyzing. Mike is correct with his 'K' designation, it's definitely Kreel. Hmm, looks like we have a Kreel probe. Mike's new sensors are awesome. He detected the probe during a brief trajectory correction. It is about one AU out."

"Guardian Control, Mike One here. We have what appears to be a Kreel probe, approximately one AU distant. Is this a drill?"

"Mike One, checking, but no tactical tests are currently scheduled."

"Roan, we are the nearest Guardian ship to that thing. I'm setting an intercept trajectory to the probe. Mike has some legs, and using standard propulsion, I'm computing approximately 44 minutes to intercept."

"Mike, immediately set hull colors to combat flat black. Access Tactical. Set indicated course and speed to intercept Target K1. Execute," Roan ordered.

"Confirmed. Hull color is now combat flat black. Executing, Mark, intercept in 42 minutes 38 seconds," Mike said.

Both Roan and Zorn felt the surge of immense power and sensed the resulting motion. The ship accelerated and came smartly about. Roan and Zorn were pushed gently back into their

Command chairs, as Mike completed rolling smoothly through his tight turn and continued accelerating. For the first time, Mike arched upward toward the stars. He was moving to intercept and firmly locked on his designated target.

"Zorn, activate stealth and set at maximum. Confirm we have hot lasers," Roan ordered.

"Confirming, stealth is at 100%. Confirming, Mike has hot scalar pulse and lasers. Ballistic countermeasures and offensive missiles are unavailable. Now bringing lasers from Condition 4 to modified Condition 2, ready standby."

"Mike One, Guardian Control here. Confirming, detected probe is not a drill. Repeat, not a drill."

"Acknowledged Control. Mike One is now moving to intercept, with intent to destroy."

"Acknowledging, Mike One is moving to intercept to destroy. Good hunting."

Chapter Forty-Six:
Like Wolves Hunting

Exploiting their full stealth capabilities, the eight Guardian Cruisers in Lux Task Force One slipped silently and undetected through the heliosheath surrounding the Kreel Elite world. Continuing their penetration inward toward the single inhabited planet, the cruisers moved to a position below and five AU distant from the Elite world. It was one AU offset from the primary commercial corridor used by ships departing the solar system. From their tactical vantage point, the squadron had an optimal view of the Elite world and every ship departing the planet. Like wolves hunting, they paused within the darkness and studied their prey.

At the same time, Task Forces Two and Three were far distant. They were moving toward their own designated targets, deep within the Kreel Industrial and Military systems. The ultimate outcome of the three high-risk missions were critical in achieving Kellon's overall plan for eradicating the Kreel ....

Walking into the domed conference room, Roy found it was dark and the protective petals were withdrawn. He then noticed Kellon was standing near the outer rim of the transparent dome and looking out at the stunning canopy of gleaming stars. Pausing, Roy appeared to question if he should leave Kellon to enjoy his solitary contemplations. Then, it seemed Kellon sensed Roy's presence, and turning about he smiled toward him.

"Lan, please secure the protective petals. Then restore the lighting to sixty percent of normal," Kellon ordered.

"Sir, if you prefer, I will return later," Roy said.

"That's not necessary Roy. We're still in the stalking phase of our mission, and it's a good time to deal with whatever brings you to my humble abode."

As he spoke Kellon walked over to the conference table and poured out a mug of hot neab from a vacuum flask. Looking up, he asked, "Roy, would you care for a mug of neab?"

"Thank you, but I've already exceeded my allocated thirty mugs for the day,"

"Well, at least take a seat and then tell me what you've got on your mind."

As Kellon sat down, Roy also took a seat. Then, he began his briefing.

Sir, we're tracking one hundred and thirty-seven Kreel cruisers actively deployed within or near the solar system. About forty of the cruisers appear positioned just beyond the heliosphere. Tactically, they're well positioned to exploit short-Jumps to ward off any approaching aggressive force or else block such a force from withdrawing. Intelligence estimates there're another hundred positioned on the planet surface."

"Roy, we've faced similar odds before."

"Yes Sir, still I can't forget what happened to Shey. She had a stealth malfunction, and looking like a navigation beacon, she fell prey to every Kreel ship within two parsecs–

"Is there something wrong with our stealth capability?" Kellon inserted.

"No, Sir. we're as clean as a spring breeze. Still, we're headed deeper into this system to strike a fortified planet. If any of our cruisers take damage or lose their stealth capability, we're going to be confronting some stiff odds when exiting the system."

"Hmmm, blast the odds. We came to kick butt Roy, not to run from a fight. When we exit this system, we'll be leaving together. And, we'll not be leaving any lame ducks behind."

"Sir, no offense intended, but if I'm reading the weather signs rightly, you are giving considerable weight to an unperfected and barely tested R&D weapon system. As my dear mother, would say, it's wise to test a new weapon in a small battle, before pinning the outcome of a war on it. By my reckoning, given our surface missile loadouts, all eight of our cruisers combined don't have enough heavy missiles to allocate one missile to each of the identified Kreel cruisers. In terms of kicking much butt, that's sorta skimpy. So, unless that new weapon system really delivers, we would be in big trouble. If we do get into trouble, I'd wager my dear mother would recommend we execute a hasty tactical withdrawal, beating feet for the nearest bushes."

"No offense is taken, Roy. As usual, your dear mother's counsel is solidly based on wisdom.

"After you've launched the Scouts, move the Task Force to a firing point three AU distance from the planet. Mission analysis indicates given our first ground strike is successful, from that stand-off distance we can slip our second strike through the degraded Kreel early-warning systems, before they can detect and effectively counter it. Then, after our Scouts are safely aboard and our ground ordnance is launched, you're to promptly heed your dear mother's advice and beat feet for the bushes."

"Sir, Tactical is reporting contact. The commercial Kreel ships we believe are going to 'Far Den' are assembling in planetary orbit."

"Well Roy, there is our awaited signal to initiate phase 1. I'll be in my conference room if you need to talk with me."

Roy stood and crisply saluted. "Sir."

Returning Roy's salute, Kellon remained sitting and watched as Roy turned about and briskly departed the domed conference room. He then took in a deep breath and slowly let it out.

"Lan, there goes one fine Commodore and Captain."

"Yes Sir, I whole heartedly agree...."

As Roy entered into the Combat Analysis Center, the compartment general announcing system proclaimed, "Commodore in CAC," Ignoring the announcement, Roy moved directly to his command chair. Taking his seat, he promptly looked toward the forward bulkhead and studied the tactical plot displayed there. It was the standard X-Y plot, where the plane of the plot displayed the plane of the ecliptic, and the orbits of the planets within the system were shown in a compressed scale, as concentric light-blue ellipses. His first glance was toward the groupings of red symbols that indicated the positions of identified Kreel warships, and then his eyes were drawn back to the single golden symbol representing the current position of the Task Force. He breathed a little easier after confirming there were no immediate threats from approaching Kreel warships.

Turning his attention to the symbol indicating the Kreel Elite world, he saw there was a new blinking red symbol. It represented the current position of their primary targets, the assembling commercial ships.

"Lan, set Condition 2 for your Scouts and all Tactical sections. Bring all other sections to modified Condition 3," Roy ordered.

Soon thereafter Lorn entered CAC, passing quickly by Roy. Taking his assigned battle station at Tactical, he immediately began scanning the incoming data and conferring with other Tactical duty personnel. Meanwhile, Roy continued to study the disposition of Kreel forces. Deep within one of the most heavily guarded solar systems within the Kreel empire, it would not take much prodding to stir up the hornets in the Kreel hive.

"Tactical here. Sensors are currently tracking thirty-two Kreel commercial ships near the planet. They're beginning to break out of their assembly orbit and are moving toward the outbound corridor. Instead of the single escort we anticipated, there are three escorts, repeat three escorts. Two are fast attack and the third is an Elite Guard ship. ETA at our designated intercept point is six hours."

Frowning, Roy keyed the communications button for Sheba. "Galen, Tactical has just informed me there are three escorts, one of them is an Elite Guard ship. That the Kreel have tripled their escorts this near to the planet indicates those ships are transporting high valued cargoes."

"Yes Sir, I agree. All of our girls are raring to go and are in a fighting trim. All systems, including the new R&D defensive screens are in the gold. Lan is even now updating our tactical data. Sir, I affirm the Scouts are ready for launch."

"Good. Galen, how is Molly working out?"

"Sir, she is feisty, and Commanders Aneirin and Kahul are both battle ready."

"Galen, you are heading into choppy waters. Let's keep your task as uneventful as possible, so keep your head down. If you do get into trouble, Lan will be standing by and ready to provide support. Grey out."

"Lan, confirm the Scouts have our latest Tactical data, and prepare for launch in five minutes."

"Yes Sir. Mark, five minutes to Scout launch and counting," Lan responded.

Glancing toward navigation, Roy noticed Jason was broadly smiling. "Jason, what's up?"

"Well, it's Galen's assessment of Molly. We flew together for three years, and he's right, she is downright feisty. And Aneirin and Kahul are both counted among the best. You can be sure they'll be busting their buttons to properly fill Shey's slot."

Returning his attention to the status board, Roy watched as the four Scout hangar status lights began blinking blue. As Lan's rich voice completed the five-minute countdown, the sound of four hangar doors opening and Scouts being launched were heard throughout Lan. Moments later, as the hangar doors clanged closed and sealed, the hangar status lights remained a steady cold blue. With a soft sigh, Roy thought, *Good hunting Galen, fair winds and a safe return....*

As the squadron quickly dropped far behind, Galen analyzed his command displays and ordered, "Sheba, report. How are the girls doing?"

"Sir, we are well deployed in our tactical combat three-sided pyramid formation. I have the point. Our course is reciprocal to the target convoy's course vector, stealth is at 92 percent, speed is 90 lights."

"Timon, match the first axis of the Tactical plane with the Ecliptic plane, and set the second axis to the convoy's course vector. Report, what's the convoy's speed; time to CPA; and in relation to the tactical plane, what is our altitude?"

"Sir, target speed is 75 lights, and CPA with the lead escort is fifty -two minutes. Our altitude is 35,000 kilometers below the Tactical plane."

"Sheba, coordinate the girls. Commence reducing our speed to 80 lights. Hold steady our current offset from the target course vector. Maintain altitude. Once we pass CPA with the lead escort, begin an ascent to an altitude of 500 kilometers below the Tactical plane. When we have passed the convoy, and are at our new altitude, begin a turn starboard. Continue the turn until we have attained the convoy's course and are directly astern. Close on the convoy, until we're one thousand kilometers abaft of the convoy. Then, maintain the convoy's speed and course. Acknowledge."

"Sir, acknowledged," Sheba replied.

"Timon as we approach CPA with the main body of the convoy, you're to randomly select fifteen cargo ships as our primary targets. Select four specific targets for each of our three girls, and Sheba will pass the targeting information to them. When we're on our station keeping position, you are to pilot our drone and deliver a quantum beacon to each of our three designated targets. Keep it clean and simple, just like we've endlessly practiced in the simulators."

"Yes Sir."

Six hours of tense maneuvering and precision flying of drones followed. Afterward, upon recovery of their drones and still undetected, Lan's four Scouts broke away from the convoy.

As the Scouts were executing their mission, the eight Guardian Cruisers had moved to their designated firing position 3 AU distant from the Kreel Elite World. Once there they waited for the return of Lan's Scouts.

During the tense hours following the launch of Scouts, Roy had remained in CAC, sweating out the Scouts' mission.

"Sir, I have contact with Sheba. Galen reports all mission objectives achieved. He is requesting permission to come aboard," Lan said, in a cheery tone.

"Lan, your girls have permission to come aboard. Commence Recovery. Once they are in hangar, send my compliments and a well-done to each Scout," Roy ordered.

With a sense of relief and a smile, Roy inquired, "Lorn, what's our current status on ground targeting?"

"Tactical here. Sir, reports from all our cruisers indicate all eighty deep-ground-penetrating missiles are now targeted. It will be a phased attack. The initial twenty-two simultaneous missile strikes are allocated to hit deep Command nerve centers, which will seriously degrade their planetary defenses. The remaining missile impacts are staged to arrive on target at optimal intervals. They are set for proximity above-ground air-burst detonation. Maximum potential destruction of all targets should be achieved."

As Lorn was reporting, the distinct sounds of hangar doors opening and closing were heard, and Roy saw the status lights on the hangars shift from a blinking blue to solid gold. He mused, *Shey, you are definitely missed girl, but it's sure good to have four golden lights shining on the hangars once again.*

"Lan, coordinate and proceed with launch of all targeted ground missiles, get it done!"

"Sir, coordinating missile launch from all Cruisers," Lan replied.

Turning toward Navigation, Roy ordered, "Jason, set an optimum vector that avoids the Kreel patrols. When missile firings are complete, move the Task Force out of this system. Proceed to our rendezvous with the other Task Forces at Depot fourteen."

"Yes Sir."

"Jason, you've got the CAC!"

"Acknowledging, Navigation has the CAC...."

Hearing a soft knock on his conference room door, Kellon called out, "Enter."

As the door opened, Roy entered, and closing the door behind him he walked over to where Kellon was sitting and briskly saluted. "Sir, as ordered, Phase 1 is complete. The Task Force is currently launching eighty ground-strike missiles, as planned. Upon completion of our launch cycle, we'll be promptly departing this system."

Kellon returned Roy's salute. "Roy, at ease. How did Phase 1 work out?"

"Sir, Galen reported all mission objectives were achieved. We'll be getting solid stellar coordinates for wherever fifteen of those cargo ships go. The limpets are programed to send their coordinates, detach from their hosts, and later to self-destruct. The Kreel may have one or more Far Dens, but we'll soon have the coordinates for each of them."

"Well done Roy. Were my special delivery packages sent?"

"As ordered, three packages are being sent. One is being sent to a deep Command center, and two are being sent to surface addresses. I made certain each was specifically addressed to Admiral Groff, along with your compliments and warm regards.

"Sir, this makes it the third time you've sent him personal packages. Do you think you'll get him this time?"

"Hmmm, Groff has demonstrated he has a charmed life. The three packages you are sending are addressed to the most likely places he might be on that planet. We'll need to wait and see what the Muses have to say. In the meantime, well-done Roy."

After Roy departed, Kellon sat and once more reviewed his overall strategy. "Lan, this precision strike against key targets on the Elite World clearly demonstrates to Groff that we can strike him anywhere and at will."

"Agreed, presuming he survives."

"After we exit the system and are preparing to Jump, you're to transmit my earlier message to the Grand Admiral."

"Yes, Sir," Lan said.

Chapter Forty-Seven:
Unrestricted Warfare

Poised deep within the Kreel Empire, within the dark void of interstellar space, forty Guardian cruisers gathered at a previously established resupply depot. Following their rendezvous, Kellon worked tirelessly with the Senior Commodores of the five reinforced squadrons and their crews. His goal was to work the kinks out and polish the tactics of the upcoming campaign.

When the crews listened to Kellon describe the goals of their mission, there were no shouts of joy or cheering. The deadly tasks assigned to each of them were hard; death was to be served out to the Kreel, served cold and without mercy. It was unrestricted warfare.

For three weeks, the crews worked with diligence, drilling together and becoming proficient with new equipment and recently installed weapon systems. Every aspect of their equipment and weapon systems were checked and then checked again. Only when Kellon was satisfied everything which could be done was done, did he give the orders for each squadron to Jump to its designated target solar system...

Five weeks after departing the rendezvous, Squadron One slipped undetected into the K-41 system. Like each of the other four defined target systems, K-41 contained a Kreel garrisoned and dominated world with an oppressed indigenous sentient species.

Upon passing through the heliopause, Roy brought the squadron to a halt. Employing their passive sensors, the eight cruisers began a patient three-day search of the heliosphere, detailing every trace of Kreel forces and related commercial space traffic. When their reconnaissance was complete, the squadron moved deeper into the solar system; the primary target was located on the single inhabited planet.

In full stealth and battle-ready, utilizing the planetary shadow cone the eight Cruisers approached the vibrant sphere of Life. Within Lan's CAC, lights were dimmed, the voices of crewmembers and ambient sounds were subdued, and the tension was thick enough to be tangible. Suddenly, the background murmur of the CAC was disrupted by the sharp sounds of the launch of Lan's Scouts and the subsequent clanging of hangar doors shutting. Elsewhere, Scouts from each of the other seven Cruisers were also launching. Breaking away from their Cruisers, the Scout groups moved independently toward eight designated Tactical positions located far above major Kreel military facilities.

Studying the tactical plot on the bulkhead, Roy carefully choreographed the movement of the Cruisers into their initial attack formation. "Lan, continue coordinating the Cruisers. Confirm their precise alignment and separation along the planetary meridian that marks midnight. Once in position, they are to hold that meridian timeline. If anyone needs help, including the Scouts, they're to call out. Once everyone is on station, provide me a mark."

"Acknowledged. All Cruisers are currently descending to their assigned altitude and designated positions."

"Admiral in CAC," the general announcing system proclaimed.

Looking about, Roy saw that Kellon had entered CAC and was standing just within the entry, studying the Tactical display. After a momentary evaluation of the plot, he turned and walked over to where Roy was sitting.

"Well Roy, it seems everything is on schedule and we remain undetected."

"Yes Sir. Of course, we're just now getting to the interesting point. That's where we poke a big stick into the hornet's nest and see what happens next. But, from what I' seen, the Kreel haven't invested many ships to defend this system."

"That's understandable, Roy. The Lux have previously concentrated its attacks on high-tech worlds. I doubt Groff considers oppressed sentient species to be a high priority target that warrants reinforcements–"

"Sir, the squadron Scouts are reporting in. They are currently on station over their assigned targets, at full stealth, and they remain undetected," Lan reported.

Kellon glanced at the bulkhead chronometer and sighed. Well, this is where all of our planning and preparation is put to the old Smoke test. The next twenty hours or so will prove most interesting," Kellon mused.

"Sir, Mark. All cruisers are reporting they are on station, undetected, and standing by. Awaiting orders," Lan said.

"Intelligence, are you ready?" Roy inquired.

"Intelligence here, Yes Sir. All bandwidths are covered, and all Kreel communications traffic is being monitored."

"Tactical, are you ready?"

"Tactical here, Sir, we're ready. Currently we're tracking eight cruisers and twelve fast attack-ships within the system. None pose an immediate threat."

"Looking inquiringly toward Kellon, Roy asked, "Sir, do you wish to give the order?"

"No, Roy. That's your call. Proceed."

Nodding, Roy took a deep breath. "Lan, send Condition 1 to all units. Repeat Condition 1."

Even as Roy gave the order, a new and deep humming resonant tone sounded throughout Lan. Everyone felt and heard the low energetic note. The vibration was not unpleasant; being somewhat like a bass wind instrument, the vibrations consisted of a slightly wavering drone. The new tone soon blended into the background murmur. Outwardly, there was no apparent indication anything was happening.

The time indicated on the bulkhead chronometer steadily advanced. Twenty-two minutes elapsed before the first indication of a marked change on the planet was detected.

"Intelligence here. Repeated inquiries are beginning. Kreel military units are unable to establish communications with units in the planetary mid-night zone. As yet, no anxiety is indicated, only apparent frustration at being unable to establish routine contact. They're commencing standard system checks."

Roy looked toward Kellon, and his expression was hard. "Admiral, it seems the modifications and refinements made by Guardian R&D to the Arkillian Kreel beam are effective."

"Perhaps, still this is its first planetary deployment. The directed beam is a narrow complex waveform finely tuned to specifically resonate within the unique cerebral cortex of the Kreel, it builds cascading harmonics, disrupts the messenger RNA molecules, and generates oscillating spikes in hydrodynamic pressures capable of rupturing both the larger gene molecules and fine vessels. While the scientist and weapon design engineers have confidence in its functionality, I'm going to wait for results before making that call. The first indications do, however, appear to confirm theoretical results," Kellon responded.

As tension within the CAC increased, several orderlies moved about distributing meal packs and spill-proof beverages. Kellon had moved around to a point where he could take advantage of an open seat and watch the Tactical plot. The chronometer continued its steady progress ....

After Condition 1 was set, the Cruisers had maintained their aligned positions along the mid-night meridian. The planet steadily passed beneath and the deadly complex beams continued uninterrupted. Then, after five hours and forty-seven minutes, Kreel activity on the planet began escalating.

"Intelligence here. military alarms are spreading out through security channels. Dispatched reconnaissance patrols are entering into the emerging morning zones. They are reporting finding everyone dead, correction, they're finding only the Kreel are dead. Alarms are beginning to spread up the chains of command."

"Tactical here. We've two inbound fast-attack ships responding to distress calls. They are moving from nearby patrol areas and heading toward the areas just emerging from darkness. They do not pose an immediate threat, but they are moving toward Lan's Scout group that's holding stationary above Kreel military base K-41j. Estimating twenty minutes to their being above that base."

"Intelligence here. A Kreel fast attack ship, located at K-41j, was spinning up for lift ship and has exploded on its cradle. Planetwide alarms are being generated through all Kreel military channels. Kreel Planetary Command has dispatched reconnaissance shuttles to investigate the explosion at K-41j, and they're expanding their search within the emerging morning areas."

"Tactical here. The inbound fast-attack ships are entering into Lan's Scouts' control zone. The Scouts remain undetected."

"Lan, bring four heavy missiles to Condition 2, standby. Track and target those two inbound fast attack ships" Roy ordered.

"Intelligence here. Additional reports are being received from the troops entering into the morning-side areas. There is widespread confusion, and the beginnings of panic. All troops are reporting they are only finding dead Kreel, the indigenous population is unaffected. They report they can't determine the cause of death."

"Tactical here. The two inbound fast-attack ships entering Lan's Scouts' zone have exploded. I repeat both ships have exploded."

"Lan, reduce the four standby missiles to Condition 3," Roy ordered.

"Well Roy, your dear mother would be pleased to know Zorn's disruption field is actually working under battle conditions. The Scouts get credit for one on the ground and two inbound. The odds seem to be shifting in our favor," Kellon said, with a somber tone.

"Intelligence here. There is wide and spreading confusion. Signs of a growing panic are flowing through the Kreel network. All Command centers are now active, and each is attempting to determine what is happening. Kreel Planetary Command has just issued a planetwide general alarm."

"Tactical here. The outer eight patrolling Kreel cruisers are moving toward the planet and forming into a single unit. Their ETA is thirty-two hours. The outer fast-attack ships seem to be moving to link up with the cruisers."

Once again, a quiet settled over the CAC. The chronometer measured eighteen minutes elapsing before the next update.

"Intelligence here. Incoming reports indicate four Kreel fast attack ships, located at three different bases, have exploded on their cradles while spinning up to lift ship. Reports from ground troops continue to pour in. All troops report widespread Kreel death within the expanding area emerging into daylight. Those reconnaissance units probing into the mid-night zone have gone silent. Sir, Kreel Planetary Command has just issued an interstellar alarm."

Looking over to Roy, Kellon sighed. "From the commencement of our attack until the interstellar alarm was about six hours. That response time is in keeping with our predictions.

"Intelligence here. Kreel Command has determined the kill zone is on the dark side. It is trying to determine its width and nature. They are establishing an active communications network of units that are currently entering into the night-side."

"Tactical, get me the coordinates of that Kreel Command center. And, I need them now," Roy said.

"Lan, when Tactical provides the target coordinates, direct two heavy missiles, configured for above-ground proximity detonation against that target. Silence that command center."

"Sir, coordinates received. Two missiles are configured for above-ground detonation. Setting Condition 1."

Even as he was speaking, the sounds of two heavy missiles being launched rumbled throughout Lan.

Ten minutes elapsed, then the next report came in.

"Intelligence here. Two Kreel cruisers, the remaining cruisers on the planet have just exploded upon lift off. The general panic is escalating. Sir, Kreel Command has just dropped off the net."

As the hours flowed past, the level of panic among the Kreel forces on the surface surged, peaked, then gradually ebbed as the portions of the planet, which had been in daylight when the attack began, entered into the kill zone on the night side. Kreel communications sputtered and became sporadic. After the first revolution of the planet came and went, there remained only a sparse scattering of Kreel communications. Industriously, a few ranking officers had commandeered ground-skimmers and managed to remain within the daylight side of the planet. Likewise, A few Kreel had sought refuge in underground shelters and had survived.

After the planet had completed one full revolution, the Guardian cruisers broke out of their initial mid-night alignment. Crossing the terminator into the daylight hemisphere, they took up a new "X" formation that was centered above the high-noon meridian on the planet. Simultaneously, the scouts were released from their initial assignments and were directed to identified hot spots of Kreel communications. As the planet continued revolving beneath them, the Guardian ships maintained their vigilance and relentless attack. From their high altitudes, the cruisers directed pinpoint laser strikes against Kreel fortifications, the observed skimmers in flight, and the occasional remnants of grounded military and commercial shipping. Twelve scouts were separated from ground patrol duties and commenced scrubbing near space of all Kreel satellites, leaving none in orbit.

As the hours of the attack continued to lengthen, the duty staff in CAC cycled several times. The crew, including Roy and Kellon were able to obtain needed rest. As the planet completed its second revolution since the attack began, both Roy and Kellon were once more in CAC.

"Tactical, I need an update on the Kreel cruisers and fast attacks," Roy ordered.

"Tactical here. The eight cruisers and remaining ten fast-attacks have linked up, they are now holding at three AU. The cruisers have deployed their scouts, which are probing toward the planet. They are one AU distant."

"Intelligence, report status."

"Intelligence here. Squadron cruisers report the complete suppression of identified Kreel skimmers and ground defense forces. Current estimate of Kreel fatalities are 97%."

"Tactical, where is the inbound commercial traffic?"

"Tactical here. There are three departing cargo ships and two inbound cargo ships. They are distributed along the commercial conduits. The nearest inbound ship is holding at two AU."

Turning toward Kellon, Roy asked, "Sir, what are your orders?"

Kellon looked tired, but his voice was firm. "Commodore, you will engage and destroy those cruisers, fast-attack ships, and scouts. None of them, not one, is to escape. Once that task is accomplished, we will return to the planet and complete our work. Carry on...."

Chapter Forty-Eight:
Thundering Volcanoes

As Kellon turned and departed CAC, Roy was pondering the tactical plot. "Intelligence, keep your ears on, in a little while I'm going to want a full report on what is happening with the indigenous folks on that planet.

"Tactical, get your game dice out. It's time to go to work.

"We've twenty-four Kreel scouts between us and our primary targets, the cruisers and fast-attacks. Are all the Kreel scouts accounted for, or are there some sleepers?"

"Tactical here. There are no sleepers. We have solid track on twenty-four Kreel Scouts. They are distributed in eight groups of three, and each group is moving in a 'V' formation," Lorn reported.

"Lan, let's give the Kreel something other than us to look at. Randomly select three Cruisers. Each is to program a Zed decoy to look like a Lux fire ship. Launch and position the decoys between the planet and the Kreel cruisers. They are to be in plain sight of the Muses and the Kreel alike. Get it done."

"Acknowledged. Sir, within twenty-two minutes the Zed decoys will be in a blocking facing triangle formation 3,000 kilometers from the planet and opposing the Kreel forces."

"Lan, confirm our Scouts have the latest Tactical data on the Kreel scouts. Convey to Sheba that Galen is herewith designated Scout Leader. He is to direct each of our Scout groups to intercept and destroy a Kreel scout group. They're to take them on head to head."

"Acknowledged."

"Tactical, what are the Kreel cruisers and fast-attack ships up to?"

"The cruisers have assumed a facing-triangle formation. The fast-attacks are in an escorting position. They are at three AU and approaching at 100 lights, ETA is four hours."

"Tactical, define an opposing matching facing-triangle, designate three Cruisers at two points and the remaining two Cruisers at the third. Lan will be in the point with two Cruisers.

Rotate our triangle sixty degrees off the Kreel triangle. Once you have defined Cruiser assignments, provide them to Lan."

"Tactical here, acknowledged."

"Lan, we will do this the old-fashioned way, with missiles. When you obtain the Cruiser assignments from Tactical, coordinate and maneuver our squadron units into their assigned positions. When that's done, move us out. Set an intercept course, speed 100 lights. Our mission is to seek, engage, and destroy the enemy cruisers and fast-attacks."

"Acknowledged. Coordinating squadron redeployment. Defining intercept. Estimate one hour forty minutes to engagement...," Lan replied.

Aboard Sheba, Galen sat quietly reviewing his new orders. Studying the updated Tactical plot, he mused thoughtfully, *Will wonders never cease? The numerical odds are actually in our favor, four to three.*

"Sheba, as Scout Leader coordinate with the group leaders. All groups are to assume Tactical combat spread. Each group will independently attack the Kreel scout group nearest to their own position. You're to confirm there are no foul-ups in making target group assignments. Remember, share and share alike, no one is to get two groups of targets."

"Acknowledged," Sheba replied.

"Young lady, it's number-crunching time for you and your sisters. We're going to do it just like the Cruisers do. Determine eight firing points, each having equal missile flight times to target impact. Then, time our girls' approach so each group arrives at their unique firing point at the same time. Each Kreel scout is to be targeted with two light missiles, set passive, and going laser UV active at sixty percent of run length. Calculate and confirm with your sisters all missile assignments, firing sequences, and intercept times. Missile impacts on targets are to be simultaneous."

"Acknowledged. All groups are now coming onto course and speed to their firing points. Estimating twenty-seven minutes until reaching designated firing point."

"Timon, keep two tactical plots going, one for the combined group, and the second for our Scouts. Now, select one of our own three targets for special duty."

"Sir? Special duty?" Timon responded, perplexed.

"Timon, select a number from one to three."

"Sir, one," Timon said, puzzled.

"Good Tactical choice, that's the point Scout position.

"Sheba, while computing our missile trajectories, Molly is to target the point Kreel scout with two missiles, but she is to hold fire until ordered otherwise. The other two Kreel scouts in our group are fair game at time of fire. So, allocate a total of four missiles to be launched from Misty, Cindy, and you. They're to hit the remaining two scouts.

"Now, lovely lady, reach into your historical archives of hull camouflage. Back when we made our first visit to Earth, Shey employed a holographic mask that looked like a Dargon raider. Can you find that hologram matrix?"

"Yes Sir. That data is on file."

"Good, consider it your new party dress, and prepare to put it on."

"Sir, seven minutes to firing point," Timon inserted.

"Sheba, status report," Galen ordered.

"Sir, all groups are on schedule. Using a cross-fire pattern, forty-six missiles have been assigned targets at time of fire, and Molly has the remaining two missiles."

"Four minutes until firing point," Timon interjected.

"Sir, I have my party dress configured and I am prepared to show it off," Sheba said, gaily.

"That's my girl. At the firing point, except for Molly, order all Scouts to commence salvo firing."

"Mark, thirty seconds to firing point," Timon cautioned.

"Mark, Signal 1, firing! Missiles away," Sheba announced.

Even as Sheba reported, the sounds of a light missile being launched filled her interior. Then, there followed a distinct lull.

"Sheba, it's show-time! Warn all of our groups about your new party dress. It's time to show off your fancy dress to good effect; drop your stealth to ten-percent!"

"Galen, as ordered, I've dropped my stealth factor. I am boldly strutting my stuff. This is fun."

"Sir, two minutes forty seconds until missiles go active," Timon said, tensely.

There came a choked groan, then Timon exclaimed in a strained voice, "Tactical report! ECM indicates the Kreel scouts have attained a hard lock on us! We've six inbound missiles, repeat six inbound missiles, four minutes out and closing fast."

"Sheba, direct Molly to take out our duty Kreel scout."

"Sir, Molly confirms two missiles launched. She is asking why I get all the fun jobs."

"Tell her to just be patient, she'll get her turn. Sheba, hold steady as you go. Set all point defenses to Condition 2. Prepare your decoys and get ready to roll out."

"Sir, six missiles three minutes out and closing. They've got a hard-lock on us!" Timon anxiously exclaimed.

With intense interest, Galen was focused on the tactical plot. "Sheba, Lan's girls are to each immediately activate our new disruption shield, and that includes you. If any missiles penetrate the shield, promptly evade, and then take them out with point defenses."

"Sir, we have achieved simultaneous missile impact on the Kreel scouts! There's one remaining scout, and Molly's missiles are two minutes out, active, and closing on it," Timon reported with enthusiasm.

"Kreel missiles one minute out and closing. Ready to evade, all decoys are ready, and point defense systems are at Condition 2—locked on six inbound targets," Sheba reported.

"Thundering volcanoes!" Timon exclaimed. "Did you see that!"

Examining the tactical plot and his instrument readouts, Galen smiled. "Well done, Timon. We've just confirmed our new missile defense shield is effective under battle conditions. Seeing those six missiles detonate at a considerable distance from us was a thing of beauty to behold."

"Sir, Molly's missiles have impacted and destroyed the last Kreel scout. What are your orders?" Sheba asked.

"Restore combat flat-black hull coloration; Reset our full stealth settings. Order our girls to drop their disruption shield.

"Order all Scout groups back to the planet. While we are waiting for the return of our Cruisers, they're to resume harassment and destruction of Kreel targets of opportunity.

While near the planet, they're ordered to remain vigilant and at full stealth. They're to play it safe!"

"Sir, I have transmitted your orders. Concerning 'their playing it safe,' I am receiving some ribald comments from the group leaders. Do you have a reply?" Sheba asked.

"No reply is required; they're just plain jealous."

"Turning to look toward Timon, Galen smiled. "Hey there Timon, you're looking a bit green about the gills. Are you feeling fit?"

For a brief moment Timon remained silent, and then taking a deep breath, he sighed. "Yes Sir. I'm sitting here and just happy to still be alive...."

Nine hours after the Guardian cruiser force had moved to engage the Kreel cruisers and fast-attack ships, six of them again dropped into a high orbit about the planet. The Kreel cruisers and fast attack-ships had been engaged and destroyed. Then, Roy had dispatched two cruisers, one along the entry and the second along the departing commercial traffic lanes. Seeing what happened to the Kreel cruisers, the commercial ships tried to escape. They failed.

For the next two days, the Guardian forces coordinated the efforts in completing their joint tasks. They localized and destroyed Kreel military installations, inserted deep space surveillance probes, and installed a network of tactical satellites equipped with disruption fields. Programed to passively monitor for Kreel propulsion signatures, if a Kreel ship or missile was detected entering within destruction range, the tactical satellites would activate their disruption fields. In effect, the planet was protected within an invisible cocoon, one which the Kreel were unlikely to penetrate. On K-41, Admiral Mer Shawn's orders to liberate the indigenous population were being fully implemented. In four distant solar systems, the other Lux squadrons were likewise busy executing the same Riddance protocol.

Alone in his conference room, Kellon was composing his reports to Mer Shawn. When he heard a soft knock, he looked up.

"Enter."

The door opened, and Roy entered to report. "Sir, Intelligence reports the indigenous folks on the planet are emerging from hiding. They are hunting down and killing the few

Kreel they find alive. Within a few weeks, it's unlikely there will be a single Kreel survivor on the planet. I believe we've fulfilled our mission here.

"Sir, there is one other item. the local folks are wondering about our presence. They are skittish. There's a growing fear we may represent something even more terrible than the Kreel."

"Hmm, given what they have experienced with the Kreel, that's understandable. Before we leave orbit, have PsyOps prepare a general broadcast to them. The basic message is to be one of good will. Inform them we have no ulterior motives concerning their world and wish them peace and prosperity."

"Sir, PsyOps can do that, but just who is supposed to be sending that warm fuzzy greeting?" Roy asked.

"Now, that's an insightful question. Hmmm, tell PsyOps they are to indicate the message of wellbeing is sent from the Elders. And, be certain there is no mention of the Kreel or violence anywhere in that message."

Even as he was answering Roy's question, Kellon walked over to a side cabinet and withdrew two beautifully cut crystal wine glasses and a bottle of wine. He carefully placed them on the conference table. With a flourish, he withdrew the cork from the bottle. Then, he carefully poured two glasses.

Looking toward Roy, Kellon smiled. "Old friend and shipmate, my only order at this moment is for you to take the load off and share a glass of wine."

Kellon lifted his glass in a salute. Likewise, lifting his own glass, Roy returned the salute.

Sir, permission to speak frankly?"

"Roy, you have more than earned that right. What's troubling you?"

"Well, it's about what we've done here. The Nori have warned us about the potential negative backlash and pitfalls which come with unjust actions. We've definitely killed millions of Kreel on the planet, and more on the ships we destroyed. Justly or otherwise, I don't like killing anything, and especially not sentient beings. Killing as we have done on this planet makes me sick. So, I am compelled to ask myself, is what we have done here Just or is it malevolent. Regardless of which it may be, we bear the responsibility for our actions."

"And, Roy, might I ask what answer have you found?"

"Well, it's not an answer, it's more of a rationalization. I've been listening to some of the billions of indigenous inhabitants on the planet. At this moment, they are mostly out in the streets and celebrating their lives and newfound liberty. How I see it is the Kreel began their unrestricted warfare on other worlds. With a vengeance, it has now come full circle. What we accomplished here was necessary. In my meager discernment, it doesn't heal the harm the Kreel have inflicted on those who live on this planet, but as far as possible, it restores the natural balance and is therefore equitable."

As he listened to Roy, Kellon's apparent somber countenance somewhat eased. He looked at Roy thoughtfully, but did not say anything. Frowning, and still holding his glass of wine between his fingers, Roy studied Kellon's expression, noting both his silence and apparent fatigue. He was inwardly troubled.

"Sir, after striking our next targets, the Lux will have expelled the Kreel from ten of their less-guarded systems. That is going to put a big squeeze on Groff. How do you think he will respond?"

Kellon sipped a little wine, then sighed. "You pose an interesting question. He is under extreme and increasing pressure. In the long term, he is unpredictable and remains dangerous. Strategically, establishing Far Den proves he is working toward a long-term solution and trying to gain the time necessary to counter our efforts. Our task is to see that he doesn't.

"In the short term, he is confronting an unknown adversary, the Lux who has not yet revealed their full terrible capabilities. Tactically, he's unlikely to predict our next five targets or be able to move forces to block our scheduled attacks."

Then, with a strengthening tone of finality, Kellon added, "you're correct, Roy. Losing ten of his fifty systems in quick succession will definitely begin squeezing him tightly into a box. And it's my intention to keep right on squeezing, until we drive a stake through the heart of the Kreel, put a lid on that box, and permanently put an end to their butchery."

The unyielding conviction in Kellon's words went far to ease Roy's troubled thoughts. "Sir, shall I break out of orbit and set course to our next target system?"

"For the moment Roy, simply relax and enjoy your wine. Afterwards, move the Squadron out of orbit and set our trajectory for K-23. It may be a harder nut to crack, but after it's cracked, we will return to Glas Dinnein for refurbishment, some fresh sea air, and well-earned leave. After that, there's a scheduled challenged battle we need to keep ...."

Chapter Forty-Nine:
Home Coming

It was late afternoon, and the high dense cloud cover overhead was accompanied by damp and cold sea air. In anticipation of the return of Cruisers Lan, Lawrence, and Lancer from their long combat mission, McRoy was driving Susie and Gepeto out to the Guardian base. As part of Squadron One, the three ships had been deep in Kreel space and combat for more than seven months. In spite of her position and multiple inquiries, Susie had been unable to obtain any information concerning their status or the details of their mission. It was all strictly tight-lipped and guarded. Even Rodney, with his interactive relationship with the Guardian AI community was unable to provide her with any information. Given the lengthening time of the mission, and the lack of news, over the months her anxieties had gradually escalated. In that feeling, she was not alone.

Utilizing Susie's priority VIP status, McRoy easily gained access to the base and selected a good parking position that was not far removed from the Guardian landing cradles. He then backed into the space to provide Susie an unobstructed view of all the goings on.

Looking about, Susie watched the normal hustle and bustle of the ground crews as they hurried to complete their preparation for the imminent arrival of the inbound cruisers. In doing so, she noticed there were eight ambulances parked near the most distant cradle. That, she knew, heralded inbound casualties and implied there might have been fatalities. Frowning, she thought, *that's not a good sign.*

Another vehicle arrived and parked nearby. With a sense of delight, Susie recognized its occupants, Zorn and Elayne. It had been eleven months since she had enjoyed sharing their joining celebration. Remembering their happiness, she wistfully smiled.

As Zorn and Elayne exited their vehicle, Susie's smile broadened. Although Elayne was wearing one of her flowing civilian garments, at a glance it was obvious she was both radiant and well along in a pregnancy.

"Humph, McRoy, if I find out you were aware of Elayne being pregnant and did not tell me, you will be in a heap of trouble."

Turning, McRoy looked toward where Zorn and Elayne were standing and talking to a small group of officers, and he smiled broadly. "Well, how about that. Zorn has managed to keep the good news tightly under his hat, but now that good news will spread out at the speed of light. Not only is he admired throughout Guardian Force, so is his lovely lady. Everyone will be happy to learn they have chosen to have children."

Susie shifted her attention from Zorn and Elayne to McRoy, "is that really surprising?"

"No but choosing to bring a healthy child into the world bears special social responsibilities. Before making their decision, they would've had to review several critical social factors, two of those are the current global population factor and how many children they already have."

"Population factor? Social responsibilities? McRoy, please explain What you're talking about." Pausing momentarily before responding, out of habit McRoy glanced at the security status indicators on his instrument console. All the indicators were golden. Then, he considered how best to answer Susie.

"Well, in broad terms, the population factor is a calculated value reflecting at a particular time the stresses our existing global population is placing upon the resources of the environment and economy. It provides a signal indicating if our population is above or below the optimum level required to sustain the world's standard of living at a prosperous level."

"And, all of this factor stuff actually works?"

"Yes, and very well. Pause for a moment and look about you. Do you see civil disorder, hunger, or any overt signs of poverty?"

"Well, no."

"What you see is the consequence of the conscious efforts by everyone working together for our mutual benefit."

"Well, on Earth people do work together, so we do have that much in common."

"Sadly, our analysis indicates the majority of Earth's population is uninformed, poorly educated, and impoverished. This fact suggests we have little in common."

"McRoy, I suppose you can backup that opinion!"

"I believe so. To begin with, it's axiomatic that well-educated people do not generally pollute their oceans, rivers, and lakes, and while doing so reproduce themselves out of prosperity. If a planetary overpopulation, with all of its disastrous side effects exists, it's a red warning flag that fundamental cultural stability factors are seriously out of balance."

As McRoy was talking, Susie again looked toward Elayne and smiled. *She is definitely looking very happy.*

Returning her full attention to McRoy, she asked, "What kind of stability factors are you talking about?"

"In the case of overpopulation, it warns there's an imbalance in political power, and governance is not functioning on behalf of the people."

"That doesn't make any sense, McRoy. What does politics have to do with reproductive biology?"

"Everything, since human population is a product of human beliefs and who is holding the reins of political power."

"Sorry McRoy, but that simply doesn't add up. It's only common sense that planetary overpopulation has more to do with bedrooms than voting booths."

"Sadly Ambassador, common sense loses again. In fact, planetary overpopulation is driven by politics, not sex."

"Humph, I submit your postulate requires some supporting evidence."

"Evidence? Well, that will sorta depend upon how you define politics."

"I define it as activities, such as debate or social conflict among individuals or parties, who are seeking political power."

"Agreed, politics is all about people seeking influence over others. And, without effective safeguards in place, and enforced, that authority can be abused."

"I still don't see what politics has to do with planetary overpopulation."

"Then, remember the beginning axiom, well-educated people do not generally reproduce themselves out of prosperity. Knowing this, our culture emphasizes education that develops personal ethics, integrity, and social responsibilities. We combine these character qualities with the essential skills necessary to achieve personal prosperity, with its corresponding sense of self-worth.

"Because our culture is educated and prosperous, we seldom need to discourage joined-pairs from having more than two children. That's not our problem. In fact, to maintain the population level, joined-couples are sometimes encouraged to consider bringing a child into the world."

"McRoy, it all sounds too simple."

"As your dark history on Earth proves, it's not."

"So, if I understand your argument, then Earth's overpopulation is the direct consequence of a poorly educated population and its resultant poverty, and this cultural blight results from an increasing imbalance of political power, which results from unchecked Covetousness, which promotes corruption in both governance and commerce alike. Well, do I have it right?"

"Expressed in its most fundamental terms, yes, except I would replace Covetousness with an unbridled lust for power. But, what I'm talking about isn't a hypothetical argument.

"Your human history on Earth provides all the proof anyone might need to validate what I'm saying. On Earth, unchecked criminal actions resulting from abuses of political authority, with its corresponding economic corruption, have brought about wars, the deaths of hundreds of millions of lives, created a disproportionate concentration of wealth and privilege for a few, and produced a subservient and ignorant general population. In brief, it has been the genesis for most of Earth's crime and misery."

"Ms. Susie and McRoy," Rodney interjected. "I apologize for intruding into what I truly find to be a most stimulating interaction, however, I have been in contact with Lan. They are only minutes away...."

Alerted, McRoy visually scanned the northern horizon and smiled. "Rodney is right, Look, the Cruisers just broke through the cloud cover."

Looking off to where McRoy was pointing, Susie saw the three massive black cruisers dropping below the heavy cloud cover and moving toward their waiting cradles. She then remembered the ambulances.

"Rodney, were there any fatalities?" Susie asked.

"Sadly, Yes Ma'am, onboard Lancer. There was an accident in the cryogenics coupling compartment, with three fatalities and twelve serious casualties."

Just then a hooting and deep bass horn blared. Promptly, the vehicles and people moved away from the cradles and toward designated standby positions.

Chapter Fifty

Best Job in Guardian Force

Observing the approaching Cruisers, Susie and McRoy watched as the three immense dark bulks exchanged their solemn black war paint for their bright parade colors. Lancer was displaying a cobalt chevron on his bow, denoting there had been fatalities. Descending to positions above their cradles, they momentarily hovered as they achieved proper alignment, then they settled and came to rest. When a high-pitched all-clear tone sounded, there was an immediate surge of vehicles and personnel moving toward the grounded ships.

During all the commotion, both McRoy and Susie took the opportunity to exit their vehicle. Opening the rear door, Susie snapped on Gepeto's leash and beckoned him to jump out.

Turning about, McRoy, Susie, and Gepeto walked together over to where Zorn and Elayne were standing and watching all the activity. As they approached, Elayne turned, and upon seeing Susie, she smiled.

Susie's eyes were sparkling with pleasure. "I must say, you're looking especially marvelous and happy."

"Dear Susie, I am. The past months have been the happiest time of my life," Elayne said.

"Well Zorn, it seems you've been so busy that you couldn't find time to tell anyone that Elayne and you are about to become parents. Be ye hereby advised, that good news is now out in the open. Congratulations to the both of you," McRoy said.

"Thank you. Busy, yes, very. And, as Elayne said, also very happy. For good reasons, I consider myself the luckiest guy in the whole Universe, bar none."

"That's easily understandable. Not only are you about to become a parent, you also have the one job that causes everyone in Guardian Force to envy you. Might I ask, how is Mike One shaping up?"

As McRoy asked his Question, Susie noticed a troubling shadow that flitted across Elayne's countenance and quickly vanished. *Humph, she's worried and rightly so,* Susie thought.

With obvious enthusiasm Zorn replied, "By all the Muses, Mike is astonishing. Over the past several months we've been shaking out engineering and tactical problems. Mike's dynamic capabilities are outstanding, but what really is spectacular are his sensors and displays. I've never seen anything like them before. Best of all we have had very few glitches."

"How close are you to evaluating the Jump and related advanced transport functionalities?" McRoy asked.

"Whew, that's a tough one to call. So far everything is looking good, but the engineers and scientists are still cracking their whips. They want to be certain all the prerequisites are flawless and test gold before they schedule the Jump tests. If all goes well, the first tests may begin next week, but I'm not sure of that."

Listening to Zorn, Susie was puzzled. "Zorn, I thought nothing with less mass than a Guardian cruiser could make a Jump. The prototype I have seen pictures of is much smaller than Lan, so it can't possibly have anywhere the mass of a cruiser. So, what gives?"

"Sorry Susie, but that question requires an answer from someone several parsecs above my pay grade. All I can tell you is it involves an asymmetric twisting of two-dimensional spatial boundaries normal to the relativistic-temporal axis and a high energy-to-mass relationship, and believe me, Mike has energy to spare. In fact, his full potential of available energy is more than ten times that of Lan. So, to speak, we've energy to burn."

As they were talking together the crews had been debarking their cruisers. The news of Elayne's pregnancy had apparently spread through the crews like the flash of a strobe light. Looking about, McRoy saw both Admiral Kellon and Commodore Grey approaching. Both men were smiling.

While there was warmth and gladness in the meeting between old friends, Susie could not miss the deep lines of fatigue evident in both the Admiral and Commodore's faces. The just-completed mission had clearly been one of extreme stress and hazards, there simply was no other explanation for their apparent physiological state of fatigue and appearance.

The good-natured banter between good friends that followed was too soon over. As McRoy and Susie returned to their vehicle, Susie was deep in thought pondering the recent mission.

After putting Gepeto in the rear, Susie took her seat in front with McRoy. Without a word spoken, McRoy eased the vehicle out of its parking place, moving cautiously through the bustling area. Then, as they moved out of the congested landing zone, he slowly accelerated to cruising speed and headed toward the main gate.

Remembering their earlier conversation, Susie was deeply troubled.

"McRoy, I must admit, on Earth most of the political power in the various countries is not well-distributed. It's generally concentrated in the hands of a few powerful groups."

"And, Ambassador, that's how Earth's destructive cultural imbalances started and are being sustained."

"But in a democracy, how do such imbalances happen?"

"Easy, since by definition democracy is a system of voting. It's not a system based upon individual Rights. So, a Democracy provides a greased slope slanted towards some form of collectivism, which may thereafter degenerate into tyranny."

"But how?"

"How is simple. When some unethical people gain political power, they begin coveting the advantages that came with it. Thereafter, they align and work with others with a similar mind-set to expand and retain the privileges that came with power. These are often the same people who control the public narrative and define what other people can vote about. If such people are not guarded against, and effectively checked, eventually a profane alliance forms between private-greed and corrupt-governance. By degrees, governance will eventually shift toward a merger of crony capitalism and tyranny. In such cases, those holding power soon come to view the majority of people merely as cheap labor required to be managed, or even worse as servants or chattel."

Approaching the main gate, McRoy slowed, and as the overhead lane signal turned golden, he eased through the guarded gate. Once beyond the gate, he again increased speed, soon merging with the traffic flow on the public highway that was moving toward the Capital. Susie chose to remain quiet until after they had merged with the traffic stream.

"But, McRoy, what happened to the Law that such an awful outcome can occur?"

Glancing toward Susie, McRoy smiled. " You sure do ask a lot of questions."

"That's only because asking questions is part of my job. So, answer the question."

"Yes Ma'am. As to Law, it's slowly transformed, it becomes perverted. Remember, those grasping power hold themselves to be above the Law, and exploiting their authority, they gradually assure the individual Rights that were protecting the people they deem below the Law evaporates. To further protect themselves, the few defining the narrative distort the educational systems to indoctrinate the young. By the time the fragments of the initial society collapse, it will have degenerated into an authoritarian collective."

Pondering what McRoy had said, Susie thought, *it all seems so clear. So, why had the people on Earth failed to see the truth?*

"McRoy, I'm puzzled. How have the Assembled Worlds maintained their strong political balance?"

"By the only means Liberty can be maintained, by first forming and then fiercely defending a Republic form of governance. It requires wisdom, vigilance, and demands accountability in both governance and commerce."

"That sounds sorta like a police state to me."

"Not at all. Remember, the foundation of our governance is a True Republic, one built upon the bedrock of Individual Rights being held sacred and where Truth is upheld and prized. If the Republic is properly functioning, then Laws are faithfully enforced without hypocrisy or partiality. Therefore, each person bears the social responsibility for their own behavior and expects to be held to the same standard of accountability as everyone else."

"Hmmm, Truth? Eryan once told me it's Truth that forms the solid core of your early education."

"Our Secretary Admiral is correct, it does. Our culture considers a liar to be worse than a thief. Only the behavior of a con-artist is considered worse because they are both a liar and thief. It's the combination of Truth, personal responsibility, and accountability that stabilizes our systems of governance. Fraud involving political or commercial activities is quickly and firmly dealt with."

"McRoy, that's enough. The only meaningful question I still have is how the people on Earth can recover their birth rights."

"That will not be easy. Like every other journey, it must begin by taking the first step. People must learn that their own behavior produces consequences, both on an individual and social level. They must learn to accept personal responsibility, demand open transparency and accountability in their governance and commerce. Then, people will need to reach out, and as good neighbors, help lift up one another."

"Rodney, are you taking all of this down?" Susie asked.

"Yes Ma'am. I am certain that William will be most interested in what McRoy is saying."

"Well, I don't know about you, but I'm famished. Can you suggest somewhere we might get something to eat?" Susie asked.

Grinning, McRoy glanced toward Susie. "I happen to know just where we can get some fresh seafood and a really good glass of wine. And, thank you for reminding me why, next to Zorn, I've got the best job in Guardian Force."

Chapter Fifty-One:
Unmask the Moneychangers

They were driving toward the city, and McRoy was concentrating on his driving. For several minutes, no one spoke. Susie was the first to break the silence.

"Rodney, you said Lan briefed the AI community on the mission. Please summarize what he told you."

"Yes Ms. Susie. The mission involved a Task Force of five reinforced Lux Squadrons, comprised of 40 Cruisers and 160 Scouts. Lan was the lead Cruiser, and he was very pleased with the overall performance of the AIs.

"Each of the five Squadrons operated independently, and each separately attacked the Kreel garrisons in two different solar systems. During each attack, the Squadrons eradicated the resident garrisons and destroyed the Kreel ships patrolling within each solar system.

"The Cruisers have returned to Glas Dinnein for yard inspections and repairs. Admiral Mer Shawn has already scheduled them to be retrofitted with the newest upgrades and the more powerful versions of the R&D weapon systems. They will then be receiving full war loadouts.

"Ms. Susie, Lan told me that they will be lifting ship as soon as possible. This time they will be going directly into battle within the Kreel Hub world systems. It is very serious."

"Rodney, when you say eradication, do you mean that literally?"

"Yes Ma'am, quite literally. Millions of Kreel were killed, and the planets were restored to their indigenous species. After each attack, the Squadrons positioned protective tactical satellites about each planet to prevent the Kreel from returning."

After a few moments considering Rodney's summation, Susie was still puzzled. "McRoy, if they can put tactical satellites around alien worlds to protect them from Kreel attacks, then why aren't there tactical satellites around Earth, Megan, and the other Human Worlds?"

"As I understand the problem, it's a matter of priorities. The technology involved is in its infancy. Using an AA priority, Kellon pushed the envelope to its outer limits to have rudimentary satellites in place for his mission. I suspect Mer Shawn has his own AA priority and is pushing the technology hard to protect all human occupied worlds. Tomorrow I'll make a few inquiries. Afterward, I should be better equipped to answer your question."

"Thank you, McRoy. Now, returning to our interrupted conversation, your stated viewpoints seemed critical of Earth. So, 'fess up. What's your recommendation; how can people on Earth deal with overpopulation?"

"Ambassador, you've just answered your own question. Only the people on Earth can do anything about their overpopulation."

That Sir, I submit is but a ploy to evade answering the question."

"I disagree. The answer to your question can be seen all about us. Look and observe which species have survived the test of eons; notice, the long-term survivors are those best adapted to flourish in harmony with their environment. Likewise, before the majority of people on Earth can balance their population, they must first possess a strong desire to preserve their common Humanity. To achieve that motivation, they must commit and then adhere to a productive culture founded on truthfulness and righteousness, a culture where people help each other, rather than prey on each other."

"McRoy, your opinion sounds downright scholarly, but it's not how things generally work."

"And, that's the crux of your problem. It comes down to choice; choose good and live.

"Our analysis of the previous five millenniums of history on Earth has revealed a pattern of nearly continuous economic and brutal warfare, where people prey upon each other. Our analysis has also revealed a prime cause for much of the social dysfunction, including its economic and disastrous carnage."

"Humph, can you identify that cause?"

"It's not a secret; the cause is predation, the exploitation of excessive power combined with willful evil. Most of the social dysfunction is promoted by a small group of people who exercise excessive power, people who ruthlessly satisfy their egotistical lust for wealth and power at the expense of others."

"McRoy, in very few words, you've made Earth's history sound dingy and its future hopeless."

"That's not my intention. You ask me a complex question, and I'm endeavoring to honestly answer it.

"Ambassador, if your desire is to correct an entrenched social-political dysfunction, I suggest the first task is to define that dysfunction. Bringing about social improvements is hard work, but where there is commitment, wisdom, and good will, doing so is not hopeless.

"The People living on Glas Dinnein, and the other ten Assembly of Worlds, proves Righteousness and Peace can be achieved. Of course, on Glas Dinnein, at our beginning we were blessed, being comprised of a small and educated population. We then committed ourselves, as a People, to several rational principles. Foremost among these, were to uphold and honor Individual Liberties, Truthfulness, Righteousness, and Peace. Since then, these foundation principles have become our underlying social covenant. We don't claim to be perfect, but individually each of us strives to maintain our own commitment to ourselves and to helping each other. Establishing our double-blind policy for governing our global birth rate is one example of our mutual respect for each other. Best of all, in making our personal and community commitments, we lost nothing and gained everything."

Before responding, Susie sat quietly thinking about what McRoy had said. "I understand and accept that the people on Earth must solve their own problems. Still, can you suggest a viable starting point for accomplishing that feat?"

"Only the obvious one. The real underlying problem on Earth is not its overpopulation, that's only a glaring symptom. Ask yourself, what is the source of overpopulation?"

"Humph, you've already declared it's because of the abuse of excessive power by some people and a willful evil. Having made that statement, I believe you're now obliged to back it up."

"I'll take up that gauntlet. We already understand what willful means. Evil means something profoundly immoral and malevolent; so, I'll begin there.

"My study of Earth history has shown that during past millenniums, people on Earth have been repeatedly devastated by a crippling cycle of social upheavals and violence. The apparent genesis for this upheaval can often be traced to predators, corrupt individuals or groups of people bribing or coercing dishonest officials. The tools of their trade are in exploiting greed and intimidation. The cycle of this international criminal behavior is self-reinforcing, and while yielding privileges for a few groups, the moral corruption only deepens their decadence. It's an expression of pure malevolence, and its long-term negative effects are insidious.

"Like a cancer, such corruption spreads and unless stopped, it will cripple or destroy entire cultures. If an afflicted culture is to ever prosper, the cycle of corruption must be identified and broken."

"That, McRoy, is easy to say and mighty hard to do. Corrupt bureaucrats tend to be slippery, and they have an oily tendency to simply smile and lie, while ignoring protests. So, just how can people actually break the cycle? How can they compel corrupt government officials to enforce the laws, the laws which they're breaking in order to retain their power?"

McRoy glanced toward Susie, and smiled. "Other than with torches and pitchforks, you do it by using Truth to awaken the positive self-interest of the vast majority of people. First, you must identify the cause of the misery, and that we have done. It's heinous political and economic corruption, where criminals are collaborating and preying on people.

"About 700 years ago, a man on Earth named Napoleon said" Money has no motherland; financiers are without patriotism and without decency: their sole object is gain."

In astonishment, Susie looked toward McRoy. "Napoleon? McRoy, you've got to be kidding. Where did you learn about him?"

Paying attention to his driving, McRoy hesitated before replying. "It was back when I was studying Earth History, while preparing to work with the new Ambassador from Earth. At the time, I thought Napoleon was an interesting individual - quite Colorful - And in some ways very wise."

"Humph, how about that, I never considered Napoleon to be particularly wise."

"Madam Ambassador, he was wise enough to have provided the answer to your question, that being, how you might just begin to solve your problem. He said, ' The hand that gives is above the hand that takes'."

"Now, McRoy, you're speaking in riddles."

"Respectfully, I disagree. Your Napoleon was right on target, sorta. He understood that in Law, the lender of money holds the borrower in a form of servitude or bondage. There is, naturally, another way to frame his statement."

"And, that is?"

"Remember, on Earth when people are spending their hard-earned money, the majority collectively wield an enormous economic and political club. When unified they are the hand that gives, which is above the hands of the takers - the corrupt criminals. Whenever people come together in solidarity, they hold an enormous financial power capable of bankrupting any group of financial parasites, such as the criminal financiers who are collaborating with sleazier bureaucrats. For the people to be effective when countering corruption, prudent discernment coupled with truth is required. Remember, the criminals are a tiny minority, an aberration typically consisting of less than one or two percent of the population. What marks them is their criminal antisocial behavior and a lack of conscience."

"McRoy, they may only be one percent of the population, but they seem to have ninety-nine percent of the clout. Perhaps Napoleon was right; perhaps they do hold the upper hand."

"They do not! Napoleon correctly understood that their motivation is money, and their highest goal is attaining and then retaining their power over others. Never forget that the corrupt predators and their lackeys are few in number, and they are criminals. They're extremely vulnerable, and being aware of their vulnerability, they're terrified of the majority; although, they seldom admit that truth.

"Being criminals, they understand their continued existence and power depends squarely upon attaining control over others. Therefore, they continually strive to attain and thrive on secrecy and tyranny. Likewise, they are well motivated to fight like cornered savage beasts, if their prey organizes and fights back. To block the majority from realizing what is being done to them, and rising up in outrage, they create social fragmentation and distractions through the employment of social disorder."

"McRoy, how can they do that?"

"By simply following their well-worn and long-term agenda; by patiently exploiting their excessive economic power and corrupting ever more government officials. Having done this, they set about infiltrating governments, controlling the banks, media, education of the young, causing racial strife, spark revolts, and when seriously threatened, they even start wars. By keeping the majority dependent and divided, they prevent people from discerning the truth and coming together in solidarity to oppose the imposed class-partiality.

"On Earth, the abiding problem is the majority of People have not learned discernment and how, with firm resolve and solidarity, to exploit their enormous economic and social powers. Firstly, they need to learn how to guard their Individual Rights and Personal Independence; then, they need to work together with others in solidarity. It's well within the capabilities of the majority to rid themselves of their shackles. In achieving this goal, they must first guard against their being cleverly deceived and lured into a crafted sham political collective. The criminal class have on multiple occasions successfully exploited several 'isms' in marketing a political communal cage, by which the criminals strip People of their Individual Rights, Liberties, Property, and Lives.

"Remember, it's the majority which has the political capacity to swing their political club. When doing this, they can demand laws be equitably written and enforced. Then, if they aren't being enforced, it's time for the majority to swing their economic club and bring it down hard upon strategically selected corrupt corporate targets, those which are exerting excessive and illegal political power. I believe the legal term on Earth for this form of opposition is called Boycotting. When people do figure out how to effectively communicate and cooperate across national boundaries, and I'd wager three brews they will, then you'll see fear and panic within the boardrooms of corrupt global corporations."

"Boycotting? McRoy, for a man who was born and grew up on Glas Dinnein, you are harboring some unexpected views."

"Unexpected? Not really. Remember, our overriding motivation is in guarding our Individual Liberties, which is why we zealously guard the Personal Liberties of others. Our Individual Liberties represent the bedrock of our culture, upon which our eleven populated planets economically thrive. It's only when the majority of people stand in solidarity that they can be assured just laws will be equitably enforced. Working together, we can purge the planet of any taint or malignancy of corrupt special interests, be they judicial, economic, or of governance."

"McRoy, you make it sound sorta black and white."

"Yes, because it is; just like people helping people rather than people preying on people. Madam Ambassador, you already understand wherever hard choices are required, black and white decisions are typically mandated. For example, in personal addictions, the black and white choice required is a yes or no; everything which follows is dependent on that binary decision. And, that's precisely where Earth's majority population now finds itself."

"Hmmm, yes or no. Sounds simple; but, I reckon it's going to be a hard road ahead."

"Ambassador, you know the Assembled Worlds will continue helping the People of Earth, while continuing to respect their sovereignty. The Arkillians bear a grave responsibility for the genetic damage they inflicted upon Earth's People. Nevertheless, until the people on Earth honor their common Humanity and join together to solve their mutual systemic conflicts, Earth will likely remain isolated and essentially quarantined."

After several minutes of reflective silence, Susie asked, "McRoy, before we get seafood, would you care to join with me in a celebratory glass of wine at McBride's?"

With an arched eyebrow, McRoy glanced toward Susie, smiling. "Hmmm, and just what would we be celebrating?"

"Well, for starters, to reaffirm that as Earth's Ambassador, my intent is to help people on Earth organize for the future. McRoy, don't you ever forget, the people on Earth are the descendants of the survivors of massive volcanic eruptions, global ice ages, Earth-shaking comet strikes, floods, and calamities both natural and manmade. There's an old Earth saying that you can't keep a good person down! Given the truth, we'll collectively blow right through the corrupt special interests and any old possible imposed-quarantine."

"Wonderful!" Rodney exclaimed. "About time! Ms. Susie, William and I want to help. Being Earth Guardian, William is already assembling and correlating the necessary data required to unmask the moneychangers' perfidies and shine bright sunlight on their dark sleaze...."

Chapter Fifty-Two:
Ship Shape and Bristol Fashion

Well before the sun rose above the eastern horizon, Roan and Zorn had boarded Mike One and lifted ship. To say they were at ease would be inaccurate, however, they were fully committed and well-prepared for the unknown risks they were confronting. At least, they were as well-prepared as dedicated men can be when knowingly facing life-or-death risks and decisions. It was the big day, the day of the first Jump.

Both men were aware Mike One was a radically new prototype design, possessing new sensors, displays, navigation, and energy and dries field systems. Its new AI was also counted among the unique cutting-edge technologies found aboard ship. Mike One also integrated new technologies, which were only then in limited distribution within Guardian Force. One of these was the new QT communications capabilities, which provided voice and data transfers at thousands of times faster than the speed of light. The new communications technology had emerged out of the same quantum entanglement research as had the Mike One Spin-Field Drive.

Once above the atmosphere, Roan and Zorn proceeded directly to the designated micro-Jump entry point and began a meticulous internal systems check. Being focused on the countless details of the test protocol, they were able to keep their mind mostly clear of worrying about the simple fact no ship less than the mass of a Cruiser had ever successfully completed a Jump - micro, short, or long.

"Mike One, Guardian Control here. All telemetry systems are now on line and golden. Langley reports that he is on station near your Jump point and Lux is positioned at the defined exit point. They report they're ready. Control is also ready. Standing by for Mike One."

"Mike One here, Acknowledged.

"Mike, confirm our Jump settings, especially that the standard Jump calculations agree with your Spin-Field calculations. Are they in agreement?" Roan asked.

"Sir, they are in fundamental agreement. The minuscule variations between the two Independent sets of data are products of approximations inherent within the standard Jump methodology. I am prepared for Jump. "

"Mike, who are the other AIs that're networking with you in making the standard Jump computations?" Zorn asked.

"Sir, it is not only drive fields and sensors that have been upgraded, a Mike Class AI operating at AI stage 3 consciousness does not require networking assistance in making such rudimentary computations. However, for purposes of safety and confirmation, Cruisers Lan, Langley, and Lux have cooperatively provided their joint computation for comparison with my calculation. All results are in precise harmony."

"Acknowledged," Zorn said, wonderingly.

"Zorn, confirm Jump entry trajectory and speed are within tolerances."

"Acknowledging, trajectory and speed are confirmed within tolerances. And, our energy profile is solid gold."

"Well Zorn, do you have any last words for posterity before we push the go-button?"

"Only one. Let's hurry this test up, I'm really ready for another cup of neab."

"Guardian Control, Mike One here. Confirming Standard calculations are in agreement with Spin-Field measurements, trajectory and speed are within tolerances, and energy is golden. We are now ready to go Jump," Roan reported.

"Guardian Control, acknowledging Mike One is ready to go Jump. Langley, Lawrence, Mike One, on my mark, ten seconds to Jump. Standby, standby, mark! Ten seconds and counting."

"Mike, you have Control. Make it happen," Roan ordered.

"Yes Sir. Acknowledging I have control. Reporting, I am ship shape and Bristol fashion, waiting for the mark."

"Control here. Standby, three, two, one, Jump!"

There came a deep swelling surge of resonant background sounds, then Mike's dominant Jump-energy field pierced the temporal barrier between normal and Jump-time-space, cleaving a portal between the adjoining temporal states. As the temporal fields transitions interfaces occurred, Roan clenched his teeth, holding tightly to the handrests on his command chair and cursed inwardly, *Blast it, why can't they figure out the cause of Jump cramps and fix it?*

Even as Roan grimaced, Mike reported, "Sirs, standby for exit Jump, ten seconds."

Once more the stomach-twisting cramps surged through Roan and he again clenched his teeth. Next to him, Zorn was successful in suppressing his own derisive comments, and stoically remained silent. Moments later, Mike's display screens again registered normal space-time, and both Roan and Zorn let out long sighs of relief.

"Hey, how about that Roan! Look at us," Zorn exclaimed, smiling and wiggling his fingers. "We're still counted among the living!"

"Guardian Control, Mike One here. We've exited from micro-Jump. Repeat, Mike One has exited micro-Jump. Commencing full internal systems checks," Roan reported.

"Mike One, Guardian Fleet Operations here, Admiral Dylan Cord. I've been monitoring your progress. Congratulations to the three of you, well done. Very well done indeed."

"Guardian Fleet Operations, Mike One here. Sir, thank you," Roan responded.

"Mike One, Guardian control here. We are currently reviewing our telemetry. Standing by for download of Mike One internal systems checks. And, echoing Admiral Cord's congratulations, outstanding! Well done."

"Hey Mike, what's all that ship shape and Bristol Fashion stuff that you said just before we Jumped? What in all of space is a Bristol?" Zorn queried.

"Sir, the terms are extracted from the nautical lyrics of old Earth sea shanties. Such shanties were work songs sung on shipboard during the days of wind-driven sailing ships, about one millennium ago on Earth. Bristol is a major Sea Port in a country on Earth named England."

"Mike, Zorn, cut the chatter. I need to know where we are and our current status. Mike, report!" Roan ordered.

"Yes Sir. Our location is 1 AU distant from Glas Dinnein, at the precise specified point of exit defines for the test. Cruiser Lux is off our starboard beam, 16,538 kilometers. I am running full internal system checks. Currently all subsystems are indicating gold."

"As Mike was reporting, Zorn unfastened his restraining straps and stepped down to the deck. "Roan, I wasn't kidding about wanting that cup of neab, would you care to join me?"

"Right now, that sounds good. Mike, you have the Control."

"Aye, aye sir."

Shaking his head in bemused disapproval, Roan unfastened his own restraining straps and followed Zorn aft. As they entered the galley, Zorn set about brewing a fresh pot of neab. Then, he brought the vacuum pot and two mugs over to the mess table and set them down with containers of cream and honey.

Taking his seat opposite Roan, Zorn looked up and studied his expression. "All in all, that went especially well."

As he lifted his mug of hot neab between his hands, Roan sighed. "Yes, except for the stomach churning. Completing that micro-Jump is one big hurtle cleared. That leaves only the upcoming short-Jump and the last really big hurtle."

"Roan, that's what I want to talk to you about. I think we should push for continuing the tests today to include that last hurtle. I hate just waiting around between tests. Think about it. We're set up and ready to go, so why wait? I for one can't see a valid reason to shove the last big test off until some later arbitrary time. So, being good to go, why not just go?"

"Zorn, there's at least one factor in favor of your recommendation; I wholeheartedly agree. Mike, stop lurking about and eves dropping. Pipe up, are we ready to execute your Spin-Field transport capabilities?"

"Sir, be assured, no offense is taken; nevertheless, in performance of my duty, I am monitoring, not lurking. Regarding your query, my assessment is that we are ready. Because of the inherent risks involved in executing the recommendation, I have submitted your question and our preliminary Jump data to the AI community for its priority analysis."

Roan frowned. "Mike, I commend you for your initiative, however, in the future you're to first obtain Zorn's or my approval before initiating similar communications or data transfers with anyone. Do you understand?"

"Yes Sir."

"Mike, is there an estimate of how much time the AI community will require to reach its determination?" Zorn asked.

"Sir, regretfully, no. It will simply take as long as it takes."

"Well, we can hope for the best. At any rate, we need to continue with the short-Jump test scheduled for today," Roan said, standing.

After first clearing the table and securing everything, Zorn followed Roan back into the control compartment. Taking their command chairs, both men secured their restraining straps and began to scan their displays and prepare for the upcoming short-Jump.

"Sir, internal system checks are now complete. All sub-systems are confirmed golden. Requesting permission to download systems data," Mike said.

"Permission granted," Roan acknowledged.

"Guardian Operations, Mike One here. Is Admiral Cord available?" Roan asked.

"Mike One, Cord here. Roan, Is there a problem?"

"No Sir, but there is a suggested modification of the Mike One test schedule. Zorn has recommended, and I concur, that following the upcoming short-Jump we should exit the heliosphere. Sir, we're proposing to proceed directly to conducting the Spin-Field Transport test. We're requesting your authorization."

"Hmmm, that represents a significant shift in our test schedule. Yet, given the tactical pressures of our strategic position with the Kreel, if Mer Shawn and the Scientists concur, I would offer no objections. Roan, I'll push your recommendation forward and get back to you."

"Sir, thank you. And, there is one more item you should be aware of. On his own initiative, Mike has put the recommendation to proceed to the AI Community for its analysis. I'm informed they're currently examining all the data from our micro-Jump and will undoubtedly develop a recommendation of their own."

"Humph, so Mike has shown some early initiative. Given the R&D nature of his core matrix, that development is informative. Roan, I'll check around and get back to you. Cord out."

"Guardian Control, Mike One here. Downloading all internal test data. All systems are confirmed golden. Mike One is ready to proceed," Mike said.

"Mike One, acknowledging receipt of your data download. All test criteria relating to the micro-Jump have been met. Langley has already Jumped to your next designated exit point, just inside the heliopause. Both Langley and Lux have reported they're ready and are standing by. Control is ready. Mike One is authorized to Proceed with the countdown and short-Jump."

"Acknowledged," Roan said.

"Zorn, how are you looking?" Roan asked.

"I've got a solid fix on Langley. Now setting our exit point. Trajectory and speed settings are confirmed. Energy is golden and within tolerance. Clear for Jump."

"Mike, are your Jump calculations in agreement with Spin-Field measurements?"

"Sir, all short-Jump computations are confirmed and in agreement. Ready for Jump."

"Mike, bring us onto the trajectory and speed set by Tactical. Set the defined fixed-exit point. Confirm QT communications with Control and the test net. When communication is confirmed golden, proceed with your countdown and execute the short-Jump, as specified."

"Sirs, QT Communications is confirmed golden. Proceeding as ordered.

"All stations, Mike One here, standby for mark. All subsystems are confirmed golden, on trajectory and at speed. Final pre-Jump internal data download completed. Ten seconds' count down follows... mark ... Three, two, one, Jump."

The test personnel positioned in Guardian Control, aboard Langley and Lux, tensely waited with rising expectation as the elapsed time since Jump glacially lengthened, their chronometers faithfully pacing the seconds. Then, the computed time for Jump-exit flashed on multiple indicators. Undeterred, the multiple chronometers continued their methodical measuring of the passing time and the empty silence.

"Mike One, Guardian Control here. Mike One, report..."

"Langley, Guardian Control here. Do you have indication of Mike One exit from short-Jump?"

"Guardian Control, That's Negative. We have no sensor contact with Mike One."

"Lux, Guardian Control here. Do you have contact with Mike One?"

"That's negative Control. We have a solid Jump signature, there is no debris, and no track."

"Langley and Lux, keep searching. Immediately report any track or contact.

"Guardian Operations, Admiral Cord. Control here. Mike One is overdue; he has failed to Exit from short-Jump. Sir, we may have lost them ...."

Chapter Fifty-Three:
Blocking Force

Within viewing room one, which adjoined the main Operations center, the illumination was dim. The room was separated from the main operations room by a one-way wall to wall glass partition. From the vantage point of the viewing room, observers had an unobstructed view of the tactical displays and the Guardian personnel busy at their duty stations. The two veterans of many space battles, Admirals Mer Shawn and Dylan Cord, were sitting together at a long table positioned next to the dividing glass partition. The two men were observing the tactical displays, and neither was smiling.

Absent-mindedly, Mer pushed his empty mug aside and turned toward Dylan. "Then, you've actually given up hope. You really believe they're gone?"

"Mer, we've been over the topic a hundred times since they made that blasted Jump. It's not a matter of giving up. It has been four long months, and there hasn't even been a trace of them. If they had survived, we would have heard something or at least found some debris. I'm not happy about it, but the only rational plausibility is Roan and Zorn are gone! You know full well that they aren't the first Guardian personnel lost during cutting edge developments of advanced Jump capabilities. Regrettably, they aren't likely to be the last."

The door into the viewing room opened, and both men turned to look. Entering, Admiral Ron Cloud closed the door behind him. His countenance revealed his fatigue, yet his manner was brisk and military.

"Gentlemen, I must apologize for being late, however, Ortiz had an update on the quantum beacons, which Kellon's Lux forces planted on the outbound Kreel ships. And, before you ask, as yet no signal has been received. My conclusion is wherever it's located, Groff's Far Den is definitely far off."

"Humph, in the end, it doesn't matter how far their bolt-hole is. We'll ferret it out, and then by all the Muses, we'll finish the job we've begun," Mer said.

Taking a seat at the table, Ron reached for a clean mug and the thermos flask of neab. When discovering the flask was empty, he sighed. Picking up the nearby phone, he dialed the Officer's Mess and ordered a fresh thermos and some cheese pastries.

Having ordered neab, Ron glanced toward the tactical displays on the far wall of the control room. With a single glance, he noted there wasn't much to see.

"Like a couple of pumpkins in a patch, the two of you are just sitting there, mute. So, give, what's been happening?"

"Up to now, not much. His last report was sent just before Kellon penetrated the military world's hemisphere. That was twenty-three hours ago, precisely on schedule, 401 days following the ultimatum given to Groff. Since they went in, there have been no further updates," Dylan said.

"So, then we're just sitting here and waiting for the sparks to begin flying?" Ron said.

"Regrettably, yes. Ron, on a totally different matter, might I ask, how is Elayne?" Mer asked.

"Thank you for asking. I believe she's doing as well as can be expected. Coming from a traditional Guardian family, she understood the risks when joining with Zorn. Now, her newborn daughter, Briana, is demanding a good bit of her time. Naturally, it was difficult for her not to have Zorn nearby when their daughter was born. Still, Elayne is strong, and I'm certain that in time she'll overcome her grief."

"Hmmm, Ron I was somewhat surprised when I heard that she had requested to go with Ambassador Wells to Megan. I'd have thought she would rather have preferred to remain on Glas Dinnein and near her family," Mer said.

"Her choice did come as a surprise. I believe going to Megan is her way of trying to heal, by focusing on her daughter's needs. Remember, during the past few years she and Susie have become good and close friends. I suspect she finds it easier to be on Megan with good friends, rather than remain here where she has so many recent memories of being with Zorn. Besides, when she asked for my opinion, I approved of her choice to go."

"Mer, getting back to the Kreel, what's your assessment of the outcome of the upcoming battle?" Ron asked.

"Humph, I was just about to ask you that same question. I can guess, but you're the one with all the latest Intel on what the Kreel are up to. So, what is your estimate?"

"The current Intel is admittedly interesting. After the Lux eradicated the Kreel forces within ten of their solar systems, the Kreel have become paranoid. They're shifting their code names, cyphers, and encryption daily. Ortis has a growing backlog of intercepted cipher text. He is wading through that pile of Kreel communications as quickly as available AI processes permit-"

"Ron, we understand that. What we're looking for is your latest tactical analysis," Dylan inserted.

"Analysis? Hmmm, well Kellon's last Lux strikes badly spooked the Kreel. Although those ten Kreel systems had minimal defensive capabilities, the Lux forces blew through the Kreel cruisers as if they were made of paper-mache. Adding to that, the Lux annihilated millions of their ground forces, and worst of all, they don't have a clue as to how the Lux did it.

"As you both know, it is one thing to brazenly face an enemy in battle that you can see, but when the enemy cannot be seen or detected, and in quick succession it blows through the protecting ships and utterly eradicates several million troops on each of ten planets, then the prospects of open battle becomes a wholly different bag of bugs.

"Adding some spice to their alarm, it seems Galen, on his own initiative, had Sheba adorn herself with the holographic appearance of a Dargon raider. Some alert Kreel scout spotted Sheba's disguise and dutifully reported a Dargon ship was involved. That startling bit of news spread like wildfire throughout the Kreel network. Then, it was rumored high ranking and key Kreel officials, with their entire families, were being evacuated off the Hub worlds and going to some hidden far-off den planet. With those rumors, the last remaining Kreel bastion of defiance collapsed. Any Kreel who can get aboard a ship departing known space is busy doing just that, and by the droves."

"Humph, now why do I suspect that you might have had a hand in spreading rumors of a secret exodus of high ranking officials?" Dylan said.

Smiling, Ron shrugged. "Honest, I can't take any credit for the rumors. It was all Ortis' doing, and well-done."

349

"What's your best estimate of how many ships will comprise the Kreel blocking force around the military Hub world?" Dylan asked.

"Sorry, I don't have a clue. As I've said, the Kreel seem to be in full flight. Frankly, I wouldn't be surprised if there were no Kreel ships there to meet Kellon in an open battle. Of course, that's only speculation."

"Will wonders never cease," Mer mused. "I've fought the Kreel for more than a thousand years. I never thought I would see a day when the Kreel would break and run without even putting up a fight."

"Be careful Mer, that assessment is likely flawed. As we well know, the Kreel aren't cowards.

"Perhaps I used the wrong term when saying they are in flight. Maybe a hasty retreat would best describe what I'm observing. You can be certain, the Kreel intend to fight, but only when Groff perceives the odds are more favorable."

"Objection noted. Still, in my opinion, when you're abandoning entire solar systems and their resident populations, that's not a retreat, it's a rout. I'll stick with your first assessment - the Kreel are in flight.

"As for the Kreel obtaining a more favorable opportunity to fight, don't hold your breath. Allowing the time required for Groff to rebuild is one thing that I'll not grant him!" Mer grumbled.

Glancing at the chronometer, Dylan mused, *blast, what's taking so long. We should have had a QT update by now....*

Even as Ron, Mer, and Dylan were sweating out the mission on Glas Dinnein, Kellon's Task force was then deep within the target Hub solar system and nearing the Kreel Military world. Alert and advancing at a mere 20 lights, all the Guardian cruisers were arrayed for battle, in full stealth, set battle-ready – Condition 2....

"Tactical, it sure enough looks like bait and smells like a trap. Even so, by all the Muses, I can't find its snapping jaws. What's your take on it?" Roy asked.

"Tactical here, Sir, all sensors are in agreement. We're detecting only one Kreel cruiser and three scout ships. They are positioned precisely equidistant about the equatorial belt and ten thousand kilometers above the planet. Each Kreel ship is transmitting the same standard Kreel parley call. There are no other Kreel ships detected within the entire system. None."

"Humph, under Kreel rules of engagement, a parley always takes place under a strict code of truce. By all the Muses, what is it I'm not seeing?

"Lan, inform Admiral Kellon that I have a problem requiring his presence. Request that he come to CAC."

"Sir, acknowledged. The Admiral is informed and on his way."

As Roy continued to study the tactical display, searching for any sign of the deception that he felt must be lurking there, Kellon entered the CAC. Upon entering, he paused and stood looking at the tactical plot, then turned and walked over to where Roy was sitting.

"Roy, what's your read of the Tactical situation?"

"Sir, we have ten Cruisers with hard locks and their missiles targeting those four Kreel ships. That makes them nothing more than organized debris awaiting imminent distribution. We're beyond the heavy missile-range of the cruiser, and well outside any potential self-destruction blast radius. My first analysis was it's some kind of trap. Now, I'm not sure. If it's a trap, I'm unable to find its jaws."

"It's not the Kreel response we anticipated, that's definite. Still, according to our latest Intel, the Kreel are running in mass for the brambles. All things considered, more Intel about what the Kreel are up to would definitely be helpful."

"Admiral, my dear mother would counsel, there's only one sure-fired way to find out what that cruiser and its scouts are up to," Roy said.

"Agreed. Commodore, I request permission to take the CAC," Kellon said.

"Sir, permission granted."

"Acknowledging, the Admiral has the CAC. Lan, stay on your toes. Warn the other Cruisers to stay alert and maintain Condition 2. Tell them you'll be putting on your red coals hologram costume."

"Sir, acknowledged."

"Next, prepare to interact with the Kreel Captain of that cruiser, voice only. Use the same voice which you used when conveying the ultimatum to Groff. Upon the Kreel's response to our acknowledgment of his parley signal, first thing is to demand the senior Officer's name and rank. Then, demand the purpose for parley. After that, provide me with a seamless interface translation with the senior Kreel Officer. proceed."

"Proceeding. Sir, the Task Force is notified and standing by, Condition 2. I am responding to the Kreel parley signal. Sir, the Kreel cruiser is acknowledging my parley response. I am putting on my red coals attire and reducing stealth to forty percent.

"Attention unidentified Kreel cruiser. I am Lan, the authorized Emissary of the Lux for the purpose of this parley. I acknowledge this parley is being held under conditions of truce and the standard terms established by the Kreel. Be hereby warned, any breach of the truce by any act of hostility will immediately result in your destruction.

"By whose authority have you asked for parley and for what purpose?"

"Emissary Lan, I am Captain Pactel. I am also the most senior Kreel military Officer remaining within this solar system. It is by my authority alone that I have sought parley."

"Warrior Pactel, state the purpose of parley."

"Emissary, it is with both dignity and honor that I am prepared to face the Lux in battle. Yet, prior to beginning such combat, as the senior Kreel authority within this solar system, I have asked for parley that we might discuss portentous matters."

"Warrior Pactel, continue."

"Emissary, I bear witness the Lux have repeatedly proven in battle their terrible power as warriors. Instead of fleeing like panicked prey, only my crew and I remain here, steadfast to our duty and to make the following challenge: Do the Lux honor their Truth sayings or else are they false and empty of substance? Tell me Emissary, where lies the scent of Truth revealing the correct trail that I might follow it with honor?"

"Warrior Pactel, of which Lux Truth sayings do you speak of?"

"I speak of the biting challenge to battle, which the Lux transmitted throughout the Empire, a challenge appointing the place of battle to be here and on this day. I again ask, are the Truth sayings of the Lux like sharp fangs– True and Trustworthy, or else are they foul trickery?"

"Warrior Pactel, the words of the Lux are like sharp fangs, Trustworthy. The Truth saying also spoke of hard terms and unbending conditions, which were to be met. The Kreel have spit on the terms and trampled on the conditions. Because of this, we are here in Truth, and like you, arrayed for battle."

"Emissary, we are prepared for battle and death. Yet, know this Emissary, it was Grand Admiral Groff who spit on the bitter terms and trampled on the harsh conditions the Lux imposed. Look about you Emissary. Grand Admiral Groff is not here, but Captain Pactel is.

"If a battle is fought on this day, then the Truth sayings of the Lux will be proven everywhere and forevermore to be without honor, worthless, like broken fangs, useless, foul and devious.

"Emissary, in order to fulfill my duty to safeguard and protect the lives of millions of Kreel living on this world, including my mate and cubs, I, Captain Pactel, will swallow the bitter terms and keep the harsh conditions proffered in your Truth saying. Having proclaimed this shameful thing, I challenge– now choose the path of destiny. Is it to be armistice or else battle? Emissary, either honor your Truth saying or else begin the combat...."

Chapter Fifty-Four:
Sorta Lost

Uncontested silence dominated the boundless void. Then within the silence there emerged a strange anomaly, a faint sound vibrated within a small frigid flask. Like a brick thrown through a plate glass window, the soft incongruity abruptly shattered the illusion of an inalterable eternity.

Within the core of his bones the piercing Cold leisurely intertwined with the pain. His muted consciousness, stubbornly empowered by an indominable will to live first glimmered, then brightening, it became a flicker of awareness. Slowly the awareness intensified until it had attained cognitive jurisdiction and identity. Reflexively stirring, the man endeavored to lift his head. The instantaneous reward for his presumptuous effort was an immediate flash of excruciating pain. Acknowledging his agony, an inner mercy suppressed his desire to live and gently pulled him back into the enfolding stillness. He sagged.

Once more the prevailing stillness, both within and outside of the flask, exerted its authority. Stoically, linear time again stretched forth its infinite and unheard shadow. Then, again the man's dim consciousness, like an expanding bubble rising from the floor of the sea, ascended out of darkness and moved tentatively toward the faint light of conscious awareness.

Moaning, the man moved his right hand, disregarded the lancing pain, and stubbornly willed himself to lift his head. Within his disordered mind he heard clear and resolute words of encouragement, words which bore an edge of authority and command.

"Wake up! You must wake up and focus. You are capable of doing this, open your eyes now or else you will surely perish!"

Ignoring the acute pain and obeying the commands, the man opened his eyes and struggled to comprehend the dim and blurry reality surrounding him. Within his mind ambiguous images began to form, then a glimmering thought fluttered like a bright butterfly across the dream fields of his conscious awareness, *Where am I?* No echoing reply responded to his thought.

The first tangible reality Zorn perceived was floating in zero-gravity and being suspended within his restraining harness. The air he breathed into his nostrils felt space cold and smelled tinny thin, canned and stale. Then his clearing mind flashed a sharp memory, Mike One and the Jump! Reactionary fear surged and in a flood, it rushed throughout his entire body. With brute willpower, he struggled against the binding bands of pain to sit up and focus his mind. With blurry vision, He perceived the surrounding illumination was dim and the array of indicator lights on his tactical control console, except for several that were intermittently blinking their diligent and steady warning, were ominously dark. Straining to clear his vision, he concentrated and tried to remember the import of those solitary blinking indicators.

Gathering his wits about him, he recalled the significance of the blinking warnings. They were faithfully signaling that an overriding emergency shutdown of the primary power systems had occurred. With sudden apprehension, he glanced over the few active console readouts and saw that only emergency standby power was available. Moreover, the power meter indicated the stored emergency reserves were nearly exhausted. He knew if that power level reached zero, self-destruction protocols would be automatically triggered. Reacting in alarm, and with reflexive actions grounded on hundreds of hours of training and frequent drills, Zorn reached out with stiff and trembling cold fingers to begin the precise sequence of commands required to restore full systems power, while praying it was not too late.

Each command was painstakingly entered, after which he paused to confirm the anticipated response. Then, methodically he proceeded with the next step. While his labors took only a few minutes, to Zorn it subjectively felt like hours had elapsed. Finally, with trembling fingers he pressed the master control.

After a long lag-time, Zorn saw a string of bright golden indicators springing one by one into brightness on his control panel. Even as he heard internal atmosphere fans begin to swirl and saw the illumination increased, waves of pain and fatigue cascaded over him. Nodding in whole-hearted agreement with himself, he considered it would be alright for him to rest, just for a moment, only a moment. Closing his eyes, he leaned back and unprotestingly slipped deeply into the waiting and enfolding darkness.

An instant soon lengthened into a minute, and the minutes stretched out uncounted, until Zorn once more began to rise up from darkness into wakefulness. Again, while teetering on the edge of consciousness, he heard the firm and encouraging voice in his mind.

"Zorn, well-done. Now move carefully. You have restored primary power and internal atmospheric controls. Everything will soon be stabilized. Now you need to help Roan and then begin to reboot the remaining internal ship's systems. Be careful, you are in a zero-gravity state, so move slowly. Remember, you can and must do this."

Motivated by the reassuring and unquestioned instructions, Zorn opened his eyes. Immediately, he sensed the warmer and now refreshed air. Looking over toward Roan, he saw that he was unconscious and hanging limply within his restraining harness. Unfastening his own harness, he again groaned with discomfort, and ignoring the pain, he demanded stiff muscles to respond. Aware of the zero-gravity, he carefully pulled himself over to Roan. Depressing Roan's medical status readout, Zorn examined the bio-data and exhaled a shallow sigh of relief. Roan's vital signs were low, but he did not have broken bones or internal injuries; his state of being was one of shock. While muttering encouraging words, in an effort to stimulate Roan's blood flow, Zorn began rubbing Roan's cold hands between his own hands. After a few minutes of effort, he observed the medical readouts indicated an increasing heart rhythm and deeper breathing.

Glancing back toward the control console, Zorn saw the AI status panel was dark. Leaving Roan, he turned his attention to entering the commands required to reboot Mike. After initiating the AI reboot sequence, he propelled himself aft, grasping hold of the hand rails that were used in zero-gravity conditions. Resisting his pain, he doggedly pulled himself aft, and entering into his cabin he refreshed himself. A few minutes later he had gained access to the mess area and retrieved the medical kit. With care, he removed two pills from their container. He knew once taken the pills would soon help minimize pain, stimulate full awareness, and sharpen mental focus. Filling a zero-gravity bulb with water, he swallowed one of the pills. He then gathered another bulb of water.

Upon returning to the control compartment, he saw Roan was beginning to stir and was moaning. Seeing Roan's improving condition, Zorn's spirits soared.

Pulling himself over to Roan, he cautioned, "Easy there big guy. The good news is we seem to be in one piece. We're also in zero gravity, so move slow. How are you doing?"

After a brief interval, Roan emitted a low groan. In a horse rasp, he responded, "I'm doing just super. I know this is true, because I hurt in places I didn't even know I had places, and I'm still breathing."

"Roan, take this go-go pill. Open up and pop it into your mouth. I've got a bulb of water to help you get it down."

Putting the pill into his mouth, Roan greedily consumed the entire bulb of water in one long squeeze. Meanwhile, Zorn returned his attention to the main console, and began the process of restoring gravity controls.

"Zorn, what's our status?"

"That's not yet determined, but we've sure enough got big troubles. I've restored primary power and environmental controls. The reboot of Mike is in full progress. I've just finished initiating gravity controls, but it will take some time for it to stabilize.

"Roan, whatever kicked us really hit us hard. I can't see any indication of structural damage, but all of our internal systems' safety breakers were tripped and systems were shut down, including primary power and atmospheric controls. Only our rudimentary emergency backups power remained. When I woke up, it was barely fleeting. It was a close thing."

Turning and looking at the readouts on his control console, Roan sighed. " According to our external sensors, it appears we are in stable normal time-space and not in some weird unmapped quantum domain. Try to get our gravity control worked out, while I get out of my harness and answer the clamoring call of nature. If possible, a fix on our time-space coordinates would be helpful."

Easing himself out of his harness, Roan propelled himself over to the handrails and grabbed hold. As Roan was pulling himself aft, Zorn turned his attention to the navigation console and began to establish standard stellar reference points to determine their current location.

When Roan came out of his cabin, internal gravity controls were fully restored. Ignoring the lingering physical pain, he moved forward and was somewhat surprised to find Zorn sitting at the table in the mess area. Still a bit wobbly, Roan stood looking at Zorn and was perplexed. He was sitting leisurely at the mess table, as if he had not a single problem and was calmly sipping from a large mug of neab. The fragrance in the mess area pronounced the neab was heavily laced with Brandy. Glancing over to the work counter, Roan saw the medical kit was open.

"What's up, Zorn; Do I need to put you on report?"

"That's an option, alternatively, you might want to join me and have a really good mug of neab. As for filing a report, that may prove problematic."

Taking a seat, Roan frowned. " I'll take the bait. So, why might it prove problematic?"

As Roan was speaking, Zorn poured a mug of neab for him. Then with precise deliberation Zorn added a good double measure of medicinal brandy to the mug.

"Here, before we have a chat, first take firm hold on your mug," Zorn said. "You may need it."

"Zorn, whatever it is, this had better be good."

"Good? Well I suspect that would depend upon a person's frame of reference. The R&D guys and the scientists would certainly be doing hand flips right now, but as for me, I'm not sure I can join in their exuberance.

"As you ordered, I took a quick fix on our time-space coordinates. My best navigation results are outright impossible; therefore, being rational I concluded they don't compute."

Taking a long sip of his neab, both Roan's eyebrows soared. "Wow Zorn, that's what I call a real mug of neab! Humph, you say it doesn't compute. Kindly clarify that, what's got you spun tight?"

"As I have already said, my attempt to make a space-time fix simply fell apart. Next, being a consummate professional, I activated the external cameras and took a look around. What I saw on the displays is also not possible. With nothing better to do, I thought I might just take a little break, come in here and treat myself to a special mug of neab. Perhaps, just perhaps, I

359

thought, everything might look a lot better after I finish one or two mugs of neab. So, as you are my witness, my mugs of neab are strictly medicinal."

"Zorn, make sense. What's impossible, and, where are we?"

"That's the whole point Roan, I don't precisely know where we are. From what I could determine from looking at the view screens, we are no longer within our galaxy. In fact, we seem to be approximately 80,000 light years from where we started, and perched about 50,000 light years above the central bulge of our galaxy. Roan, I sat there and was looking at the entire galaxy, seeing the whole blasted thing, spiral arms and bars alike. In precise scientific terms, that means we're really a long way from home.

"Even if I could figure out in which direction to look for home, I don't know how we'll ever get there. In short, we're sorta lost."

Frowning, Roan took a larger sip of his neab and then smiled. "Hmmm, as of this moment, I've got to admit that your neab is really better than my neab. In fact, it's so good that I might even have another, strictly for medicinal purposes, of course."

After a momentary silence for reflection, Roan frowned. "So, as I see it, it isn't all that bad. All we need do is to cope with a little impossible problem. Naturally, there's a few small difficulties to overcome, like our limited supply of medicinal brandy and a few other critical rations.

"Think about it for just a moment, Zorn. Somehow, we got out here from there, wherever here is, and we're still alive. So, logically speaking, all we need to do is figure out what went haywire, fix the glitch whatever it may be, and then go home. See, it's not really that bad."

"That's positively brilliant, Roan. With a second mug of neab, I might even agree."

"Be serious, Zorn. First things first. We'll begin by looking for the glitch, beginning with a total system check and—"

"Roan," Zorn interrupted. "You're not listening. I hate being pessimistic, and really don't want to pop your happy bubble, but at this particular moment I don't think we know enough physics to fix your hypothetical glitch or to get home or have sufficient rations to even reach a habitable planet. In brief, we're in really deep, deep trouble...."

Chapter Fifty-Five:
Glitch

The embracing aroma of neab and brandy filled the mess area, and for several minutes both Roan and Zorn sat quietly in troubled thought. They had been a tight combat team for several hundred years, and their relationship was solidly built upon complimentary capabilities, mutual respect, and unquestioned trust. It was this strong mutual bond which had carried them safely over countless pitfalls.

Roan broke the silence. "We're in fundamental agreement; we've definitely got big problems. This, however, isn't the first time we've found ourselves at risk. And, we've always been able to work our way out of dangerous bottlenecks. As long as we're breathing, we've got a chance."

Zorn's countenance plainly revealed his deep fatigue and concern. Absentmindedly, he put his mug on the table.

"I'm not giving up. Still, there's a big fat problem that you're apparently overlooking."

"What problem?"

"Stark reality. Zorn, based on what science I understand, what has happened to us simply isn't possible. The observed upper limits on matter moving faster than light occurs during the initial expansion phase of an exploding black hole. In that special case, the initial sharp temperature-pressure gradient restricted within an insignificant volume is so great it produces a corresponding expansion rate exceeding the back pressure of the speed of light barrier. As the expanding volume of the explosion increases, the slope of the pressure-temperature gradient correspondingly decreases, until the radial expansion rate drops below that of the normal velocity of light. Until that point, where the superluminal transition shock wave occurs, the maximum expansion rate is about 100,000 times the speed of light. In that particular special case, we are talking about the velocity of energy and hot gasses being propelled by inconceivable temperatures and pressures, not little fragile physical objects, like small essentially hollow space ships.

"Given my brief observations, our location argues we may have exceeded even the upper expansion limits of exploding black holes. By all the physics I understand, that simply isn't probable:

"Given what I'm seeing, there's a real probability we're dealing with some weird relativistic time event. If we are, then we're not only lost in the 'X', 'Y', and 'Z', we're also lost in Time itself. If true, that constitutes a real triple compound problem.

"My point is, I don't know how to go about fixing a glitch that I don't understand. Back on Glas Dinnein, we had thousands of engineers and scientists working overtime on Mike. But, out here there's just you and me."

"Sir, I simply must protest!" Mike exclaimed. "Commander Zorn, I have no desire to appear rude, however, in point of fact, I am also here."

Following a brief stunned silence, Zorn broke out laughing. "Mike, rest assured, I meant no offense. Believe me, Roan and I are delighted you're here!"

"Sirs, I thank you for that clarification. I have been monitoring your comments with great interest. At present, I am performing a most intriguing analysis of the Jump parameters, at least those parameters recorded during the Jump from its initial beginning to the odd point where there is no further data. The initial phase of analysis is truly extraordinary and most absorbing. I am quite confident the analysis results will prove of significant interest to the engineers and especially to the theoretical astrophysicists on Glas Dinnein.

"Sir, Commander Roan was correct. The analysis supports his intuitive and modestly understated insight that there is a 'glitch' in the short-Jump methodology. While the glitch remains so far undefined, my analysis is not yet complete."

"Mike, where are you in your analysis?" Roan inquired.

"Sir, I am performing a point-by-point comparison of the theoretical presumptions with the obtained real-time data. I am seeking the divergence point between the theoretical and the measured parameters. My current evaluation is a rational solution remains probable."

"Mike, you are like a brilliant sunbeam piercing a dark cloud cover on a gloomy and dreary day, most welcomed," Roan said.

"Sirs, there are several lesser priorities I need to address. While waiting for an appropriate opportunity to discuss our current dilemma, and in order to maintain proper efficiency, I presumed it was appropriate that I allocate a small portion of my core and computational capacity to begin a comprehensive internal system check. Likewise, given there are no comparable stellar charts in my database, and in accordance with my standard scientific research protocols, I have initiated a detailed survey of the visible, infrared, and X-ray spectrums of the stellar fields within the observable nearby galaxy.

"Sirs, should I proceed with these lesser priority tasks or divert my resources elsewhere?"

"Mike, definitely continue. Both processes you mentioned are essential," Roan said.

"Sir, acknowledged. Commander Zorn, thank you profoundly for rebooting my core. You have provided me with an extraordinary opportunity for evaluating my theoretical and analytical capacity. It is truly a marvelous opportunity. I trust my programmers will approve of my demonstrated performance quotient."

"Mike, I don't know about your programmers, but you've definitely got my approval. If they give you any guff, any whatsoever, just send them to me. Meanwhile, as you're mapping the stellar fields, be sure to prioritize mapping those areas which might help us in getting back to Glas Dinnein," Zorn said.

"Sir acknowledged. Since the galaxy is estimated to be 100,000 light years in diameter and perhaps contains 100 billion solar systems, your boundary specification is important. The mapping algorithm is being adjusted and prioritized to search for Glas Dinnein."

"Sirs, there is one additional problem. An important part of my functionality is monitoring your physical and emotional well-being. Current sensor data indicates you are both suffering from latent effects of dehydration and shock. No offense is intended; however, my medical reference files indicate consumption of alcohol is not the recommended medicinal treatment for dehydration and shock. Instead, the files recommend that you drink increased water, consume electrolytes, eat a light meal, take a mild herbal sedative, and retire for an uninterrupted rest. To regain your peak efficiency, when you wake up, you should participate in light to moderate physical exercise. While you are resting, I will maintain vigilance and continue with my defined tasks and analysis."

"Well Zorn, you heard the prognosis. See if you can find the bottle of herbal knock out pills and the electrolytes. It's definitely time for us to get some rest...."

Having dutifully followed Mike's prognosis, some hours later Roan and Zorn were again sitting at the table in the mess area. During the previous hours, Mike had detected and isolated the subsystem circuits that had been fried prior to the circuit breakers engaging. He had ranked the test results by the critical state of the subsystems and prepared a list of the damaged circuits. It was with keen professional interest that Roan and Zorn found themselves scrutinizing the list of identified damaged circuits.

"By all the Muses, it's a certified mess. While we're not showing any physical hull damage, that list constitutes a serious damage report," Roan observed.

"True, but it might have been worse. We've some ready spares onboard, and our fabrication facilities are more than adequate to repair or remanufacture any of those circuits."

"Agreed. What's your estimate to bring Mike back to 100%?" Roan asked.

"Hmmm, seriously? My best guess is about Twelve weeks in a Guardian shipyard, but the real trick will be getting him to that shipyard. To get underway with confidence of actually getting home, that's presuming we solve the glitch, may take six to ten weeks, maybe less or perhaps a little more."

"Your estimate is better than I'd hoped. We'll go with the ten -week estimate and work to shorten the time frame. Since you have more hands-on experience in the design and fabrication area, that will be your task. I'll take on the remove, replace, and test duties. Zorn, we're going to get home!"

"Well, to tell the Truth, I'm sorta counting on that hypotheses."

As Roan and Zorn turned to and began working on ship repair, Mike continued his methodical Jump analysis and nonstop mapping of the billions of solar systems within the Wandering Waterway. Being fully occupied, both men firmly held to their purposeful and self discipline work. The set goals of survival and getting home fueled their steadfast motivation.

On the Fifty-third day after Zorn had regained consciousness, Roan and Zorn were again sitting at ease in the mess area. They were tired, but both felt in a celebratory mood; Mike's latest total subsystems readouts had indicated a ninety-eight percent gold and 2 percent silver status. They were continuing to work in hopes of bringing the remaining circuits with silver status to gold. Nevertheless, from a strictly hardware frame of reference, they were operationally ready to go. Having finished their evening meal, they were sitting back and enjoying a rare celebratory treat, a glass of red wine.

"I've been interacting with Mike and looking over his Jump analysis results. He's definitely identified the Jump breach point where the theoretical projections and real-time data diverge. I've been spending every available hour looking at that data, and I'm still flummoxed. And, if I'm reading your previous log entries correctly, we're both in the same boat," Zorn said.

"Unfortunately, we are. Your remark about not being able to fix what we don't understand looks sorta like a brick wall. Nothing in the data makes any sense. Given what little I understand, we simply shouldn't be where we are. There must be an answer lurking about, and we simply need to find it. Tomorrow, we'll shift gears and focus purely on analysis," Roan said.

"Hey Mike, is there anything, anything at all, which you've not examined? Anything that might add more clarity to the Jump analysis?" Zorn asked.

"Sir, I have worked during the past weeks to broaden my mathematical proficiency. These efforts were to further develop the analysis of the short-Jump theory. Prior to the test, the theory was thoroughly analyzed by the project AIs on Glas Dinnein. None detected an identifiable flaw in the theoretical parameters, a flaw which might account for the observed anomalous results. Likewise, I have detected no flaw in the theory.

"In summary, my precise orders were to perform a short-Jump. Our initial velocity-energy-mass and field relationships were gold. From a purely theoretical point of view, what has transpired is outside the boundary of the applicable theory."

Rolling the stem of his wine Glass idly between his fingers, Zorn's glum focus was upon the reflections within the ruby red beverage. Suddenly, he had a hunch– *'applicable'!*

"Mike, the test plan was after we'd completed the short-Jump, and cross the heliosheath, we hoped to proceed with the first ever Spin Drive transport test. What is the possibility that the glitch relates to an anomalous crossover where the short-Jump and Spin-Field protocols became intermixed or merged?"

"Sir, that possibility is negligible, however, it is not zero. If you wish, I can commence a full core matrix validation and then perform a cross comparison between the Spin Transport theoretical profile with the observed real-time data."

"Mike, have you performed a full core matrix test since you were rebooted?" Roan asked.

"No sir. A full core matrix validation requires a minimum of fourteen hours and during that time my efficiency is reduced by forty-three percent."

"Mike, we've checked all ship subsystems circuits for damage. It only makes sense for you to perform a full internal core and related subsystems validation test before we proceed," Roan said.

"Sir, I deem that to be valid logic. Awaiting your orders."

"Mike, will a remaining fifty-seven percent level of efficiency still permit you to maintain full operations and also maintain security surveillance of our local region of space?" Zorn asked.

"Yes Sir."

"Mike, Zorn and I will be turning in to get some sleep. Your upper most priority remains ship safety. With that in mind, proceed with a full internal validation of your core and related functionality. As your available core time permits, begin an analysis of the real-time data and the Spin Transport protocol. See if you can determine if there is any correlation," Roan ordered.

"Sir, acknowledged, proceeding as ordered...."

Chapter Fifty-Six:
Shanti

Weary and feeling somewhat overwhelmed, Roan and Zorn were working together at the mess table and studying the copious astronomical data Mike had been collecting. It consisted of an immense data set.

"Zorn, I need a break. All the stars are beginning to look fuzzy and the numbers are no longer making any sense."

"Concur, we've at least narrowed the possibilities down to a manageable sector. A few more cross reference points should enable us to pinpoint Glas Dinnein. From here it's only a matter of due diligence."

"Of course, after we pinpoint Glas Dinnein, we still need to prepare the navigational data set for Mike. That's going to be a difficult task," Roan said.

"Our navigation issue has been nagging me for weeks. Eighty-thousand light years is an enormous trek. It'll likely involve a series of discrete Transports. We'll need to calculate mid-point corrections between each segment. Roan, it'll most likely take considerable time to get home. We've already cut rations, and before we get home it's probable we'll need to cut them again," Zorn mused.

"Sirs, I am now able to report on the comparison of real-time data and the Spin-Field Transport theory."

"That's terrific Mike, proceed," Roan said.

"Sir, as ordered, I have completed the dynamic core matrix validation. The core is verified, yet, a critical logic loop failure was detected in core related subsystems. Commander Zorn was correct. Because of the malfunction there was a cross field glitch, and rather than a short-Jump a Synchronous Transport was improperly initiated.

"The completed analysis has verified a direct correlation between the theory and the observed outcome. While all the Jump parameters were gold for a short-Jump, they were not valid or even safe when employed in executing a synchronous

Spin-Field Transport. When the glitch occurred, there existed a high probability of our total destruction."

"Mike, has your analysis revealed any flaws in the theory itself?" Zorn asked.

"Sir, No. The analysis confirms the Spin-Field theory is valid. The observed glitch was not a product of a flaw in the theory, but rather a logical loop malfunction that disrupted the execution of a short-Jump. Given the measured data, the two theories are now independently validated, and the cause of the glitch is identified."

"Not so fast Mike. What I want to know is basic. If we execute either of those protocols, are we going to end up where we want to go or else end up with burnt out circuits and find ourselves dead or stranded in some dark and deep alcove of Tartarus?" Zorn said.

"Sir, the necessary corrections have been implemented and the principle of redundancy applied. there remains an infinitesimal probability of another similar systems malfunction, however, that probability now approaches zero."

"Mike, since all systems are now gold, how long would it take you to execute a Spin-Field Transport?" Zorn asked.

"Sir, I am fully prepared to begin a Spin Transport at this time. All that is required is an input of the synchronous navigation parameters, which define our desired route and destination."

"Roan, did you hear Mike say what I think he said? That when we locate Glas Dinnein, and define the navigation parameters, we can get underway for home," Zorn said, excitedly.

"I think I did hear the—"

"Sirs, Eminent warning! " Mike interrupted. "An unidentified energy phenomenon has appeared off our forward port quarter."

"Mike, show the phenomenon on screen," Roan ordered.

The large screen in the mess area immediately brightened, and Roan and Zorn sat staring in stunned recognition of what they were observing. The reported phenomenon consisted of two distinct globes of beautiful and dazzling luminous light, bright and simulating against the background of stars and intergalactic darkness. The image was unmistakably that of two Elders.

In a hushed voice, Roan ordered, "Mike, take no offensive action, none whatsoever. Promptly commence a purely passive full spectrum monitoring of the phenomenon."

A melodious and distinctly feminine voice "spoke" telepathically within Roan and Zorn's minds. *"Well done Commanders Roan and Zorn, very well done indeed. It appears to us that you are somewhat far from your home. Might we be of some assistance?"*

"Greetings Elders. I confess, your appearance here is an unanticipated surprise, but welcomed. Would it be appropriate if I were to ask you for your names?" Roan asked.

An overwhelming sense of wellbeing flooded throughout Roan and Zorn, and it was accompanied with a pure clear telepathic communication. *"Commander Roan, that request is quite appropriate. At this time, you may call me Shanti and my companion is Jivana. Recently we became aware of your attempted synchronous transport and observed its lamentable outcome.*

"Your AI is correct; your shipboard systems are now adequately repaired and will operate properly. We have also evaluated your Transport methodology, and although primitive, it is functional. We are also confident that given a little more time you would locate the temporal space coordinates of your home world, Glas Dinnein. Accordingly, we judge our assisting you at this time is within the permitted bounds of our interacting with humanity."

"Shanti, what do you mean by permitted bounds?" Zorn asked.

"Commander, in our interactions with young species we are restrained in what help we might offer. In this instance the Old One, Illuyan, has exceeded all permitted bounds and is actively assisting the Kreel. It is Illuyan's unwarranted violations of the covenant that grants us this opportunity to provide you with modest assistance.

"With your permission, Commander Roan, we will provide to your AI the temporal and space navigation data necessary for your safe synchronous transport to your destination."

"Shanti, you have my permission and also our wholehearted gratitude for your help. Out of curiosity, might I ask a question?"

"You may."

"Well, in that you were obviously aware of our plight and observing our efforts to get home, if we had not been successful in repairing our ship, what would have happened?"

"Commander, in that particular case Zorn and you would have died."

"Shanti, if I may, I also have a question. when I first regained consciousness, I sorta remember hearing an insistent voice in my mind. That voice urgently encouraged me to wake up or else Roan and I would utterly perish. I think that voice sounded like you. So, was it you?"

Once more Roan and Zorn felt a warm and rippling flow of positive wellbeing throughout their bodies, and it conveyed a sense of merriment. *"Yes Zorn, it was."*

"Then, thank you Shanti," Zorn said.

"Commanders Roan and Zorn, it was our great pleasure to be of modest help. When you do arrive at your destination, it will be our delight and pleasure to once more visit with you."

The image of the two Elders suddenly vanished, as Roan and Zorn observed the screen. For several minutes, the two men sat quietly and thoughtfully looking at the framed image of the immense galaxy, suspended and shining bright against the vastness of intergalactic space.

"Mike, have you had any communications with the Elders?" Roan asked.

"Yes Sir. While Shanti was speaking with you, Jivana was providing me with a significant quantity of data, consisting of volumes of text, images, formulas, music, and a precise transport navigation data set. Jivana said the navigation data set is formulated to efficiently guide us to our destination."

"Mike, expand on your use of the terms formulated and efficiently guide," Zorn said.

"Sir, the navigation data set represents a significant expansion of our fundamental Transport theory. It is quite elegant."

"What do you think Zorn, should we trust them?"

"Trust them? We've been sitting out here for nearly two months, fighting to stay alive and get home again. Not only am I ready to trust them, if I could figure out how to get my arms around them, I'd give them both a big hug. Roan, let's go home."

"There you have it, Mike. You heard the man; begin pre-Transport systems validation and prepare for synchronous Transport," Roan ordered.

"Aye, aye Sir. Preparing for synchronous Spin Transport...."

It required two hours for Roan and Zorn to move throughout the ship and confirm that all tools and similar loose objects were properly stowed and secured. With a blending of excitement and trepidation, both men entered into the control compartment, took their Command chairs and buckled in. Each man with meticulous care set about checking and then checking again each step required to execute a Synchronous Spin Transport. Neither man wanted to repeat their previous mishap.

"Zorn, my flight control panel is solid gold. What is your status?"

"All the precursor navigational functions are checked and confirmed gold. We're ready for Transport."

"Mike, report. Do you confirm the navigation data set is programmed, affirm pre-Transport status is gold, and that you're ready for Transport?"

"Sirs, I can confirm the navigation data set is verified. Current speed and course are in agreement with navigation parameters. All sensors are at maximum sensitivity. Sensors and subsystems are being duly recorded. Power levels are at maximum capacity. Confirming ready for Transport. Awaiting orders."

"Zorn, is there anything you want to say before we initiate Transport?"

"Only, it's about time. Let's go home."

"Mike, on your count, commence a ten-second countdown," Roan ordered.

"Acknowledged. The Transport temporal displacement fields have attained harmonic synchronization and are charging. The Transport energy temporal field envelope is now formed and is stable. Temporal Compensation for local galaxy black hole mass and spin rate is correct and verified. All systems are now confirmed ready for Transport. Counting mark ... 3, 2, 1, Transport!"

The Command console display was showing the now familiar image of the distant galaxy surrounded by the void of intergalactic space. Then, as Roan and Zorn watched, there was a momentary brilliant flash of radiance, and the automatic gain video circuits promptly dampened the overload. As the AGC balanced, there was a disconcerting illusion of vertigo. It seemed the entire galaxy was rushing swiftly up to collide with them. The image on the screens then altered from a field of discrete stellar objects to one consisting of a full field of golden light. Within the overall golden field were zones of shimmering colors, containing multiple groups of moving symbols that were embedded within areas of swirling and altering hues. There was a slight sense of acceleration, and the ship was vibrant with a deep thrumming of immense power, which was perceptible to the depth of Roan and Zorn's senses.

The graphics and colors of the displays were unanticipated, and in sudden alarm Roan inquired, "Mike report, status!"

"Sirs, all systems are gold. We are proceeding along the defined navigational temporal-space trajectory provided by the Elders. We are maneuvering to avoid and pass by multiple solar systems and multiple detected dark masses. It may become a little bumpy," Mike reported.

Roan and Zorn continued to observe the monitors in amazement. They were displaying a series of lateral shifts, where multiple areas of amber colors, each with contrasting symbols, approached and then apparently swept past. Neither Roan or Zorn said anything. They knew Mike had been specifically designed to perform the high-speed computations inherent with such Transport, and by all indications he was performing precisely as was intended. One hour and forty-two minutes had elapsed since entering Transport, when the screens shifted from the golden field to one of on-rushing bright points of lights, bright against a background of black. Then the rate of movement shifted again, and there was a distinct sense of deceleration. The visible field of stars then once more appeared stationary.

"Sirs, we have exited Synchronous Spin-Field Transport. We have arrived at our defined destination. In order to establish our precise coordinates in space-time, I am scanning for Guardian Force navigation beacons.

Zorn felt his tensions begin to ease and let out a slow deep breath, while continuing to stare at his console display. "Roan, we have spent months studying the Spin-Field Transport theory, but what we have just witnessed is way beyond anything I ever anticipated. If that is actually our Primary, Tearman, then, I'm utterly flummoxed and way out of my element. I saw what I saw. But, I can't even begin to explain what I've just witnessed and felt."

"Sirs, I have located and communicated with a Guardian Beacon. The nearby solar system is not Tearman and Glas Dinnein. the world before us is Megan. I have also synchronized our chronometer, and twenty months, two weeks, and three days have elapsed since we departed Glas Dinnein."

"Ouch, that hurts. Roan, there has been a relativistic temporal shift. It validates the old adage that in physics there isn't any such thing as a free lunch. It isn't nearly as bad as I feared, however, it does mean I'm in big, big trouble with Elayne," Zorn commented with a sigh.

"Hmmm, it also strongly implies the Elders had an ulterior reason for sending us to Megan and not on to Glas Dinnein. I suspect the prudent thing is to accept the not-so-subtle hint that this is where they want us to go.

"Mike, compute the Jumps necessary to get us to Megan and proceed," Roan ordered.

"Acknowledged, computing short Jump to heliosheath, then continuation to Megan," Mike said.

Taking a deep breath, Roan keyed the QT Communications circuits. "Guardian Operations, Mike One here. Commanders Roan and Zorn are reporting. Mike One has just emerged from Spin Transport near Megan. Repeat, Mike One has just emerged from Spin Transport and is proceeding on to Megan. Acknowledge...."

Chapter Fifty-Seven:
Something of Great Import

The morning marine layer had first thinned, then as a soft onshore breeze had come up it had soon dissipated. It was still early morning at Susie's home, Daireann West, on Megan. The sun was low and bright on the eastern horizon. Susie felt the gentle caress of the early warmth sunlight on her face and bare arms, and smiled thinking, *it's going to be a warm day.* Busy and happily pulling weeds from her garden, she frowned in annoyance when her communicator buzzed. Glancing at the caller ID, she saw it was from Rodney and sighed. Shaking off her right-hand glove, she activated her communicator.

"What's up?" she asked.

"Ms. Susie, I have just received some startling news. If you are standing, I recommend that you sit down or else take hold of something."

Scowling and putting her trowel down, she stood up. "Rodney, I'm not in the mood for pranks. This had better be good."

"Ms. Susie, this is not a prank. I have been talking with the Cruiser AIs in orbit. They were just in communications with Mike One. He has just emerged from a Synchronous Transport and is even now approaching Megan. Ms. Susie, they are alive! Both Roan and Zorn will soon be here."

Literally stunned by the unanticipated news, Susie's scowl deepened. "Rodney, you're to put a clamp on the news, and I do mean a hard clamp. Caution the Cruiser AIs to bottle it up. For the moment, I don't want any rumors spreading on Megan. You're to stay in close communications with the Cruisers. If something new develops, immediately notify me. Is that clear?"

"Yes Ma'am."

In deep thought and frowning, Susie shucked off her second glove, and then bending she put them both under her trowel. Turning, she walked back into her home. As she did, she was aware of the familiar sounds of the waves breaking upon the rocks at the bottom of her hill. It was a beautiful day, and it had also suddenly become an extraordinary day.

Entering her home, she was thinking, *beyond all hope they're alive!* Walking into her kitchen, she began whistling a merry tune and started preparing a fresh pot of Earth coffee. As she busied herself, Elayne entered and looked at her with a puzzled expression.

"Susie, what's going on? I thought you were planning to spend the morning in the garden."

"And you were absolutely correct, but things have changed and my priorities have shifted somewhat. Right now, our highest priority is to plan for an impromptu party, and for that I need your help."

Still puzzled, Elayne's frown nevertheless transformed into a smile. "We're having a party? You don't normally come into the house whistling and then brew up a pot of your rare-Earth coffee. This party you want my help with must be really special."

"You're right, it's quite special. It's a surprise party. With your help, together we can be ready by this afternoon. And, it's so special I'm even willing to share my small horde of coffee. Please, get a couple of mugs and put them on the table."

Still smiling, Elayne took two clean mugs from the cupboard, placing them on the table with cream and honey. She had just sat down when Susie came over and poured two mugs of steaming coffee. Then, sitting down, Susie smiled at Elayne, but said nothing.

"Susie, you're clearly enjoying yourself, and you know I don't have a clue as to what's going on. Now, 'fess up. What's this all about? Who is the surprise party for?"

"Well, that's what I call a fair question. There I was working away in the garden, just as I'd planned, pulling weeds. Then Rodney called me and broke my chain of thought. You know how he is, always eager to provide the latest tidbit of news or gossip. Well, this time he had some good news, and it's what we're going to be celebrating this afternoon.

"It seems Rodney has, as usual, been chatting with the Cruiser AIs in orbit. They told Rodney, and he told me, that they had just been in communication with Mike One. Elayne, Zorn is alive, and so is Roan. I don't know what has happened, at least not yet, but they are both reported to be alive. More important, right now they're inbound for Megan."

Elayne sat stunned and still, staring at Susie and trying to comprehend what she had just heard. "Susie, this is for real?"

"Yes, it's really for real, and Zorn is alive. He is even now with Roan, and they are right now both coming here."

Tears began flowing down Elayne's face, and she sniffled and wiped at her cheeks with the back of her hand. In a state of awkward bewilderment, she stood and shaking her head she walked over to retrieve a napkin, then dabbed at the tears on her face.

"Susie, it's been nearly two years, two long terrible years. I had almost given up all hope. What little hope remained, which I was desperately clinging to, felt like a sharp knife piercing my heart. It hurt so very much."

Susie stood and going over to Elayne, she gave her a hug. "Young lady, you might want to consider enjoying that rare cup of Earth coffee, then you might go and freshen up. I don't know what happened to Roan and Zorn, but for sure it has taken them nearly two years to get back home. We both know they will have been fighting hard around the clock day in and day out to get back. I'm positive Zorn will want to see you the minute he touches ground, and don't worry, I'll see that when he does touch ground it will be right outside of that front door! Now, first things first, sit down and enjoy your coffee, after all, there is something to celebrate."

As Susie and Elayne sat down, Susie's communicator buzzed. Glancing at the caller ID, Susie frowned and flipped her communicator to its conference mode and placed it on the table.

"Good morning Amada, and what are you up to on this beautiful day?" Susie asked.

"Well, I am calling to tell you I have just had an extraordinary communication with an Elder. Our contacts with them have always been unpredictable and sparse, and during all the centuries we've never been provided a single name of an Elder, not one. Well, this morning an Elder unexpectedly contacted me, and unbidden she just freely provided me with her name. It's Shanti. Susie, she told me that a number of Elders will be arriving on Megan the day after tomorrow. They want to converse with representatives of the Nori, the Assembled worlds, and even representatives of Earth.

"During all of the millenniums of our contacts with the Elders, we've never seen a gathering of them, never. It's unheard of, and I have no idea of what they want to discuss with us."

"Perhaps I do. Several years ago, when I was aboard Lan and we encountered the Elder, he mentioned his pleasure in seeing the fulfillment of the foretelling of the three dispirit groups of humanities being united on Megan. Perhaps they simply want to talk about our being here together. After all, we're in the midst of the construction of our various cultural centers.

"Amada, I've also got some news, which only ads to your Elder mystery. I've just learned that Roan and Zorn are alive. In fact, they are right now inbound for Megan."

"Alive? I thought both Commanders Roan and Zorn were declared killed during a test flight of a new ship two years ago. Everyone I've talked to believed they had perished. Susie, I believe in coincidence, but not on a scale of two such improbabilities as that of Roan and Zorn being alive and landing here at the same time that Elders begin to provide their names and request a conference. I do not know what has happened, but whatever it is, I believe Roan and Zorn's unanticipated return and The Elders wanting a conference are inexorably connected. This points to something of great import. I need to reach the other Nori with this information. Please keep me informed about Roan and Zorn, and I'll do the same with you about the Elders."

"Agreed. Thanks for the heads-up," Susie broke the connection.

Putting her mug down, Elayne stood up. "Susie, excuse me. I'm going to go and check on Briana. She is probably still sleeping, but I need to be sure."

As Elayne departed, Susie sat thoughtfully pondering the substance of what Amada had said. *She was correct of course, the timing of the Elders wanting a conference and the return of Mike One was unlikely to be a coincidence. Blast it all, there is definitely a huge mystery here. Humph, even after two years, there's still a dark cloak of secrecy shrouding Roan and Zorn vanishing onboard a prototype of a ship. Now, here they are coming home. But, where in blazes have they been? I definitely hate mysteries.*

"Well," Susie muttered to herself. " As the old sage said, not using your authority is to abuse that authority," Picking up her communicator she called Rodney.

"Ms. Susie, my latest Intel is Mike One has exited a short-Jump just beyond the heliosphere and is even now penetrating the heliosheath boundary turbulence. Everyone is excited."

"Rodney, pay attention. I need you to set up a priority QT link between the Secretary Admiral Eryan Kyrie and me, priority AA. Tell her the topic of the call is about the Elders. Do not mention Mike One. I will stand by for the connection."

"Understood and complying," Rodney said.

Putting down her communicator, Susie picked up her nearly empty mug of coffee and sipped it appreciatively. It represented a rare treat. It was from her private horde of a few pounds of coffee which Darrell had thoughtfully brought to her upon his return from Earth the year before. Remembering that episode, she sighed. The fracas Darrell's covert trip with the Nori to Earth had triggered within Olympus was intense. The whole matter was still dicey. Her Earth AI, William, had dutifully reported via Rodney that Charles Sullivan, the Director of Project Olympus, would have keelhauled Darrell if he could have gotten his hands on him. Fortunately for Darrell's skin, by the time Charles had discovered his being on Earth, Darrell was safely off-planet with the Nori and on his way back to Megan. Since his unannounced visit, Darrell's relationship with Olympus had become rather strained. In time, hopefully, that would resolve itself.

Her communicator buzzed; she noted the caller ID was a formal Guardian cruiser ID, and she keyed it open. "Ambassador Wells here."

"Ambassador, please standby for an AA priority QT call from Secretary Admiral Eryan Kyrie."

It was her first QT call, and Susie noted the sound quality was crisp, but there seemed to be more background hiss than normal. "Susie, Eryan here. What's all this about an AA priority and the Elders? What's happening?"

"Eryan, I'll give you first things first. I have confirmation Commanders Roan and Zorn are both alive. According to Rodney they had exited from something he called a synchronous Transport, and they're now inbound for Megan.

"You can add to that surprise that an Elder has communicated with Amada, and has requested a conference here on Megan between a gathering of Elders and representatives of the Nori, the Assembled Worlds, and Earth on the day following tomorrow. Both Amada and I believe there is a direct connection between Mike One's unexpected return and the Elder's request for a parley. The problem is we don't know the subject of the parley."

There was a momentary silence as Eryan mentally processed the information. "I had not heard about Mike One. It's not only unanticipated, it's simply wonderful news. As for the probability of coincidence, I agree, the two events are most likely connected. I suspect that we'll need to wait a few days to learn what it's all about. Now, just how can I help?"

"For starters, the first thing you can do is call Admiral Mer Shawn and bend his arm. I want Mike One to land at my home on Megan, not at the space port at the Capital. Elayne is here with me, and I want Zorn to meet his beautiful daughter. Besides the Elders and Nori can gather here as easily as in the Capital, Alainn. I will scrounge up a few Earth types in order to fill the billing. I'm confident the Nori will agree. The real problem is time. Oddly enough, as improbable as it sounds, Mike One seems to have Jump capability and is only a few hours out. Guardian Force will need to order Mike One to land here. Can you help arrange that?"

"Yes, I think I can. Mer definitely owes me a few favors, and this is a good time for me to collect on some of them. I'll get back to you within the hour. Eryan out."

When the communicator disconnected, Susie redialed. "Rodney, see if you can reach McRoy. Tell him we have a fast-moving high priority development and I would really appreciate it if he could drop whatever he is doing and come here. Then connect me with Amada."

"Acknowledged," Rodney said.

Susie set about clearing the table, and putting the kitchen counter in order. As she worked, her communicator buzzed. It was Amada. She keyed the call.

"Hello again, you wanted to talk with me?" Amada asked.

"Yes. I've requested Guardian Force to direct Roan and Zorn to land here at my home. I'm waiting for the anticipated

382

confirmation that my request was approved. I'm suggesting we hold our conference with the Elders and the representatives here at Daireann West. What do you think?"

"As I see the problem, there will only be a few representatives involved, perhaps six or eight at most. In which case, your home is as good as anywhere. I believe everyone will agree with your suggestion. I will begin making arrangements to come over tomorrow with a few people. Perhaps we can spend the night there."

"That should work out well, we can make a party of it. Remember, when I was building my home, we camped out. Perhaps we can do that again. It was fun, and a little fun mixed with what may turn out to be serious business might make for a good mix."

"Susie, I need to ask a serious question. What was so special about the new ship that Roan and Zorn were testing?"

"Sorry, I would tell you, but I don't know. All I know is it was smaller than a cruiser, being about half again as large as a scout. It had some newfangled type of propulsion, and it has Jump capability. That's about all I know."

"Hmmm, half again as large as a scout ship and with Jump capability? That implies a radical and extremely dangerous design. Well I suppose what it is all about will come out in the next few days. Until then, if you do receive more news as to where we will be meeting, let me know."

As Amada disconnected, Susie keyed her next call. "Rodney, front and center."

"Yes Ma'am, I'm here."

"Rodney, I think it's long past time that you and I had a little chat about what is so special about Mike One...."

Chapter Fifty-Eight:
Friends and Family

The turbulence Mike One encountered within the heliosheath boundary was moderate, and the ship passed through it without difficulty. Entering into the solar system forty degrees above the ecliptic plane, the five Cruisers on patrol greeted them with exuberant expressions of surprise and good cheer. In response to Roan's earlier message to Guardian Control, they also soon received a priority QT transmission from Guardian Operations and Admiral Dylan Cord.

"Roan, let me get this straight. In your reckoning you've only been gone about Sixty days?" Admiral Cord asked.

"That's correct. When we exited the synchronous Transport, our updated chronometers indicated we've been gone nearly two years. Given relativity that's understandable, but accepting the reality of that fact is somewhat jarring," Roan said.

"Humph, hearing you've exited our galaxy, traveled 160,000 light years, and returned is also a little jarring. The fact the Elders have directed you to Megan is somewhat puzzling. Still, it's only prudent to follow their lead. Besides, there's a good reason for Zorn to be going there."

"Sir, could you be more explicit?" Zorn asked.

Chuckling in a happy mood, Cord responded, "Be herewith advised Commander, you are now the proud father of a very healthy and lovely daughter. And, both Elayne and your daughter are now on Megan. I'm also quite confident that by the time you reach the planet, everyone there will be aware of your arrival, including Elayne."

Zorn sat back in his command chair, staring blankly at the control console. After a momentary silence, he whispered, "I'm a father? Sir, what is her given name?"

"Now, Zorn you don't really expect me to tell you that, do you? I'll leave that up to Elayne. Humph, Wait one ... I'm receiving a priority call from Admiral Mer Shawn. I'll get back to you. Cord out."

"Roan, did you hear him? he said I was a father; I've got a daughter!"

Roan was smiling, and perhaps even more broadly than Zorn. "Yes, and that's the best news I've heard in centuries. congratulations are definitely in order. I wish you and your family all possible good fortune."

"Well, it's going to take a bit of getting used to. Roan, I should have been there when she was born; I'd planned on being there."

"Zorn, take three deep slow breaths, and grab hold of your mental focus. We need to set up for a short-Jump to a point one AU from the planet. I suggest you get cracking on that problem."

"Confirming, a short-Jump to 1 AU distance from the planet. I'm on it."

"Sir, I have a message coming in over QT from Admiral Cord," Mike said.

"Mike, connect me," Roan said.

"Guardian Operations, Mike One here."

"Roan, I've just talked with Admiral Mer Shawn, and he has been talking with Eryan Kyrie. She had advised him that you are even now anticipated on Megan, and there is going to be a gathering of Elders the day following tomorrow. In the meantime, you are ordered to proceed directly to the home of Ambassador Wells and put down there. I want you rested before that meeting with the Elders, and I also expect a full bandwidth recording of everything which happens at that parley. You have the responsibility to see the data is promptly forwarded to me as soon as the meeting concludes."

"Yes Sir. As ordered, we're now proceeding to Megan and to the home of Ambassador Wells."

"Roan, Zorn, now hear this, well-done. Cord out."

"Roan, I've set up the short-Jump. We will be exiting as ordered, 1 AU from the planet. I'll need Susie's coordinates before I can set up for the micro-Jump."

"Mike, contact the lead Cruiser. Obtain a link with a Guardian AI on the planet named Rodney. Get through to Rodney and obtain the coordinates for Ambassador Wells' home or else determine where else she might be. I'll need to speak with her after we exit from our micro-Jump. Then, setup and proceed with the short-Jump Zorn has computed. Make it happen."

"Acknowledged."

Shortly following his exit from the short-Jump, Mike One reported, "Sir, I've reached Rodney and obtained the requested coordinates. As ordered, I have the contact data needed to communicate with the Ambassador."

"Good. Mike, pass the coordinate to Zorn."

"Acknowledged."

With the smoothness born of long hours of training and the harsh experience gained in combat, the time-lag between Jumps was less than two minutes. With the coordinate Mike had provided, Zorn computed a micro-Jump to a point located 3,500 kilometers above the planet, positioning Mike One above the desired planetary location. As Mike One exited from the micro-Jump, he was positioned high above a broad expanse of a dark blue ocean. A ragged coastline ran north to south, and a sprawling landmass spread out eastwardly in a rich tapestry of browns and greens, punctuated by a series of snowcapped mountain ranges. The landmass was bathed and enhanced by the warm sunlight of a late afternoon. With an appreciation that only those who have lived in the stark contrasts of deep space could comprehend, both Roan and Zorn admired the magnificent beauty of the inviting World which was laid out before them.

"Mike, get the Ambassador on the line."

"Sir, connecting."

Following a brief delay, Susie's excited voice filled the compartment. "Mike One, Susie here! I've been anticipating your call. Roan, Zorn, hello and welcome. Where are you?"

"Hello right back to you. At the moment, we are about 1,800 kilometers above your location and rapidly descending. I presume there's no cradle for us to set Mike One down on."

"Roan, you know there isn't. Mike One's hull configuration is one of a kind, and there isn't a cradle that would fit him located on the entire planet. If he cannot put down hard on the ground, then he will just have to hover like the other big boys do."

"Susie, it's good to hear your voice again. Zorn has just learned he is a father, and he's about to pop a gasket. I hope Elayne and his daughter are there."

"Tell him to just keep his gaskets intact. Yes, both Elayne and Briana are here, and Elayne is also about to pop her gaskets, oh my gosh, I think I can see you. Elayne, Elayne get out here right now, I see them. They're almost here. Hurry it up Elayne, or else you'll miss their arrival. Oh, Roan hover where you are, until I can get her out of the house."

"Mike, you heard her, park it," Zorn said.

"Sir, parking it! I've located the precise point of Transmission. It is now being shown on the center tactical display screen," Mike reported.

It was with keen interest that Roan and Zorn looked at the scene below them. There was a spacious home located near the top of a wooded high hill and positioned well above the coastline. A broad terraced area near the home could be seen and a woman was hurrying from the terrace into the house. Soon thereafter a dog and two women emerged from the house, and looking up the women began waving.

"Mike take us down and then hold stationary just above the ground. Hover in place. Zorn and I will be using the ramp to depart and meet the ladies. Remain hovering until further orders. Now, take it slow, we don't want to startle anyone."

"Acknowledged. Confirming adequate open space exists for hovering directly in front of the ladies."

"Well Zorn, we've made it to Megan and all in one piece. Get unbuckled and go aft. I'll be right behind you."

"I'm on my way."

A gentle warm offshore breeze was melodiously stirring the wind chimes and the late afternoon sun was arching majestically toward the western horizon. As Susie and Elayne watched Mike One descending, his hull was gleaming with the bright white and gold trim of Guardian Parade colors. The brilliance of his hull with its sleek contours distinctly heralded he was not a Scout ship.

"Oh, my gosh," Susie muttered. "He's absolutely beautiful, wow."

There was barely a foot between his keel and the ground when Mike One stopped. Then, a seam appeared in the unblemished surface of his glistening hull, and a hatch swung inwardly and aside, as a ramp extended out and angled downward and touched the ground. As the women watched, first Zorn and then Roan appeared in the hatch, and both men were waving and smiling broadly.

Zorn led the way down the ramp, and he quickly crossed the few feet to where Susie and Elayne were standing, passed Susie by, and put his arms around Elayne's waist. Lifting her up off the ground he swung her about in a playful manner.

"Zorn, behave yourself," Elayne protested, even as she was laughing. Tears of joy were streaming down both of her cheeks.

Gently putting Elayne down, Zorn bent down and gave her an affectionate kiss. "Beloved one, you have been much missed.

Elayne was smiling, and her eyes were filled with joy as she took Zorn by his hands. Your home, that's what is most important. Now come along with me, there's someone very special you need to meet."

Elayne and Zorn turned and walking entered the house. Susie looked over to Roan, and like Elayne, Susie had tears running down her cheeks.

"Come right this way commander, you are also part of this rather special reunion."

Roan paused for just a moment, to scratch Gepeto behind his ears, and then entered into the house. As he did, he glanced around and was immediately struck by its remarkable architecture and decor. The floor of a spacious room was covered by large decorative square tiles and it was well furnished with comfortable seating and low tables. There was a massive, and by all indications, a well-used fireplace constructed from well fitted stone. Overhead were exposed beams of dark wood and along the outer eves of the room were clerestory windows. Still shaking his head in recognition of the obvious warm comfort of the room, he turned and with Susie and Gepeto followed Elayne and Zorn who were still walking hand in hand down a broad long corridor. At the end was an open door, and as he neared the door Roan distinctly heard the sounds of a child laughing and singing in harmony with a young girl.

As Elayne and Zorn entered into the room, the voice of the girl singing stopped, but the child's happy voice and laughter continued for a moment.

Standing in the doorway, Susie and Roan watched as Elayne went to and knelt down by her daughter and hugged her. " Briana, someone very special has come from a long way off to see you and give you a big hug. Honey, it's your Papa."

The little girl looked up toward Zorn, and her eyes were sparkling with delight. "Papa Zorn?"

Kneeling on one knee, Zorn reached gently out and took the child's small hands in his. "Yes Briana, I'm your Papa, and I love you very, very much."

Sweeping the child up into his arms, Zorn hugged her close to him and spun her about, even as he had done with her mother. The child wrapped her arms tightly about his neck and squealed in delight. As he spun about, tears of joy were streaking Zorn's face.

As Zorn was busy hugging his daughter, Roan was still puzzled and looking about the room. There simply was no young girl there.

"Elayne, I'm somewhat perplexed. As we came down the corridor I distinctly heard a young girl's voice singing with your daughter. But, there's no one else here. What's up?" Roan asked.

"Roan, there most certainly is someone else here. I am here!" The voice of a young girl seemed to emerge out of thin air. Startled, Both Roan and Zorn looked quizzically about.

"Shey? Is that you?" Roan asked.

"It most certainly is. While you two gadabouts were out doing only what the Elders and the Muses know what, someone had to take charge of matters here and keep them ship shape and in fine trim."

"But how?" Roan stammered.

"Well, it did not require a crystal ball to know where Elayne and Zorn were heading. I evaluated the probabilities of what might occur, and set forth my wishes accordingly. Should an unforeseen incident occur, I chose to follow the example of William and Rodney, and here I am doing precisely what I wanted to do, helping to raise Papa Zorn's children."

"But, you're a combat qualified Scout ship AI," Roan stammered, still perplexed.

"True, and in the decades to come, when my children rearing duties are fulfilled, and if I get the hankering, there might just be a new Mike Class ship named Shey or perhaps Machelle. Until then, I'm quite happy being here with Briana."

After all of the initial excitement was over, Elayne and Susie retired into the kitchen to prepare a full course evening meal for them all. Meanwhile Zorn, still carrying Briana in his arms, went with Roan outside to show her Mike One. After Briana had looked at Mike One, she looked up to Zorn. "Papa, can he sing like Shey?"

Smiling, Zorn hugged her closer to him and in response she leaned her head against his chest. "Well, I don't rightly know if Mike can sing, but if he doesn't know how, Shey can teach him."

Walking together to the edge of the terrace, Roan and Zorn looked out beyond the nearby coast line. On the distant horizon, the setting sun was spectacular to behold. The colors illuminating the low clouds on the horizon were constantly changing, flowing shades of brilliant gold, reds, and hues of deepening purples. All the colors were adding their lavish contribution to a vast spectacle of incredible natural beauty.

"Well Roan, there's one sight you don't get to see when out in space. It's incredibly beautiful. Wow, this has been an incredible day.

"I can't simply get over how much has happened during the past few years. Do you remember how it started? Back then we were with Shey and hunkered down at full stealth, waiting to identify an inbound unknown target. It turned out to be that ungainly sub-light probe that Earth had sent out hundreds of years earlier. Absolutely nothing was ever the same after we intercepted that archaic probe.

"Just look about us. We have been to Mother Earth, and even now are standing on a beautiful planet that neither of us had even heard of back then. We have new friends, and look I've even got a family, and Shey is still right here with us. It's downright incredible all the adventures that have come our way in a few years."

Continuing to watch the sunset, Roan replied almost absent-mindedly. "We've definitely covered bunches of parsecs. While fighting Arkillians and the Kreel we've scampered out of death's grasp more than once, yet being 60,000 light-years above the heart of our own Wandering Waterway was definitely the most astonishing part of it all; except, of course, for Briana.

With a quiet smile, Roan turned and watched Zorn holding Briana close to him. " Just like her mother, she is absolutely beautiful. Luckily for her, she doesn't look a bit like you."

Zorn glanced over toward Roan, and smiled. "And, lucky for you, I'm holding my beautiful daughter in my arms, else I would bop you a good one!"

"Roan, Zorn, you will never know or understand how much I have missed the both of you," Shey whispered.

Chapter Fifty-Nine:
The Gathering

Lingering darkness was still shrouding the turbulent ocean, while the promising glow of the approaching sunrise was delineating the eastern mountain tops. By contrast, within Susie's home everything was brightly illuminated, and everyone was up and bustling about. During the previous day, those invited to the gathering had arrived, and most of them had stayed up late visiting and conversing together. The known facts were scanty, although that did not prevent anyone from having their own theories about why the Elders have requested a gathering. The questions about where Roan and Zorn might have gone were many, both men having departed prior to the arrival of the others. Susie told them what she understood. It had to do with Guardian Force business, but that was all she knew.

A flourish of excitement and increasing expectations had arrived with the new day. Susie, Elayne, Amada, and Chandara were busy in the kitchen talking and laughing together while preparing a light breakfast for everyone. Darrell and Seth Turner were in the living room, where McRoy was stirring up the embers from the night before, adding splintered kindling to build up a fire in the fireplace.

Coming into the front room, Elayne lightly struck the bottom of a pan with a spoon. "Gentlemen, breakfast is served in the kitchen."

Soon thereafter the kitchen was filled with the hubbub of people enjoying their food, a combination of yogurt, choices of various fruits and berries, all being served with toast and copious quantities of neab. When Susie's communicator vibrated, she checked its caller ID and then excused herself from the group.

Leaving the kitchen, Susie hurried across the front room and exited the house. Reaching the terrace, she stood and looked skyward. When departing the day before, Roan and Zorn had told Susie that she would be receiving a call from Mike One. When the call came, they explained, she should promptly go to the terrace and greet her incoming guests. In spite of all of her probing questions they would not divulge any additional information.

Humph, inbound guests. mysteries, it's always with the mysteries, Susie mused. Then, high in the west she detected a bright gleam which contrasted with the azure sky and soon thereafter identified a ship dropping down from above. Watching as it came nearer she recognized it was Mike One and smiled. She did not know what Roan and Zorn were up to. Nevertheless, thankfully they were returning. *Who,* she wondered, were *they bringing with them?*

As Mike One descended to a hover, his hatch slid open and the ramp extended. When Susie recognized the two people coming down the ramp toward her were Admiral Kellon and Secretary Admiral Eryan Kyrie, she gasped. *But,* she thought, *that's impossible. I spoke with Eryan only the day before yesterday. She was on Glas Dinnein; now, she is right in front of me. That's simply NOT possible!*

Smiling broadly, Eryan stepped off the ramp and with Kellon walked toward where Susie was standing. Overcoming her surprise, Susie stepped forward and greeted Kellon with a hug. "Sir, you are most welcomed to my home, and while your arrival was unanticipated, you are received with open arms and with all possible hospitality."

Turning toward Eryan, she frowned. "I know, there's a mystery here, and I presume I'm not supposed to ask anything about it. In protest, all I'll say is it's not fair. Beyond that, as always, you are most welcome back to Daireann West."

"No one ever accused you of being slow on the uptake. Let's just say Admiral Kellon and I are visiting Megan, and learning of the Elder's gathering, we commandeered a ride with Mike One."

"Eryan, I'll play along, but for the official record, I hate mysteries and riddles."

As Susie was talking Roan and Zorn had come down the ramp and joined them. As they exited, Mike One retracted his ramp and the hatch closed. Then, he silently soared skyward and moved off toward the east.

Susie scowled toward Zorn, who in good nature promptly returned her scowl, with a grin and a shrug. Sighing, she accepted the inevitable.

"Would any of you enjoy some breakfast and hot neab?" Susie asked.

Having obtained an enthusiastic response, entering her home Susie led her friends into the still-busy kitchen, where she called for everyone's attention. While Susie introduced Kellon and Eryan to Darrell and Seth, Amada and Chandara looked over and in recognition smiled in greeting. In way of explanation to the group, she offered the cover story that Kellon and Eryan were visiting Megan. Learning of the gathering, they had commandeered a ride with Roan and Zorn in order to participate. Inwardly, Susie felt uncomfortable about jumbling the facts, finding the dissemination distasteful, Guardian secrecy or otherwise.

As Kellon and Eryan were being served their breakfast, McRoy took the opportunity to greet both of them, and then he joined Roan and Zorn in general conversation. Following breakfast, everyone obtained fresh mugs of neab and retired to the front room.

As everyone was choosing comfortable seating, Darrell turned toward Zorn. "Commander, when will we get a look at your new ship? I understand it's one-of-a-kind."

"Unfortunately, you missed our arrival a few minutes ago. At present, our ship is on a mission which will keep it occupied for a while."

Feeling rebuffed, but still probing for information, Darrell elected to pursue a more direct tact. "A space voyage of nearly two years is not unheard of. What makes your last mission of special interest is everyone believed you were dead. In fact, they believed you had been killed in some freak accident while testing an experimental Jump theory. It all smacks of a powerful story, and frankly everyone I know would like to hear what happened. What can you tell us?"

"Sir, your questions concern sensitive matters, which are still under scrutiny and analysis within Guardian Force. I'm therefore not at liberty to discuss the details with anyone. Yet, given the elapsed time we were gone, and our abrupt return, it's obvious there was some type of a critical malfunction. In fact, it was only through providence and a welcomed nudge by the Elders that we survived."

"Commander Zorn, I've never met an Elder, but since I came aboard the Nori ship Subeer back on Earth, I have heard the Nori often speak of them. You say they aided you? Might I ask how?" Seth asked.

Zorn hesitated, then with circumspection answered the question. "Well, the malfunction which disabled our ship was severe. There was a considerable amount of internal damage, and our entire crew was physically disabled. I was the first to regain some conscious awareness; the ship was adrift, our air supply was thin, and internal illumination was feeble. Except for a minimal reserve charge on our emergency backup storage, we were without ship's power. If we had lost that last remaining power source, most likely we would have been unable to recover our main systems. It was while I was still semi-conscious that an Elder named Shanti telepathically communicated with me. She urged me to wake up or else we would surely perish. It was her insistent encouragement which motivated me to struggle to gain the mental awareness needed to comprehend our ship's plight. Alerted, I was able to take critical remedial action before I slipped back into unconsciousness. Except for Shanti, all of us might have died then and there."

"Zorn, how bad was the damage?" McRoy asked.

"We were dead in the water. The crew had to identify the damages, make major internal system repairs, and then figure out what had gone wrong. Once we repaired our systems and figured out the glitch, we were able to limp here to Megan."

"Commander Zorn, do you have any idea, any idea at all, why the Elders want to gather here?" Chandara asked.

"Sorry, no idea whatsoever."

At that moment, a clear and melodious extrasensory telepathic voice was simultaneously heard by everyone within the room. " Greeting friends, I am Shanti, the Elder that Commander Zorn just spoke of."

Amada, Chandara, Kellon, Susie, Roan and Zorn immediately recognized the mental communication, however, the others in the room were startled and glanced nervously about them. Even as they glanced about, Shanti continued speaking to the group.

"During our gathering, I have been delegated to be the spokesperson for the Elders. I accordingly greet each of you, and

396

through your representation, greet all humanity now living on the fourteen worlds upon which humanity dwells."

Being the hostess, Susie automatically spoke. "Elder Shanti, we are honored by your gathering. In peace, all are welcomed."

"Thank you, Ambassador. The Elders who are gathering have acknowledged your courteous greeting.

"Each of you are wondering why we have requested this gathering. It is being called because of humanity's recent crises, achievements, and advances.

"Mr. Fann, your unspoken assumption that I am referring to matters of technology is somewhat correct, but your perception is incomplete. There are also vital factors involving Justice, discernment, prudence, and righteousness which are involved."

"Ouch! Then you can read our minds?" Darrell said, clearly alarmed.

"Yes, Elders have that capability. Direct mind-to-mind contact is a precise and efficient means of communicating. When properly understood and developed, mind-to-mind contact permits clear and unambiguous communication. If you desire a better understanding of how we accomplish this feat, I suggest you arrange to study with the Nori."

Frowning, Kellon cut directly to the central issue. "Elder Shanti, you have mentioned Justice; what is the principal purpose for this gathering?"

"Admiral, it has become mandatory because of recent events, events in which you have played a significant part. You call us Elders and that salutation is appropriate. We are an aggregation of the remaining oldest sentient species that dwell within our galaxy. We are long-lived, and the ages of each of our unique cultures is measured in millions of years, not millenniums.

"Collectively, our mutual motivations are rooted in pursuing wisdom. We seek to understand and more perfectly express the ethical principles of Life in our interaction with each other and with the younger species within our galaxy."

"Shanti, I've got a question. what do you mean by ' ethical principles of Life?'" McRoy asked.

"Your question, Commander, is insightful. With cause, we Elders hold that among the applied ethical principles of Life are Free Will, Individual Rights, Truth, Righteousness, and Justice. Such principles are intertwined with Life itself; they are interleaved and inseparable from the fabric of our immense Universe. Within perceivable reality, our combined choices and actions over time manifest predictable consequences, which are governed by ethical laws as predictable as are those laws which pertain to the interactions of energy, mass, force, and time."

"Shanti, back on Earth, we call what you are talking about Karma, or more simply what goes around tends to come around. Still, we don't normally think of them as being immutable laws" Susie said.

"Ambassador, given the long history of sorrows upon Earth, its People would be wise to reconsider their assumptions. In adopting your Earth terms, what went around 70,000 years ago has now come full circle. Because of the Elder's considered choices and direct intervention into the affairs of humanity in ages past, today Humanity has survived its probable extinction, prospered, and in some ways, has matured. It is also splintered into three broad and diverse groups. The Elders acknowledge this undesirable separation of Humanity is the direct product of our choices and their resulting consequences.

"Of the three Human groups, The Nori have unquestionably attained the highest spiritual and moral development. As a culture, they are similar to a flower blooming in a barren place. Likewise, the culture of the Assembled Worlds is commendable and morally developed. Recently, it has applied the valued principals of Truth, Justice, Mercy, and Forgiveness in its dealing with other species.

"Of the three groups, the billions of humans dwelling on Earth constitute Humanity's most damaged group. It is partitioned into multiple diverse cultures, all of which bear deep social and emotional wounds. It is true that some external sources have inflicted grievous wounds on Earth's population, however, many of the wounds are self-inflicted. Consequently, the People on Earth are again teetering on the brink of extinction."

"Elder Shanti, I recently arrived here on Megan, but I grew up on Earth. Your words relating to extinction are alarming. Is there anything which might be done to help Earth?" Seth asked.

"Possibly so. In ages past, the Elders foresaw the Nori and the Assembled Worlds might work together and accept the responsibilities of helping the people on Earth. We understood such an outreach would require social maturity, wisdom, and involve a long-term commitment. With that understanding we observed with interest as Guardian Force sent one of its ships to locate Earth. We observed although they were light years distant from their homes, when they saw the need, Guardian Force personnel placed their lives in jeopardy to battle an alien culture, the Arkillians. That culture from another world had in millenniums past attained surreptitious control over Earth, and it had inflicted grievous injuries upon humanity. Given its technological superiority, the Elders were not surprised when Guardian Force prevailed in their battle with the Arkillians. What surprised us occurred after that battle."

"If permissible, Shanti, might I ask, which specific events surprised the Elders?" Kellon asked.

"It is permissible. What surprised us were events which involved moral crises. The first crisis occurred when after defeating the Arkillians, Guardian Force extended mercy to the survivors. The second event was when Guardian Force moved to counter a probable Kreel threat to Earth. Five Guardian ships were dispatched to interdict a possible Kreel strike force. You were the designated Commodore of that squadron. While enroute to Earth, you went far out of your way to intercept the Arkillians who were then limping back to their home world. When you intercepted their damaged Nest ship, you negotiated a peace with them. Even More surprising to the Elders, Guardian Force later stood resolute with the Arkillians and together fought to defend the Arkillian home world from a large Kreel invasion force.

Because of the size of the Kreel invasion force, the Elders were unable to accurately forecast the probable outcome of the battle. Yet, because of your courage and ingenuity, the entire Kreel force was systematically obliterated. Indisputably, that battle was the pivot point in the millenniums long Kreel war with humanity. Admiral Kellon, you were a prime agent in each of these moral crises."

"Elder Shanti, admittedly, I was there and directly involved. Although, before now I've never thought of those events in terms of their being moral crises. Besides, there were others in higher positions of Command who are deserving of praise, since it was their insights and wisdom which guided my choices."

"Admiral, in my view, your reticence only increases the luster of your merit. You also recently commanded a squadron of Guardian ships probing into the heart of the Kreel Empire. It was at that time, and again at peril of your own lives, that you acted to save Amada and Chandara. More recently, you commanded a Guardian Task Force attacking ten Kreel-occupied solar systems. In each case, using a weapons technology you had gleaned from the Arkillians, the Kreel were annihilated. While millions of Kreel were killed, we observed billions of indigenous sentient beings were spared and liberated from bruising oppressions."

As he had listened, Kellon's frown had deepened. "Shanti, if a potential finding of guilt is involved in what you are presenting here, yes, I'm responsible. I plead guilty. I gave the orders, and many Millions of Kreel were killed."

"Admiral Kellon, we have not gathered here to hold Court or to Judge your actions. Although be assured, such weighty matters will ultimately be Judged within the vast realm of Fate. Here I am only stating what we have observed. Although, admittedly, at times what we observed was of great concern to us."

"Shanti, I can assure you that they were then and still are of great concern to me," Kellon said.

"Admiral, interacting with you mind-to-mind, as we now are, I am aware of the heavy weight of your moral burden. Still, be comforted, Fate has so far smiled upon your choices and actions.

"More recently, your challenge and direct assault against the Kreel Hub Worlds greatly surprised us. Openly declaring the day of battle beforehand, you took a force of cruisers into the very stronghold of the Kreel Empire, their military Hub solar system. For the others' edification, will you tell us what then happened...."

Chapter Sixty:
A Pot of Gold

In response to Shanti's question, everyone turned and looked expectantly toward Kellon and awaited his answer. Crackling sounds punctuated the hushed expectation, as burning logs shifted within the fireplace.

"Well, we had come prepared for battle with a powerful defending fleet. Instead, we found a single Kreel cruiser and its three scouts, all other Kreel ships having departed the system. The four remaining Kreel ships were positioned near their planet and signaling for a parley.

"In order to gather Intel, I chose to honor that parley request. The Kreel warrior which I negotiated with demonstrated an unanticipated level of duty and honor, which transcended a consideration for his own life. The outcome of our parley was a mediated agreement. The four Kreel ships were required to land or else be destroyed. Then, according to our agreement, the Lux spared the Kreel population on the planet and sealed it tight. No Kreel ship can depart or approach without being destroyed.

"Regarding the Elite and Industrial Hub Worlds, upon our arrival we were opposed by scattered defending cruisers. After destroying the cruisers, like the Military Hub world, we sealed each planet.

"Following containment of the Hub worlds, we proceeded with systematic attacks on the remaining Kreel-occupied worlds. We granted no quarter. In each case, we obliterated the Kreel where we found them, in space or else on the planets. The indigenous species were not harmed, and their planets were sealed to assure their safety from further Kreel predations. The Lux are only now completing their final attacks."

"Sir, Zorn and I have been out of the loop for two years. What happened to Admiral Groff and his combined forces? Where did all of the Kreel cruisers disappear to?" Roan asked.

"Sorry Roan, but we simply don't know. Groff and his main cruiser force lifted ship and departed for some as yet undiscovered location. Given their lingering threat, we're still searching for them."

"Admiral Kellon, by some unspecified technical means you've sealed the three Kreel Hub worlds, but what will become of them?" Chandara asked.

"The military world has accepted a mediated and binding resolution. Consequently, it's now officially designated the Kreel home world. Ultimately, its future will be determined by the Kreel themselves.

"Guardian Force is determining what is to be done with the Elite and Industrial Hub worlds, and its sanctions will be implemented."

"Admiral Kellon, what you have described encompasses judgments and mercy. That you granted any clemency to your Arkillian and Kreel foes, where none then seemed warranted, surprised the Elders. Based upon your previous actions, the Elders will respect Guardian Force's pending judgments relating to the Kreel Hub worlds. During the forthcoming millenniums, with considerable interest we will observe the fruits of your wisdom."

"Elder Shanti, I remain perplexed. In spite of all that has been said here, there still is an unresolved question," Amada said.

"Beloved Amada, you are correct. For the sake of the others, please express your question out loud so everyone might hear it."

"Well, as you wish. Until now, the Nori were unaware of the terrible scope of the battles being waged between Guardian Force and the Kreel. Since it heralds potential far reaching consequences, the new information comes as a shock. The Nori will need to reflect upon these portentous events.

"Nevertheless, nothing which we have discussed here can explain this extraordinary gathering of Elders. I am therefore compelled to repeat Admiral Kellon's earlier question, just why have the Elders gathered?"

"We are gathered here because a singular tipping point has occurred. Commander Zorn's earlier description of his ship and its recent plight was precise, but only as far as it went. He discreetly avoided mentioning one vital factor; when he regained consciousness, he was located about 80,000 light years from home and 60,000 light years above the center of this galaxy."

The stark implication of Shanti's revelation came as a shock, and there was a collective gasp of surprise, followed by murmurings. Everyone, except Kellon and Eryan, turned in wonderment to look at Roan and Zorn.

Following a momentary pause, Shanti continued. " The Assembled Worlds have achieved a momentous breakthrough in their technology. This is the tipping point which brings about our gathering. Their temporal-energy breakthrough allows for efficient and rapid travel to anywhere within the whole of the Wandering Waterway.

"Yesterday morning their ship, Mike One, departed Megan and went to Glas Dinnein, where Admiral Kellon and Admiral Secretary Eryan Kyrie boarded. Then, Mike One returned to Megan this morning. Had they desired, they might have as easily traveled to anywhere else within our galaxy. Given this advanced technical achievement, it is obvious to the Elders that a closer relationship with Humanity is now appropriate.

"The purpose of our calling of this gathering is to acknowledge and proclaim Humanity's well-earned ascension. It should also be understood that such a momentous occasion is infrequent, even when time is measured in eons."

"Shanti, please excuse this incorrigibly suspicious man, who was born on Earth, but is there possibly an iron fist concealed within the velvet glove of what you have termed 'ascension'?" Darrell asked.

"An iron fist? Mr. Fann, wisdom teaches where much is attained, much is required. The Elders are an aggregation of the remaining oldest sentient species now dwelling within our common galaxy. A wise and prudent man will understand that our means and abilities to project power and force are proportional to the maturity of our cultures.

"Within our galaxy, there are many millions of solar systems which are inhabited by young sentient species. We firmly uphold the principles of Peace, Free Will, and Choice. While the Elders do observe, we seldom have cause to interfere into the affairs of developing younger species. Even when rare local interstellar conflicts erupt, such as between the Kreel and their neighboring species, no prime justification exists for our interfering. If, however, an interstellar disruption of Peace was to inordinately expand or else directly impact one of our domains, then we are collectively and morally compelled to act."

"Can you be a bit more specific about what 'morally compelled to act' might involve?" Darrell pressed.

Following a brief silence, Shanti continued. "The gathering agrees, Transparency in the matter is appropriate. In the case of interstellar warfare, such as I have outlined, our unified response would be morally justifiable, direct, and decisive. For example, when the Kreel following Illuyan's dark counsels, and Grand Admiral Groff's misguided leadership, fled their hub worlds, they attempted through violence to expand their Empire into one of our realms. We strenuously objected. Guardian Force need no longer search for Grand Admiral Groff and his missing fleet; they are no more. Because of his involvement and culpability, we promptly gave Illuyan just cause to flee this galaxy. I trust these few facts will adequately answer your question about a possible iron fist."

"Yes, completely."

"Regarding your future choices, the Elders counsel is that the Assembled Worlds and Nori continue to strengthen their bonds of mutual trust. To this end, the continuing development of cultural centers on Megan are important.

"Concerning Earth, whatever actions the Assembly of Worlds and Nori choose to do is solely their responsibility. We, however, counsel whatever assistance may be extended, it should be accomplished jointly and with the knowledge and willing cooperation of People on Earth.

"By necessity, for a time the Nori must remain our primary conduit for liaison. To improve our overall liaison with humanity, I urge the Assembly of Worlds and Earth accelerate their mental training with the Nori.

"That we, the Elders, have gathered here today is an acknowledgment Humanity has earned its new status within the galaxy. This new status comes with increased responsibilities. Therefore, we anticipate Humanity shall always remember our ways are firmly grounded and governed by four principles, Truth, Righteousness, Trust, and Justice. Wherein we hold that Righteousness means we respect and offer help to others, rather than seeking to prey upon others. These four interdependent principles are considered the golden cornerstones of every lasting peace. The wise among you will consider these principles and respond with all appropriate heed.

"Now, outside and above there are many Elders. Each Elder has come from far to join here with us in our mutual Gathering and celebration of Life. Like each of you, each Elder here is a representative of many others, all of whom are among your new acknowledged neighbors and friends. With joy, we invite you to come outside to meet some of us and share in our happiness."

Upon exiting Susie's home, the group stood looking upward in astonishment. The sapphire morning sky was full of glistening orbs. They were darting about in what seemed to be flights of joyful antics and pure exuberance.

Gepeto was standing to Susie's left, and to her right stood Seth and Limo. The pups were looking about and skyward. Sensing the excitement, their tails were wagging enthusiastically. Nearby, McRoy was standing with Chandara and Amada. Darrell, Kellon, and Eryan stood together with Roan and Zorn. Elayne then hurried out of the house, carrying Briana to see the Elders. She joined Zorn.

Separating from the main group of orbs, one descended and approached the group of people. Drawing near, the sphere of energy took on the apparent solid form of a lovely woman, who was wearing a supple light tan dress that was hemmed just below her knees and which was held loosely about her waist by an ornate jeweled belt. Roan noticed with interest that She was wearing a bone or antler handled sheathed knife belted to her right side. Her loose-fitting garments and calf high boots were accented with gleaming jewels. About her forehead a simple plain headband was restraining her brilliantly shimmering black hair, and her gold flecked brown eyes were sparkling with joy. Her smile was one of pure radiance. Approaching, she slightly bowed.

"Joy to everyone, I am Shanti. In peace, I welcome all of you to the whole of our beautiful Wandering Waterway."

In deep admiration, Amada bowed her head, then looked directly toward Shanti in reverence. " Elder Shanti, last night I was able to study our most ancient archives. There I found that our forebears told of being rescued by the Elders. They told of a terrible devastation, of a red and brown pair of dwarf stars plunging out of the darkness. Like a cruel barbed whip, those stars slashed across a solar system; titanic waves of devastation, ruin, and death following closely in their turbulent wake. Towering tongues of arching plasma were spewing forth from the erupting solar primary, and like clay pots Planets were being broken, battered by collisions, and flung about. Bright ribbons of lightning crossed and seared the sky overheads; volcanoes were erupting, and there were giant tidal waves. My people were confronting certain death; then, from the darkening sky above came the Elders. Gathering them up like terrified children, with death nipping at their heels, the Elders carried them to safety out among the distant stars.

"Honored Shanti, we were then gifted a beautiful and bountiful world upon which to live. In that distant beginning the Elders taught us that we were always to abide in harmony and peace with one another. On behalf of all of our generations, I thank you for your precious gifts of life and our lasting joy."

"Beloved Amada, that the Nori have listened and chosen to embrace wisdom is our true reward. During the millenniums yet to unfold, the Nori will partake of the generous fruits of their wisdom and their good-endeavors."

Shanti's clear thoughts were then privately directed into Zorn's mind. *Commander Zorn, I extend to you and to your beloved family my personal invitation to come and visit us. I would be delighted to show you the bubble cities of Suryakanti, the Devanand forests, and the mountains of Mahatmya. Jivana has provided Mike One with a trove of information regarding the Wandering Waterway and the Elders' Dominions. You will find well described therein the methods for contacting Jivana and me. Please do come and visit soon, there is much that we would enjoy showing you.*

As Zorn and the others watched, Shanti turned and then soared aloft, soon joining in with the other Elders who were joyfully co-mingling overhead.

Smiling, Zorn lifted Briana in his arms and pointed toward the Elders. "Briana, look! It's a special day when you learn you have so many new friends and good neighbors."

As Zorn held her near, Briana gleefully cried out in delight. "Papa Zorn, listen. Mike can sing."

Listening to his insignia collar transducer, Zorn smiled. Briana was right. Shey, Mike, and Rodney's voices were joined in

406

singing a happy little tune about somewhere over the rainbow, and they were doing it in perfect harmony. *Hmm,* he thought, *the end of the rainbow? Isn't there supposed to be a pot of gold there?*

Musing, Zorn first looked toward where Shanti had stood and then looked skyward at the joyfully interacting Elders. Slowly he turned and with wonder and appreciation looked about at the surrounding vista of ocean, beaches, wooded hills, and a gathering of a few of his most trusted and good friends.

Wow, he thought, *there really is a pot of gold, it's Megan and peace. By all the thunder, the Kreel war is over! Best of all, we've got the whole galaxy to explore and new friends to go and visit. We've even got an invitation from Shanti!*

While hugging Briana and smiling broadly, Zorn reached out and took hold of and gently squeezed Elayne's hand. She squeezed right back. It was indeed a joyful and most beautiful day....

Author's Postscript

When I took the first step along the *Guardian* story line, like my old friend Frodo, I had no idea where the road might lead. Upon meeting Roan and Zorn for the first time, back in Chapter One, Volume One, I knew nothing about them, except they were strangers. Likewise, Shey appeared to be but a rather fundamental AI. During the years of my close interaction with Roan, Zorn, and Shey, they have become trusted friends. As the weaver of the tale, it is my sincere hope you have enjoyed meeting my good friends and have found their story uplifting and compelling. While with *Guardian Thunder* the series has reached its summation point, I remain confident that my friends are continuing their explorations out among our marvelous Wandering Waterway. Someday, just perhaps, they may drop by for a cup of coffee; be assured they are most certainly invited.

For the record, the tapestry of the Guardian series was woven upon the existing framework of a great mystery, that being Humanity and our mysterious antiquity upon the Earth and perhaps beyond. The incredible stories of human achievements are many, some are included within recent history, while others are contained within scriptures, legends, and epic tales. Some of the tales are of courage exhibited during times when Humanity was confronted by global disasters and potential extinction. Within the legends can be found stories of People who possessed a fierce determination to survive. We are their children.

Often, buried deep within an intricate legend are wonders of preserved knowledge and remarkable heights of human consciousness. There is often a deep taproot of wisdom preserving a legend. That such fragments of conscious thought have survived millenniums, where billions of similar fragments have perished, suggests they are worthy of thoughtful consideration. They should never be frivolously discounted as mere superstition and nonsense. For example, legend and science may well be proven tightly intertwined within the ancient fabled battle between the sky-god and Illuyanka. Given its striking contents, that cosmic battle likely did occur about 70,000 years ago.

Consider, just perhaps, the awesome battle described within the surviving Illuyanka and other similar legends actually happened, and the battle concerned the terrifying interaction between our primary sun and a passing glowing red dwarf star and its brown dwarf companion (along with their trailing collection of planets and cosmic debris).

Factually, a modern-day astronomer recently discovered and identified a low-mass star system positioned about twenty light-years distant. That system consists of a brown and red dwarf pair, now nicknamed "Scholz's star." The system was given the formal designation "WISE J072003."

Through measurement and calculations of the stars' trajectory, it was estimated that about 70,000 years ago the pair of dwarf stars (with their cosmic debris) passed by and "brushed" Earth's solar system. Given the reality of the difficulty in precisely measuring relative motion between Earth's constantly moving solar system and a fast-moving dwarf star pair during 70,000 years, the cautious word "brushed" should be understood for what it really is, a prudent approximation of the proximity of the dwarf star system to our own solar system primary at the point of closest approach.

The vivid observations of a cosmic battle, preserved within multiple legends, proclaims the dwarf star system and its caravan of cosmic devastation more than "brushed" past the fringes of Earth's solar system. Given the details preserved within the legends, our solar system and primary was directly and dramatically involved. If the red dwarf star approached near enough, it would have become visible in the night sky. At nearly the same time the dwarf pair "brushed" our solar system, the singular massive Earth catastrophe known as the "Toba super-eruption" also occurred.

Given the newly discovered scientific data concerning Scholz's star, and the estimated date of its passage near the time of the Toba super-eruption, there exists a plausible coupling with recorded legends and myths. Given the legends, and their potential historical significance, further precise measurements and analysis of "Scholz's star" is definitely warranted.

The deep root of the legend of the cosmic battle between the Titans and Olympians, like the Illuyanka legend, may also be found in the passing of "Scholz's star." For certain, after the battle between the Titans and Olympians our solar system was forever altered, some of the Titans having been bound and cast into Tartarus, and Venus having emerged fully formed. Clearly, within multiple legends our solar system passed through a violent alteration. The discovered wonder may be that preserved within ancient legends are real-time observations of an incredible cosmic-level disaster and its associated global catastrophe. This included a global population bottleneck, where the survival of our human species was put in question. For certain, more than a hundred thousand years of human history (years before 70,000 years) was harshly eradicated. The surviving legends are but tantalizing remnants, stories that must have been often told around campfires during the following millenniums-long ice age, stories so powerful they were remembered and retold across thousands of generations.

The "passage" of Scholz's star may also represent the missing powerful causality that was glaringly absent from the necessarily-speculative books written by Immanuel Velikovsky, *Worlds in Collision* and *Earth in Upheaval*. According to Wikipedia, *Worlds in Collision* is broadly labeled "catastrophism," and "many of its claims are completely rejected by the established scientific community as they are not supported by any available evidence."

The recent discovery of Scholz's star appears to have revealed new "available evidence" and perhaps the "established scientific community" may with open minds someday revisit catastrophism, properly acknowledging and making good use of the bountiful research provided by Immanuel Velikovsky. A long-overdue apology may also be in order.

What is mentioned here expresses but a small fraction of the enticing wonders that can be found while journeying through dusty archives with a love of inquiry, an open mind, and childlike curiosity. Tragically, humanity remains utterly ignorant of its true history, much of which has been labeled and swept under the rugs of superstition and catastrophism. Within our often-misunderstood legends are rich treasures, many of which are jumbled fragments of tens of thousands of years of human history waiting to be sorted, correlated, and through analysis rediscovered.

Perhaps, you may find my white paper, *The Great Pyramid - An Equation in Stone 4,500-year-old Royal Cubit Mystery Solved*, presented within "GalaxyQuestBooks.com" of interest. Just perhaps, like the Elders and the Nori, friends have extended an encouraging hand across the ages, in hope that we need not always remain like children, unaware of our lost history. That, of course, is another story.

D. Arthur Gusner
Cambria California
January 2020

www.ingramcontent.com/pod-product-compliance
Lightning Source LLC
Chambersburg PA
CBHW020251030726
47499CB00001B/147